PROMISE OF DESIRE

Jared swung one long leg over his saddle, dismounting fluidly, and then reached up to assist Deirdre. His palms closed around her waist, and he realized as he lifted her down, that his hands nearly encircled her waist. Jared let her slide against his chest as he slowly lowered her to the ground, letting his hands slip from her waist up to the soft curve of her bosom.

Breathless, Deirdre stared up at him, her hands pressed against his shirt as her feet finally touched the ground. Beneath her fingers, she could feel the hard curve of his chest. He smelled of sun and sweat and skin, mingled together in a scent that was intoxicatingly male. And she knew she was lost. She watched his mouth lower to hers, knowing what was to come, and found herself hungry for the taste of him. She lifted onto her toes, anxious to receive his kiss. When it came, it plundered her senses with its intensity.

She leaned into him, molding her body to his, surrendering to the power of their kiss. She remembered how he had suckled at her lip last night, and, desirous of having him feel the same melting warmth trickling through him that he had brought to her, she captured the corner of his mouth between her teeth, gently nipping at it. With her tongue she traced the outline of his mouth. Her efforts were rewarded, for Jared groaned, a rumbling from deep in the back of his throat. His arms slid around her, crushing her against him.

"Deirdre," he whispered against her mouth. "My God, how I want you . . ."

Books by Elaine Kane

DESERT FLAME
TEMPTED
PROMISE ME

Published by Zebra Books

PROMISE ME

ELAINE KANE

ZEBRA BOOKS
KENSINGTON PUBLISHING CORP.

ZEBRA BOOKS are published by

Kensington Publishing Corp.
850 Third Avenue
New York, NY 10022

First Printing: June, 1996
10 9 8 7 6 5 4 3 2 1

Printed in the United States of America

For Jim,
my love, my life, my friend,
my lover, my husband.
My soul set free.
I love you.
w/

One

Deirdre Ramsey crossed the darkening marble foyer with even steps as she made her way to the heavy double doors leading into her father's study. Her hands on the door handles, she took one deep, steadying breath and opened them. The solicitor stood behind her father's heavy rosewood desk, a pile of unread correspondence in one hand, a sheaf of papers in the other. Short, rotund and red-faced with a thinning patch of yellowish hair atop his head, he was exactly as Deirdre would have imagined a solicitor to look. But not at all what she would have expected of her father's solicitor.

Dropping her father's unopened mail, he cleared his throat and straightened to his full height, which was not much more than it had been when he'd been bent over. "Lady Ramsey," he began. "Allow me to begin by expressing my sincere sympathy at the death of your parents."

"Thank you, Mr. . . . ?"

"Benchley. Stewart Benchley."

Deirdre nodded. "Thank you for coming all the way to Ramshead."

"As your father's solicitor, it is part of my duty."

Deirdre stood very still, waiting for Mr. Benchley to explain why she had been requested to meet with him now. She couldn't imagine what he could feel to be of such importance that it must be dealt with today. Not when she had just been informed that the ship her parents were on had gone down while returning from Scandinavia, and that everyone on board had died. What was so important that it could not wait until this horrible day was over?

In a businesslike manner, Mr. Benchley straightened the papers he still held in his left hand. "Perhaps you should have a seat, Lady Ramsey." Deirdre closed the distance between them and seated herself in one of the matching wing-backed leather chairs positioned before the large desk. Clasping her hands protectively in her lap, she stared at the familiar piles of paperwork that littered the desk top. It did not seem possible that her father would not be coming back to riffle through them, something he occasionally did when he was "playing at being a respectable gentleman" as she would sometimes overhear him say. The solicitor remained standing, and when he cleared his throat loudly Deirdre blinked, her mind returning from its musings.

"Unfortunately, your parents' death is not the only bad news I am here to convey to you, Lady Ramsey. I have not been your father's solicitor for very long. He contacted me just before he and Countess Ramsey left for the Nordic countries. My responsibility, as I understood it, was to sort out your father's somewhat muddled financial records. A rather daunting task, since he provided me with what can only be described as scanty records—" Mr. Benchley broke off for a moment, his gaze following the piles of correspondence and records that lay scattered across her father's desk, stacked on the floor, along windowsills, and upon every available surface in the room. As if overwhelmed by what he saw, the solicitor did not speak for several seconds.

"The problem is, Lady Ramsey, your parents spent all of their money and have gone rather seriously into debt." After a pause he continued. "Debts amounting to £30,000 pounds sterling, to be exact. I realize you may not understand clearly just how much money that is, so I have prepared a schedule," he explained in precise, clipped tones that suited his profession perfectly. "Apparently, prior to your father's retaining me, he employed a financial advisor to whom he gave discretion over his various accounts. This advisor, although I assure you I use the term loosely in this instance, allowed your father to sign several documents which pledged his belongings as collateral for moneys borrowed. Naturally, with your father's demise, those loans are now being called in, and there are no liquid assets with which to pay them." He stopped here, allowing the young woman before him to absorb the full import of his words. "The schedule lists all the items which have been pledged, and which your father's lenders will collect as well as the debts themselves. You might wish to review it soon."

He handed her the sheaf of papers, but when Deirdre made no motion to look at them he cleared his throat in discomfort. "I'm sure we can review the list tomorrow, Lady Ramsey." She nodded, a movement so slight that the lacy collar on her riding habit didn't move a hairbreadth. The solicitor gathered his leather portmanteau and papers and excused himself. At the door, he looked back into the darkening room, recalling the information he'd studied in the carriage on the long trip here today. The earl and countess of Ramsey had left only one child. Female. Age seventeen, to be eighteen in another month. Lady Deirdre Antoinette Ramsey. That was all.

How little that said about the stricken young lady who sat stonelike in the large chair, hands clenched around the papers that listed nearly the entire contents of her family's home. The last light of day filtered through the windows, lighting her dark upswept hair and somber profile. Even pale and drawn, her looks were befitting of her legendary parents. When he had arrived he'd prepared himself for histrionics and weeping, pleading, shock, possibly even swoons. It had never occurred to him that such difficult news would be met by a young woman with stoic silence.

With a sigh, Mr. Benchley decided to wait one more minute, thinking that perhaps Lady Ramsey would have questions. He was not a man who enjoyed the conveyance of unpleasant news, but he took pride in performing his duties well regardless of the circumstances. This instance, he reasoned, was no different than others, simply more unfortunate. And he would perform his job to the best of his abilities. He must, at any rate, since the earl had paid him generously and Stewart Benchley needed the money. Gaining a client with the prestige of an earl had not been easy, and he intended to do everything possible to keep the new countess happy.

Lady Ramsey continued to sit silent and straight-backed in her chair. Mr. Benchley opened his mouth and closed it twice before finally deciding to speak again. "I expect the first of the collectors to arrive within the week. Unfortunately, we will not be able to put them off once news of your parents' deaths appears in the papers." He waited at the door another moment, now quite certain that there would be no response from the figure in the darkening room. At last, he closed the door behind him and left her alone.

When the solicitor had finally gone Deirdre closed her eyes and concentrated on holding herself very still, as if by doing so, she could halt the rush of events that had swept her feet from under her and shaken her to the core in the last two hours. First Bert had come in from the fields to deliver the news that her parents were dead. Now this stranger had just informed her that their possessions were to be taken, given, bartered, or otherwise dispersed to the far ends of England as well. When she had ridden off to smell the coming of spring on this beautiful, cloudless morning, her life had been intact and all had seemed right with the world. Why hadn't there been any warning that this horrible maelstrom lay in ambush for her?

For a moment, an image of her parents flashed through Deirdre's mind. She so easily pictured them laughing gaily over their good fortune at having cheated old age and a mundane death. They would have been toasting one another with

French champagne as their ship listed heavily and went down
into the icy waters of the North Sea. Squeezing her eyelids
even more tightly closed, she pressed back the lump of tears
that gathered suddenly in her throat. Her parents were always
happy, always in love, always gay to the bitter end.

It did not surprise her so much that her father had failed
to oversee his finances well. She could imagine him even
now, looking at her in shock. "My darling Deirdre," he
would say, "I paid the man quite handsomely to see to
everything. What use for me to have reviewed his work? I
wouldn't presume to tell him his business."

"Oh, Father," she whispered brokenly into the chill of the
dark study. "Why didn't you come back?" But she couldn't
bring herself to be angry with him. Her life until today had
been perfect, easy, and beautiful. She had adored her parents.
It just hurt so terribly to know that they were gone forever.

The service for the earl and countess was held two days
later. It was thinly attended. Ramshead lay well beyond a
comfortable ride from London and Deirdre's parents had not
catered to the *ton*. They had, in fact, eschewed society, preferring the company of each other. A few acquaintances from
what might qualify as neighboring estates came, the staff,
Deirdre, three somewhat distant relatives Deirdre had been
unaware existed, and a handful of her parents' friends, few
of whom Deirdre had seen at all over the past six or eight
years.

But if the services for the earl and countess of Ramsey
had warranted little attention, the dissolution of their property had the exact opposite effect. In fact, Mr. Benchley's
prediction about the collection of her parents' belongings
turned out to be quite liberal. The day following her parents'
burial, Ramshead fairly overflowed with people. Deirdre
stood at the French doors of her bedroom suite watching
the continuous flow of people into and out of the house in

the fine May weather. Those coming carried only the papers verifying their loans to her father, but no one left empty-handed. Only her own rooms and a few of the more common necessities of a household would be unclaimed by the end of the day. Blessedly, she didn't recognize anyone, but she watched the decimation of her home with a morbid fascination that had held her hostage to the window all day.

"There goes the vase Mother brought from Venice," she said to no one at all as a tall, thin man whom she'd already watched remove several paintings from the house carried the Venetian urn to his carriage. Deirdre remembered when her mother had brought it back from Italy. She had been six. As the urn disappeared into its new owner's carriage, a new participant in the denudation of her home arrived. He rode up the gravel drive as though he had done so a thousand times. Until now, she hadn't given a thought to who these people were. They were curs, and that was all she needed to know. But something about the way this man held himself was unlike the other strangers who had come to rape her home. He didn't slink like the others, and she wondered if that made him all the more audacious or whether it might be something else. Probably, he was just more accustomed to this form of unsavory profit-taking, she decided. She had no reason to feel generous toward anyone who approached her home today.

Heartsick to the core of her soul, Deirdre turned away from the window and clenched her hands at her side. These strangers didn't know or care the first thing about where these things came from or what they meant. Did they care that each item was a memento, a memory of some place or occasion her parents had shared? They were only possessions to these people. Objects to boast over. *Did you know this vase came from Morgan Ramsey's estate,* they would say. *Quite a bargain, it was!* The thought made her empty stomach heave as sour bile threatened at the back of her throat. She had yet to shed a single tear; yet to whisper one word to anyone of the sorrow that racked her soul, and her entire body throbbed with the effort of having held her loss and confusion tight within her for the past three days.

The compulsion to escape came over her with the rush and power of an ocean wave against the shore. Suddenly, she couldn't bear the thought of watching one more person crow over his find or listen to them snarl to Mr. Benchley that they required interest payment as well; especially this latest enigmatic stranger. Crossing the room, she practically threw herself into the hallway. But there she found herself exposed to a new sort of nightmare—one from which the relative quiet of her rooms had insulated her. The hallway was crowded with collectors and people who could only be gawkers, curiosity seekers.

Vultures, she thought. Everywhere people were examining the personal objects of her home as though it was a flea market. They stripped her house bare to the bone, and not one gave Deirdre so much as a glance as she raced down the stairs and out the wide double doors away from the sickening devastation of her proud parents' home.

"Lady Ramsey!" Mr. Benchley called, chasing after her with a stride that indicated such speed was extremely unfamiliar to him. "I was just about to send a message to your rooms. It is imperative that we speak. There is an opportunity which I believe—"

Deirdre was intent on putting every vile opportunist at least a hundred yards away from her, and she particularly did not want to hear *anything* the solicitor had to say. "No, Mr. Benchley," she called back to him without stopping. "I need some air." Her voice shook ever so slightly with the pent-up emotions that threatened to break the tight bonds in which she'd held them since Mr. Benchley's arrival.

Doggedly, the solicitor followed her, managing a half hop every third step to keep apace with his fleeing client. "Lady Ramsey, I know this is terribly difficult for you," he gasped as he increased his speed to gain on her. "I assure you, I am only attempting to do my job as your father would have wished."

Deirdre only increased her gait, lifting her black silk skirts to accommodate the stone steps leading to the garden terraces as she fled. "I know you are, Mr. Benchley. But I need to be alone now."

"I quite understand, my lady. But this cannot wait."

"And the last time you had something which could not wait, it was the news that my parents were lucky not to be in debtors' prison!"

Mr. Benchley gave up racing after her, and stood sulking on a wide expanse of lawn. "I merely delivered the facts, my lady. And, at least, you were not caught unawares."

Deirdre stopped at last, her escape blocked by Mr. Benchley's words. She had reached the edge of the fruit garden, which at least afforded her some semblance of privacy. One side of the garden was protected from view by a long stucco wall and another by a row of ancient cypress trees. All along the wall espaliered pear, apple, and quince trees created perfectly formed leafy diamonds dotted with spring blossoms that would soon bear fruit. "Please go on then, Mr. Benchley," she sighed. "Give me your bad news."

The solicitor squared his somewhat unsquare shoulders and actually smiled. "I'm pleased to say that rather than bad news, I am here to give you some very good news. Quite unexpectedly, I received an offer which will provide a very equitable solution to your situation." Deirdre's brows came together as she listened. "After all," Mr. Benchley continued, warming to this new position as the bearer of *good* news and thinking of the hefty commission he was about to collect, "you still must continue your life. You will want to have a Season so that you may find a husband suited to your position. You have the very good fortune of being a countess, since your father specifically provided for the passing of the title to you. And you have every opportunity to find someone who will take care of you. Being a woman, you have the advantage of completely recovering from this dire financial situation through marriage. However, in order to accomplish this you will need an income— for gowns, a chaperone, rental of a London town house, and so forth."

"Mr. Benchley," Deirdre said, stunned almost to laughter at the absurdity of his concerns, "I have no interest in having a Season. My parents saw no reason to mix with the *ton;* in fact, they described it to me as quite boring. And the very last thing on my mind right now is finding a husband! I intend to stay here and carry on exactly as I would have if my parents had not died."

"But that is impossible," Mr. Benchley argued. "Ramshead is a very large estate. Just to maintain the house and its outbuildings requires at least six thousand pounds per annum, but the maintenance of the grounds nearly doubles that. You have no income. When the debts have all been paid, you'll be lucky to have a few pieces of furniture left. How will you pay for food or firewood or candles, much less provide wages for the staff? I've reviewed the estate books quite extensively with the steward. It is an impossible situation."

"I thought you said you had *good* news, Mr. Benchley. This sounds suspiciously like very bad news," Deirdre commented, glassy-eyed.

"Oh, I do!" he exclaimed, breaking into a wide smile. "I have found a buyer for Ramshead. Or more accurately put, he has found me."

All of the controlled, reasonable traits which Stewart Benchley had thus far admiringly attributed to the young Lady Ramsey evaporated into the crisp spring air. Deirdre stared at her father's solicitor in disbelief. "Sell Ramshead?"

"I have discussed it, although very briefly, with Mr. Bert Manning, the estate's bailiff, and he is in agreement that selling the estate would provide you with—"

"Bert agreed with you? He agreed that I should sell my home?"

Mr. Benchley shifted uncomfortably from one foot to the other. Lady Ramsey was acting quite strange, verging on the hysteria that he had initially anticipated from a distraught female and then dismissed as being quite unlike her. "It is just that, as I explained to you, you will need to provide an income for yourself. You are a young, very eligible woman. Certain things will be essential and . . ."

"No!"

"But you are unmarried and you will need a—"

"No!" Deirdre turned a half circle on the thick carpet of spring grass before facing Mr. Benchley again. When she did, the tears that she refused to shed shone like diamond drops in her sapphire blue eyes. Tears mixed with a rising anger born of loss and an unbearable hurt. "I have watched these vultures come hour after hour to haul off bits and pieces of my parents, although no one was the least interested in attending their funeral! If these people need to be paid and there is no other form of payment, then let them take my parents' possessions. But Ramshead, Mr. Benchley, is my home. It is all I have ever known and all I have ever wanted. As you have explained to me, my father has left me two things. The family title and the family home. Ramshead is the one thing of theirs which no one will take away from me. Ever."

"But the offer is for cash and it is—"

"NO! Tell this man, whoever he is, that Ramshead is not for sale. Not for any price. Find out how much my father owed him, and I will find some other way to pay him."

"It is not a matter of owing," Mr. Benchley tried to explain.

"I don't care. I don't care what it is a matter of. Ramshead will not be sold." Deirdre turned and fled, determined to escape all the horror of the past week at last. She ran past the fruit garden and on into the orchards, unmindful that her slippers and gown were being ruined by the wet grass. They would never take her home. She didn't care if she had no idea how she would pay off a debt of such size that all of Ramshead would be a fair trade. It didn't matter. Anything else they could have, but never Ramshead. She had agreed to selling all the other. Agreed to paying her father's debts because it was right that they be paid. But never Ramshead, because she had told only a half-truth to Mr. Benchley.

Ramshead was not merely her home. It was her soul. The very essence of who she was and what she knew of herself. Her first breath had been of this air, her first playground the soft cushion of the terraced gardens, her first explorations had been through the mazes and gardens of Ramshead. And without it, she feared she would lose herself.

Stewart Benchley watched Lady Ramsey's black-garbed figure disappear beneath the low branches of the peach trees. Then, gathering himself for more unpleasantness, he straightened his cravat, flicked a stray blade of grass from his stockings, and walked back to the front of the house. The gentleman who awaited him lounged casually against one of the ten pillars that lined the entrance. The solicitor was not in the least misled by this casual demeanor. The marquess of Jersey was anything but casual. His message had arrived quite unexpectedly early this morning, and since then Benchley's day had been a maddening scramble to assess the value of the estate versus the offer the marquess had made. The offer, though, was quite fair. Not excessive, as would be expected of a businessman of his reputation, but neither was it the offer of a man who sought to benefit by the misfortune of a young, parentless woman.

"Lord Jersey," Benchley greeted the marquess with a bow.

"Mr. Benchley, I presume."

"The same. I received your correspondence early this morning, and . . ."

"Shall we walk, Mr. Benchley," the marquess suggested, striding slowly away from the commotion of the house without waiting for the solicitor's reply.

Why was it that everyone wanted to exercise themselves, Mr. Benchley thought irritably? He was already bound to need a medicinal for aching muscles from pursuing Lady Ramsey, and now the marquess felt the need to walk as well! He caught up with Lord Jersey and began again. "As I said, I received your missive and I regret to inform you that while I strongly recommended to Lady Ramsey that she accept your offer, she has not."

"Then she has found some income?"

"No, my lord." Benchley sighed. "I explained the predicament to her, but she was unmoved. Quite unusual for her." The marquess shot the solicitor an interested glance. "Excuse me, my lord. I fear I was deliberating a point to myself. I simply meant that Lady Ramsey has been the picture of calm throughout this unfortunate turn of events. Nearly excessively so. Yet when I suggested that she accept your offer, she became quite irate. Not at all like her, from what little exposure I've had to the countess," he amended.

The marquess seemed to consider this information for several minutes. "My offer will stand, Mr. Benchley."

"Stand, sir?" the solicitor repeated in surprise.

"The new countess is how old?"

"Seventeen, my lord. Eighteen on the summer solstice."

"And quite sheltered, from what I understand."

"She has been raised here. I believe she has rarely been even so far as London."

"Then she is in for an abrupt awakening. She will soon discover that her life will be far easier when she has hooked some wealthy gentleman looking for a title. And she will find, as all women do, that life in London is quite glamorous. She will have no need for a large estate that gobbles up her husband's money and cramps her gown allowance. It is much too far from London to afford her a place for weekend entertainments. Her friends will not come so far. The *ton* is nothing if not spoilt, Mr. Benchley." The marquess looked over the main house with its unfashionable twining roses everywhere and acres of verdant farmland complete with herds of black-faced sheep and Hereford cows. This was no place for hunts and weekends that afforded the aristocracy with opportunities for their *tête-à-têtes*.

"She will change her mind," he assured the solicitor. "Contact me as soon as she is ready to sell. However, should the countess change her mind rather quickly, as I suspect may be the case, you may provide the paperwork to my solicitor, Mr. Charles Ellis of Ellis & Fitzwalter. I am leaving next week for America and shall be out of the country for several months."

"As you wish," Benchley agreed with a nod. "But I don't understand why you believe she'll change her mind, my lord."

The marquess pinned him with an emotionless grey stare. "Women always do." Turning on his heel, he strode across the drive to the groom, who held his prancing black thoroughbred. Swinging into the saddle, the marquess of Jersey departed without so much as a backward glance.

$\mathcal{T}wo$

Deirdre leaned her forehead against the cool pane of glass in her bedroom window. She was tired to the core of her soul. Tired of the insanity that had descended upon her life and refused to go away. It was as if, when the first stone in her life had slipped from its position, the entire wall upon which she'd built her life had begun to crumble, until now she felt as if the thunder of its shattering would deafen all of London. The strange thing, she realized, was that there was not one single person who seemed to hear or see the rubble that had become her existence.

Deirdre let the cold glass pane numb the headache that threatened at her skull. Her life had changed so drastically over the last nine months that sometimes she wondered if Ramshead even existed. It seemed so far away now, so long ago that she was there. Her parents' death was still a raw sore in her heart, and thoughts of the two weeks she had spent closing her home following their funeral still made her flinch. Determinedly, Deirdre pushed the quick flash of memories away. She should be glad to be here, she told herself. It was a godsend, really, that her mother's younger sister had appeared at Ramshead's doorstep soon after the burials and insisted that she could not stay at Ramshead alone. Deirdre hadn't wanted to leave, but she hadn't wanted to stay either. Ramshead was changed suddenly. It was her home and yet not her home. A respite, Selda had told her, was just what she needed. And it had been easy to let her aunt convince her to come to London for a while. But she found everything very different here. Nothing was familiar. No one was like her. And lately Ramshead seemed so far away. She missed her home.

"Deirdre dear." Aunt Selda knocked daintily on the closed bedroom door. Before Deirdre could answer, the door opened and Selda bustled in. "Goodness, you'd think you were at a funeral!" she insisted, moving around the room to light one taper after another. "Oh!" she gasped in dismay. "I'm so sorry, my dear. I know everything reminds you of your loss, but one day you really must begin to put the past in the past and enjoy your new life. Look at you, you're still in your wrapper!"

"I think I'll stay home tonight, Selda," Deirdre said quietly.

"Nonsense! The thing you need least is to stay home. Why you'd just lock yourself up here in the dark. My dear, impossible as it may seem to you, the very thing for you is a night out. Now, which gown are you going to wear?" Without waiting for an answer, she pulled the biscuit watered-silk from the armoire and laid it across Deirdre's bed. "This will be perfect, sweetness. I'll send Avis up to help you finish dressing. Don't dally now, Deirdre. Peters has just pulled the carriage around. Your uncle and I will be waiting. We're already fashionably late. It won't do to be rude."

In a rustle of taffeta, Selda was gone. Deirdre stared at the exquisite gown that lay across the coverlet on her bed, then turned back to the window. Pressing her nose against the glass like a small child making an examination of the world, she stared down at the wet cobblestone street. A brougham passed by below her, its passengers protected from the spring rainstorm as they headed, no doubt, for some soiree or ball. All of London was out tonight, though this fact made it no different from every other night. It was the height of the Season, and no one who was anyone would be caught without an invitation somewhere. But Deirdre would have loved nothing so much as to stay, exactly as her aunt had said, locked in the darkness of her room.

She needed desperately to heal. Yet the hurt refused to go away. Week after week, month upon month, Deirdre's wounds lay open and sore. Her parents' death. Seeing her home stripped of its possessions. Sending away all but a few of the people who'd cared for her. And leaving. Leaving the only home she'd ever known. The place where her soul resided still. The place, she was realizing, where she belonged. If she closed her eyes, she could see Ramshead as it was the day she left. It was midsummer, and a steaming haze hung over the hills like a fine gauze. A day when she should have been riding or picking through the flower beds with shears, wearing a wide-brimmed straw hat. Instead, she was inside, walking ever so slowly down the main hall from one end of the house to the other. The sound of her slippered feet on the marble floor had echoed off the bare walls and tightly locked windows as she ran gloved fingers across the dust cloths draped over the remaining furnishings. Items that had been deemed beneath the taste of the London scavengers.

Ramshead had been a stranger to her when she left. So different from the days when bouquets from the cutting gardens were set in every room and the windows thrown wide to welcome the sunshine and fresh breeze. Her heart had ached that day. And it still did.

Another knock came at the door and Avis slipped in through a slit that would barely have admitted a mouse. Silently, she began to glide Deirdre's gown from its hanger. "It's a wet one tonight, my lady," she commented in her trilling, birdlike voice. "I've told Martin to have your cape ready."

Deirdre turned away from the window and smiled gently at Avis. She couldn't help thinking of a little brown wren every time she saw her. It wasn't just the maid's tiny stature or her coloring, although those were a perfect imitation of the little bird. It was her way of flitting around the house, her hands making quick, pecking motions, her black eyes darting about—never on any one thing for more than a second. Avis was one of the few things that had come with her from Ramshead. Her slight size belied her age, which Deirdre knew to be nearly thirty. She'd been at Ramshead for as long as Deirdre could remember. Her earliest memories of Avis were in the kitchens, where Deirdre would sneak treats and seek companionship. Eventually Avis had been promoted to her mother's service, but Deirdre's parents were gone so often that Avis had doubled as Deirdre's maid as well.

When she had turned thirteen, her mother had thought to hire a true governess to see to Deirdre's social education and provide a chaperone. But Deirdre had protested violently until her father convinced his wife that their daughter was doing perfectly well without a matron, who was just as likely to do no more than squelch her warm nature. Instead, her father had installed the entire staff of Ramshead as her educators. Bert, as bailiff, was to teach her horsemanship, mathematics, and the finer points of reading. Sanders, the steward, was in charge of etiquette. Avis and Maris, the highest-ranking maids, were responsible for teaching her behavior befitting a lady, including dressing and conversation. The earl laid on these responsibilities with the dire warning that should his daughter ever appear to be in anyway lacking in these regards, he would be forced to bring in tutors, chaperones and other dour, difficult types.

No one in the household wanted such a thing, and, as a result, everyone was suitably enthusiastic in their duties. As providence would have it, Deirdre was an exceptionally bright pupil, and it wasn't long before they were required to hire help from outside the household, a fact which was surreptitiously hidden from Lord Ramsey. But Bert, Sanders, Avis, and Maris carefully selected only tutors and other instructors who met their rigid standards of humaneness, thus sparing Deirdre one of the normal trials of childhood among the aristocracy.

Deirdre let the drape fall into place in front of the bay window and walked to the center of the room, putting herself in Avis's capable hands. There was no use arguing with Selda. Besides, she was probably right. What use was staying in?

Silently, Deirdre stepped out of her wrapper and into the pool of silk formed by her gown as Avis held it ready. She slid her arms into the close-fitting sleeves and stood very still as Avis applied a hook to the long row of tiny clasps that ran from neck to hip. As each loop fell into place, securely closing her into her gown, Deirdre felt herself close as well. She sealed her loss inside of her, fitting a loop over each vulnerability, each thread of pain. It was the only way she could face the crowds of people she did not know. They cared nothing for her hurt. Their concerns were the style of her hair and how she comported herself as a conversationalist. They didn't know her, nor did they truly care to. So Deirdre had learned to lace herself as securely closed as the back of her gown.

Jared perused the Whitmores' ballroom and its occupants with a bland expression. But as Robert Harelton handed him a replacement for his champagne his thoughts hardly matched his demeanor. Why on earth had he come home? Unlike America, London never changed. It remained stagnant, trite, utterly predictable, and completely boring. At least he had Jerseyhurst to look forward to. He'd brought back crates of new seed types and journals full of breeding notes, all of which he planned to put to good use at his family's ancestral estate. Unlike other landed nobles of the realm, Jared was not satisfied to let his estate function as a weekend retreat for entertaining the gaggles of London society. He made the estate work, and more important even than that, he made it profitable.

"Here's to your return, Jersey," Robert announced, raising his own glass in a toast.

"Here, here," Viscount William Marlot echoed, slugging back his entire flute in a single gulp. "Now, tell us what's up in Philadelphia." Jared enjoyed his champagne as he watched the newcomers being announced at the top of the wide staircase above them, neither eager nor reluctant to discuss his latest trip with his friends.

"Is it true that Hamilton has the upper hand with their Congress? It would be quite a sweet for your shipping concerns if England was to have special trade concessions," William commented.

"I believe that Hamilton will lose in the end," Jared explained. "But I prefer that."

"Just because your friend Jefferson opposes him!"

"Jefferson has the longer perspective," Jared explained nonchalantly, "and I'm interested in trading with America for three or four decades, not one. Which is why I'll be happier if Jefferson wins out. The secretary of the Treasury is a smart man, but he's not looking out for America's best interests. I'd say he needs to break some of his emotional ties to England."

"You sound like an American yourself," William countered, his thin, angular face turning red with frustration.

"And if I didn't have Jerseyhurst and my title to worry about, I might be."

"Well, you're here now, and I, for one, am damned glad to have you back," Robert stated, brushing aside William's political rantings. Following Jared's gaze to the top of the stairs and back again as another group waited to be announced, he lifted both eyebrows in feigned surprise. "Don't tell me that you've already settled on your next paramour, Jared," he commented dryly. "You've only been back in the country two days!"

"What's wrong with you Robert?" Will chimed in. "If he's been here two days, I'm sure Jersey has at least three ladies hoping to win his exclusive favor."

"Ah, but I didn't say 'hoping'," Robert countered. "Were we to include those who *hope* to win his attentions, they'd be numbered in the dozens. Far too broad a basis for consideration. No, I am speaking strictly of attachments—those whom Jared has selected for his dalliances until America seduces him back to her shores."

"So who is it?" William asked, turning a mischievously questioning eye on his friend.

The ribbing didn't affect Jared's demeanor in the least, a fact which he knew would merely serve to draw more *bon mots* from his friends. "Around the two of you, a man can't engage in the simple exercise of noticing who arrives without being labeled a womanizer."

Robert gave Jared an incorrigible grin. "When the man is you, Jersey, of course not! What's more the miracle is all the determined mamas who believe you're still in mourning. They'd claw one another to ribbons for the chance to make their sweet daughter the virgin who charms you out of your blacks." They were about to continue their deviltry when the slightest narrowing of their friend's eyes turned the attention of all three men to the party just entering the ballroom. Following the marquess's gaze, Robert smiled broadly. "Dare I believe my eyes? A delectable female turns Jersey's head!"

Jared watched as the party of three descended the curving, marble staircase. Two were clearly man and wife and of a middling age. Jared vaguely recognized the gentleman's face from other balls and, very likely, from White's. Between, and slightly behind them, was a woman he had very definitely never set eyes on before. His first thought was that she was incredibly beautiful. His second, for reasons unfathomable to him, was that she seemed very alone despite the fact that she was not.

Rich mahogany hair was piled into heavy curls atop her head, except for two strands that curved along the slender curve of her neck. She had skin that reminded him of fresh cream, and her scooped-neck silk gown exactly matched its color, inciting Jared's fertile imagination to conjure highly provocative images of what lay beneath its bodice. She was perfection to look at, every inch of her, yet something was missing in her demeanor. Her face was devoid of the excited flush of a young woman enjoying the London Season. She glided fluidly down the staircase, every movement perfect, almost magical, yet without the enthusiasm of the unjaded. The hopeful.

"Don't bother with that one," Will muttered, noting the direction of his companion's attention. "She may be the crown jewel at every soiree in the city, but in this case, looks are deceiving. She's definitely not your type." Jared raised his brow, prompting his friend to continue. "Don't deny you have a type, Jersey."

"Perhaps you should enlighten me," Jared commented softly.

"Temperamental, sleek, very discreet, and very *willing*. Definitely willing."

"They are all willing when it comes to Jersey, Will. It takes no brilliance to know that. And don't mind him," Robert explained, winking at Jared. "William is feeling more than a touch bitter these days. It seems Constance Parfitt has given him the slight of late. Besides, she *is* stunning."

William turned to glare off into the crowd and snapped another champagne from a passing tray. "Well, she isn't your type, Jersey, whether you take my advice to heart or not. A beauty, there's no questions about that. But underneath that lovely skin of hers, she's no different than a sixteen-year-old having her first season. No," he added after a quick pause, "she's worse. At least the *ingenues* twitter and giggle and fawn over a man with gratitude every time he asks them to dance or offers to fetch them a champagne. But the Ice Beauty had nothing to say. She doesn't generally care to dance and stands quietly with the older set, sipping her champagne and never smiling with more than the corners of her mouth. You'd be bored to distraction before the first dance was over, if you could even get her to accept a dance. But see for yourself, Jersey. See for yourself." With that, William turned and headed for the French doors of the smoking room.

"I swear Lady Constance is driving him over the brink, although I fear he's not wrong about that one," Robert repeated, nodding toward the bottom of the stairs. "Of course with her, it doesn't matter in the least if she's got an ounce of charm."

"And why is that?"

"Well, she's a countess, after all, and gorgeous. It won't matter to some that she's without a shilling and cold as a witch's tit. There are plenty who still consider her a prize."

"Countess of . . . ?"

"Ramsey. You must have heard the story. I could swear you were still in England when her parents died."

"I was," Jared commented dryly as he watched the stunning brunette with deepening interest. "In fact, I put down an offer on Ramshead."

Robert stared at him in surprise. "And she didn't take it?"

"No, but I'm certain she will now." Without another word, Jared strode in the direction of the countess of Ramsey.

As he made his way around the rim of the crowded room, his mind was making quick calculations. If he could conduct a little business, the night might not be a complete loss. He had almost, but not quite, forgotten about Ramshead. It had been over nine months since he'd made his offer. Clearly the young countess's solicitor had failed to apprise her that his offer stood. If the countess of Ramsey was destitute and unhappy—a likely circumstance based on

Will and Robert's claims and his own intuition, he offered her a solution that would cheer her pretty little brain and wipe all her petty cares away forever.

Deirdre positioned herself, requisite champagne in hand, far enough into the ballroom that she would appear to be joining in the festivities, yet close enough to the door that she could avail herself of a speedy exodus should she need one. Her usual routine was to stay as close to two hours as she could stand and then discreetly slip outside, where Peters would be waiting to take her home.

Uncle Felix had departed for one of the numerous parlors where the assembled gentlemen could enjoy a harder liquor than champagne and a few rounds of whist as soon as he had fulfilled what he considered to be his duties at such an event. Those duties entailed the delivery of a glass of refreshment for each of the ladies and the securing of at least one other woman acquaintance for purposes of light conversation.

A tiny smile on her face, Deirdre nodded politely as Marvella Bowers described the events along the Pall Mall that afternoon. Marvella's taste for detail was oppressive and Deirdre listened somewhat selectively, certain that she could follow the story very well by catching every third or fourth sentence.

Apparently, Marvella was beside herself with joy over the fact that one of the city's most eligible lords had just returned from abroad. Her daughter, Justine, Marvella declared, was the perfect match for the marquess. And the stir of seeing this prize male exercising one of his famous stallions along the Mall was enough to make even a matron like Marvella swoon. Listening with only one ear as she was, Deirdre wondered if she'd missed the part about this marquess falling to his knee before Justine beseeching her to marry him lest he perish for want. The entire discussion seemed a bit overdone to Deirdre, even for Marvella.

Still vaguely listening to the older woman, Deirdre sipped her champagne and scanned the crowd. She recognized every face she saw. They were the same people at every soiree, play, opera, or outing, every evening. Among the guests this evening were at least ten men who had called on her during the first month she was in London. None of them bothered to seek out her attentions tonight, nor had they at any time in the recent past. But while most young ladies enjoying their first Season would find it distressing that such highly eligible suitors as Lord Hale, the earl of Erskine, and George Dimock, who would one day be the marquess of Newport, had dropped all signs of interest in them, Deirdre could only summon up relief. Their insouciant conversations about the weather, the current state of the king's health, and whom had been seen with whom where and for what unsavory purpose had seemed completely nonsensical to her.

Her studies at Ramshead had not included learning how to carry on a pointless conversation that left no one better off and many injured. Tonight, she thought with a sigh, was unlikely to be any different from all the past nights, when she had graciously declined the attentions of men with whom she had nothing in common. She had just decided that one hour should be more than long enough to have made her appearance when her gaze fell upon a man she was certain she had never seen before, although there was something vaguely familiar in his demeanor.

He was looking directly at her, his grey eyes reflecting a daunting, crystalline intelligence that held her gaze from across the room. He was handsome and elegantly attired completely in black except for the snowy white of his shirt and jabot, which stood out in stark contrast to his sun-bronzed face. It was a face, like his build, which was devoid of softness. Lean cheeks and a broad forehead would have made his looks too hard were they not softened by the lightness of his eyes. His mouth was firmly set in a cynical expression that had settled into subtle lines along either side of a patrician nose, and his jaw, like his shoulders, was squared.

He was all hard lines. Not sharp or brittle, but sculpted, and at least a head taller than any other man there. Beneath the fine linen of his jacket, which stretched tight across a frame built for agility and finesse, she could see the outline of thick muscles that bespoke a life of physical activity. As he watched her, he began to move purposefully through the crowd. With each step, people moved back a pace, clearing a path for this man when others would have been ignored. He emanated a subtle power that was palpably different from the usual men who frequented such events. Yet he was completely in control. Fleetingly, Deirdre imagined him as a black-haired pirate storming the ball. *He's a renegade,* she thought. *Just as out of place here as I am.*

The thought unsettled Deirdre. Why should she think this man was somehow like herself? Most disconcerting of all, however, was her distinct impression that he was bearing down directly upon *her.* Of course, that was a ridiculous thought, she told herself, all the while her gaze never leaving his. But she never had the opportunity to discover whether he actually was seeking her out or not.

"Deirdre! It is you, isn't it?" All thoughts of the strange man in black disappeared as she blinked in confusion. Suddenly there in front of her was a face from far in her past.

"Anson?"

With a smile that would melt ice, Anson Reece leaned over and planted a kiss on her cheek. Then, as if remembering that such liberties were reserved for only the most intimate relationships, he sheepishly ducked his head. "Forgive me for being familiar, Deirdre, but my enthusiasm for discovering a long-lost playmate overwhelmed me." Deirdre blushed warmly, more than a little afraid to believe her eyes. Here, at last, was a familiar face.

Selda watched the exchange between her niece and this young man with sharp interest. In the first place, it was quite unseemly for any young man to be kissing Deirdre in public, and, second, she hadn't seen Deirdre smile so genuinely in the year since her parents' death. Just as she was about to demand that the gentleman introduce himself properly, he turned to her and smiled.

"Lady Derby, please let me introduce myself. I am Anson Reece. My parents were very close friends of Deirdre's parents, and Deirdre and I have known each other since we were children. Ah, I see you looking at me with suspicion. I must beg your indulgence of my bad behavior. I was so delighted to see Deirdre that for a moment I lost all sense of propriety." With another glowing smile, Anson swept Selda's hand into his and planted a kiss upon it. Selda's ruffled feathers were instantly smoothed.

Turning back to Deirdre, Anson presented a toe and bent low before her. "May I have the honor of this dance?" Blushing again, Deirdre happily acquiesced.

As the pair joined the other dancers, Marvella burst into excited chatter. "Well, if that isn't providence, I don't know what is."

"Why providence, my dear?" Selda asked.

"Just look at your niece."

Selda had to admit that Marvella was quite right. For the first time since her arrival in London, Deirdre seemed to be enjoying herself. "Well, he is an attractive young man. And very well mannered."

"Indeed. You know it has seemed to me that Deirdre doesn't do well with strangers. And here is a man she has known all her life. They seem similar in age, and he's quite charming as well, don't you agree?"

"Oh, yes," Selda replied, with a vigorous nod. "Quite charming."

"We must encourage this," Marvella declared.

Selda watched the couple dancing and talking. "Yes, we must."

Anson swept Deirdre around the dance floor. "You waltz very well," she told him somewhat breathlessly.

"As do you."

"I'm afraid yours is a false compliment, sir. I had very little practice at it until I arrived in London. At Ramshead I was taught the older dances. I had to rely upon my own imagination regarding the waltz."

"And with whom did you waltz?"

"Anson!" she cried with mock indignation. "That is a private matter. I most certainly shall not answer such a question."

"I hope it wasn't some other strapping young lad you were entertaining!" Deirdre gave him a coy look that she fervently hoped would discourage further questions, for she would rather not admit that her dancing partners at Ramshead had consisted of broomsticks and mop handles. To her great relief, he changed the subject. "I remember the day we took a picnic out to your favorite pond and fished for hours," he said, smiling down at her with green eyes that sparkled warmly.

"So do I!" Deirdre exclaimed. "The trout pond was always one of my favorite places to go. From there you can't see any of the buildings at Ramshead. It was my wilderness. I could take off my slippers and stockings and do whatever I pleased there."

"Take off your stockings!" Anson exclaimed in shocked amusement. "Why Deirdre, how very unladylike of you!" Deirdre laughed in delight and gave her head a toss that sent the mahogany curls piled atop her head dancing in the blaze of the chandeliers' candlelight. "What was the name of that pony?"

"Pony?"

"He was black as midnight, and he wouldn't listen to a single command."

"His name was Cobweb, and he may not have obeyed your commands, but he was most deferential to me."

"Cobweb. You would have done better to name him Spider!"

"He wasn't named Cobweb for his color," Deirdre explained laughing. "He was named after one of the fairies in *A Midsummer Night's Dream.*"

"A bluestocking, eh?"

"I was studying Shakespeare when my parents gave him to me. It seemed a very good name at the time."

"And ingenious." Anson took her chin between his finger and thumb, and, tilting her face up toward his, said, "You were always very smart and quite pretty. But I had no idea you'd turn out to be such a beauty."

"Thank you," she said, looking up at the man she had last seen as a little boy. He was tall and well built. He wore his blond hair tied in a queue at the base of his neck and was nicely dressed in a burgundy evening jacket and green breeches. His face could easily be described as handsome, with its straight nose and slightly cleft chin. Everything about him, from the way he spoke to how he stood, bespoke a relaxed personality. She could not think of anything about him that there was to disagree with or dislike.

Anson led her from the dance floor and back to her aunt. After securing a fresh glass of champagne for Deirdre, he turned to the assembled group of women and, in a matter of minutes, had Selda and Marvella, as well as Justine, who had joined her mother, engaged in a witty conversation about the rumors of new lanterns that were fueled by gases.

Deirdre joined here and there in the discourse, but her gaze drifted around the crowded ballroom, seemingly in general disinterest. In reality, she was methodically searching every group, every corner, every couple on the dance floor. He should have been easy to spot, being so distinctly unique from the other men at the ball and so much taller, yet nowhere could she find the man she had seen across the room. At last she abandoned her search. He had obviously either joined her uncle at the gaming tables or taken his leave. Perhaps such events bored him just as they did her. What a strange thought! She knew literally nothing about the man, and yet she had already assigned him a personality as well as likes and dislikes. Deirdre gave herself a mental rap on the knuckles. Silly!

The evening passed enjoyably, a fact that surprised Deirdre. She had forgotten how nice it felt to be in the company of someone familiar. Anson's asking her to dance and fetching her champagne the very second her glass was empty was quite different from being swept from one stranger to another. She found herself dancing more dances than she had at all the balls of the past two months combined. The orchestra played one waltz after another, and Anson insisted on dancing to at least every other one. After each, Deirdre was so parched that she fairly gulped down her champagne. And Anson dutifully refreshed her glass each time she emptied it. His jests about her hoydenish ways at Ramshead brought back wonderful memories of days she wished had never ended, and she laughed happily over the memories, feeling warm and relaxed for the first time in months.

"Ah, midnight!" Anson declared, as the pendulum clock at the top of the stairs chimed the hour. "Let's celebrate! Deirdre, let me have your glass refilled."

"I've already had far more than I'm used to, Anson. I'll be abed 'til noon!"

"What's the harm in that?" Anson asked, laughing heartily.

"Deirdre is quite an early riser, Lord Reece. I doubt that a pounding head has ever been the cause of a late start for her," Selda declared, with a shake of her own somewhat aching faculty.

"The morning after is well worth the fun of the night before," Anson proclaimed, launching into an entertaining discussion of some of his more painful experiences while overimbibing champagne.

But Deirdre found it difficult to concentrate. She had no similar experiences to relate, and the room had suddenly become stiflingly hot. Dancers swept by at what seemed to be dizzying speeds. Acrid smoke hung in the air from the hundreds of candles that blazed in the chandeliers, and her arms seemed cumbersome and uncooperative. The room tipped and swayed and she felt her stomach lurch. She took a sip of champagne, hoping to settle the queasiness in her stomach, but instead it proved to be her undoing.

The sparkling wine tasted sickening in its sweetness, and the scent of the spirits brought a sudden nausea sweeping over her. In a moment the feeling passed, only to come back a second later with devastating force. Panicked by her state, Deirdre tried to concentrate on recalling where the ladies' retiring room was located and exactly how far away. The room was, she recalled in despair, up the staircase and down a long hallway. Then she noticed three sets of tall, open doors, leading to what could only be a terrace of some sort. Escape from the heat and smoke foremost in her mind, she neither waited to tell anyone where she was going or why. She simply stepped around Selda and Justine and began to make her way through the crowded room, her only thought that she not embarrass herself by being sick in front of everyone.

Her entire being became focused on reaching the open doors of the balcony as she fleetingly wondered whether she was already drawing attention. In the next instant she dismissed her concern, aware that whatever attention she might attract in her mad dash for the door could hardly be worse than emptying the meager contents of her stomach on some unsuspecting lord or lady, something she was certain was going to happen if she did not hurry.

She reached the nearest of the doorways without a moment to spare. The cool air hit her with a sobering sting and immediately she felt better, but the effect was short-lived. The refreshment of the air was not enough to battle the inordinate amount of champagne she'd consumed, and a minute later she realized she was very definitely going to be extremely ill. Without giving a thought to the misting rain or how her actions must appear, she bolted for the darkest corner of the marble balustrade and bent over the railing. Her retching was the most horrid noise she'd ever heard, and there wasn't a doubt in her mind that every single person in the ballroom was listening with rapt attention to every vile sound she made. But it was such a blessed relief to have her stomach empty of the champagne that she barely cared.

When her stomach had finally disgorged enough of the champagne to cease heaving, Deirdre straightened and took a shaky breath. She felt weak-kneed, and her mouth tasted absolutely foul, but overall she was not nearly so ill as she had been. It was then, just as she was thinking that perhaps she had not been detected by any of the other guests, that she realized with an agonizing certainty that someone was standing just behind her. Frozen in place, Deirdre tried to envision the worst possible person to have seen her. *Marvella,* she thought. I'm going to turn around and find that Marvella has seen the entire thing, and then she will go inside and move slowly from group to group announcing to absolutely everyone that I was sick over the Whitmores' railing.

Closing her eyes, Deirdre breathed in more of the damp night and squared her shoulders while she contemplated a strategy.

"I believe you could make use of this," a deep, decidedly male voice said. Deirdre found a square of linen at her shoulder and, without acknowledging its owner, took it. Mortified though she was, she neatly wiped her mouth and inspected the bodice of her gown. It was only then that she turned around.

Three

Instead of Marvella, Deirdre found herself standing only inches away from the very man she'd searched so diligently for earlier. He was even more daunting at such close proximity. As she looked up at him, a break appeared in the thick blanket of clouds, and the light of the full moon poured down onto the terrace, illuminating them both. In the moonlight, his face was a series of sharp planes that lent a hard, unreadable edge to his allure. But his eyes caught the light. Their grey mingled with the opalescent moon rays, making him seem more untamed beast than mere man.

"I'll take my handkerchief if you are finished with it."

"Oh. Oh, no," she stammered, wadding it into a ball in the palm of her hand. "Please, let me have it laundered. I will see that it's returned first thing in the morning."

"It *is* first thing in the morning," he reminded her dryly.

"So it is."

"You should return to the ballroom before you're missed."

"I'm rather certain that I haven't been missed," Deirdre countered, thinking of all the lords and ladies who no longer bothered to speak to her. "But I was probably noticed. I'm afraid I nearly bowled over one woman," she explained gravely.

"Matrons expect young girls to seek solace for their broken hearts on terraces."

Deirdre's spine stiffened mutinously. "I did not come out here to cry over some matrimonial disappointment!"

"Perhaps you'd rather have them know that you were emptying your stomach upon the Whitmores' hedgerow? I suggest, Countess, that you learn to temper your intake of spirits quickly."

Before Deirdre could form a reply, he turned and strode back into the ballroom, leaving her to wrestle with her rising indignation. Her struggle didn't last long. She had made a fool of herself, and she roundly deserved the cryptic cut he had laid on her. Squaring her shoulders, she tilted her chin upward and reentered the ballroom, ready to take whatever strange looks and biting comments might come her way. Thankfully, the ball was breaking up, and, in the crush of collecting capes and finding one's carriage, no one seemed to have noticed either her departure or her return.

The rain had turned from mist to a downpour by the time Peters pulled the carriage under the Whitmores' portico. Felix handed Selda into the snug interior first, then helped Deirdre inside. As always, Peters had placed warmers filled with hot embers and wrapped in foot blankets under the seats, and three fine woolen lap robes lay ready for them.

"Horrid rain!" Selda declared as she wrapped herself in the warm wool. "But it was a fine evening despite the weather, don't you think, Felix?"

"Indeed. Lots of talk among the gentlemen tonight."

"The marquess, I suppose. I dare say he caused quite the stir among the ladies."

"With the men as well, I assure you."

"Do you think it's jealousy?"

"That, and intrigue. Do you know of anyone who is as difficult to read as Jersey? Or as unlike anyone else. He's part nobility, part peasant."

Selda nodded. "Polished beyond description, yet . . . rough."

"Barkley said he rode out to Jerseyhurst about a year

ago and found the marquess up to his knees in cow dung. Composting, or some such thing he declared. He'd rather spend his time collecting seeds and working out breeding charts than socializing, you know. And they aren't even breeding charts for horseflesh! It's cattle he's breeding. Cattle and strange new crops from America and Lord only knows what!"

Seated across from Felix and Selda, Deirdre listened intently to the conversation. Beneath her lap blanket, the handkerchief in her hand was being worked threadbare by her fingers. "Who are you talking about?" she asked at last.

"The Marquess of Jersey," Selda responded enthusiastically. "No one could have failed to notice him tonight, except perhaps you, my dear niece. You have the most extraordinary ability to spend the entire night at an event and be completely unaware of who has come and who has gone."

"He does keep very much to himself and a small group of intimates," Felix noted in her defense. "But I must agree he's hard to miss."

"What does he look like?"

"Tall. Dark."

"Hair as black as pitch with skin the color of a Spaniard's," Selda added. "And very intimidating."

"Confident."

"Almost frightening."

Felix inclined his head. "I agree. But he's not a roughian. Jersey's a marquess, after all, and carries himself every bit in accordance with his title."

Deirdre's fingers found a corner of the abused handkerchief and began to tug at it. Her fingertips touched the outline of a monogram and her heart jumped. "The kind of man people move out of the way for," she ventured quietly.

"Exactly!"

"An enigma," Selda stated with a decisive nod.

"Everyone wants to claim him as a friend, yet very few can," Felix explained. "He's undoubtedly one of the richest men in all of England."

"When he walks toward you, it's almost as though he's stalking you," Deirdre added.

"Then you *did* see him," Selda said.

Deirdre nodded. "Very tall and dark. Black hair, bronzed skin."

"Precisely. And cold grey eyes that never look at you."

"Unless you cross him," Felix tempered.

Deirdre looked out the carriage window. She was certain that the gentleman her aunt and uncle spoke of was the same man whose soiled handkerchief she held. But his eyes had been nothing like either Selda or Felix's description. The image of him standing only inches from her on the terrace appeared in her brain. He had looked right into her soul with those eyes, absorbing every response and action she made as he watched. They had been anything but cold. Rather, they'd sparked with intelligence and a restrained power. She could not honestly say they were friendly eyes, but neither were they cold. Although she could not fathom why, she was certain that an intense warmth had flickered in their depths. "What is his name?"

"Lord Jared Montgomery, marquess of Jersey, earl of Rochefort," Felix intoned importantly. "And, as I said, one of the wealthiest men in all of England."

"I do believe that the marquess cannot be blamed for his demeanor," Selda continued with a sympathetic sigh. In the darkened interior of the carriage, Deirdre gave her aunt a querulous look. "The past few years can not have been easy ones for him."

Felix pondered this for a moment. "He seems to have taken it harder than most, I dare say."

"Felix!" Selda protested. "The marchioness was adored by all. Can you think of any . . ."

"The marchioness?" Deirdre asked, quietly repeating her aunt's words.

"It's a devastating story, my dear. The marquess was once married to a woman who was the toast of London. Lady Daphne Montgomery was stunningly beautiful. She was also vibrant and personable. Why the moment she walked into a room it came alive.

"They led quite a life. I don't think there was an event of importance at which Lord and Lady Montgomery were not in attendance. If they did not appear at your ball or come to your hunt weekend, it was the deadliest of cuts. Many a noble's most intricately planned entertainments were laid waste for want of the marquess and marchioness as guests."

A nameless gloom fell over Deirdre as her aunt spoke, one which she determinedly shook off. "They must have been very much in love."

"My dear, they were inseparable."

"What became of her?"

Selda shook her head. "She was killed in a carriage accident. It must be three years ago now, don't you agree Felix?"

"Just three years, I believe, even to the month."

"You're right. It was terrible weather, even worse than tonight. Lady Jersey was traveling alone, which was quite unusual. The roads were in very bad condition, as they always are at this time of year, what with the rains. The carriage overturned and fell down a steep embankment." Selda paused, shaking her head. "It was all so unfortunate."

Deirdre looked from one to the other of her relatives. At last Felix completed the tale for her. "The marchioness had just insisted upon having oil lanterns installed on the inside of their carriage. It seems that oil spilled everywhere. At any rate, by the time the news of the accident was received by the marquess and he rode to the scene, there was nothing left of the brougham or his wife but ashes."

"He wasn't even able to see her one last time," Selda declared in anguish.

"How terrible," Deirdre whispered.

"He still mourns for her. One never sees him in anything but black, and his appearances at functions are very rare now. He simply can't bear to attend without her."

"He has become quite reclusive," Felix agreed. "So much so that when he does make an appearance, as he did tonight, it causes a stir for weeks."

The occupants of the carriage fell silent, each pondering for themselves the devastating story. They would be home soon, and as Deirdre looked silently out the window, Selda watched her niece carefully. It did not occur to her for a moment that Deirdre had given more than a passing thought to the marquess. Jersey was not worth the trouble of considering. Marvella, dear friend though she was, was not at all sensible about such things. She'd gone completely poppycockish about the possibilities for Jersey and Justine, as if there was the slightest chance of such a liaison! It wasn't that Justine was not attractive enough, though Selda mentally tempered her compliment with a note that the girl would do well to lessen her taste for bows and baubles on her dresses and intersperse the relentless pink and powder blue of her fabrics with some less childlike colors. It was simply that Jersey would probably never get over his loss. Of course, Marvella claimed that one day the urge to secure his lineage would strike the marquess, and he would marry again. So far as Selda could see, however, it would be a marriage of convenience, and she wanted none of that for her niece.

But Selda would dearly have loved to discover if Deirdre had any interest in the young Lord Reece. She knew little about Lord Reece, but she was certain that Deirdre had enjoyed herself more tonight than she had in all the time she'd been in London. And Anson Reece appeared to be congenial, well-bred and good-looking. Selda did not, how-

ever, make even an offhand inquiry of her niece. She'd
learned better than to question Deirdre about potential suitors. Each time she'd done so in the past, the results had
been disastrous. Whatever man she inquired about was
never acknowledged by Deirdre again. That had been when
gentlemen still called upon her niece, and many months had
passed since anyone, man or woman, had bothered to leave
their card for Deirdre.

It wasn't that her niece was rude. To the contrary, she
was delightful company to both herself and Felix. But she
preferred to be alone. She spent most of the day with her
nose in a book or tending to Selda's hothouse plants, upon
which she had performed nothing less than miracles. She
rode, but only at unfashionable hours early in the morning,
when sensible people were still abed or breakfasting. Deirdre claimed that the air was fresher at seven in the morning,
more like Ramshead. She had to be dragged out of the
house in the evenings and insisted upon ending her nights
ridiculously early. Selda was quite convinced that no one
knew what to make of Deirdre, and so they stayed away.
None of this appeared to bother Deirdre in the least. But
Selda worried for her.

Deirdre only allowed Avis to help her out of her gown
before she sent the tiny maid off to bed. It was nearly two
in the morning, and Deirdre was reluctant to keep Avis up
any longer. With the lamp turned low in her room, Deirdre
diligently brushed her thick tresses until they gleamed,
washed her face at the basin, and slipped into the white
batiste nightgown Avis had laid across the carefully turned-
down bed. But in spite of the late hour, Deirdre wasn't
sleepy. Her mind returned again and again to the evening
past and images of flinty grey eyes that were at once judg-
mental and inquisitive. At the side of her bed, now carefully
folded and straightened, lay the marquess of Jersey's hand-

kerchief. One corner, that which lay exposed on the nightstand, bore the intricately intertwined initials $\mathcal{J\,M}$ embroidered above a family crest. At last, abandoning any thoughts of sleep, she snatched up her wrapper and candle and slipped from her room.

Gliding soundlessly down the stairs, she headed for the kitchens at the back of the house. From the hallway she could see light shining from beneath the kitchen door, and, as she pushed through the swinging door, she inhaled the delicious aroma of warm chocolate.

"I'll have a cup ready for you in a minute," Avis announced without bothering to look up from the kettle as she dropped a lump of chocolate into the steaming milk she stirred.

"How did you know?"

Avis smiled at her, webs of fine wrinkles radiating from the outer corners of her small brown eyes. "How have I always known? Haven't you, since you were tall enough to see over the top of the counter, always wanted a spot of chocolate to warm you on rainy nights? Or was that another little girl whose growling stomach I warmed?"

Deirdre pulled a three-legged stool next to the hearth, a soft smile curving the corners of her mouth upward as Avis handed her a cup and saucer and then filled it with the steaming drink. Without hesitating a moment, Avis threw herself into cleaning up after herself, her motions quick and darting despite the hour. "Now, tell me how was the ball? And don't sip that chocolate too soon or you'll surely burn your tongue."

"It was . . . different."

"Then you're glad you went, despite yourself."

Deirdre blew on her chocolate as she pondered Avis's point. "Yes, I am glad I went. I met a man."

Avis's glance darted to Deirdre and just as quickly she looked away. "So what kind of man would turn the head of a lass as stubborn and unsociable as you?"

"Avis! I'm not unsociable. I just don't have anything in common with those people. They're strangers. Not like you or Aunt Selda and Uncle Felix."

"Aye, I know. I just worry after you. You're not makin' a new start, Deirdre, and ye must. Now, tell me about this gentleman."

"There were two really," Deirdre hesitated. "No, only one. But I met two men. One is Anson Reece. Do you remember Lord and Lady Reece? They came to Ramshead to visit Father and Mother."

Avis stopped her cleaning just long enough to try to recall. "Was it a long time ago that they came? I can't recall a soul visiting the last five or six years."

"I must have been seven or eight. Anson and I went out to the trout pond and rode on Cobweb."

"I might remember a visit," Avis agreed, moving to poke at the fire and spread the embers. "Was he the one who caught your eye?"

"No, not really. It was just nice to spend the evening with someone familiar. He was easier to talk to than a stranger."

"But the one you're thinkin' of, he was a stranger."

"A stranger, yes. But he was different." Then after a moment, she asked, "Have you ever met someone whom you'd never seen before, never spoken to before, never even heard of before, yet you felt as though you knew him?"

"I can't think of a time that I have," Avis replied, stopping her constant flurry of activity to peer intensely at Deirdre. "And did you dance with him?"

"No," Deirdre explained, suddenly feeling acutely uncomfortable at the look Avis was giving her.

"Converse with him?"

Deirdre gave an embarrassed roll of her eyes and deposited her cup on the butcher table. "In a manner."

"You didn't let this Lord Whatever-his-name-was kiss you, by any chance?"

"No! Of course not."

Avis put down her cloth and walked over to her charge, who was now fidgeting with the white ribbon ties of her wrapper. She laid her hand on top of Deirdre's, the soap-reddened skin a sharp contrast to Deirdre's smooth, pink-tipped fingers. "It's just that sometimes when a young woman gets that moonish look, it's more because she's had her first kiss than due to the lad who's kissed her."

"Well, you needn't worry about that because I didn't kiss him. Far to the contrary, he lent me his handkerchief after I threw up my supper in the bushes." Avis stared at her blankly, a look so uncommon for the active maid that Deirdre couldn't suppress the giggles that bubbled up. "It wasn't a very good way to meet him, was it?"

At last Avis said, "How very kind of the gentleman to help you."

"Oh, Avis." Deirdre shook her head as the giggles subsided. "It *was* kind of him. There he was, daunting and intimidating one moment, then telling me to wipe my face like a good little girl the next! Not the best of meetings." She smiled, then added with a shrug, "But I did feel, even then, that we were somehow alike. It was a very, very strange feeling." Yawning, Deirdre wrapped Avis in a hug. "Thank you for the chocolate. And don't worry about me in the morning. Get your rest, it's nearly dawn as it is."

Warmed by the chocolate and her talk with Avis, Deirdre slid between the sheets of her bed just as the first fingers of sunlight began to streak the sky. She dreamed of the ball, of Ramshead, and of the marquess whose slate grey eyes seemed to seek something from her.

Four

Jared stretched his legs to their full length beneath the study table and stared down at the papers before him, his coffee growing cold as he concentrated on the situation at hand. Just after dawn, he'd sent a message to Charles Ellis's home. The solicitor had arrived, as requested, at eight. By nine, Jared was in possession of every fact available on his subject and now, as the clock struck ten, he mentally reviewed his plan. Before him sat three stacks of neatly organized files. One contained all the information Ellis & Fitzwalter had accumulated over the past year on Ramshead and Morgan Ramsey's debts. Another contained what scanty information was available on Deirdre Ramsey, and the third pile was a small collection of writing papers crowded with ciphers and notes made in Jared's own hand. He tapped the documents containing the information on Ramshead with the tip of his quill, deep in thought.

Impressively, every one of Morgan Ramsey's debts had been paid in full—some even with interest—by his daughter. The estate had been decimated in order to do so, but, according to Charles, the young Lady Ramsey had insisted that every last one be paid.

Jared stared out the tall study windows at the Pall Mall, indifferent to the occasional carriage or horse and rider that passed by. Though few Londoners knew or cared, Jared was well aware that Ramshead was one of the finest estates within a hundred miles of London in any direction. Certainly Morgan

Ramsey never understood the value of his inheritance. The books Ramsey's solicitor had provided for Jared's perusal last summer had revealed a frugally managed estate. Yet when needed, money had been invested to maintain the integrity of the land and herds. Apparently the bailiff was the guiding hand behind Ramshead. Born on the estate, Bert Manning had learned the expert techniques his father passed on to him. Morgan Ramsey's father, James, had been passionate about his land and invested a lifetime making Ramshead a highly successful working estate. Unfortunately, his son, unlike his bailiff's son, had cared only that the estate provide him with the wherewithal to live the lifestyle of the nobility.

Jared pursed his lips in irritation. Even with the profitability of Ramshead at his disposal, Morgan Ramsey had run through every shilling of his inheritance, all the income of Ramshead and twice that again in debt. At least the fool had let Manning have a free hand in managing the estate. And because he had, there wasn't a property in all England that held more appeal for Jared than Ramshead.

According to Charles's information, Ramshead was completely closed now. The servants, all except for two, had been paid a severance and had taken employment elsewhere. Only Bert Manning and Seamus MacDonald, the head groom, remained. Having lived their entire lives on the estate, neither had any inclination to leave. Besides, they were both of an age which merited being pensioned by now, though Jared didn't believe for a moment that a pension had been set aside for them. The fields lay fallow, the prize cattle and sheep sold off, the entrance locked. According to his calculations, Jared had determined that it would take £5,000 just to put the estate back in working order. And Lady Deirdre Ramsey didn't have a guinea to her name.

Lady Ramsey. He carefully reviewed his assessment of the countess, an integral piece of the puzzle. She lived with her mother's sister and brother-in-law. The childless couple apparently doted on their niece, although their interaction with her prior to her parents' deaths could barely qualify as minimal.

Last night had proven Robert Harelton and Will Marlot correct about the young countess. She was beautiful, but her behavior at the Whitmores' had proven there was little of merit in her personality. Beauties such as her should be full of fire, Jared thought with disdain. But they never were. Sparkling jewels held no appeal for him, be they of stone or flesh. Inevitably they were either icy and cold or brittle and easily shattered. Still, beauty like that was powerful. If she'd had the intelligence to understand her position, she could have had all of London at her feet. Like Daphne.

Unbidden, his wife appeared in his mind, looking just as she had when he'd taken her out on the night before she died. The silver gown she'd worn to the Kenilworths' ball was nothing more than gossamer. Scandalously low cut, it left little to the imagination. The gown matched the color of her hair perfectly. Her pale-as-snow skin was set off by a diamond diadem at the base of her long, slender throat, large diamond teardrops on her ears, and a triple strand that was clasped about one delicate wrist. Not a man alive could have gone unaffected, and none did that evening. She had been the queen of London at the Kenilworths'. The men had been nearly insane, dancing and flirting outrageously, despite the knowledge that she was his wife. And the ladies had stayed away. They whispered behind their fans all night, too envious to speak to her, too daunted to stand beside her.

Jared's shoulders tightened, his jaw clenching at the memory. Shoving back his chair he paced the study, his long legs eating up the floor. Daphne was gone. She was gone.

Ten minutes passed before his pace slowed and his thoughts returned to Lady Ramsey. Stopping mid-room, he rested a forearm on the mantel and stared into the cooling embers of the morning fire, Daphne now safely returned to the recesses of his mind.

As he'd walked toward Deirdre Ramsey last night, he'd

found his interest momentarily stirred. She'd met his gaze
with her own forthright stare and he'd sensed—what? Insight? But that impression had evaporated as he'd watched
her waltz and drink herself sick with Anson Reece. A
woman like Deirdre Ramsey was useless. The past three
years Jared's tastes had turned to women who offered hot,
fiery passion without an attached list of requirements, and
who accepted the same in return. Not naive, undisciplined
virgins. He shook his head. His momentary interest in Deirdre Ramsey last night had been nothing more than the result
of four weeks crossing the Atlantic and another two getting
resettled, albeit temporarily, in London. Since leaving Vir-
ginia, he'd not had an opportunity to relieve his growing
needs. He needed to give that immediate attention before
he did something he'd later regret. And he would do well
to get his business with Lady Ramsey taken care of and
leave her to the milquetoast gentry she obviously preferred.

Over breakfast, Charles had provided all the necessary
information on Lord Reece as well. Twenty-four and accu-
mulating a mountain of debt at the gaming tables, he was
living a lifestyle which he could ill afford. Why the chit
chose to set her sights so low was beyond his understanding.
She probably believed she was in love with the sap. The
thought momentarily turned Jared's stomach. Reece could
offer Lady Ramsey no assistance in saving Ramshead from
decay. Nor would he provide her with a lifestyle similar to
the one she now lived with her aunt and uncle.

Clearly Lady Ramsey was not looking for someone to
assist her in reclaiming Ramshead. She was not looking
very clearly at anything from what Jared could tell. She
claimed to have no interest in selling her estate, yet neither
was she working to keep Ramshead from turning into just
another downtrodden estate of former greatness. Jared, on
the other hand, had no intention of allowing that to happen.
In one fluid movement he rose, looped a finger over the

collar of his black riding coat, and stalked out of the study, his mind focused on Ramshead.

Thirty minutes later he strode through the wrought-iron entrance gate of the Derbys' Mayfair town house. Taking the steps two at a time he reached the door just as it flew open and Deirdre Ramsey, a potted plant in each hand, barreled into him. Jared heard the wind rush out of her lungs with a whoosh at the force of their collision and his arms closed around her, pulling her against him as she teetered backward in surprise. He was amazed at how small she felt, no more than a wisp in his embrace, and for an instant he felt lumbering in comparison. Her head barely reached his chin. In fact, it fit nicely just beneath it, and through his jacket he could feel the press of firm breasts against his chest. She smelled faintly of flowers, but more predominant than flowers was the scent of grass. Damp, dewy, morning grass.

Pulling herself out of his grasp, pots still in hand, she stared up at him in surprise. The first thing he noticed when he looked down at her face was that she looked nothing like she had the night before. And nothing like what he had expected. Rather than being pale and puffy as women tended to be early in the day, she was radiant. Her cheeks were flushed with color and her blue eyes bright and awake. In the morning light, her hair was of an even richer tone than the ballroom's candlelight had shown it to be. She'd obviously pinned it up hastily, judging by the long strands that had escaped her efforts and lay loose about her shoulders. Jared lifted a finger to her forehead and wiped away a smudge of potting soil. "We seem to be constantly meeting under unusual circumstances."

Her skin pinkened with embarrassment, and she looked down, balancing one pot on her knee as she worked her fingers to a better hold on the rim. "You took me quite by surprise, my lord."

"Had I suspected that anyone would be dashing out of

houses at this hour of the day, I'd have been more wary in my approach."

"The day is nearly half-gone, sir. And the morning is the best part of it. I can't imagine that you would expect a household to be lounging when it is nearly noon."

"I admit to knowing more that would be than those which would not."

" 'Tis their loss then."

Jared cocked a brow in silent acquiescence to her point, then nodded down at her pots. "Are these being banished from the household?"

"Not at all. Euphorbia requires a great deal of sunlight and the front of the house is south-facing. The weather has warmed and they will continue to bloom longer if they are set here. Besides, they will brighten the entrance to the house."

Both eyebrows now raised, Jared watched as she placed the pots of brilliant yellow flowers on either side of the steps, dusted the stray soil from her fingers, and turned back to him. Working hard to keep his expression bland, Jared nodded toward the hem of her fawn-colored riding skirt. "You are missing your slippers, Lady Ramsey."

Flushing, Deirdre looked down at her feet as though noticing for the first time that they were completely devoid of either slippers or stockings. She curled her toes and then looked back at him with no hint of her discomfort other than the bright red spots on either cheek. "You must have come for your handkerchief," she said, lifting her chin ever so slightly. "I've laundered it for you. If you'd like to come in, I'll get it."

Not bothering to correct her assumption, Jared followed Deirdre inside. In the foyer, she requested that tea be brought to the drawing room and asked that her aunt be informed that she was with a visitor. Jared noticed that the butler was not in the least concerned that a good three inches of bare ankle was in plain sight beneath his mistress's skirt hem. Still somewhat taken back by this person who was far different from the girl he'd lent a handkerchief to the night before, Jared allowed Deirdre to show him into the drawing room.

As soon as she was in the room she took refuge behind the pianoforte in the far corner, where her bare feet would be less noticeable. Then she pinned him with a direct gaze. "Thank you again for being so kind last night."

"Was I kind?" Jared replied.

"I'm afraid I haven't much experience with wine. Until I came to London, I only drank it when my parents were at home . . ." Her voice trailed off as the tea arrived, and she turned to toy with the muslin curtains covering the bank of windows until the butler was gone. The door had barely closed when there was another knock and a tiny, wiry maid slipped in. Without a word, she handed the laundered handkerchief to Deirdre, deposited a pair of tan slippers beside her feet, and departed. Lady Ramsey slipped the shoes on as though it was a completely natural thing to do in the presence of a gentleman caller and then crossed to the tea. "Would you like milk?"

"No, thank you."

She poured a cup, handed it to him, and went to retrieve the neatly pressed and folded linen square. "Thank you again."

Jared put his teacup down on the table, silently reassessing his impression of Deirdre Ramsey. The barefoot, somewhat disheveled woman with blossoms in her cheeks and sparkling sapphire eyes standing before him was markedly different from the one he'd watched last night. Softer. Definitely warmer. And refreshingly devoid of airs.

But that was of no matter, he told himself. Nothing had changed. He still had only one interest in her, and that was Ramshead. The sooner this transaction was completed, the better. He could throw his energies into getting Ramshead back in working order, and she could marry Anson Reece.

And she wouldn't need to worry about whether or not he had any money. She would be set for life after he paid her for the estate.

He pushed the revolting picture of Deirdre married to Anson Reece out of his mind. Turning, he walked to the opposite end of the room.

"Lady Ramsey, could we sit down? I have a second reason for coming to see you. A business matter."

Deirdre tried to cover her surprise, nodding as she walked to a seating arrangement before the fireplace. She sank into a chair and indicated that Lord Jersey take the opposite seat, watching as he placed his untouched cup of tea on the silver tray she'd just served from and walked toward her. Why did he make her feel so off-balance? She felt inept before him, uncertain of herself and discomforted beneath the scrutiny of his gaze. When she'd slammed into him on the front stoop, he'd looked at her with an intensity that made her knees go weak and her head swim. Her body pressed up against his had seared like a firebrand that burned through her clothing to her flesh and left a mark. Even his scent had been startling, filling her nostrils with its musky tang. And that stare. It was as though he peered into the very windows of her soul, assessing her. Deirdre could not discern what he saw there, good or bad. Nor did she understand why she so desperately wanted to draw the curtains of those windows and prevent him from seeing whatever it was he sought. Normally, she would not care what a stranger thought of her. Why, then, did she care with him?

The tone in his voice had changed in the last minute, as had his entire demeanor, and as he bore down on her, his expression reminded her of the way he had looked the night before, when she'd been certain he was searching her out. Like then, she felt he wanted something. But what could he possibly want from her? She watched him sit down, stretching long, powerful legs clad in skintight black breeches and knee-high boots into the space between them. He dwarfed the chair with his size. The embroidered cushion supported by spindly cabriolet legs didn't look substantial enough to hold him, yet he relaxed into it with a natural grace. Folding his hands together, he rested his forearms on the small, padded arms and looked her squarely in the eye.

"I have a business proposition for you, Lady Ramsey. I understand that your father left a substantial debt when he died, a debt which you paid in full." Deirdre felt a chill run down her spine, but she nodded in wary acknowledgment of his statement. "Paying that debt has left you with limited options, but I have an offer which will provide you with a beneficial solution. I would like to buy your estate, Ramshead. I assure you that my price will be equitable."

Deirdre cocked her head ever so slightly, as though she wasn't certain she'd heard him correctly, but before she could muster a response, he continued.

"I will pay you cash for the estate. A situation which will see you set very comfortably for life."

He continued, but Deirdre heard little of what he said. Her spine felt as though it had turned from bone to iron in the time it took Jared Montgomery to utter thirty words. Blood rushed to her head, roaring through her temples. Her face went hot with the flush of anger as she stared at the man lounging comfortably in her uncle's drawing room. Had she, only an instant ago, been moved by this man's gaze? She could not believe she had allowed herself to be affected by him. He was not the handsome, enigmatic stranger she'd romanticized him to be. He was nothing but another uncaring opportunist set on picking the last of her flesh from the bone. Staring at him in disbelief, she listened to him recount the benefits to her of selling Ramshead. She concentrated, wanting to memorize exactly what he said. *Vulture,* she thought. Her fingers curled around the arms of her chair until they ached. Every inch of her body tensed with fury. How dare he sit here, in her aunt and uncle's drawing room, as relaxed as though he was discussing the weather. He wanted her home.

"If you agree, I'll see to it that everything is taken care of," Jared continued. "My solicitor will be certain to see that you are fairly represented."

"I have a solicitor, thank you, Lord Jersey."

"I am aware of Mr. Benchley. However, I have—"

Deirdre could no longer stand it. She could not bear to listen to one more sentence, one more word, uttered from his mouth. She'd thought they were all gone, the heartless, self-interested people who'd so callously stripped her home as if her parents' belongings were nothing more than the contents of a peddler's cart. But she'd been wrong. So long as she had anything, they would come after her. And Jared Montgomery was one of them.

"You have what, my lord?" she demanded, coming out of her seat. "You have a misbegotten opinion of yourself? You have the insolence of an ill-mannered child? You have the effrontery to come here without so much as a proper introduction and calmly declare that you have the wherewithal and intention of purchasing my *home*? Ramshead *is not for sale*. Not to you or anyone," she declared, her chest heaving as her fury grew unabated. "I have no idea upon what presumption you have come here and insulted me with such a suggestion. Who told you Ramshead was for sale? Or do you imagine," she continued without waiting for his response, "that no woman would bother her silly head with an estate?

"You probably believe that all I care for is a wardrobe full of new gowns each season and a fine pair of bays to pull my carriage!" Deirdre blinked as she realized by his lack of response that this was precisely what he believed. Her temperature rose another degree at the unspoken insult, and she stamped her foot in frustration and anger. "Well, you are quite definitely and completely wrong, my lord! I haven't a care for balls and gowns and society. All the soirees in London in a hundred seasons shall never equal one hour at Ramshead in my mind. Not one hour! Ramshead is *not* for sale!"

Her breath coming in gasps, Deirdre glared at Jared Montgomery. He had not moved an inch while she stood over him giving him a dressing down, but now he rose from his chair. His eyes, which had taken on the color of rain-heavy storm clouds, remained locked on hers. As he stood, she was forced to tilt her head so far back that she couldn't help but notice with dismay how broad his chest was, or that the top of her head did not even reach his shoulders. *No matter,* she told herself. *David slew Goliath, and I will not let Jared Montgomery believe that I am a mere wrinkle in his plans.*

"You love Ramshead so much?" he asked in a voice low with suppressed anger.

"It is my home, sir. It means more to me than any person or possession."

"You love it so much you would rather let it rot than see someone else return it to the glory that you knew in your childhood?"

Deirdre's jaw dropped. "I will never allow it to rot! Ramshead is beautiful. In the spring—"

"When was the last time you saw it?" he demanded icily.

"June. It was early June when I left."

"I suggest you visit your home again. You haven't seen it as it is now. It's empty and abused—"

"You're wrong!" Deirdre retorted, her entire body beginning to shake. "The bailiff is there. He writes to me each month. He has assured me the house is fine."

"Fine?" Jared pinned her with a look of sheer ridicule.

"Yes! Oh, it's empty, Lord Jersey. Stripped of its furnishings by people who prey upon the misfortune of others. People whom you probably consider your friends. People, in fact, like you."

"Beware whom you label, Countess," he warned, his eyes flashing lightning streaks. "You know nothing of me."

"And you know nothing of me! Yet you came here presuming much, my lord. Very much."

Jared stared down at her. "There is nothing to know about you, Lady Deirdre. Nothing that isn't very clear."

"Is that so, my lord? Forgive my transparency. Pray tell what you see."

"I see your father's daughter. Someone who possesses little regard for the land except that it provides an income."

"How dare you say such things of my father!"

"How dare I?" Jared retorted, his voice thick with sarcasm. "Was it out of sheer delight in doing so that you stripped Ramshead of everything to pay your father's debts?"

"No, but—"

"It is a fact, Lady Ramsey, that your father used every penny Ramshead earned to travel and keep himself in style."

"Bert took perfect care of Ramshead."

"Yes. And despite his dedication, your father mortgaged everything he could. He spent it all and left you penniless. No, he left you worse than penniless. He left his only daughter to pay his debts for him."

"He didn't know he was going to die!" Deirdre fairly screamed at him.

"No." His reply was so soft it had the impact of a striking mallet. "And if he were alive today, Ramshead would already be sold. At the very least he would have done just what you've done, stripped it and then locked it up and come to London for the Season. He'd have worried about what to do about the mounting bills tomorrow."

"I am not incurring debts, sir."

"You are living off your uncle's goodwill."

"Only until—"

"Until you find a rich husband. Until you lure some poor sop who lusts after a title and a beautiful wife into a trade.

He gives you his fortune and, in return, you give him a title and your virgin body."

Deirdre glared at him, speechless. She hated him. She despised every word of what he said, every thought he had about Ramshead, her father or herself. Most of all she hated those lead grey eyes that stared at her with icy disdain. What did he know about her? And how dare he stand here and tell her that she would trade her body for Ramshead.

"I am offering you an alternative, Lady Ramsey," he said, his voice deadly calm. "Accept my offer, and you won't have to sell your body to the highest bidder. I'm willing to pay you a fair price for Ramshead, and that's a small fortune. It's much more than just the price of a plot of land I'm giving you. My offer is your freedom. But you are too naive to see that, aren't you?" He stared at her and Deirdre felt his eyes searching for the slightest chink in her armor. A way to disarm her. "I will have my solicitor draw up a formal offer. I suggest you consider what I've said very carefully, Lady Ramsey. Very, very carefully." Without another word he left.

Deirdre stood numbly in the drawing room long after she heard the front door abruptly close behind the marquess. Tears burned behind her eyes, but she refused to give them quarter. She would not let his words hurt her. He understood nothing about her. And he was wrong. She loved Ramshead. It was only for the sake of Ramshead that she was even here. She was keeping it safe by being here. She was.

"Was that the marquess?" Selda asked, bustling into the room still in her morning gown.

Deirdre continued to stare straight ahead, afraid that one look at Selda would be her undoing. "Yes, that was the marquess."

"My goodness," she said in surprise. "What was he doing here?"

"He came after something of his."

"Something of his?" Selda was silent for a moment, pondering this news. "How very strange." Tilting her head to one side, she regarded Deirdre's pale features. "Are you feeling well, my dear? You look rather ill."

Deirdre looked away, not certain she could stand up to a close inspection. "I'm fine."

"Good, because Lord Reece has left his calling card and a note." Deirdre didn't respond, and after a moment Selda continued. "You really should see what his note says."

Deirdre shut her eyes and sighed. She wanted nothing but to run to her room and lock the world out. But Anson Reece was her friend, and she would not ignore him. Taking the proffered envelope, Deirdre opened it and read the enclosed message. "Anson wishes to take me for a carriage ride this afternoon."

"How lovely. Will you accept?" Selda asked, working diligently to invest a degree of enthusiasm into her niece.

"No," hung on the tip of Deirdre's tongue, but her aunt's face was full of excitement.

"It sounds quite nice," Selda encouraged. "It's a lovely day out, and a bit of fresh air might help your pallor, my dear. After all, he is an old friend of yours. It would be nice to spend a few hours with someone you know well. You seemed to enjoy his company so much last night."

Deirdre reread the note. Perhaps Selda was right. Some fresh air would clear her brain of Jared Montgomery's accusations. And Anson was her friend, not a stranger she would have to smile at and pretend interest in all manner of boring conversation. She smiled at Selda and nodded in agreement. "I think you're right. It would be lovely to go for a carriage ride this afternoon."

"There," Selda responded happily. "You see, the blush is already returning to your cheeks. Come and sit down with me for a minute." Taking a seat on the settee, Selda patted the cushion beside her. "You haven't yet told me about Anson's visits to Ramshead. Did his parents come often?"

Feeling better, Deirdre sunk into the small couch. "I remembered him as soon as I saw him last night. But I only recall Lord and Lady Reece visiting once." She shook her head, perplexed. "Perhaps they came another time. Otherwise, how could Anson remember so many things about Ramshead, and about me?"

"Perhaps you have confused Lord Reece with other children who visited."

Deirdre smiled softly and patted her aunt's hand. "Very few people ever visited Ramshead, Selda, much less children."

Selda savored this bit of information without much surprise. "It was a lonely childhood for you, wasn't it?"

"I was very happy, Selda."

"So you've always said, my dear. But lonely, too. You had no sister or brother to keep you company, Deirdre, and your parents—"

"No one could have had better parents than I," Deirdre responded emphatically. She took a deep breath, remembering, and leaned against Selda's shoulder. "You know what they were like. So happy. So carefree. When I was very little, I thought of them as magical beings. Beautiful and special."

Selda listened in silence, then gave Deirdre a quick squeeze. "You must send your acceptance to Lord Reece without delay," she warned, changing the subject. "It's nearly noon now. I'm certain he'll want to come for you at two."

"How are you so certain?"

"Because that is what's done."

"Ah, what is done." Although Deirdre nodded, it was an action somewhat lacking in acceptance. "Now I'll know." Planting a kiss on Selda's cheek, Deirdre went to her room. Ten minutes later her note of acceptance was dispatched to Lord Reece. At exactly two o'clock, Parker greeted Anson at the door.

Bathed and dressed in a Wedgewood green gown and matching cropped jacket trimmed with citrine braiding at her wrists and collar, Deirdre felt refreshed and far removed from the morning's angry encounter with Jared Montgomery. Greeting Anson in the drawing room, Deirdre's mouth curved into a mischievous smile. "I'm afraid you have proven my aunt to be the undisputed authority on the *de rigueur* appointments of society."

Anson grinned broadly. "I have no idea how I've managed such a feat, but I am delighted to have done so if it pleases you."

"She claimed that you would arrive at two since it is the approved hour for social events such as carriage rides," Deirdre explained blithely.

"And she's correct, of course. But I confess I was so pleased that we could spend some time together that I nearly came earlier." Taking her hand, Anson bowed over it and pressed a kiss to its back. "You look even more beautiful than you did last night."

Deirdre blushed at the compliment. "Thank you. Have you had a busy morning?"

"I'm afraid I lazed about this morning. I admit to being a bit of a night owl. I prefer not to see the sun until it is well overhead."

Anson's comment brought Jared Montgomery crashing unbidden and unwelcome into her thoughts. Hadn't he claimed that most people were not early risers? Angrily, Deirdre shut the thought out of her mind. "Shall we go?" she asked, anxious to quit the room where she'd last seen Lord Jersey. With a nod, Anson collected her gloves and hat for her and handed her out the front door.

Despite yesterday's heavy rain, it was as lovely an afternoon as Deirdre's morning ride had promised. Anson's coachman turned in the direction of the Pall Mall and Deirdre breathed in the crisp spring breeze. The leaves were nearly fully out, spreading light patches of shade across their path, and the flowers along the Mall filled the air with a delicious scent that lifted her spirits tremendously. She was glad that Anson had asked her to come. It was so nice not to think of the man beside her as Lord This or Earl That. Here was someone whom she could think of simply as Anson, and the familiarity felt good.

"How long have you been in London?" he asked, giving her a soft smile.

"It will be nearly a year soon. It doesn't seem possible that so much time has passed."

Anson reached over to lay a reassuring hand over hers. "I'm sorry about your parents, Deirdre. I didn't have a chance to tell you so last night. You must have been lonely these past months."

Deirdre inhaled a shaky breath and fixed a smile on her face. At least Anson had known her parents, and that made his concern real. Other men had offered her the same consolations, but they were strangers, and she could not help but read their concerns as false. Anson was different. He was her friend, and she could trust him. Not like Jared Montgomery. It would be a lovely afternoon, she thought, relaxing back into the carriage squabs. "I have never minded being alone. I don't really think of it as being lonely. There is always so much to occupy my mind that the time seems to fly by."

Anson gave her another smile. "I confess to needing a bit more entertainment than that. But then I have lived in London since I was only eight. My family estate went to my brother, a blessing since I haven't the mind for that life." Anson turned as an approaching carriage passed them. Lifting his gloved hand in a greeting, he smiled brilliantly at the two young ladies who occupied the open hack. "The ladies Bromleigh," he explained when they had gone by. "I've known them since we were children. Wonderful ladies." Then, giving Deirdre another of his charming smiles, he turned his attentions back to her.

Five

Jared pushed the last of the paperwork toward Charles Ellis and ran his fingers through his thick, black hair. Rising from the table covered with the files on Ramshead and Deirdre Ramsey, he walked to the study windows and braced one hand against the sash as he let the slanting rays of late afternoon sunlight warm his chest and arm. "Well, what do you think, Charles?"

"I think the countess could not do better, no matter where she looked for relief from her predicament." The solicitor continued to review the stack of papers, searching for any error or imperfection in the legal documents he had spent the majority of the day preparing. He had handled the marquess of Jersey's financial matters for well over a decade, and his knowledge of the marquess's vast holdings was extensive. Ellis & Fitzwalter acted as financial and legal advisor for the marquess's shipping concern, as well as handling the bookkeeping and audit of Jerseyhurst's revenues, and a variety of Jared's personal matters. Charles was well aware that equal parts ability and discretion ensured his firm's continued association with the marquess. But Charles Ellis prized more than just the highly lucrative business of managing the financial concerns of the marquess of Jersey. He valued the personal respect which had grown between them the past twelve years. Jared Montgomery was a man he admired greatly. He had overcome circumstances which most men would have merely wallowed in until they were destroyed. He had used adversity to his gain and become, in the course of a decade, one of England's wealthiest men. "I'll present the formal offer to Lady Ramsey first thing in the morning, unless you'd like it delivered this evening."

"No, tomorrow is fine. And deliver a full set to her solicitor as well. You can review it with the countess when you deliver it, which will give Benchley an opportunity to familiarize himself with the offer before he meets with Lady Ramsey." Recalling the paunchy solicitor from their last meeting at Ramshead, he added, "Benchley doesn't move too quickly, so I'm depending on you to cover all the details with the countess." Jared moved to the crystal brandy decanter and poured two drinks. Handing one to Charles, he looked each document over one last time, ensuring that everything was in order.

"The countess should find nothing disagreeable in the offer," Charles repeated.

One corner of Jared's mouth curved into a sardonic half smile. He doubted very much that Deirdre Ramsey would be pleased with his offer. "More than likely she'll toss it straight into the hearth," he speculated. He didn't need to look up from the papers to know that Charles reacted with surprise. Not that it should matter how Deirdre behaved when she received the offer. He'd executed innumerable business transactions in which the other party had been less than agreeable. It was simply business, and feelings were not involved. In fact, remaining emotionally detached from a business proposition was the only rule he believed in adhering to at all times. Ignoring it assured absolute disaster. Experience had taught him that lesson well, and he didn't intend to subject himself to its costs ever again.

The problem was, he had expected to dislike Deirdre Ramsey. Despite her beauty, he had assumed he would find everything about the cold, immature, self-interested chit distasteful. Instead, he found himself continually surprised by her, and his dislike was proving difficult to sustain. "She's very . . . different," he commented to Charles as he made a notation in the margin of one sheet.

Charles took a sip of his brandy. The marquess had never discussed a lady with him before. Of course, he reasoned, this was purely a business transaction, and therefore quite different from the various arrangements Charles had handled regarding the financial needs of certain ladies whom the marquess had taken a personal interest in over the years. It was disconcerting to find himself in the position of commenting on the more subjective side of Lord Jersey's affairs. Still, he felt a response was expected. "I have not had the pleasure of meeting the countess."

"It doesn't always qualify as a pleasure," Jared stated flatly. "And I don't think that meeting her once will tell you much about her at any rate. From what I have been able to discern, it's when she's not expecting to be seen that you see what she's really like." For an instant a pair of tiny bare feet and comely ankles flashed through his mind, along with a dirty face. The appealing picture was followed abruptly by the memory of her belligerent, hardheaded tirade and momentarily he wondered which she was—forest nymph or cantankerous shrew.

"I've found it quite true of most people, your lordship, that their best face is always the one shown in the public domain."

Jared glanced up from his perusal of the contracts. "True. But in the case of our little countess, I'm not sure if the one that's hidden isn't the best face." Laying the last of the papers down, he took his drink and returned to the window. There was something notably different about Deirdre Ramsey. Something which defied generalizations such as Charles had just made. Her social persona wasn't created to impress people, as were most. Instead, her goal seemed to be to hide herself, to be as bland and uninteresting as possible around those she should be most concerned about winning over.

In her uncle's drawing room today, she had been as different from the woman he'd watched last night as day was from night. One part of her had been as warm and light as a forest pixie, and the other part! Jared could only shake his head. Was it only last night that he'd thought she lacked fire? What a little spitfire she'd been today. A hotheaded hoyden! Jared couldn't remember the last time anyone, let alone a woman, had dared to speak to him in that tone. But he knew it had been well before he was out of short pants. He'd intended on giving her a tongue-lashing she'd not soon forget and he would have if her hair hadn't come loose as she stood over him, lecturing and stamping her foot in anger. But it had, falling in thick, dark waves that curved around her full breasts and spiraled all the way to her waist, and after that he hadn't been able to concentrate on his anger or her rantings.

Instead he'd watched mesmerized as her cheeks flushed raspberry and her eyes sparked like twin blue embers alive with passion. He'd watched each movement of her lips with total fascination, noting that just beneath them he could see the straight edge of pearl white teeth and the occasional flick of a moist, pink tongue. Her mouth had proved deeply distracting. So distracting that he'd settled for a mildly caustic rebuttal. But even when he'd stalked out of the Derbys' house, the image of her mouth still haunted him, making him increasingly certain that it was the most eminently kissable mouth he'd ever seen.

Jared tightened his grasp on the crystal glass in his hand. He was a fool to think of Deirdre Ramsey as anything but an inconvenient business associate. And he was *not* going to mix business with pleasure. Not ever again. What had Will said about her? *Cold as a witch's tit.* Remember that! he ordered mentally. Jared shook the thought of her lips out of his mind. He would buy Ramshead and save it from deterioration. By adding it to Jerseyhurst and his other holdings in England, he would establish not only the best cattle-breeding program in all England, but the finest crop farming as well. He could stock his ships to the deck boards with grain and livestock and sell it to America or France or any country that would buy it. With the proceeds of those sales, he would further improve England's livestock and crops. He would have an impact on his homeland's future.

Staring out the window, Jared focused on a carriage moving leisurely across the Pall Mall, and his brain began to smoke at the sight. There was no doubt who was in the carriage as it passed directly before him. Anson Reece and Deirdre Ramsey. How could she be so stupid, he fumed as his emotions once more defied his control. What did she think Reece had to offer? He watched the useless dandy twirl a strand of her hair between gloved fingers as he leaned close to whisper something in her ear.

For a moment, Jared relished the idea of breaking each of those fingers one by one, followed by a good whack or two applied to Deirdre Ramsey's behind. She had immense nerve. Not four hours ago she had been ranting at him about how she was never going to sell her family's estate, and here she was letting a boorish lout like Anson Reece pursue her. Nothing matched being intimate in an open carriage on the Mall for fueling the gossipmongers' fires. By supper the pair would be "an item," and by tomorrow speculation would be in full swing, with every eye watching. If she wasn't going to sell Ramshead, then she ought to be expending all of her talents on finding a wealthy gentleman to marry. But Lady Ramsey, he was beginning to suspect, had some very naive notions about how the world was and what was required in order for her to have her every whim.

The carriage continued on, its occupants engrossed in each other. Jared turned away from the sight in disgust and downed the remaining contents of his glass in a single gulp.

"Your lordship?"

Jared stared blankly at Charles, who stood with the decanter in his hand.

"I asked if you'd like another."

"Yes," Jared responded, depositing his glass on the silver tray beside his solicitor. Preoccupied, he watched the brandy being poured, then retrieved his tumbler. "Charles." The solicitor came to attention, well aware of the change in his client's tone. "Be certain the countess and her solicitor understand that this time my offer will only stand for thirty days. If Lady Ramsey cannot reach a decision within that time period, she will have to live with her choices—detrimental as they may be."

"I shall, your lordship."

Deirdre peered out the carriage window into the darkening evening as they made their way to another ball. What was wonderful about spring, she thought to herself, was the utter unpredictability of the season. Last night had been cool and rainy, but tonight was its opposite. The cloudless day had dried much of the dampness from the air and ground so that even now, when it was approaching nine in the evening, the night was lacking any chill. As Felix had handed her into the landau, she'd felt a warm breeze touch her face, portending the arrival of summer. If she'd been at Ramshead, she mused, the air would have borne the scent of lilac and dog roses, and she'd have run through the house opening windows to let the delightful smells in and banish the stale winter air from every room. She would remind Bert that he must do so when she wrote this week.

Peters pulled up before the Caveneshes' home and Deirdre was handed out by a liveried footman. Positioned, as always, between Selda and Felix, Deirdre waited as they were announced, and then began her descent into the crush of satin gowns and colorful evening coats. Her own peach-colored gown was embellished with brocaded lace and sprays of embroidered floral bouquets. Selda had suggested it because the gown was so summerlike in its design. It must be true, Deirdre thought, because she felt more enthusiastic about tonight than she had in months and months of balls and parties. Tonight, however, she knew there was something to look forward to. Anson had promised to be there, and, because of that, she anticipated enjoying her evening. This ball, she told herself, would consist of neither of her previous alternatives. In the past, a ball represented either hours spent relegated to the corner with the elderly ladies, widowed either by death or the draw of cards in another room or, worse, an evening spent in the company of boring, unknown lords who thought themselves and the dull complexities of their day fascinating. She considered herself indebted to Anson for rescuing her from such a fate.

As Felix handed her a glass of champagne, Deirdre scanned the room for Anson. There he was! Rising on tiptoe, she craned her neck as much as she dared so she could get a better look at the blond-haired gentleman standing with three other young men on the far side of the ballroom floor. No, she realized in disappointment, it wasn't he. Deirdre glanced about for a clock, but the ballroom was without a timepiece, and she was reluctant to ask Felix the hour, knowing he and Selda would make too much of her question. As it was, the entire conversation over supper had focused on Anson. Anson's parents. Anson's home. Anson's family history. Deirdre had done her best to answer their questions, but as she had told Selda before, she really only knew that his parents had been friends of her own. They had visited Ramshead once, although she thought she recalled her father and mother going to visit the Reeces on occasion while she remained at Ramshead. Felix related that he thought he'd met Anson on perhaps one or two occasions, but neither he nor Selda knew much about him, which, of course, had to be remedied if he was to be considered as a suitor.

Dejected by Anson's absence, Deirdre sighed. *Was* Anson a suitor? she asked herself. She certainly enjoyed his company, and she felt much more at ease with him than with the other men who'd plied their suit. He was handsome and very charming. Would he make a wonderful husband and companion for her?

It was the first time Deirdre had ever thought of a man in those specific terms. Without question, she looked forward to seeing him, which was a marked departure from her feelings toward other men. She supposed that it depended upon how Anson felt about her.

Thoughtfully, Deirdre put the rim of her champagne glass to her lips and then stopped. The smell of the sparkling wine was a sudden and potent reminder of the previous night's catastrophe. Squelching a tinge of queasiness, she lowered the glass to waist level. She had no desire even to sip on the liquid, which until last evening she'd enjoyed in limited quantities.

"Ah! There are the ladies Bowers," Felix announced, nodding in the direction of a small alcove. He ushered Deirdre and Selda to the other ladies, and let out a sigh of relief as though he had now fulfilled an arduous task. Giving Marvella a gentlemanly bow, he then repeated the action to Justine. "Don't tell me your father has begged off this lovely event, Lady Justine."

"Oh, no, Papa is here," Justine bubbled. "But I believe he's availed himself of the whist tables, Lord Derby."

Felix's eyebrows shot up as though he was surprised by this most common of occurrences. Lloyd Bowers, as they all knew, viewed the balls of the Season much as Felix did. The whist tables held much more appeal than the ballroom, and he wasted as little time as possible in getting his women settled so that he could get six cards into one hand and a port into the other with minimal delay. "I think I will see how he's doing," Felix declared as though it was a novel thought.

"That would be fine, my dear," Selda replied, giving him a light pat on the arm. "We'll be right here." The ritual departure played out, Felix and Selda exchanged affectionate looks, and Felix started off in the direction Justine had indicated the whist games were proceeding.

"Deirdre," Marvella beamed as Felix's wine-colored dress coat disappeared into the swirl of silks and woolens. "I'm so very happy for you!" Deirdre tilted her head and regarded Marvella with some confusion. "Come now, my dear," she continued in a conspiratorial tone. "You and that handsome Lord Reece . . ."

"We are friends, Marvella. Acquaintances from childhood."

"Well, I know that, of course. Wasn't I standing right beside you when he nearly swept you off your feet in his delight at seeing you again? But, really, Deirdre, you've no need to keep your news quiet from me."

"News?" Deirdre repeated.

"After all, you were seen by at least a dozen people on the Mall this afternoon. And quite intimate, I've heard."

"Intimate?"

"Now, now." Marvella patted Deirdre's gloved forearm. "Don't look so shocked. This is *London.* And the Season as well. I think it's absolutely wonderful that Lord Reece has made his feelings so evident. Why everyone is whispering that you'll be betrothed before the month is out. And you do make a lovely couple."

Deirdre closed her eyes and shook her head to clear it. As usual, Marvella had succeeded in making much more of her relationship with Anson than had yet developed. Marvella had an amazing ability to recreate completely any occurrence or situation to suit her whimsy which was very clearly what she had done with Deirdre's afternoon carriage ride with Anson. If anything was to develop between Anson and herself, Deirdre wanted it to be kept very private. The last thing she would want was for all of the *ton* to discuss in minute detail her budding association with Anson.

"Marvella," Deirdre began, thinking that she must squelch Marvella's overenthusiasm before Anson finally arrived. "I believe that . . ." Deirdre let her intended comment trail off into silence. Marvella, Selda, and Justine had gone completely still, and, judging by the size of Justine's eyes, Deirdre needed to check the top of her head for newly sprouted corkscrewed horns. Deirdre gave the three ladies a queer look before suddenly realizing that they weren't staring at her at all, but at something directly behind her.

A male voice, deep, rich, and familiar spoke just over her shoulder. "Countess, may I have the pleasure of this dance?"

Deirdre's heart leaped, yet she held herself frozen, her back still to the man who spoke. Why, after their argument this morning and the obvious animosity that had sprung up between them, was he here? And standing so close to her back that she could almost feel the warmth of his chest against her shoulders.

Struggling to regain her composure, Deirdre slowly turned to face Jared Montgomery. He gave no indication that he even knew the other ladies were there, but looked directly at her. His gaze was dark and unreadable, though she did not sense any hostility there. Nor was there the slightest indication that their last conversation had been anything but amicable. Holding out his gloved hand, he cocked one dark brow in a bold challenge. "Countess?"

Deirdre knew she could not possibly refuse without causing a stir that would be weeks in settling. She understood at least that much about London society. A refusal would be no less than a cut direct, and to the most sought-after man in the *ton*. Slowly, Deirdre inclined her head, her gaze never leaving his face. The challenge accepted.

Jared lifted the champagne flute out of her hand, depositing it into Selda's care with no more than a short nod of acknowledgment. Deirdre placed her hand on the exquisitely cut sleeve of his black evening coat and walked, as though being escorted to the gallows, onto the dance floor.

"You like to be the center of attention, don't you, my lord?" she said curtly when he did not stop until they were in the very center of the room, where every person in attendance would be afforded an excellent view of them.

"To the contrary, Countess, I much prefer my privacy. But since they will watch every move we make anyhow, we might as well provide them with a clear view." The orchestra leader tapped his baton, Jared bowed to her and then slid his arm around her waist and drew her closer to him as the musicians began the waltz.

Finding her face nearly upon his shoulder, Deirdre had no choice but to look up into his impenetrable face or be labeled a loose young lady devoid of morals. "Are you always the center of attention?" she asked.

"Unfortunately, my past and my present have combined to present society with a certain fascination for watching my every move," Jared explained, though the depreciatory slant of his mouth said much for his dislike of such attention. "Rest assured I don't normally make it a habit to attend these functions."

Interested by this vast departure from the lifestyle Selda and Felix had described to her when they had discussed the marquess, Deirdre contemplated the tall stranger with whom she was dancing. He was as graceful as a cat—his dancing flawless—as they moved around the ballroom. He held her comfortably, neither clinging to her as some men did, nor holding her limply as though wishing she were across the room rather than mere inches from him. Yet Deirdre felt the power of his arms and the heat of his muscled chest with an intensity that left her breath ragged and uneven.

The shadow of a smile touching his mouth, Jared raised one eyebrow and tilted his head, indicating the floor. "I'm disappointed to find you wearing slippers this evening," he told her blithely.

Deirdre blanched, completely taken aback by his statement. He chuckled at her dismay, then continued softly. "I believe I prefer you as you were this morning. Barefooted and with dirt on your face. Tell me, my lady, how are your euphorbia faring?"

Frowning at this unfamiliar warmth, Deirdre took a moment in deciding how best to approach this new tack of his. "They're fine," she ventured at last. "As I said, they will do better facing west."

"Are you familiar with other plants?"

Deirdre gave him a wary, sideways glance. "Some. Most. Why?" She was finding his conciliatory attitude highly suspicious.

"One of my gardeners tells me he is having some problems with the roses I brought from northern France last year. I thought you might have some advice for him."

"I know nothing about roses," Deirdre lied, her chin coming up mutinously. "My lord," she finally announced in vexation, "if your aim is to make jest of me, we can end this dance now. If, on the other hand, your purpose is to enlist my affections in your favor because you believe I will change my mind about Ramshead, you are mistaken. Either way, I see no point in continuing our discussion. You cannot have any real interest in your roses. And I, as I stated this morning most emphatically, am not interested in selling Ramshead."

"Why are you so certain that my only interest in you is your property?"

"Because," Deirdre explained, her ire growing by the minute, "that is what you want. Tell me honestly, sir. When I first saw you last night, you appeared to be making your way to me. Were you?" Jared nodded. "Was your interest in me then to discuss Ramshead?" Again, the marquess inclined his head in agreement. "Then this morning, you called on me for the express purpose of making an offer on Ramshead. An offer which you were certain I would accept."

"That is true."

"You see," Deirdre declared, victorious. "You want to buy Ramshead. Since your two previous attempts have not met with success, you are now trying a different tactic. That is all this is, a tactic."

Jared smiled broadly, and she couldn't help but notice that the grey of his eyes softened, growing almost warm. "I admit that I'd like to purchase Ramshead. But only because you are not doing anything to show me that you actually intend to keep it."

Deirdre glowered at him, all her defenses locking into place at his criticism. "You know nothing at all about it. How can you say—"

"I can say it because it's true," he interrupted. "And I assure you that I do not ever pursue something without knowing exactly what I am dealing with."

Her chin came up in saucy defiance of his statement. "You haven't dealt with me, my lord."

"But I know a great deal about you. Much more than you think."

"For example."

"For example," Jared said, thinking that this hotheaded vixen had more brass than most of the men he knew combined. "You closed down the estate, which was a mistake. You have no means of income, so you cannot provide the infusion of funds needed to start new crops or herds. And you are not actively looking for a husband who would enable you to keep Ramshead."

Deirdre went white-faced in disbelief. "Because I am not interested in finding a husband, you deem me uninterested in keeping my home?" she sputtered, incredulous at his brazen opinion.

"Yes."

"You are the most arrogant, ignominious man I have ever had the poor fortune to know. I can only think that you demand such attention from your peers because you have no compunction about what you say or to whom."

"On the contrary, if anything at all, I hope I command their respect because I am honest in what I say. Whether or not it is easy to hear is another matter."

"Oh! And who, pray tell, would you have me marry to prove that I value my home?"

"Anyone with a great deal of wealth. One hundred thousand pounds in cash and assets of another £100,000 would be sufficient, so long as he agreed, prior to the marriage, that he was willing to provide for the upkeep of your estate."

"So, I am to sell myself as you suggested earlier today?"

"It is an option, although not the one I recommend."

"Besides, there aren't five men in all England with assets equal to the amounts you suggest. And one of them, from what I understand, is you."

Jared shrugged. "You didn't ask me if I thought it a practical solution. Were I in your position, I would take my offer and marry whomever I pleased."

The waltz ended, and Deirdre spun on her heels, intending to blatantly march away from Jared Montgomery—a display which, she spitefully hoped, wouldn't be missed by a single pair of eyes. Her exodus, however, was halted by Jared's iron grip on her elbow. "As I said, sometimes the truth is not easy to hear."

"Take your hand off of me, sir. I do not care to continue this conversation any longer."

"But I do," Jared stated flatly. "Except it isn't going to be here, where we will afford everyone an entertaining display." Continuing his firm grip on her, Jared steered her out of the ballroom and down a busy hallway. They passed two closed doors through which Deirdre could hear a multitude of men's deep voices, and then he turned her abruptly to the left, stopping in an alcove leading to another room shuttered by twin doors.

Yanking her arm from his grasp, Deirdre glared at him, her chest heaving as her breath came in shaky, furious gulps.

The tight control he'd maintained over his growing anger broke, and Jared's eyes narrowed, a sardonic curl touching one corner of his mouth. He had taken more than he cared to from the little chit. And he was filled to the gills with her aspersions and stiff-necked pride. "Tell me, my little shrew," he asked in an acid tone, "what exactly have I said that is not the truth?"

Setting her jaw, Deirdre pinned him with a mutinous glare. She wanted desperately to fling down example after example of how wrong he was and flout his challenge in his devilishly handsome face.

But she couldn't.

She could not find one chink or flaw or misstatement in his words. What was worse, he knew it.

"We don't have to be at odds, Deirdre," he continued more smoothly. "But in order for that to happen you have to trust me."

"I have no reason to trust you," she declared arrogantly. "You are a stranger."

"I see," came his soft reply. "Then you only trust people you know."

"Naturally. A stranger has no reason to treat me kindly. Nor has a stranger any understanding of who I am. Why would I trust someone like that?" Despite her imperious demeanor, Deirdre was aware of a strange sense of regret that blossomed deep in her bosom. A bleak despair that there were so few places to find trust. Her anger dissipated with the suddenness of a spring rainstorm and she looked away from him, unaccountably disheartened by her own words. "I should return to my aunt," she murmured softly.

"I'd like to show you something first." Picking up a large

candelabra from the hall table behind them, Jared put his hand on the handle of one of the doors beside them. "Do you know the Cavendeshes well?" he asked.

Deirdre let out a nervous laugh. "My lord, I don't know anyone in London other than Selda and Felix and a very few of their friends."

"Andrew Cavendesh attended Oxford with me. I came here quite often as a boy, so I know all the secrets of this house." Jared opened the door and stood back so that Deirdre could precede him into the darkened room. The moment she stepped inside she could smell the green plants. Behind her, Jared lifted the candelabra high, revealing the most beautiful room Deirdre had ever seen.

It was an enormous, glass-enclosed conservatory, filled with exotic plants of every shape and size. Somewhere out of sight a fountain filled the room with the soft music of spilling water. Her companion forgotten in her fascination, Deirdre followed the tiled walkway as it curved through the greenery, breathing in the warm scent of soil and water and a forest of plants. In the flickering light of the candelabra, she let her fingers trail over the leaves and petals, naming those plants she recognized as she went. "Bellflower. Delphinium. Ummmm," she murmured, inhaling as she dipped her nose to the petals of a white trumpet. "Lilies." She leaned over a bush resplendent with enormous red flowers with long yellow stamens at their centers. "I've never seen anything like this," she said softly.

"It's called rose mallow. I brought it from America as a gift for Andrew's mother, Lady Cavendesh." Deirdre looked up at him, soft surprise lighting her eyes. Jared set the candelabra on the tiles well away from the swirling hem of her gown. "I thought perhaps you would like this room."

"I do." Deirdre straightened and gazed up into the inscrutable face that moments ago she would have happily clawed to ribbons. How could he be this warm, enticing gentleman, and yet still be the cold, angry predator she'd faced? He stood very still beneath her perusal, and it occurred to her that he was watching her watch him.

He stepped closer, and she tilted her head back to look up at him. He smelled of spicy cologne, soap, and leather, all made stronger by the warmth of the conservatory. "Would you trust me if I asked you to?" he whispered.

Deirdre drew her brows together in anguish. "I . . . I don't know."

"Try."

"When?"

"Now." His arms closed around her at the same time his mouth dipped toward hers. Despite the fact that she knew he was going to kiss her, she did nothing to stop him. His lips brushed hers with a kiss that sent a spiral of liquid warmth pouring into her stomach. Deirdre didn't move. She felt his breath against her cheek and caught the vague scent of brandy. His lips came against hers again. This time they did not skim lightly over hers, but covered them, hot and moist, and so utterly delicious she ceased thinking altogether, letting the heat pour through her, warmer and warmer, until her limbs burned with it.

Mindless of exactly what she was doing, she rose onto her tiptoes, pressing herself against him. In response, Jared's arms tightened about her, crushing her with his embrace. Breathless, she moved her lips beneath his, parting them to make way for she knew not what. His tongue flicked gently across the inside of her lower lip, and the sensation caused her knees to go weak. Again, his tongue caressed her lip and then delved more insistently into the recesses of her mouth. A moan escaped, unbidden, from deep within her, and she ran the palms of her hands up the lapels of his jacket until she touched skin and the tips of his hair lying at the base of his neck.

"S-stop," she begged, her lips still pressed against his. "Please." Jared raised his head the slightest bit and stared down at her, his eyes smoky and intense. Then, loosening his embrace, he let her step back. "We should go back. My aunt will be concerned . . ."

Without a word, Jared bent to retrieve the candelabra. Turning back to her, he leveled a considering gaze at her. "Are you glad that you trusted me?"

"I don't know," Deirdre answered honestly. "I still don't really know you, nor you I."

"But you really believe that your trust should be given on the basis of a familiar face and not on the basis of what is proved?"

Deirdre nodded.

Moving back to the end of the room, he held the door for her. "If only the world was so simple, Deirdre."

Six

The dancers spun across the floor to another waltz as Jared reentered the ballroom with Deirdre on his arm. Sensing the turning heads that noted their return, he chided himself for his indiscretion. He hated the gossip that a moment's absence could cause as much as he despised an aristocracy that preferred busying itself with the creation of scandals where none existed, over exerting the least amount of energy in real work. In addition, Deirdre was not like the women he had taken as lovers over the past three years. They were experienced widows who knew how to deal with the *ton*. Deirdre was having her first Season, and one indiscreet action could ruin her. The more powerful matrons could destroy a young lady's future with a look or a word, and she was receiving the first indications of such looks now. Glancing down to judge the effect of the lifted eyebrows and blatantly speculative stares on Deirdre, Jared discovered that the woman on his arm appeared not to be cowed in the least. Her chin aloft in regal disregard of the reactions their entrance was garnering, she walked at his side with graceful self-possession. She looked straight ahead, as though there was not one person of consequence in the room beside the two of them. A slow smile spread across his face, and something akin to pride swelled inside him.

As they approached the alcove where he'd left Deirdre's aunt and two other vaguely familiar ladies, he heard Deirdre sigh with relief. The sound, coupled with the reason for it, made his jaw clench in disgust. Standing beside the three ladies, his head nodding in response to some comment, was Anson Reece.

Deirdre removed her hand from Jared's arm as they reached the group and gave Anson a sparkling smile. "I'm so pleased that you were able to come! I had begun to fear some other matter would keep you from being here to-night."

The muscles in Jared's back tensed as he watched Deir-dre's obvious pleasure at Reece's arrival, and he scowled in annoyance.

"I promised you I would come, didn't I?" Reece re-sponded, flashing an intimate smile as he bowed over Deir-dre's hand. "A promise made must be a promise kept."

"Anson, have you met Jared Montgomery, marquess of Jersey?"

Reece turned to Jared, smiled agreeably, and bowed. "Marquess. It's a pleasure."

Jared responded with a tight-lipped, barely discernible nod. He could hardly contain his desire to grab the man by his collar and deposit him unceremoniously in the street. Reece reeked of liquor, and judging by the slightly sloppy smile on his face, he was as sotted as a fiddler.

Too inebriated to notice the slight or the dangerous dark-ening of Jared's eyes, Reece apprehended a passing servant bearing a silver tray of champagne glasses and retrieved two flutes. Jared helped himself to a glass after Reece had taken his pair. "A toast," Reece said, handing one of the glasses to Deirdre and lifting his own. "To my very dear Deirdre and the wonderful afternoon we shared." Then, leaning intimately close, he added, "And to many, many more days shared together."

Deirdre smiled, blushing slightly at his boldness, and joined in raising her glass along with the others in the small group, but she only touched her lips to the rim of the glass and didn't actually drink. Jared's glass remained at his waist.

Ignoring Jared's slight, Anson gave Deirdre an over-dramatized look of concern. "Are you not well?"

"I'm sorry, Anson. I just don't have a taste for champagne tonight."

"Ah, well," Anson responded as he tipped his glass and emptied half of it. "A woman should have a more delicate constitution than a man."

Jared watched Anson Reece's every move, his dislike of the man growing by the second. He was worse than Charles's report had indicated. His drunken state gave him airs of self-importance. He clearly thought himself impressive and invulnerable. Fatal flaws.

Jared's eyes narrowed as he cataloged the man's weaknesses. He was the type who inevitably charmed young ladies and then left them pregnant and penniless while he pursued his pleasures elsewhere. A man like Reece would never have the money to keep a mistress—a dubious benefit to the woman he would wed. He would brag about his lovely wife and heir. Even show her off if he had the money to dress her well. Then, without a second thought, he would take his fill of available women, luring housemaids and nannies into his bed while his wife turned her head to keep up appearances.

Jared watched Reece as he regaled the ladies with incredible tales. Only his desire to know every one of Reece's weaknesses kept him from putting a great distance between himself and the cocksure fool beside him. As he listened to Reece's lengthening stories, Jared's eyes focused on a dark, bluish red hickie on the back of his neck. Another one showed just above his cravat. Love nips, left by some doxy who thought she had a young lord on her line. Reece had arrived late because he was earlier satisfying himself with some convenient trollop. And Deirdre could not see it. She couldn't see Anson Reece for the useless embarrassment he was. She was laughing and smiling along with the other women, entranced by his faux charm.

Because he was familiar.

Because Anson Reece was not a stranger.

Disgust rose like bile in Jared's throat. This ball, this city, this revolting display of idiocy represented everything he detested about London. Repelled by what he knew, Jared turned and left.

Deirdre felt Jared turn his back and walk away. His immediate dislike and disapproval of Anson had been obvious, a fact that she had found both irritating and hurtful. But she didn't want Jared to leave angry. The truce that had begun between them and ended in a kiss felt too sweet to lose again so soon after it had started. Thinking to stop him, she started to call his name, but Anson placed a firm hand at her elbow.

"We haven't had a dance yet, Deirdre." He leaned close to her face and fixed her with a sweet smile. Still watching Jared's back recede into the crowd, Deirdre let Anson lead her onto the dance floor. They danced to a quadrille, followed by a waltz, and by the time Anson escorted her back to Selda, Deirdre had been plied with a thousand compliments and endearments. He had a way of saying things to her which she would have considered forward and suggestive from anyone else, but when said by him seemed endearing. His entire demeanor was both masculine and gentle. His conversation was entertaining, and he seemed to be of the same opinion as Deirdre on every subject they discussed. Certainly he was handsome, with his blond hair and fine features, and Deirdre noticed the number of heads that turned as he walked her back to the alcove and fetched them each a drink.

"Champagne for you," he smiled as he held out a glass of the effervescent wine.

Deirdre shook her head. "Thank you, Anson, but I really don't seem to have a taste for it tonight."

"Then walk with me. There is a beautiful moon out tonight."

Images of Jared kissing her in the conservatory rose like phantoms before Deirdre. Her gaze fell upon Anson's mouth. She did not want to walk with him. Handsome as he was, she felt no compunction to kiss those lips. At least not tonight. And she had no doubt that a kiss was what Anson wanted. She told herself her lack of desire for Anson's kiss was due to the unseemliness of kissing two men in one night. But as she looked at Anson, it was a darker face she thought of. One with a jaw that was stronger, eyes like silvery thunderclouds that threatened always—even when they were dark with desire—and a mouth that could make her melt as it dipped toward her yet anger her with a single word.

While they danced, Anson had told her that he adored her. That she was as uncommon as a rose in winter and just as delightful a companion as she'd been when they were children. He'd smiled that sweet, boyish smile of his and told her that she held a special place in his heart. Gazing down at her with solemn eyes, he had promised that all the things he felt for her would only grow. And then he had hinted that he was anxious to have a mutual commitment between them. He would have gone on, had she not stopped him then, fanning herself and making a jest of the warm room and her tiring feet.

They were uncomfortable words, and Deirdre didn't know what to make of them. She cared for Anson very much, and she enjoyed his company. Should she, then, consider herself lucky to have someone so well suited to her responding with strong emotions of his own? He had made it clear that he wanted much more from their relationship, and somehow it didn't seem overly fast because he was not a stranger to her. But Deirdre wasn't certain just what her attachment or feelings were for Anson. She had not felt herself growing warm in his arms. She could not even recall his scent. Was he wearing cologne? Did he smell of something else? She vaguely recalled the smell of alcohol and something else. A musky scent. She cared for him, of that there was no question. But she was not at all certain what those feelings meant.

"Come," Anson urged, slipping his hand around hers in a gesture of possessiveness. "A walk will be just the thing."

Selda and Marvella were smiling encouragingly at her, their approval obvious. But Deirdre only gave Anson her warmest, most heartfelt smile and tilted her head to one side with regret. "Oh, Anson. I would like nothing more. But, I'm exhausted from so much dancing the last two nights. I fear my legs are barely holding me up. Selda," she said, turning to her aunt, "would you mind terribly if I had Peters drive me home and then return for you and Felix?"

Selda gave Deirdre a regretful half frown, recognizing her niece's usual excuse for avoiding a walk in the moonlight with a suitor. She was certain that Deirdre's feelings for Anson went beyond mere interest. This reluctance on Deirdre's part was perplexing. Although she and Felix hadn't spoken to Deirdre on the subject yet, Anson had visited Felix at his club today to formally ask for their niece's hand in marriage. There were the normal checks to be made, of course, but barring anything untoward being uncovered—which Selda simply couldn't imagine—Felix was ready to give his consent. The only issue was whether Deirdre would accept. They so wanted a good match for her, and Anson Reece seemed a wonderful young man. He was kind and very agreeable. Selda was hopeful that the two would suit. Still, if Deirdre wasn't comfortable walking with Anson just yet, Selda would not press her. "If you are tired, my dear," she smiled at Deirdre, "then, of course, you must go home. Anson will simply have to wait for his stroll."

Acknowledging that he was beaten, Anson squeezed Deirdre's hand warmly. The pressure was neither too strong nor too limp, but exactly as it should be to feel reassuring and understanding. "Then you must at least let me see you safely into your carriage."

Deirdre accepted Anson's escort with a nod. It never occurred to her that everyone at the ball would see them leave together. Nor did it cross her mind that Anson wouldn't return to the ball, thereby ending any speculation that the pair had disappeared into the night alone. As he handed her into the carriage, Deirdre did her best to give him an encouraging smile. She didn't want Anson's feelings hurt. Nor did she wish to lose the friendship of the only person in all of London that she could associate in any way with Ramshead. And there was the possibility that what she felt for Anson was the beginning of something more.

"May I see you tomorrow?" Anson asked, frowning in mock hurt at her rejection.

"Of course," Deirdre smiled. "Perhaps in the afternoon."

"You will be the only thought in my mind until then." Giving her a long, meaningful look, he pressed a kiss to her hand. Shutting the carriage door, he signaled for Peters to proceed toward home.

Anson watched the carriage pull away, a smug smile curling one corner of his mouth. Before another guest appeared at the carriage port, he slipped into the shadows, choosing to walk to the area where his carriage waited rather than chance being seen leaving alone.

Jared glared at the Jersey coat of arms that decorated the interior of the brougham above the empty seat opposite him. What was wrong with her? he raged. Hell, what was wrong with *him?* He knew better than to lead young virgins away from ballrooms. He knew much better than to keep company with asses the likes of Anson Reece. And he definitely knew better than to confuse something he wanted with lust. She was part of a business transaction, Jared reminded himself. He was not, absolutely not, going to confuse business with pleasure. *Hadn't he learned that? Hadn't he learned the idiocy of playing with fire?* Particularly of the female variety. So what had he been doing dancing with Deirdre Ramsey? Or slipping into darkened rooms to show her something that *he* cared about? My God, he'd even *kissed* her! And he'd felt like a besotted pup when he'd done it, like he'd never tasted a woman before. He definitely needed to find a mistress.

The carriage pulled up in front of White's, and Jared was out the door before the wheels had stopped turning, his long-legged stride eating up the paved walk to the front door. The minute he was inside, he was hailed by a familiar voice.

"Jersey!" Will Marlot called, his glass raised in salute. "Your timing is impeccable as always. A seat has just opened." Jared strode to the loo table and threw himself into the single empty chair.

Robert Harelton lifted one brow speculatively. "You look positively predatory, man. I'm not sure Will has done any of us a favor by inviting you to play."

"Just deal," Jared snapped. Turning to a passing waiter, he added "And bring me a brandy."

An hour later, most of Jared's fury had been defused by the cards and brandy. But the other men at the table had borne the brunt of his frustrations. Every one of the original players had quit the game except for Will and Robert. Three new men had joined the game in anticipation that the marquess of Jersey's luck was due to change at any moment, but so far their bets had proven futile to say the least.

Jared lounged comfortably in the leather chair, his black-clad legs stretched out beneath the table. His winnings stood in neat stacks discreetly to the left of his elbow.

"That's it for me," Will declared, tossing down his cards in response to Jared's winning hand. "I swear Jersey, my children—when I have them—will have you to blame for their beggared status. How you can win and win and still keep that disinterested expression on your face is beyond me." Rising, Will shrugged into his coat.

"Going home?" Harelton asked. "Or stopping back at the Cavendesh ball to see if Lady Constance might give you a dance?"

"Lady Constance may go to the devil," Will declared hotly.

Robert skewered their friend with a look of disbelief. "I see. Then you haven't a concern that she has apparently been taking calls from Archie Steele?"

"Who has it she's seeing Archibald Steele?" Will demanded. Robert lifted his shoulders in a casual shrug. "Just what I've heard." With a silent glare, Will headed for the door. The minute he was gone, Robert began to shake with suppressed laughter. "Ten pounds says he goes straight to the Cavendeshes'."

"He ought to rip Steele in half," Jared stated, unamused by Robert's teasing. "That would solve both his problem and Lady Constance's penchant for driving Will to distraction."

"He ought to ask her to marry him and be done with it," Robert countered, sobering. "He loves her, you know. But he's got some crazy notion that he wants her to demonstrate that she loves him in return. Speaking of lovely ladies," Harelton added, "the rumor is that you've had a sudden change in tastes."

Jared picked up the card Robert dealt him, added it to his hand, and made a discard. "The countess and I are engaged in a business dealing. Nothing more, Robert."

Robert Harelton glanced up at the front door as it closed behind a new arrival before casually returning to his cards. "Then you should have no problem if we ask Anson Reece to join our game."

Jared gave no indication that his friend's statement had

any effect on him. Casually crossing one ankle over the other, Jared glanced up as Reece strolled over to their table.

"Evening, Jersey."

Jared made no reply.

"Care to join us?" Robert asked.

Reece tipped to one side, regained his balance, and ran his tongue over dry lips. "Sounds like a perfect end to a perfect night." Pulling out the chair vacated by Will, he nearly fell into it.

"You sure you're up to it?" one of the other players queried doubtfully.

"If you can't play cards drunk, what's the use of playing?" Anson retorted with a grin.

"The ante is £30." Jared pinned him with a steely glare.

"No problem," Reece replied. Robert dealt and the game proceeded in silence. After Jared had won another three hands, Robert folded, and Byron Wilkeson stood in as the new dealer. As he requested that the players ante up, Reece smiled casually and called for the house manager. "I'd like to avail myself of a house credit," he stated when the man arrived.

White's accounts manager looked uncomfortable for a moment, then cleared his throat before replying. "Your credit is at the house maximum, I'm afraid, Lord Reece."

"Is it?" Reece laughed. "Well, that's unfortunate."

"Indeed," White's man responded.

Anson casually examined his hand. "You know I wasn't born yesterday. Gentlemen go over the house limit regularly. Extending me such a credit should prove no problem, I'm sure."

"I'm sorry, Lord Reece. I've a notation here not to extend further credit until a payment is made against your account." In the interest of avoiding further embarrassment to a regular, he didn't wait for Lord Reece's response, but returned to his office in the back of the establishment.

Anson leaned back in his chair, his demeanor cocky and

overly casual as he looked from player to player. Jared watched him like a hawk waiting to dive at an unsuspecting ground mole. "Gentlemen, you can see my predicament. I'm nearly £400 down right now and in need of an opportunity to recoup my losses." Pausing, Reece gave the men ample opportunity to offer backing for him to play further. When none was forthcoming, he stretched leisurely and smiled. "I'd be happy to sign a personal note to any one of you."

"What collateral are you offering?" Byron Wilkeson inquired.

"Will my carriage do?"

Wilkeson considered the offer. "Throw in that matched pair of chestnut high-steppers and I'll cover you for £100."

"The carriage is barely a year old," Anson complained. "With the horseflesh, it's worth at least £300."

Wilkeson, a shrewd gambler, shrugged. "A hundred. Take it or leave it."

"Taken," Reece replied with a dour look. Wilkeson called for the manager again, and the group waited while the appropriate papers were duly signed and witnessed. Within another four hands, Reece was through his £100, having lost two hands to Jared, one to Wilkeson, and one to sixty-year-old Silas Lamb, earl of Havenhorn.

"Best call it a night," Havenhorn admonished Reece. "Only a handful of hours 'til dawn, you know. A man your age ought not to waste his energies on cards and liquor. If I was your five and twenty years again, I'd be rolling a tender young lady under the eiderdown." Chuckling at some private memory, Havenhorn took a good-sized swill of brandy. "Thank God I'm sixty!"

Reece considered Havenhorn's counsel for a moment before reaching with an unsteady hand for his own brandy. "I do my share of rolling with willing young ladies," he boasted, privately toasting his abilities. "But there's plenty of time for both women and cards. Now, unless you gentlemen plan on denying me my right to win back my losings, I suggest we stop playing for these child-sized stakes and move on to some serious gambling."

Wilkeson and Jared both raised their eyebrows in unison. Jared felt nothing but contempt for the drunken idiot sitting across the table from him. You could almost pity him, he thought, as he waited for Reece to continue. In another five years, Reece would either be in debtor's prison or have a lead ball through his heart. Fools like Reece didn't even deserve to be called men. They had no purpose to their lives other than to have as many women and as many drinks as they could get their hands on. It was a short-lived pursuit. Men like that didn't have the brains to stay alive past thirty.

Reece gave the three men at the table a self-satisfied smile, mindless of the unimpressed glances that passed between his opponents. "I have excellent collateral."

"Better than the carriage and pair you've just lost to me?" Wilkeson queried doubtfully.

Irritated by the slight, Reece straightened and leaned forward. "Yes, Wilkeson. My fiancée's property." He waited for the impact of his offer to take effect before continuing.

"Your fiancée?" Havenhorn choked on his drink. "My, my, you *have* been busy, my friend!"

"How large is the estate?" Wilkeson queried, his gambler's nose smelling an opportunity.

"It's a large estate, a bit far from town—I'd say ten hours by carriage, but an extensive holding."

"Who, exactly, is your fiancée?" Jared had not moved an inch from where he sprawled in his seat, yet there was no mistaking the cold intensity of his question.

"Lady Deirdre Ramsey," Reece replied, his slack face growing sharp in response to Jared's glare. "The countess of Ramsey. I believe you know her. The estate is closed up now, and the house stripped, but it's certainly worth £60,000."

Jared's face hardened into a glacial mask of contempt.

Had he felt sorry for Anson Reece a moment ago? Reece wasn't merely a fool, he was a dangerous fool. A man of such utter stupidity that he didn't even bother to understand the value of the thing he bargained. Sixty-thousand pounds? Ramshead was worth twice that. Easily. But that was the least of Reece's sins. He was also lying. Jared was certain of it. Unless, the thought suddenly occurred to him, out of her utter naïveté and her silly, overly idealized view of the world, she believed that a childhood acquaintance was worthy of her lifelong commitment. If that was the case, she was in need of a lecture and a good spanking.

His anger growing by the minute, Jared considered the possibility that Deirdre had agreed to marry Reece specifically to prevent *him* from buying Ramshead. Immediately, he dismissed the idea. She was too smart not to realize that Reece could offer her no protection unless he had the assets to pay for Ramshead's upkeep. And Reece was practically a pauper. But she *would* have done it out of spite. Jared thought back to the woman who walked so proudly beside him in the ballroom, she was proud enough to do something like that. Proud enough and scared enough, he decided. But the woman who had responded so fully to his kiss would not have done something so rash.

Then a new thought crept into Jared's brain, and his fingers clenched around his glass in ill-controlled fury. Engaged or not, if Reece had the nerve to declare in front of twenty men at White's that he was marrying Deirdre Ramsey, he was, at the very least, confident that he would be engaged to her soon. Possibly as soon as tomorrow. He would have to remedy that first thing in the morning.

Then another thought struck him. This one with the effect of a thunderclap. Had he kissed her? Jared's fury roared to a new level of intensity. If he discovered that this contemptible, drunken womanizer had wiped away the remains of his own lips on Deirdre's, had so much as touched her lips with his, he would kill him. And he would consider killing

Deirdre if she willingly allowed the kiss. Only the lowliest, or most desperate of women, would kiss two different men in the space of a few hours.

The intensity of his fury at this thought was so great that Jared utterly ignored the fact that until this moment he had considered the satisfaction of male needs as a completely normal and acceptable use of women. He also ignored the fact that he had practiced such habits with zeal himself.

"Unfortunately," Havenhorn was saying, "until you marry the chit, you haven't any legal control over her property. So, I don't think it qualifies as collateral."

Jared pushed his chair back from the table, his eyes flickering contemptuously over Anson Reece, who was draped over his chair like a wet rag. "Find someone else to lend you money, Reece," he said icily. "I won't be party to stealing a woman's home from her behind her back." He stood up and walked out, the speed of his departure a testament to the fact that he couldn't stand to be in Anson Reece's company a moment longer.

Seven

The stillness of London mornings always bothered Deirdre. Lying in bed with her leaded-glass window thrown open to let the dewy morning invade her room, she could hear exactly nothing. Soon the calls of the peddlers would begin on the street below. But now, as the morning was just being born, it was utterly silent. And that was wrong. There should have been warblers and house finches filling the morning with their trilling songs. Even the squawking call of a jay or two would have been welcome. But London was too noisy and smelly for birds. And the Pall Mall or Kensington Gardens, where birds did live, were blocks away.

Running her fingers over the finely embroidered edge of her sheets, Deirdre's thoughts returned to the Cavendeshes' ball. The entire evening had been disturbing. Disturbing, and exciting, and worrisome. So much had happened there, and Deirdre needed to sort out her feelings about all of it.

She was no closer to understanding her feelings toward Anson than she'd been last night. She knew she wanted to be married one day. She imagined herself with children and a husband who would share every day's joys and tribulations with her. Was Anson that man? Closing her eyes she tried to picture Anson as a father and loving husband. She thought of her parents, who had never seemed to have eyes for anything or anyone other than each other. She wanted that intense love. She wanted her husband to look at her as her father had looked at her mother. With total devotion. Someone who shared her interests. Was that Anson?

They had shared a wonderful few days as children—Deirdre remembered that well. They had fished and rolled down hillsides. She had loved having a companion to play with; it was such a rare occurrence in her childhood. Smiling, she decided that the week he had come to Ramshead might very well have been something of an omen. She still found him pleasant to be with and, based on his declarations last night, he cared deeply for her. Perhaps he was the one for her. But when she closed her eyes and imagined what it would be like to be kissed by Anson, another man's image came to her, not Anson's.

Jared Montgomery. Why had she let him kiss her last night but not allowed Anson to? Jared's accusations had continued to bother her all of yesterday. Not even her carriage ride with Anson had succeeded in banishing their argument from her mind. So upset was she that she'd sought the mindless gaiety of the ball to push his disparaging remarks from her thoughts. Instead, at the Cavendeshes' ball, the very person she'd hoped to purge from her mind had been there. Their dance had started out the same way as all their other meetings—with an angry exchange of words. But then he had become suddenly conciliatory, as though he was not interested in arguing.

Looking out at the brightening sky, Deirdre asked herself if she didn't find something stimulating about parrying wits with Jared Montgomery. Jared never treated her as though she were incapable of speaking about anything but the weather and the latest social events, as so many other landed gentlemen did. He was smart and handsome, and she was afraid that there was more than a little truth to the concept that she enjoyed their highly animated disagreements.

And then there was the conservatory. Why had he wanted to take her there? He was the only man who had ever taken an interest in pleasing her in a way that reflected *her* interests rather than his own. Others merely assumed to know what her diversions were. Music. Painting. House calls to other unattached young ladies and their mothers. Deirdre shuddered under her covers. Those things were far removed from her interests. Or else they simply felt that she would be breathless with excitement at the prospect of hours spent listening to *their* interests and adventures.

But Jared Montgomery had noticed her love of plants. Or were plants an interest of his as well? He had implied as much when he'd mentioned his roses from France. He'd even asked for her assistance in nursing the roses. No. She shook her head and frowned. He couldn't really have meant it. The comment about his roses was simply a ploy, intended to win her sympathies and convince her to sell Ramshead.

Ramshead was his sole interest, she reminded herself. Not her. Deirdre rolled onto her side, tucking one hand under her pillow and snuggling deeper into the fat billows of her goose feather comforter. He'd seemed very knowledgeable in the conservatory. Had he really brought that beautiful flowering bush—a rose mallow, he'd said—all the way from America for his friend's mother? What a lovely gesture that was! Not at all in line with the image she had of him as a ferocious, mean-hearted monster. Nor had his kiss matched the image she'd formed of him.

His kiss. Why had she let him kiss her? she asked herself again. Why had she let him sweep her away from the ballroom? Why hadn't she protested more strenuously when she could have? She had done none of those things—instead she had let him kiss her. Knowing he was going to. Knowing she wanted him to.

Deirdre closed her eyes as an unfamiliar warmth spread through her limbs just thinking about it. It had been tender, yet . . . solid, like he was. Enticing and unlike anything she had expected or experienced before. And her own reaction— the wild, unquenchable thrill she had felt—had been wonderful beyond anything she could have dreamed of . . . and frightening as well. There had been something else also in his kiss. Something that she'd felt just beyond her consciousness. A promise—no, an implication—of passion held tight.

She shook her head hard. *Stop this!* she commanded herself, rolling once more onto her back and flinging her arms over her head. *Stop thinking about Jared Montgomery. All he wants is your home.*

Deirdre gazed at the pale yellow of her ceiling, painted to match the walls of her room, with their white trim and beautifully painted trellises of flowers that graced the two raised panels on each wall. Her gaze fell to the tall mahogany posters of her bed, with its china blue coverlet and matching armoire. These things weren't hers. Jared had been right about that. But she'd never thought of it that way before. She was the beneficiary of Felix and Selda's goodwill. This was their home and their room and their coverlet, and she was nothing more than a houseguest who someday would have overstayed her welcome. Until last night, she'd never thought of it in quite that light.

Selda had swept down on Deirdre just as she'd been handing out final wages to the servants. She'd stood at her father's desk, its top a chessboard of neat piles of silver and gold coins, for she hadn't dared give out bank drafts. She was too afraid the bank wouldn't honor them, and the people she'd grown up with and who had cared for her from her birth to age eighteen would be left without a means to support themselves until they found other employment.

In the midst of this dark and emotional procession, Selda appeared, an aunt Deirdre barely recalled having. She'd made the rest of the day go more easily. A bright smile pinned on her face, she'd helped Deirdre hand out the payments and say her good-byes. She shook the hand of every person from housekeeper to stableboy, thanking them profusely for years of service which Selda had never seen, but which she was certain had been done well. And Deirdre had been grateful.

She'd looked on her coming to London as a favor to Selda
and Felix. A way of thanking them for caring about her.
For steadfastly remaining through the week it took Deirdre
to see the property locked up. For wanting her. For declaring
that she was their niece, for goodness sake, and *of course*
they wanted her to come and live with them.

But now, very suddenly, Deirdre's eyes were opened to
another possibility. Had she come to London because she
was afraid? Had it been easier to lock up Ramshead and
come here than to face the possibility that she might not
be able to keep her beloved home? Had Jared Montgomery
been not just a little right, but completely, devastatingly,
correct when he'd claimed that she'd locked up Ramshead
and left because she didn't want to face the truth? If she
really loved her home, why wasn't she there now listening
to the sweet coo of the mourning doves announcing the
dawn?

Sitting up, she pulled a pillow into her lap and punched
it down to make a pedestal for her elbow. She propped her
chin in the palm of her hand and tucked the corner of her
lip between her teeth, nibbling in concentration. Could she
keep Ramshead? Deirdre knew the estate had always made
money. Beginning at the tender age of six, Bert had schooled
her in ciphering, using the Ramshead account books for her
lessons. When she was very young, the thick books filled
with row upon row of neatly penned numbers had been nothing more than another lesson. But as she grew older they
had taken on greater meaning, and she'd begun to understand
the information that was recorded there: £500 received for
cattle and pigs at market; £1,050 for the winter wheat crop
one year, only £766 the next, when a horrendous spring
storm wreaked havoc on the fields. There were entries each
year for wages paid out, the cost and payments of the tenants,
tools, seed, livestock. The list came flowing back into her
brain. Ramshead made money.

She remembered how thrilled she had been because her

father had spoken to the king and bragged that Ramshead harvested the finest wheat and barley in all England. And the king's man had arrived the next week to look over the harvest and purchase a large amount of the crop for the royals. But Bert had stomped around for over a week, muttering under his breath until Deirdre had wrung his concerns from him. "It may well be an honor, lassie," he told her, wagging his finger at her nose. "But 'twill be a costly one. The king doesn't have to pay a fair market price for the grain he buys! He wants it for a song! 'E's the king after all, aren't he? And we could be gettin' twice what his accountant will pay. I've tried and tried to tell your father." He threw his arms in the air and shook his head. Then, smiling down at Deirdre, he chucked her under her chin. "Ah, well, lassie. His lordship is as he is. Never been aught else, 'as he now?" And that had been all Deirdre heard of it.

Bert knew how to run the estate. He was still at Ramshead, and he'd only be leaving when the day came that he didn't rise from his bed. He loved it as Deirdre did. And he would help her. Deirdre stopped chewing on her lip and brightened. She could keep Ramshead. She would run it herself with Bert. Someday, she thought with a chuckle, she would have to thank the marquess of Jersey. In his attempt to convince her that she was helpless to save her home, he had given her exactly the impetus to do so.

Her problem as much as solved, Deirdre dressed quickly for her ritual morning ride. It was one of the things which helped her keep her sanity in the city. Donning a white blouse and ascot that wrapped high about her neck as would a gentleman's, and a dun-colored skirt with a matching jacket, she pulled her hair into a queue at the nape of her neck and slid her feet into soft leather boots. The stable behind the house smelled of the country at least—fresh bedding straw and big, round barrels of oats blended with the musky smells of leather and bridle oil.

As always, Deirdre waved away offers of help from the stableboys, preferring to curry her mare herself. She liked the feel of the horse's warm muscles twitching under her hand, and the effort of making her dappled grey coat shine was invigorating. She hummed as she slid the saddle over Iris's withers.

"It's a fine day, my lady," offered the senior stableboy.

"It is indeed, Nils."

"Off to the Mall again?"

"No, I was thinking I'd head toward the Kensington Gardens. Fewer people."

Nils scoffed at this comment in disbelief as he handed her the bridle she'd set over a hook in the wall. "I can't hardly believe the Mall is swarming with gentry at this hour, miss. You're a rare one among them if I might say so. I'd wager there's hardly a lady or a gentleman what's out at the crack of dawn like you."

"I've come across a few gentlemen." Deirdre slid the bit gently into Iris's mouth and buckled the throat latch. "And even a few are a bother. They always give me a queer sort of look. As if I don't belong out on the Mall."

"Well, they'd see you as a curiosity, my lady. As I said, yer a rare breed."

Deirdre shrugged and flashed Nils a brilliant smile as she led the frisky mare outside to the mounting block. "I wouldn't change it. Not for anything in the world."

"No, I can see that you wouldn't, miss. I can see that fer certain."

Landing lightly in the sidesaddle, she gave the stableboy a lighthearted wave and was off. Kensington Gardens was in the opposite direction from the Pall Mall and bigger. There she could race Iris over gentle knolls and along shaded paths where she was unlikely to encounter a soul. Iris was quickly infected by Deirdre's animated attitude and by the time they reached the grassy park, Deirdre's arms ached with the effort of holding the prancing mare back.

"You want to race as much as I do!" she chuckled. "All right then, let's see if we can't beat the wind." Giving the mare her head, the pair charged forward. Deirdre leaned close over Iris's neck, letting the mare's long mane whip against her face. Up over the hills and down onto a wide expanse of lawn they flew. Deirdre steered clear of the leafy copses, not wanting to encounter a footpad or beggar who might await the unsuspecting in their shelter. Faster and faster they moved, as if Iris's hooves had sprouted wings. Deirdre could smell the dew that still clung to the grass and for a moment it was as if she was at Ramshead—the wind in her hair and all around her, God's wonderful creations.

Iris began to tire, her nostrils flaring as she sucked in the fresh spring air. Still they raced on, relishing the solitude and the chance to fly unconfined through the park. As Deirdre leaned over her neck she could hear the pumping rhythm of the mare's stride, her hooves tattooing a sod-softened beat against the carpet of green beneath them. The solid repetition of hooves against the ground was soothing in its consistency. Suddenly, Deirdre leaned closer to Iris's shoulder, listening. It wasn't Iris's hooves she heard pounding the turf. There were *two* horses. She was certain of it. Her heart leaped into her throat as Deirdre turned, looking back over her shoulder to confirm what she already knew.

Another horse and rider were fast closing on them. A huge black horse, twice the size of hers. And astride him, a man bent low over his horse's neck as they raced toward her. No, not toward her. *After her!* Terrified now that, despite her efforts, she was being pursued by an attacker, Deirdre pressed her heels into Iris's ribs and the mare bolted forward with renewed effort.

Frantically looking from side to side, Deirdre tried to determine exactly where she was in the park. She didn't come to Kensington Gardens often enough to know every footpath and every entrance and exit. A broad expanse of water

appeared over a hillock in the distance and she recognized
her location as very close to the middle of the park. It was
too far to go straight on to the other side, but she was
uncertain when she would next come upon a graveled footpath leading to the safety of the neighborhoods that surrounded the park.

She dared not look back, for she could clearly hear her
pursuer closing ground behind her. Her frenzy growing by
the moment, Deirdre pressed Iris on. The mare was tiring
quickly now, laboring for breath, a layer of white froth
forming across her chest as the muscles pumped beneath
the saddle. And their pursuer rode closer and closer.

She was almost upon the pond. On its far side she could
see the dark curving trail of a footpath. Her only way across
the water, though, was a small wooden bridge built for
strollers—not a galloping horse. Still, it was her only hope
of escape. And surely her pursuer would not expect her to
race across the bridge. Inhaling sharply, Deirdre made her
move. In another instant they were over it and racing down
the crushed gravel path. The bridge might be just strong
enough for her mare, but never sturdy enough to bear the
weight of the giant stallion chasing her.

Reining Iris abruptly to the right, she galloped for the
bridge. The mare hit it at a full gallop. Beneath their weight
the boards groaned and Deirdre heard the bridge splinter
beneath their impact. Only when she didn't hear the crash
of a second horse on the already-weakened trestle did she
look back.

The horse and rider had vanished.

A short way ahead, Deirdre could see a paved street, and
on the far side of it the front doors of houses, but she didn't
let Iris slow her stride until they were only four strides from
the cobblestones. Hauling back on the reins, she let the
mare walk, leaning over to pat her sweaty shoulder and
offer Iris extraordinary praise for her bravery.

Deirdre looked around again, needing to ascertain that

her pursuer was, indeed, gone. Sighing, she wiped the back of her gloved hand across her brow. What a fool she'd been! She didn't even have a crop with which she might have defended herself had he come even with her. Her heartbeat began to stop its frantic drumming in her chest, and Deirdre drew a long, steadying breath. It was only then, after she had collected herself, that she noticed Iris favoring her right foreleg. With a groan of self-condemnation, Deirdre drew the mare to a stop.

Unhooking her leg from its saddle rest, she slid neatly to the ground and ran a hand slowly down the injured leg, searching for tenderness before she checked the hoof for a stone or piece of wood from the hapless bridge they'd assaulted. Working her way around the fetlock, she clucked. "This is my fault, you poor thing. No matter how much I wish that this was Ramshead, it's not. Why can I never accept that?"

"Some things are very difficult to accept," a husky male voice replied.

Deirdre shrieked and jumped, sending a terrified Iris into a fit of prancing and snorting. Seated astride the enormous black stallion that had pursued them was Jared Montgomery. "What do you think you are doing?" Deirdre snapped, glaring at Jared as she tried to calm the frightened mare. "You scared me half out of my wits chasing after me like that! I thought you were a-a *villain!*"

Jared's eyes narrowed as he evaluated her. "Then you do not judge me a villain?" he asked, a snap of cool fire kindling in his grey eyes.

"No!" Deirdre retorted angrily. "Obviously you are no villain, sir. But you were thoughtless to frighten me thus."

"I'm glad."

"What? That you scared me? That, sir, is the most thoughtless, mean-hearted of statements."

Jared chuckled at her ire, which only incited it further. "That you don't consider me a villain."

Deirdre merely glared at him, unable to think of an appropriate response. How could he stand there, *laughing* at her, when he had been the cause of all of this.

"Sir," she declared, placing her hands on her hips and pinning him with an irate look, "I ran my poor mount nearly to her death, destroyed the king's footbridge, and practically made myself sick because of your lack of consideration for a lady's vulnerabilities, and all you can do is be *amused?* You do not even make sense. What's more, you then accuse me of considering you a knave and a villain. Your brain is very muddled I'm afraid."

Jared leaned casually against his stallion's shoulder, which did not sport even a fleck of sweat from his exertion, and eyed her carefully. "I am certain that *my* brain is not the one which is muddled, and I hope you never have reason to consider me either knave or villain."

"Why should I think such a thing?"

"Because I think you believe all strangers are villains."

"You condemn me because I do not clutch every strange man to my bosom like a treasured friend. That is unreasonable," Deirdre countered emphatically. "I would be silly to do as you suggest."

"I am not suggesting that you do that. There is a high price to pay for indiscriminate affections. But I think that you would do well to find a new measure of a person's worth. Do you believe Anson Reece to be a scoundrel?"

Deirdre bridled at his question. How dare he question her friends! "Anson is none of your affair, sir."

Jared's eyes narrowed, and his mouth thinned to a straight line. "Why do you defend him?"

"He is my friend."

"Is he?"

"Yes!" she declared angrily, yanking Iris's reins into a knot at the mare's withers.

"Is that all he is?" Jared demanded, his demeanor no longer casual, but icily intense.

"It is none of your business what my relationship is with anyone."

"I am making it my business," Jared declared, with a quelling gaze.

Placing one foot in the stirrup, Deirdre prepared to swing up into her sidesaddle. Jared offered her no assistance. Glowering at him, she hauled herself into the unwieldy sidesaddle and gathered her reins. "And why, pray tell, is that?"

"Because you use the wrong tools to measure a person's worth, that's why. And if someone doesn't look out for you, you are going to find yourself in a situation even worse than the one you're already in."

Her temper strained to the breaking point, Deirdre hauled Iris's head around, intent on putting a large space—preferably the entire city of London—between herself and Jared Montgomery. But Jared had other plans. In one swift movement his relaxed stance disintegrated and he was at Iris's head, the reins captured in his hand.

Furious, Deirdre glared at him, sputtering on her rage. "The wrong tools? What exactly are you referring to, my lord? The fact that I even speak to a man who makes jest of scaring my wits out of me, demands to know the most intimate details of my life, and then refuses to allow me to leave when I desire to do so? But then, *I* never solicited your attentions. Had I my way, our paths would never cross again. You may not be a villain, but there can be no question that I find you difficult, demanding, unyielding, and infuriating. And I have from the first time I set eyes on you. No, my lord, my 'tools'—such as you call them—have proved unerringly accurate."

For a moment Jared only looked at her, his gaze relentless in its intensity. Then in a voice as soft as silk he said, "You did not feel those things the first time you saw me. You were curious and interested. Perhaps you've forgotten." Deirdre refused to answer, pinning him with a mutinous glare. "If you find me demanding and unyielding, you're right. I am." The admission caught Deirdre unaware, but she stubbornly refused to give quarter. "But I think you have found me to be other things as well. I have been honest with you. Perhaps recklessly so. Some of the things I've said have hurt you. I regret that. But nothing I have said is a falsehood.

"You have put your trust in the wrong people, Deirdre. I don't know who all those people are, but somehow in your life you learned to trust only those people whom you knew. Those are not always the people who deserve your trust. They can hurt you as much and more than a person who comes into your life a stranger. Listen to me. You trusted me once, in the conservatory. Did I do anything to prove myself unworthy of that trust?"

Deirdre wanted to answer "yes." She wanted to accuse him of using her trust to kiss her. But she couldn't. She had wanted him to kiss her. There had been no surprise, no forced affections. And she could not look him in the eye and claim otherwise. Biting her lip, she looked down at Jared and shook her head, ashamed. "No, you did nothing to abuse my trust."

He put one large hand on the pommel of the saddle, engulfing both of hers. Deirdre's fingers tightened over the reins as her heart stopped. Even through her kid riding gloves his touch affected her. "Look at me, Deirdre. What I am about to say is very important. A few moments ago you said that I was no villain. But soon, very soon, you may believe you were wrong. When that moment comes, I hope you will remember what you said this morning about trusting me. I think it came from a knowledge deep within you. One that you deny because I am a stranger. But I will not betray your trust, I promise you that." He surveyed her face carefully before continuing. "I ask only one thing of you. Watch me. See what I do. From that you will easily know who I am and whether I am worthy of trust. Can you do that?"

Deirdre lowered her lashes, staring down at her hands before she lifted her gaze to meet his. How intense he was. And yes, demanding. She wanted to say "no" to him. She wanted to claim that she wouldn't trust him, that she didn't know him. She wanted to decry his request and run away. He confused her, muddling thoughts that only a few days ago had been clear in her mind. She had built her life on her beliefs, and she did not want to open the way to a different way. His way. Why did he think she was so wrong to be wary of strangers? And why did he imply that those closest to her may not be worthy of her trust?

She was confused by him. A part of her wanted to understand what he was saying, but another part resisted, fearful. And she couldn't tell him her thoughts. Couldn't share the roiling turmoil and bewilderment she felt. How could she? She didn't know him. Still, what he asked was the smallest of things. And he had required nothing from her in return. Watch him. If she said no? If she said the likelihood that they would ever see one another again was slim, what would he say then? She wouldn't tell him that within the week she intended to be back at Ramshead. She wouldn't tell him that the way he made her feel frightened her. Swallowing hard, she nodded.

"Yes," she replied, turning her face away as she spoke. "I will judge you by your actions rather than because you are a stranger."

The shadow of a smile touched one corner of his mouth, softening his features in a manner that made her wish he would kiss her again. As if reading her thoughts, his hand closed around one of hers, pulling her toward him with an indefinable force for which she could find no resistance. His fingers were so gentle as he caught her chin between them, guiding her mouth to his as though parched lips to water. "Trust me." It was a husky murmur against her lips. A statement rather than a request, sealed between them by a kiss longer and deeper than the kiss they'd shared in the conservatory. The demand she'd sensed last night was unmistakable now.

She closed her eyes as his hand slid behind her head, pulling her toward him. His fingers twined through her hair and freed the ribbon that held it at the nape of her neck. The thick mass of hair fell across their faces like a curtain, shielding them from the day, the city, the world. His mouth slanted across hers, searching for a response, and as his tongue caressed her lower lip, she gave him that which he desired. A soft moan escaping from her throat, Deirdre parted her lips, making way for his tongue. It was as she knew it would be, a breathless sensation of intimate warmth. Their kiss seemed to last forever and yet be only the barest part of an instant at one and the same time, and when he drew away from her, Deirdre felt a part of her cry out as though parted from something as essential to her life as food or water.

For long seconds he remained mere inches away from her, his gaze moving from her lips to her eyes and back again, as though appraising something. Then he slid his hand from her hair, trailing two fingers along her jawline to her chin. "Don't be so quick to trust someone just because you've known him."

It was the equivalent of an ice-cold pitcher of water being tossed in her face. Instantly rigid, Deirdre straightened in her saddle, anger flaring through her veins at the inference to Anson. "Anson Reece is my friend, and you have no right to presume that he is any different than you. If anything, he is more worthy of my trust!"

"Why?" Not a question. But another demand.

"Because I have known him from the time I was seven years old!"

"On that basis alone you are willing to trust him. Allow him to parade you like a prize pigeon across the Mall. Permit him to use you for purposes that are exclusively to his benefit. Is that right, Countess?" Jared demanded, his voice taking on a merciless tone as he barked out her title.

"Yes! *Yes!* I *know* him, and I trust him. What is wrong with that?"

Jared's eyes narrowed dangerously, and he stepped suddenly away from her horse as though it disgusted him to be close to her. "More than I could ever begin to tell you."

Frustration the likes of which she'd never experienced before burned like a bonfire inside her, making her cheeks flame and robbing her of her breath. "You are the *most* infuriating man I have ever known!" she declared in a strangled voice. "Everything you say means something else. One minute you are kind and the next hurtful! Which is the false person? You cannot be both, no one is both. Just do this, Jared Montgomery. Stay away from me. You cannot have my home, and you do not want me! So don't ply me with your feigned interests and your demands. Just stay away!" She glared at him for another moment. "No, don't bother yourself!" she bit out angrily. "You won't be seeing me again anyway!"

Whirling Iris in a half circle, she fled, mindless of the probability that her departure had left the marquess of Jersey covered in bits of turf kicked up by her sudden exodus. He was the most infuriating man, or person, for that matter she'd ever had the poor fortune to come across. And their encounter this morning only served as a perfect example of why she wanted nothing more than to leave this city and return to Ramshead. At Ramshead she would never have to worry that she might run into Jared Montgomery again. There would be nearly a hundred miles between them. Not that she was certain a hundred miles was far enough away from such an infuriating man. She needed to get away from London and away from him. And she would not waste another moment.

Determined, Deirdre turned Iris onto Mayfair. The moment she got back to the house, she would ask Nils to rig the post chaise. She would speak with Mr. Benchley today, and as soon as that was accomplished she would sit down with Selda and Felix and explain that she could no longer take advantage of their goodwill and affection.

She was going back to Ramshead for good.

Eight

Deirdre flew through the kitchen door of the house like someone chasing a fire. Maggie the cook jumped and clamped her hand over her mouth to stifle a scream of surprise. "Goodness, milady! You near to gave me the shock of me life bursting in here like that!" Fanning her florid face, she added, "Do you care for some breakfast? I've got some fine smoked pheasant and a lovely soft-boiled egg with toast and jam for you."

Deirdre gave the cook an affectionate, but decidedly distracted pat on her ample fanny. "It smells delicious, Maggie. But I've no appetite just now. Avis, could you ask Sally to draw a bath for me?" she called, continuing through the kitchen and up the back stairway.

Avis followed right on Deirdre's heels, a scowl of disapproval on her face as she took in Deirdre's disheveled appearance. "It's a good thing you'd like a bath! You look as though you've been chasing rabbits through the heather just as you did growing up. When are you going to learn that London is not Ramshead, and a young woman of eighteen can't be racing around thinkin' she's a meadowlark and a fox and a pony all wrapped up into one!"

Deirdre chuckled, picturing the creature Avis described. "You're right, of course. London is no place for someone like me."

Avis followed Deirdre into her room and closed the door,

eyeing her charge suspiciously. "Then you'll not be goin' off for rides at dawn on your lonesome anymore?"

"Not much longer."

"What does that mean?"

Tossing her jacket on the bed, Deirdre quickly unhooked her skirt and began to unknot the snow-white ascot. "Just what I said. Not much longer."

Knowing she'd not get anything more out of Deirdre, Avis busied herself gathering up the clothes that were creating a rapidly growing pile on the bed and then went to the armoire to find a dress for the day. Sally appeared bearing a breakfast tray sent up by Maggie, who refused to be thwarted when she felt a meal was in order.

"A pot of chocolate for you, my lady, and buttered toast. Cook says you must at least have some of it, or you're sure to go over in a dead faint one of these days."

Deirdre rolled her eyes, but the chocolate did smell heavenly. As Sally checked the brass tub that sat in the far corner of the suite, Deirdre sat down in front of the mirror and began to work a brush through the wind-blown tangles in her hair. "Take out the navy dress, Avis. I need something for a business engagement today."

Avis cocked her brows in consideration. "And you're going . . . ?"

"To Bond Street. In fact, could you ask Parker to send a footman to Mr. Benchley's office as soon as possible and let him know I'll be coming by?"

"What shall he say is the nature of your business?"

"Oh, Avis," Deirdre said, turning in her seat to face the older woman. "It's Ramshead. I need some information, that's all." Her concern appeased, Avis went to convey Deirdre's wishes to the butler.

Just as Sally announced that her bath was ready, Deirdre conquered the last knotted strand of her hair. Slipping out of her chemise, she slid into the delicious warmth of the tub. The water was scented with lemon peel and mint leaves and a cake of similarly scented soap sat nearby. Taking a deep breath, Deirdre rested her head against the high back of the tub, her hair falling in a dark waterfall over the copper rim as she contemplated this new future she was creating. Soon she would be back at Ramshead. In her tub and her room. She would come to visit Selda and Felix, of course, conjuring up a long line of tomorrows in her mind. And they would come to Ramshead. Now that she had found some family, she had no intention of letting them slip from her life.

She imagined it all as she lathered the soap and washed. She envisioned the stunning success she and Bert would make of Ramshead. They would turn a profit with the first harvest and then, through her excellent banking skills, she would save enough to refurbish the house. In her reverie, within five years Ramshead was thriving, and she had the entire manor to herself, just as she had growing up.

By the time her bath was finished and Avis was putting the final touches to her upswept hair, Deirdre was imagining herself as a contented elderly lady puttering in the gardens of Ramshead from dawn to dusk.

Would Anson be happy at Ramshead, she wondered. She tried to picture them together there, but the image wouldn't come. Anson liked the city, that much was clear from their time together. Would he agree to live at Ramshead? She doubted so, not for the entire year. Perhaps they could come to London for the Season, she thought. Many members of the aristocracy did. But they weren't running their estates themselves, she countered mentally. They gave most of the responsibilities to their bailiffs. Well, she could do that, as well, Deirdre reasoned. But the thought left her depressed. She didn't *want* to come to London for eight months of the year. The Season demanded attendance in London during the most critical months on an estate—spring, when the fields were being planted and the sheep were lambing. And the parties lasted all the way through the summer. Spring and summer were the most beautiful times of the year to be in the country, and she knew she would be miserable if she missed them as she was missing them now. But she wouldn't want to miss the autumn either, with its harvest of colors and mellow light. Nor would she want to forgo being at Ramshead in the winter. She'd spent one winter in London. It was all rain and fog and streets amok with filth. At Ramshead, winter was long walks on crisp mornings when your breath froze in the air followed by languid afternoons spent before the hearth.

A rap at the door pulled her from her daydream and Avis set down the hairbrush to see who was there. There was a quick exchange through the slightly opened door and then Avis hurried back to Deirdre. "You have a caller, my lady." Deirdre glanced up at Avis in surprise as the maid handed her an engraved calling card.

"Charles Ellis, Esquire, Ellis & Fitzwalter. Solicitors," Deirdre read out loud. The name meant nothing to her. "Avis, I can't imagine what this concerns. And I am to be at Mr. Benchley's in an hour. Perhaps Parker should tell Mr. Ellis that I am not receiving now."

"Parker said the man claims to have a matter of grave importance to speak with you about."

Deirdre chewed on her lip, her brow knit thoughtfully as she tried to recall what reason Mr. Ellis might have for calling on her. "Are you sure he isn't looking for Selda or Felix?"

"Parker said the gentleman was here to see you. He's much too diligent as a butler to make a mistake like that."

Deirdre agreed. But she still had no idea who Mr. Charles Ellis was or what business he might have with her. "I'll be right there, then." Avis nodded and conveyed this information to Parker, who waited in the hallway. A few minutes later, Deirdre stepped into the drawing room. "Mr. Ellis," she nodded in introduction.

The man who was seated on the settee rose as she walked

toward him. Charles Ellis, whoever he was, was tall and painfully thin. His arms seemed to be ungainly in their length as he bowed formally, a folio hanging from one hand. He had thick light red hair, pulled into a queue, and was immaculately dressed in dark knee breeches, stockings, and a well-cut frock coat.

"Countess Ramsey. Allow me to introduce myself. I am Charles Ellis of the firm of Ellis & Fitzwalter, solicitors. Thank you so much for seeing me."

Deirdre smiled and nodded. She liked this man. His manner was forthright and very businesslike, and whatever his reason for calling, she was quite comfortable that he was an honest person. "It is a pleasure to meet you, Mr. Ellis. Please have a seat."

The solicitor awkwardly backed to the settee he had just abandoned, and Deirdre took a seat opposite him. "I must warn you, Mr. Ellis, if you are inquiring after my need for a solicitor, I have one already, and I am quite satisfied with his efforts on my behalf."

"I am aware of your solicitor, Mr. Stewart Benchley." Setting the folio on the low cherry table between them, he began to open it. "I have imposed on your time, Lady Ramsey, as the representative of the marquess of Jersey."

At the mention of Jared's name, Deirdre's convivial demeanor abruptly changed. Her spine stiffened and her hands, which had been demurely clasped in her lap, twined together into a tight knot that she pulled protectively against her stomach. Before she could speak, Mr. Ellis continued.

"As you know, Lord Montgomery would like to purchase your estate, Ramshead. At Lord Montgomery's request, my firm has conducted a thorough evaluation of the property. It is a stunning estate, my lady," he added as an aside. "A tribute to your ancestors." Noting the pallor of Deirdre's face save for the twin spots of bright red on her cheeks, he smiled approvingly and took out a thick sheaf of papers. "His lordship has assigned me to make the formal offer.

He will pay you £145,000 for the estate in its entirety. The price will be paid in full. There is no need for you to concern yourself with the issue of a payment schedule. His lordship was quite adamant about that. He wishes for you to be paid in cash upon the completion of the transaction."

Finished, Mr. Ellis placed the paperwork upon his knees and looked expectantly at Deirdre. When she didn't speak for a moment, the solicitor incorrectly assumed that her silence was the result of awe and pleasure. Smiling, he nodded. "It is a very fine offer, my lady. Most generous. I can imagine your relief, as well, at having your family estate turned over to such responsible hands. The marquess has—"

"I'm sorry, Mr. Ellis," Deirdre interrupted. She paused for a moment, steadying the timbre of her voice. "I know that you are simply Lord Montgomery's representative, and as such, you can know nothing about this matter except what your employer has told you. Unfortunately, it is an entirely different subject to consider why his lordship would send you here inadequately informed as to the history of this issue," she explained calmly. It was not Mr. Ellis with whom she was angry, she reminded herself. And she would not have him suffer the tongue-lashing that she would dearly love to give Jared Montgomery.

"I am aware that the marquess of Jersey would like to buy Ramshead. But it is not for sale. It has never been for sale, and I have no intention of selling it now or ever."

"But I was given to understand that—"

"I'm afraid you were misdirected by the marquess. He is fully aware that the property is not for sale. Your errand here today is nothing but an indication of his extremely stubborn disposition. I am sorry that your time has been wasted, Mr. Ellis. I will have Parker show you out."

Rising, Deirdre crossed to the drawing room door. One hand on the knob, she turned back to the solicitor who, dumbfounded, remained seated on the settee. Suddenly aware of his behavior, he jumped to his feet, scattering papers across the floor and tabletop. "And Mr. Ellis," Deirdre said, raising her chin. "Please tell the marquess that he need not attempt to change my mind in some other way." Charles Ellis gave her a confounded look. "He has already tried a personal business approach, an interested suitor approach, a 'we are very similar' approach, and an outright attempt at frightening me. Like your visit, none of those other attempts has changed my mind in the least. In fact," she said, a sudden thought coming to mind, "tell him that I am leaving London. That should settle things once and for all."

An hour later, as Charles sat before his employer's desk, he was still attempting to unravel the bizarre assortment of statements and reactions he had received from Lady Ramsey. "To say that the countess was less than receptive would be a misstatement, my lord." The marquess did not seem surprised by this fact in the least. "In all honesty," Charles continued uncomfortably, "I would advise you that she was most adamant in her pronouncement that your offer was unwelcome and not within consideration at all."

"Did you tell her the amount of the offer?" Jared asked, his fingers pressed into a steeple as he leaned back in his chair.

"Yes, sir. I was barely given the opportunity. The entire interview was quite short."

Jared eyed the disheveled state of the paperwork he and Charles had so painstakingly prepared. "Did she throw the offer at you?" he asked quietly.

"Oh my no, my lord!" Charles responded emphatically. "I, ah, I dropped them myself. The countess was most hospitable. And very even-tempered, despite her disinterest in selling the estate."

"Even-tempered?" Jared repeated, one brow coming up in surprise.

Charles nodded. "She's quite lovely, isn't she, my lord?"

Jared watched his solicitor turn a shocking shade of scarlet beneath his carrot-shaded hair. "Yes, she is."

"And different, as you said yourself. She's not at all what I expected."

"Really?" Jared asked, his interest piqued by this previously unexperienced personal insight on the part of his solicitor. "In what way?"

"Well, for one, she doesn't seem to like you at all." Both of Jared's eyebrows shot up at this, and his solicitor looked as though he had just broken wind in a distinctly loud and odoriferous manner. "I-I beg your pardon, my lord. I have spoken out of my station," Charles declared in extreme embarrassment.

Struggling to keep his composure, Jared shrugged. "Charles, we've shared many a long day of work and more than a few cognacs. I don't take offense at an honest remark, besides, I'm rather interested in your assessment of the lady. And of her dislike of me."

Charles shifted uncomfortably in his chair. "I'd rather not, my lord. As I said, I have already far overstepped the bounds of my station."

"I pay you for your insights, don't I?"

"You do indeed, sir."

"Then consider this part of your services to me."

Flushing red as a beet again, Charles found he had no choice but to acquiesce. "I can't really say exactly what things led me to assess her as a lady of unique personality, my lord. There was nothing I can specifically put my finger on. It was simply that, overall, she seemed quite refreshing. Rather unaffected." The solicitor hesitated, then plunged onward. "As for her dislike of you, it stood out in my mind because it was so unexpected. The mere mention of your name appeared to raise her hackles. And—begging your pardon, my lord—it seems a rare occurrence that a lady does not take into consideration every measure possible to win your affections. After all, you are a man of high standing, extremely wealthy, and, seemingly, uncatchable. What more toothsome goal could there be for an eligible young woman? At least that is what my Anna says."

"Anna?"

"My wife, sir."

"Ah." Jared looked out the window, digesting the fact that Charles recognized the same traits in Deirdre that he had found so appealing and so infuriating. She was a breath of fresh air. Spirited and prideful, and challenging. Her belief in herself was seemingly indestructible, for despite all the adversity she faced and the impossibility of her situation, Deirdre refused to compromise her dreams—even when they were not particularly sensible dreams.

"Thank you, Charles. And thank Anna for me as well. I had no idea I was the subject of so much conjecture." Charles choked as he sipped the coffee Jared's butler had poured him. "You can leave the papers on Ramshead with me."

Nodding, Charles straightened the sheaf before relinquishing it to the marquess. "Shall I consider this issue closed then, sir?"

"No. The countess will change her mind. It's just going to take more time than I originally thought."

Nils pulled the pair of chestnut horses drawing the post chaise to a halt before a serious-looking town house on Bond Street. "Here we are, m'lady," he declared, jumping down to help her from the light carriage.

Deirdre stepped slowly onto the street. Now that she was here, she had second thoughts about visiting the solicitor at his offices. With Selda gone to the dressmaker and Felix making his daily stop at the royal exchange before continuing on to his various men's clubs, there had been no questions about Charles Ellis's visit or Deirdre's excursion to the office of Mr. Stewart Benchley. But she wondered if she hadn't been a little precipitous in deciding to come here.

In the past, Mr. Benchley had always come to Selda and Felix's when there was some matter to be discussed. The last time that had occurred had been months ago, and Deirdre had not wanted Mr. Benchley to arrange to meet with her another day. So she had thought nothing of her plan to come to his offices. But as she stood on the sidewalk looking up at the establishment, it looked as though the modest, redbrick town house with its freshly painted black shutters served as Mr. Benchley's home as well, and she worried what people might say if anyone should see her entering the building unaccompanied.

Chagrined, Deirdre looked up at the solicitor's sign hanging from its tall post. "Have you changed your mind, m'lady?"

"No, Nils." Then lifting her skirts she made her way through the wrought-iron gate he held for her. "I shan't be long."

"Not to worry. I'll be right here, miss."

Her hand had barely touched the brass knocker when the door flew open and she found herself face-to-face with Mr. Benchley. "Lady Ramsey," he said in a slightly breathless voice. "Please come in." Safely inside, Deirdre found herself in a paneled foyer, which clearly served as a waiting room. There was an assortment of comfortable, but unmatched, chairs scattered about and a small table. "Had I received your missive earlier, I would have responded with an offer to come to the Derbys' residence. I am accustomed to visiting my clients at their homes. It was not necessary for you to be inconvenienced by a trip all the way to Bond Street."

Deirdre smiled and shook her head. "Nonsense, Mr. Benchley. It is a lovely day, and I enjoyed the opportunity to take some air. Besides, as you have said, I gave you very little notice, and I very much wanted to speak with you today."

"Well then," Mr. Benchley replied with a nod, "I believe

you will be more comfortable in my office." Holding the door, he ushered Deirdre into a nicely appointed room, similar in flavor to the foyer. The walls were newly painted and a wall of bookcases filled with books and documents arranged in precise order gave the impression of extreme seriousness. The room was immaculate, as the foyer had been and the exterior of the town house before that.

Taking a seat before Mr. Benchley's desk, Deirdre recalled his chagrin at the bedlam that reigned over her father's papers. Her father had done the right thing in hiring Stewart Benchley. He had needed someone organized to put his financial matters in order. Her father was not one to be concerned with such matters; he had other issues to see to, Deirdre reasoned. In the days after the funerals, she had imagined the look of utter shock on his face should he have returned to Ramshead to find them impossibly in debt. As with most men of his status, he turned such matters over to other people. The only difference between her father and other gentlemen was the mismanagement of funds by his former solicitor. Had it not been for that irresponsible gentleman, Deirdre assured herself, there would never have been any debts to repay and no need to sell her parents' belongings or close Ramshead.

"Now," Mr. Benchley began, settling his portly frame in the desk chair, "in what way may I be of service?"

"Are you familiar with the firm of Ellis & Fitzwalter?"

"Indeed I am, my lady. They are a fine firm. I communicated with Mr. Charles Ellis in the matter of the marquess of Jersey's offer on Ramshead last summer."

"But you haven't heard from Mr. Ellis recently."

"No," Mr. Benchley shook his head, then suddenly corrected himself. "I'm sorry, Lady Ramsey. I have been remiss! I did receive a correspondence from Ellis & Fitzwalter just this morning, but I put it aside thinking I would review it later in the day." Reaching into his top drawer, he began to pull out a large folio, the twin to the one Charles Ellis had brought to her house this morning.

"There's no need for you to bother with it, Mr. Benchley. It is another offer for Ramshead, and I have already informed the marquess that I am not selling."

Benchley covered his chagrin with a cough. "I see. Perhaps it might be wise for me to at least review it later, my lady."

"There is no point. Ramshead will never be sold. What you *can* do for me, however, is to review the last statement you had delivered to me on the accounts of Ramshead. I know that there was a crop of just-harvested barley and one of oats which Bert was to take to market."

Stewart Benchley nodded. "Mr. Manning made a good profit on both crops. Ramshead had an excellent reputation for producing fine grains."

"I know there were accounts still to be settled with the proceeds of those sales. I am just wondering what might be left of it?" Deirdre watched as Mr. Benchley went to the bookcase and removed a ledger from an upper shelf. Returning to the desk, he opened it and ran his finger down the column of numbers.

"Here it is," he said, pausing for a moment to smile reassuringly up at Deirdre. "The oats and barley garnered £821. Of that, £21 was utilized for the payment of wages to Mr. Manning and Mr. MacDonald, the stable master. Another £55 was paid to close the household accounts with village merchants and £25 was set aside to pay the wages of your lady's maid, a Miss Avis Bronley, for this year and next. That leaves £730 in the account."

"That's all there is?" Deirdre asked in shock. "But I was certain Bert said he expected us to clear at least £2,000 from the crops." Shaking her head in chagrin, she said at last, "Could you please close the account then, and pay the balance to me?"

Mr. Benchley shifted uncomfortably in his chair. "Certainly, Lady Ramsey. I will have a draft taken to the bank tomorrow and deliver the funds to you myself."

"Tomorrow?" Deirdre frowned. "Is it impossible to get the funds today?"

Mr. Benchley withdrew his timepiece from the pocket of his waistcoat and noted the hour. "I believe there is more than sufficient time to make a withdrawal today. I will deliver the funds to you at, shall we say, two o'clock?"

"That would be wonderful, Mr. Benchley," Deirdre responded, with a brilliant smile.

"May I inquire, as your solicitor, as to the use you intend for your money? I realize, it may be none of my concern, but I do feel a certain responsibility for your financial welfare given all that has occurred in the last year. I wouldn't be so forward, Lady Ramsey, if it weren't the very last of your assets."

Deirdre relaxed in her chair, happy to put the solicitor's mind to rest. "I am going to reopen Ramshead."

Mr. Benchley's reaction was not what she had hoped to receive. She thought he would be pleased at her initiative— a woman who intended to make her own way in the world and to retain her family estate in the process. Instead a look of horrific disbelief invaded his features. "Countess," he sputtered, his sanguine complexion going even paler, "I cannot counsel you to do such a thing."

"Why not? Ramshead has always turned a profit. Ever since I was a child, it has done well. You said yourself that the crops grown there are reputed to be among the finest in all England. The wool and mutton, as well, are respected. Why the king himself has purchased the crops grown there! Why shouldn't I continue that fine tradition?"

"Because, my lady, it would be impossible," the solicitor insisted. "Your purpose is admirable, Lady Ramsey. And I've no doubt your intentions are from the heart. But you would only ruin yourself." He leaned forward, placing his arms on the desk top. "Accounts of the size kept at an estate such as Ramshead are far different from a household stipend. A lady shouldn't bother her head with such weighty matters. Why wages for a minimal household staff alone will certainly cost you £100 per annum."

Although she kept her demeanor calm and businesslike, Mr. Benchley's attitude, as well as the required salaries for servants, shocked Deirdre. She did not remember that amount from the estate ledgers. She raised her chin a stubborn notch and decided that she would do without servants in the house. She was perfectly capable of caring for herself.

"Then there are cattle and sheep to buy, seed to be purchased, and laborers to be paid for the field work," Mr. Benchley continued. "It would take over £1,000 before you had even begun. You must remember the estate is closed. There are no longer cattle there. The larders are empty. Why you'd spend £20 just providing food for yourself and your staff in a month!" The solicitor ran his fingers nervously through his thinning hair. "Lady Ramsey, I know you will not like my recommendation. But I do strongly suggest that you consider the marquess of Jersey's offer."

The solicitor observed his client, who sat bolt upright in the chair opposite him, her hands balled together in her lap, her face an emotionless mask, and was reminded of nothing so much as the first time he had met Lady Ramsey. He had thought her controlled, reasonable, and poised then. Now, he believed he had been wrong in his assessment. The trauma of her parents' death had shaken her so enormously that she had chosen to deny her emotions rather than show them. Yet in all honesty, he did not understand her distress at this moment. She was a countess. She was well cared for by her relatives who had provided handsomely for her and even established a dowry on her behalf. She could certainly look forward to marrying well and living a life of ease. Why, then, was she so determined to accomplish an impossible feat? And why wouldn't she simply sell the estate? It meant over £1,000 in commission to him. "Lady Ramsey, I'm sorry if my words have distressed you."

Deirdre closed her eyes for a moment, steadying her shattered nerves. When she opened them again, she summoned a reassuring smile for Mr. Benchley. "You have only spoken what you feel is the truth. And, truly, I am grateful for your counsel. If you'll have the £730 delivered to my aunt and uncle's home this afternoon, there is nothing more I could ask of you."

"You may rest assured I will see the funds delivered."

"Thank you, Mr. Benchley."

Somehow, although Deirdre was not certain how, she made her way out of the solicitor's office and back to the post chaise.

"Home then, m'lady?" Nils inquired, handing her into the open carriage.

Deirdre concentrated on calming her nerves. "No, I'd like to go to Madame Solie's. The dressmaker. Do you know the way, Nils?"

The senior stableboy nodded. "Peters took Lady Derby there not an hour before we left for here."

"Exactly," Deirdre replied, and set her shoulders at a determined slant.

Nine

Nils continued down Bond Street in the direction of the dressmaker's shop as Deirdre sat tensed and alert in the carriage. It was impossible for her to relax. Her mind was a swirling conglomeration of disparate facts, feelings, and needs. Was everyone determined to tell her that she was helpless to keep her home? That she *must* do as every other young woman did—find a husband and spend the rest of one's days going from ball to dinner party to hunt weekend? Or was it only that men did not consider a woman capable of running an estate? She refused to believe Mr. Benchley—at least his adamant declaration that she would be ruining her life to go back to Ramshead. She loved her home. How could she possibly ruin her life by breathing life back into it?

Disquieted, Deirdre stared out of the carriage. Her brain was numb, but she felt jumpy and unsettled. Her stomach was like a tightly balled fist, her chocolate and toast sitting like a lump of iron inside it. She felt desperate. A cornered animal left with no way out, yet incapable of surrender. And the urge to fight, to claw her way through her opponents and prove them wrong, welled up inside of her.

On edge, Deirdre's gaze flitted along the shop fronts, skipping from sign to sign and doorway to doorway. She stared down cross streets and watched pedestrians leisurely making their way along the sidewalks. She leaned farther forward, her toe tapping a nervous tempo on the carriage floor.

"Not much farther, m'lady," Nils announced over his shoulder. "Another two blocks and we're there."

Deirdre glanced down a passing alley, her strange anxiety making her notice strange details. Crates piled high along the backs of shops or taverns, a rivulet of discolored water running haphazardly through the packed dirt, the sunlight glinting off the blond hair of a tall young man as he entered the alley from the back door of the tavern. Suddenly Deirdre's eyes locked on the man. "Stop the carriage!" she called to Nils as she scrambled from her seat. She barely waited for Nils to stop the conveyance and didn't wait at all for him to climb down and lower the steps. Instead she lifted her skirts and jumped, taking the impact of the cobbled stones on her toes.

"M'Lady!" Nils cried in distress as Deirdre ran for the alleyway.

"Stay there, Nils! I'll be right back!"

It was only a few meters back to the alley and as she reached it, she rose, peering over the trash as she searched for Anson. He was there, his blond queue and broad shoulders unmistakable as he spoke with someone Deirdre could not see. Laughing, Anson tossed his head back, and she caught sight of his profile, confirming that it was he. Then he stepped closer to the tavern wall, disappearing behind a mountainous pile of broken crates.

At last, something good had happened today, Deirdre thought as she began to pick her way into the alley. Wrinkling her nose at the acrid stench of spoiled meat and soured ale that permeated the air in the alley, Deirdre leaped over the little stream—the source of which was highly questionable. She needed to speak with Anson. He would give her some advice. After all, he had stayed at Ramshead, and he would be at least somewhat familiar with how it ran. His parents also had a manor in the countryside to the south of London, and although he now lived in London, he would have spent part of his years growing up in the countryside and understand more about property than she did. She could depend on him. She could tell him her plans. Plans that he would want to know about if they were to have a future as he had implied last night.

Only a few rods away now, Deirdre could hear Anson talking, his husky voice low and punctuated now and again by bursts of throaty laughter. Just as she reached the trash heap that shielded Anson from view, she caught the sound of a woman's laughter. For an instant, a thread of foreboding laced through her veins, and, intuitively, Deirdre thought to turn away. Instead, as though drawn by some macabre fascination that she was incapable of denying, she stepped around the crates.

Anson stood, though the word barely described his position, in the corner where the pile of wood met the tavern wall, pressing himself upon the delighted affections of a tavern maid. Nuzzling the maid's neck, Anson pressed noisy kisses to her ample—and completely exposed—bosom as she squealed with delighted "aaahs" and "ooohhhs."

Deirdre did not move. Her legs were leaden, and her brain rendered useless by the thick fog of disbelief that had descended upon it. Nauseated, she stared openmouthed as Anson, unaware of her presence, slid his hand beneath the girl's skirts, eliciting a sudden, deep sigh from her. It was only then, when she opened her eyes to readjust her position, that the tavern maid spied Deirdre.

"Oh, my lord!" she croaked, immediately attempting to extricate herself from Anson's embrace.

But Anson only chuckled and pulled her closer. "Don't be coy with me, wench!" he declared in a slurred voice. Freeing one hand from her breast, he used it to grab her hand and shove it against the front of his pants. "You've got my cock as stiff as a plank and I promise you it's as thick as one as well."

"Oh, nooooo, milord!" came the high-pitched wail. "It's the lady—"

"What lady?" Without relinquishing his hold of her breast, he turned, scouting about for whatever or whoever was playing havoc with his seduction, until his eyes fell upon Deirdre.

"Deirdre—" Pulling his hand from under the girl's skirts, he released her. The tavern maid hastily straightened her dress and scurried back into the tavern, her eyes never meeting Deirdre's. "My dear, don't be dismayed by that bit of baggage," he said, giving the vanished girl a dismissive wave of his hand. "Such dalliances are meaningless. The nature call of all men." Deirdre stared at him, her eyes wide and disbelieving. "You'll learn, my sweet, virtuous Deirdre, to understand a man's urges. It's just that you are an innocent—which is one of the very delightful things about you." He gave her a sheepish grin that yesterday would have seemed endearing. Today, now, it turned Deirdre's stomach. "I swear to you, you are terribly special to me. Do you remember what I told you last night? How unique you are? How I believe we were meant to be together? It's all true, Deirdre. You've completely won my dedication—and my heart as well."

Deirdre stared at him, noting every detail. The loose, white cotton shirt that clung to the damp spots of sweat on his chest. The flush that darkened his face and neck. The revolting bulge at his crotch. She wanted to scream at him that he had told her nothing but lies yesterday and the day before and the day before that. She wanted to fling at him the fact that she would never settle for a man who thought his due in this world was to satisfy his lust on any tavern wench—or worse—who caught his momentary fancy. But the words would not free themselves from her throat. Instead, she stared at him frozen by the completeness of her revulsion.

Anson smiled, that utterly charming grin that disarmed women and made them think him a sweet, considerate gentleman of the finest ilk. Reaching out his hand, he stepped toward her. "Come here, Deirdre. You look pale, and that is worrying me. I'll take care of you. You'll see."

Deirdre watched his hand reaching for her. The same hand that had, only moments ago, been doing something vile and base under the tavern maid's skirts. She tasted bile rising in the back of her throat and knew that if he touched her with that hand, she would be sick. Without a word, she spun away from him and fled, unmindful of the filth she ran through, only needing desperately to get away.

She nearly ran headlong into Nils as she darted from the alley onto the street. The dedicated stableboy had taken a position just at the entrance to the alley, intent upon preventing anyone from either entering or leaving the alley, without his knowledge. "M'lady! Are ye all right?" he asked as she veered around him and headed for the carriage.

"Please take me home, Nils," was all she could manage.

"But we're just a block from the dressmaker's shop," Nils continued in confusion. "Lady Derby is there and I thought you wanted to—"

"Please, Nils," Deirdre begged in a desperate voice. "I no longer wish to go to Madame Solie's. All I want is to go home."

Handing her into the carriage, Nils nodded, although he no more understood her distressed change of heart than he had a moment ago. "As you wish, m'lady."

Pulling herself into the corner of the squabs, Deirdre was aware that she and Nils were speaking of two different things. Nils thought that when she'd said "home" she meant back to Selda and Felix's, and that was fine. But she knew differently. It was her real home, her only home, that her heart desired. She wanted to go home to Ramshead. Back to Ramshead, where she had once been safe from all this hurt, where she would be safe again.

Shoulders hunched and head down, Deirdre curled into a tight ball as Nils turned the carriage and headed back to Mayfair. What sort of world was this? she asked herself, wretched with hurt and anger. It certainly was not the world she'd thought it to be. Not the world she'd learned to believe in. Jared Montgomery had been right. She couldn't trust even those people she knew.

Deirdre's stomach turned at the thought of Anson fondling that girl. *In the alley!* The stench and filth hadn't deterred him in the least. Had she not happened upon them, he would at this very minute be completing the act. Satisfying—what had he called it—"the nature call of all men." Deirdre tasted bile rising again in her throat. Was that what men wanted? To take some unknown woman behind a tavern in the middle of the day and have their way with her?

Clenching her hands into fists, Deirdre pressed them against her lips, willing her revulsion away. She refused to lose her breakfast over Anson Reece. And she never, ever, wanted to see him again.

She forced herself to think of something else. Ramshead. The name of her home became a chant, repeating over and over with increasing intensity. It would be her alone, she realized with a bleakness that came with understanding the finality of truth. Had she actually—only this morning— considered Anson as a husband? Deirdre thought of herself as she'd lain in bed, worrying about Anson liking Ramshead. The memory was sickening. Sickening and nearly laughable had it not hurt so deep inside her. There was no one whom she could trust. No one at all. Because if she couldn't believe in the people she had known for years, who was there to put her faith in?

No one.

The answer was like something ugly and dead dropped at her feet. Her life ran through her mind in picture book fashion. Illustration upon illustration of the people she had trusted and times she had put her trust into their hands and found herself left with nothing. First and foremost was Anson Reece. Debaucher. Liar. And, she suspected, a man who took his liquor too freely.

Then, suddenly wary of everyone she'd ever known, she considered Stewart Benchley. Her father's solicitor—and now hers. Hadn't he told her he would see to the best possible resolution of the financial crisis the previous solicitor had created? Was £730 the best he had been able to do? Or had he lied to her as well? Had he used some of the money for his own purposes? Had he mismanaged the liquidation of the estate? How was she to know? He could easily have salted away some of the profits from Ramshead for himself.

Deirdre swallowed morosely. Her instincts told her she could trust Mr. Benchley. But her instincts had told her to trust Anson as well, and clearly—very clearly—she'd been wrong to do so. She already knew that her father's former solicitor was to blame for the disaster that led to her closing Ramshead. She didn't even know the man's name, so she had no way of confirming her suspicions, but even Mr. Benchley had suspected as much when he first arrived at Ramshead with the news of her parents' financial ruin. Deirdre's lower lip began to quiver as her anger and hurt built to a crescendo. Like her, her father had trusted too readily.

As she searched for more culprits of distrust her father's face appeared in her mind, but Deirdre pushed it away emphatically. She would not consider that her father had not been worthy of her trust. It was not his fault, just as it was not her fault, for trusting people's words. Her mother and father were mythical to her. Sweeping in and out of Ramshead like beautiful butterflies. Staying only long enough to deposit the treasures they'd picked up during their latest travels. And always, always, leaving Deirdre in awestruck wonder. They could not be to blame. They were too wonderful, too special. But the flame of Deirdre's hurt had grown bright, and despite her attempts to push it away, it shed its light where she had let darkness protect her images and illusions. And its illumination would not be denied.

New memories began to fill her mind. Memories long disavowed. She remembered her father's study, a constant disaster of papers and correspondence piled into dusty towers that were left unopened and unread. And Bert, waiting in the marble hallway to catch her father's attention only to be waved off. She could see her father striding through the hall, a mirror polish on his black boots, his riding crop tucked beneath his arm as he pulled on leather gloves and herself tagging along just at his heels like a forgotten pup. "Now, Bert, my good man," her father said, "I can't imagine that there is a thing to worry about. We both know that Ramshead is one of the most profitable estates in the king's domain. How can there be a problem? You are too much of a worrier." And to Bert's response, "All right then, if it will appease you, I'll hire a man in London to handle the money matters. Although, that's just more money I'll be spending, and if you're concerned about money, it makes no sense to me."

Deirdre squeezed her eyes shut. She felt sick again. Her brain was playing tricks on her now. Confusing her. It couldn't be true. She must be able to trust her parents. Mustn't she? Her heart ached with a pain that was larger and deeper than anything she'd ever known, a pain that struck to her very soul. The basis upon which she'd built her belief in people was disintegrating before her very eyes, and she didn't know how to rebuild her world.

If she had trusted wrongly before, how could she know the right way in which to revise her beliefs now? She had been so sure of her world. So happy. Suddenly she felt as though her entire life had been a sham. Was Ramshead even real? Oh, it was there, she knew that. But for how long? Had Jared Montgomery been right about that as well? Would she have to sell her life and her body to a man she didn't love in order to save her home? She didn't think she could do that. If she didn't, and she lost Ramshead—or left it to rot, empty and deserted—then had it ever been real at all? Was the past real if it didn't last? Was it real if it was lived on false pretenses? Money that didn't exist? Friends that weren't friends? Family that wasn't there enough to be family?

Deirdre knew she could not stay another night with Selda and Felix. It wasn't her home, it was theirs. And this life she was living in London wasn't hers either. She was attending balls that she could not afford and wearing gowns that bespoke a way of life she did not really possess. She was an actress, acting out a life that had no reality behind it. No, she couldn't stay here anymore. She had to go back to Ramshead and find out who she really was. Not in her past, but now.

Nils opened the door of the carriage, causing Deirdre to jump. She hadn't even felt the carriage come to a stop. "Home you are, m'lady, just as you asked."

Deirdre stepped slowly from the carriage and blinked, looking at the house as though seeing it for the first time. It was not hers. Nothing was hers.

She went straight to her room, shutting the door behind her. Avis found her sitting on the window seat, her head tilted back against the wall, her eyes shut, and her hands clasped tightly in her lap. A soft, leather valise sat open on the bed, and the armoire doors were thrown wide. "Nils came into the kitchen sayin' you'd run into some alley by yourself and come out lookin' like you'd seen a specter."

"Not a specter, Avis. A demon."

"Of what making was this demon you saw?" the maid asked.

Her eyes still closed, Deirdre spoke in a voice that shook. "It was made of lies and filth. Arrogance and lust." She swallowed hard and shook her head. "It doesn't matter, though. Because it won't ever hurt me again."

Sitting down beside her, Avis took Deirdre's hand in hers. It was cold as ice. "Tell me what happened, child." But Deirdre only shook her head. "So you're goin' to keep this

to yourself, are you?" Avis sighed and shook her head.
"You've been lockin' things up inside yourself for eighteen
years. Every time something hurt, you'd hide in your room,
never lettin' anyone help you, never sheddin' a tear. Just
sittin' there holdin' it all inside. It's not good for you,
keepin' all that ache inside."

"I just want to go back to Ramshead," Deirdre said quietly.

"Why? There's nothing there for you. Comin' to London
with your aunt and uncle was the best thing that could have
happened to you."

Deirdre denied Avis's words with a shake of her head.
"I'm going back."

"Then tell me why."

Opening her eyes, Deirdre looked deep into Avis's. She
should not trust anyone, she thought. Not ever, not even
with this. But it was an impossible task. Avis reached out
to stroke her cheek.

"Tell me, child."

Finally, in halting, emotion-choked words, Deirdre told
Avis what she had seen in the alley. She had just finished
the vile tale when there was a knock on her door, followed
by Selda poking her head into the room. "Mr. Benchley
just delivered this for you, my dear. I'll just set it here,"
she said, noting Deirdre's pallor. She carried a pouch and
an envelope to Deirdre's dresser and then crossed to the
window seat. Selda gently patted her niece's sleeve. "I
didn't look inside the pouch, but it must be a fair amount
of money."

Deirdre opened her eyes and looked at her aunt. "I'm
leaving, Selda. I'm going back to Ramshead."

"Now, now. We can discuss this with Felix tonight over
dinner. If you're determined to go, a nice visit up there
might be just the thing for all of us. But after you've had
a chance to sleep on it, you might think otherwise. Your
uncle and I don't want to see you leave."

"I'm sorry, Selda. You and Felix have been so wonderful to me. But I don't belong here. If you'll let me have the use of a carriage, I promise you I'll see it returned in three days' time. But I need to leave today."

"Today! Deirdre, it's a ten-hour trip by coach."

"I know. If I leave within the hour, I can be at Ramshead before dark tomorrow." She gave Selda a tortured look. "Please, Selda. I need to go home."

Leaning over her niece, Selda pressed a gentle kiss on Deirdre's forehead. "Of course, my dear. Of course you may go home. Let me speak with Peters." With a reassuring smile, Selda left to make the necessary arrangements.

The direction clear, Avis threw herself into motion. "We'll not have time to pack your trunks," she declared as she made short shrift of assembling Deirdre's essentials on the bed.

Watching the spry maid flit about the room determined to set everything right brought a lump of tears to the back of Deirdre's throat. "You can't come with me, Avis. I haven't enough money to pay you a wage."

Without missing a beat, Avis moved from the dressing table to the set of drawers beside the bed. "I was just thirteen when I started working at the big house. My mum worked for her ladyship, your mother, and she toted me along to help out with the laundry or peel potatoes in the kitchen. It earned us an extra shilling or two a month. And I was there when you came into this world. You weren't the first newborn I'd seen, but you were the prettiest.

"I've helped care for you ever since. Hasn't been a day gone by that I haven't known where you were or been there to make your bed and brush that wild mane of yours. And I'm not about to start now."

"You don't understand," Deirdre explained determinedly. "I've barely got enough money to feed myself for the next few months. At least until we get a harvest in and to market. You can't possibly come."

Avis stopped her rapid packing of the valise and came to stand before Deirdre, her tiny frame vibrating with steadfast resolve. "I'm far past the marrying age, so there'll be no children for me. But I've seen every year of your life, and, so far as I can see, you're as close to being mine as I'm ever goin' to come. I'm goin' with you, and that's all there is to be said about it. There's much to be done in the next hour, so I suggest that ye get yourself changed and start sayin' your good-byes if you're truly meanin' to go."

Deirdre shook her head and managed a smile. "I'm glad you're so stubborn, Avis."

An hour later Deirdre hugged Selda and Felix as she said her good-byes. "I'll write for you to come and visit soon," she promised. Her voice caught on the edge of tears. "But right now I need to be by myself. Can you understand?"

Selda wrapped Deirdre in a tight embrace, her own tears flowing unchecked. "We understand, my dear. But you must promise us that you will write every week. We need to know that you are well." Mopping ineffectually at her tears with an already soaked handkerchief, she sniffled and shook her head. "You shouldn't be staying there without anyone. I know Avis is going with you, but so many things could happen."

Deirdre smiled softly as she squeezed Selda's hand. "You mustn't worry. Bert is there, and Seamus." Then, with a self-deprecating laugh, she added, "You know, most of my life I have been there alone except for the servants. It will be the most natural thing in the world for me." Turning to Felix, Deirdre reached up to pat a stray strand of hair back into place. "And you must take care of Selda for me." She kissed him on the cheek, then stepped back to look at them both. "I love you both very much." Felix snuffled and made much of locating his own hankie. "You have been so good to me, but I can't take advantage of that goodness any longer."

"Peters and Nils are going with you. They are under strict orders to stay until they feel you are secured at Ramshead. So there will be no arguing otherwise," Felix admonished gruffly. "Take care of yourself, Deirdre, and if you need anything at all, send a message."

"I shall." With one last hug for each of them, Deirdre made her way to the carriage and let Nils hand her up beside Avis. Maggie came bustling out, her arms wrapped around an enormous basket. "Yer can't be going off without a fittin' supper," she declared, her eyes shining with tears. "I know not a morsel of food's passed your lips since early this mornin'. You'll not get a decent meal at an inn, and the highway taverns aren't a fittin' place for ladies to dine." She shoved the immense basket under the seat opposite them and clamped chubby fingers around Deirdre's. "Take care, milady. We've all grown to love ye. We'll be waiting for ye to come back soon."

Deirdre gave her hand a squeeze, overwhelmed by the affection of everyone in the household. Nils closed the carriage door, and, a moment later, Peters gave a whistle to the team.

"I don't understand why we're letting her go," Felix told Selda as they watched the afternoon sunlight glint off of the receding brougham.

"She's just now facing so many hurts, my love. I doubt we could have made her stay even if we tried."

Deirdre estimated it to be nearing seven o'clock when Peters opened the small door in the front of the carriage and inquired if the ladies were hungry. Maggie had been right when she'd claimed Deirdre hadn't eaten all day, and now, despite her anguish, Deirdre could feel her stomach

growling. "Is there somewhere we might safely stop to picnic?" she inquired.

"Aye, milady," Peters nodded. "I know of a resting spot
only a few minutes from here."

"Then we'll stop there. Maggie packed enough for all of
us and then some, I fear." When Peters pulled up and Nils
jumped down to hand the ladies out, Deirdre discovered
they were at a lovely roadside pasture, with a small stream
passing conveniently through it and an enormous oak to
offer shade. Together, she and Avis spread the large quilt
Maggie had sent and began to unpack their supper. There
was cold pheasant, partridge, and sliced leg of mutton,
plover eggs in aspic jelly, two loaves of freshly baked bread
and a crock of sweet butter, two rounds of cheese, blueber-
ries and gooseberries, forcemeat tarts, a flagon of ale and
another of cider, as well as plates, mugs, and tableware.

Deirdre wouldn't hear of Peters and Nils eating by the
carriage, and despite the brace of pistols each man kept at
his side as protection against highwaymen, they shared a
relaxing meal. Peters explained that it would be another
hour's drive to the small wayside inn where they would
spend the night. Deirdre remembered the quaint inn from
the summer before, when she'd traveled to London with
Felix and Selda. It was a safe place for them to overnight.

Despite her initial hunger, Deirdre only nibbled at a bit
of bread and cheese. Then, declaring that she needed to
wash her hands, she wandered along the stream, filling her
senses with scents of the country and the sound of crickets
chirping in the tall river grass. Although Deirdre stayed well
within sight, they didn't let her wander far, and Avis soon
came after her.

"Peters says we'd best be goin'. He promised your uncle
he'd see us to Ramshead by nightfall and we've still a ways
to go." Deirdre nodded, but made no move just then to
return to the carriage. "Are you all right?" Avis queried.

Smiling, Deirdre pointed to a tiny flash of light in the

air just over Avis's head. "Look, Avis, fireflies." Her smile broadened, and then, as another light winked overhead, she turned back toward the road. "Yes, I'm beginning to feel much better now."

Ten

Jared hesitated for a single second before dropping the knocker against the Derbys' front door, half-expecting Deirdre to dart from the doorway with another sickly plant in her arms. Of course, she didn't appear, and when his knock was answered, it was the butler who greeted him with a bow, not Deirdre. Despite the logic of this occurrence, Jared found himself disappointed.

"I'm here to see Lady Ramsey," he stated, handing his card to the butler.

"I'm sorry, my lord. But Lady Ramsey is—"

"Lord Jersey," Selda interrupted as she descended the front stairs. "It's a pleasure to see you again."

Jared bowed graciously over Selda's hand. "I was hoping to find your niece at home this morning, Lady Derby."

"Unfortunately, Deirdre is not here. Would you join me for coffee?"

Jared's initial reaction was to decline the offer, but something about Lady Derby's demeanor raised an instinctual question in his mind. "It would be my pleasure."

"I have a problem which I am hoping you can assist me with. And there are some things which I feel I should make known to you," Deirdre's aunt explained.

Jared frowned, then deepened his frown as Lady Derby led him not into the drawing room, but to a study. Selda gestured to one of a pair of leather wing-backed chairs that sat adjacent to a low walnut table before the fireplace. "Please sit down, my lord."

Jared lowered himself into the chair, grateful that he was not once again relegated to the uncomfortably small French armchairs that occupied the drawing room. Lady Derby seated herself in the chair to his left, perching on the edge of the broad seat, her hands folded neatly in her lap. "Is something amiss?" he asked, already certain that there was.

"Deirdre has left," Selda stated softly.

Jared relaxed back into the chair and stretched his legs nonchalantly. His demeanor, however, belied his thoughts, which were anything but nonchalant. He vaguely recalled Deirdre spitting out some comment in the park yesterday to the effect that he needn't bother to avoid her because she would be gone anyway, but he'd dismissed it as nothing more than an angry arrow slung in fury. He had also dismissed it because he hadn't thought she was foolish enough to do something precipitous. Clearly, he had overestimated Deirdre's capacity for logic.

"Did she run off to elope with Anson Reece?" he asked in a voice tight with barely controlled fury.

A knock at the door, followed immediately by a manservant bearing a silver tray and coffee service, prevented Selda from answering his question, and Jared had to restrain himself from grabbing the insufferable coffee set and sending the servant racing in fear for his life. He wanted an answer, and he wanted it now. If Deirdre had done something as stupid as run off with Reece, he fully intended to go after them. He would haul Deirdre back to London by her long, thick mane of hair and then take Reece out to the Pall Mall and put an end to his miserable life. Reece was nothing but a bane to Deirdre, confusing her even further and priming her for a disastrous future.

"Thank you, Martin. Please leave us, I will pour myself." Selda nodded in the direction of the door, indicating that the footman should depart *tout de suite*. Then, in complete opposition to what she had just said, she turned back to Jared completely ignoring the coffee. "She hasn't run off with Lord Reece," she assured him. "In fact, Lord Reece has proven himself quite unworthy of her attentions. Just one of many occurrences yesterday that proved too much for my niece. She returned last night to Ramshead, and I would like to solicit your assistance in retrieving her."

Jared regarded Selda Derby carefully. "Why do you want my help?"

"You are a well-respected gentleman, Lord Jersey. It is widely known that you are reasoned, intelligent, and adroit at affairs of business. I have done a great deal of research this morning. In fact, Felix and I were up most of the night piecing together the various events which have occurred in the past several days. Our conclusion is that we have been remiss in our duties to Deirdre. We allowed unsavory characters to court her, and we assumed that she was adjusting to a new life here with us. Regrettably"—she sighed—"we presumed things we should not have. Deirdre is still young, we should have guided her more astutely. It was our conclusion, based on the information that we have been able to assemble, that you could offer us a valuable service and at the same time you would be getting something you have wanted." A raised eyebrow was the marquess's only response to Selda's soliloquy. "You are interested in purchasing Ramshead, are you not?" she continued. Jared nodded. "Then we would like you to convince Deirdre to sell it to you."

Jared barked out a half laugh. "I have tried, Lady Derby. Believe me, I have tried."

Her formal, businesslike demeanor disintegrating under the weight of her concerns for her niece, Selda rung her hands. "Lord Jersey, by your tone I assume that you are angry with Deirdre's steadfast refusal of your offer. Especially since it is an excellent offer. She is headstrong and very proud. Many, many times in the last year I have watched her be obdurate and willful when the only person she is hurting is herself."

Jared scoffed. "I could not agree with you more thoroughly, Lady Derby. But I don't see Deirdre changing her nature, or her resolve to keep Ramshead."

"She knows nothing about business, and she doesn't understand that an unmarried woman cannot live alone out in the country."

"Is that what she's planning?"

Selda nodded. "She intends to restore Ramshead to the working estate it was a year ago. An estate which she will run."

If he hadn't been so angry, Jared could have smiled at that. Only Deirdre would march off, head high and chin up, believing she could handle the management of a working estate by herself and not be in the least concerned with her loneliness or vulnerability.

"My niece is gentle and charming as well as strong-willed," Selda persisted. "Above all, she is brave. Terribly brave." Shaking her head, she fell silent, lost in thought.

"You are referring to the loss of her parents and their debts," Jared stated, watching Selda closely.

"I am also referring to Deirdre finding Anson Reece in a highly compromising position with a tavern wench yesterday."

Jared's fingers curled into fists, which he would have loved to pummel into Reece's stomach. Despite his own warnings to Deirdre that she could expect nothing better from Reece, he was furious that the fool had hurt her, and furious at Deirdre for caring enough about Reece to be hurt.

"I am ashamed to say that we actually considered his request for her hand in marriage. And," Selda continued unhappily, "I refer to Deirdre's discovery that she has only £730 to her name."

"That would make it impossible for her to get Ramshead up and running."

"Exactly. But she refuses to let go of her dream. If she does, she knows that you—or someone else—will take her home away from her."

"She intends to run Ramshead herself and on £730?" That was the most ludicrous idea he'd ever heard. What possessed a woman to attempt something so insane?

"That *was* her plan. But she left yesterday afternoon more to escape all the pain she was feeling than any real belief that she could save the estate. You know, Ramshead is the place she has always run to—it's the only place she feels safe."

"And her pain was because she discovered that Anson Reece is a drunken sot and a fool?" Jared snapped angrily. "She could have saved herself from that hurt."

"As I've said, Felix and I are to blame for that as well. I'm afraid we took Lord Reece as a good man because of Deirdre's acceptance of him. But it was not only that, my lord. What drove her away was a lifetime of hurt she has denied."

"Exactly what do you mean by that?" Jared asked, his ire provoked by the constant reminders of Deirdre's affection for a worthless miscreant like Reece.

"Her parents were—"

"She adores her parents," Jared finished for her. He leaned forward, pulling his knees up, using them to rest his elbows upon. "Although I can't find a single reason for her admiration of them."

Selda silently agreed with his assessment and was relieved at his astute appraisal. "Camille was my sister," she explained. "But I rarely saw her after her marriage to Morgan. I know Deirdre was deeply affected by their deaths. But I've often wondered why." Jared's silence was all the encouragement Selda needed to continue. "I don't profess to understand all of my niece's complexities, Lord Montgomery," Selda told him, "any more than I understood

Camille. Well," she said, hesitating, "I *did* understand Camille. I just wasn't anything like her."

"What was she like?"

For a long moment Selda looked into the dying embers of the morning fire, remembering a long way back in time. "Like Deirdre, I was the mistake in my family. That's why I insisted to Felix that we bring Deirdre here to live with us."

Jared gave Selda a sharp, questioning stare at this comment, but her mind was far too engrossed in her memories for her to notice.

"My parents resigned themselves to the idea of their first child being a girl, especially since it was clear that she would be a startling beauty. But when their second attempt produced another female—well, they were quite appalled, I fear. And I certainly was not going to be a beauty. Camille was so like her name. Perfect, delicate. A hothouse flower that needed to be fawned upon. I was always plump and plain. But I made do with much less. I never envied Camille. If she didn't have this or didn't have that, she pined in her room and wilted. I, on the other hand, was happy not to have such needs. I rather merrily went about my way.

"I suppose I seem rather stupid to you, my lord. Camille ended up wed to an earl with a stunning country estate and a lavish town house in London. They had a château in France as well, you know. I believe Camille considered the French court far superior to ours. They spent more than half of each year in Paris and Versailles. Morgan was the perfect match for my sister. He was so like her in every way. Carefree and handsome enough to take a girl's breath away. He had money and status and he loved to live life as though tomorrow would never come. If Camille wanted to attend all the finest balls and travel the continent, Morgan wanted to do so at least as much as she.

"I, on the other hand, have Felix. A baron, like our father. A lovely home in London, but no estate. We must be frugal with our income, but we have everything we need. I fear I've been found lacking when set beside my sister. But I am quite content. My only wish is that I had been able to produce a child for Felix. But, of course, it was Camille who was fertile rather than I. And it came as a terrible shock to her."

"She didn't want children?"

"No, indeed. She came to me in a frightful state with the news. It would ruin her figure. She would be confined to Ramshead for months and months during her pregnancy. She made it clear that had she known she was in the family way sooner, she would have sought assistance in eliminating the child." Jared looked away in disgust. "You have to understand her as I did, Lord Jersey. She was my sister, and I loved her. But I felt sorry for poor Deirdre.

"They never took her with them, you know. Never. And they were rarely in the country."

"I think I know what Deirdre's mother must have been like," Jared responded, images of Daphne running rampant through his mind. She and Camille Ramsey would have hated one another. They were of the same nature, and in their worlds there could only be one hothouse flower. One who was the most beautiful, the most charming, the most delightfully, maddeningly, and enticingly perfect.

"They died as they would have wished to," Selda finished with a slight shrug. "It was a wonderful life for them, but no life at all for a child I would think. Still, she insists that she was deeply happy growing up, and I believe her."

Jared believed her as well. But unlike her aunt, he understood why. It was what he found so enticing about Deirdre, and also what deeply worried him about her. Deirdre Ramsey made the best of every situation, finding what was good in it. Rather than lament a lonely, isolated childhood, she had filled her days as best she could and had come to love the world she made there. She looked upon Ramshead as her one tie to a mother and father who were rarely there for her, and she used it to shield herself from their failings. She had pride and an amazing strength to believe.

But what concerned him about Deirdre were those very same things. Her power to believe, to have faith in her dreams could be carried too far. Deirdre was not seeing people for what they were because she wanted so desperately to believe in the goodness of her parents. She was as unprotected from the vagaries of the world as a rabbit that didn't understand the use of its rabbit hole. He knew now why she so vehemently rejected his suggestion that she not trust those she knew well. If she didn't trust Anson Reece, if she didn't trust those people whom she had known the longest, she would be forced to reevaluate the two people she had known since her birth—her parents. And she would find them wanting. She would find that they had ignored her, left her to be raised by servants, deserted her for months at a time, and, worst of all, that they squandered her birthright. They had left her with nothing but a title and an estate that she had no means of sustaining. They had, in fact, left her with the worst possible choice for Deirdre. The choice to sacrifice either herself or her beloved home. For Deirdre, Jared knew it was as useless as no choice at all.

"I'm very sorry for Deirdre," Jared explained gravely. "But I'm afraid there is nothing I can do to help you." He thought for a moment. "I will have my solicitor bring you the offer I made on Ramshead. It stands for thirty days should your niece change her mind. Other than that, Deirdre will have to deal with the realities of her situation on her own."

Selda nodded in understanding. "Thank you for humoring me by hearing me out."

"Lady Derby," Jared explained, "if I could help in any other way, I would. And should I find a way to do so, you may be assured I will pursue that course."

"I believe that you would." Smiling, Selda showed Jared to the door, where she added, "I think that eventually Deirdre will see reason. Perhaps she just needs time to say good-bye to Ramshead."

Jared took a circuitous route to the offices of Ellis & Fitzwalter, choosing to ride through the park where he had seen Deirdre just the day before. He would dearly love to wring Anson Reece's neck for being so revoltingly predictable. Whatever Deirdre had seen, she could have been spared. When he'd warned her not to trust Reece, he hadn't wished that she'd learn not to trust him in the way Selda had described. He pictured Deirdre walking in as Anson Reece fondled some tavern doxy he'd pulled into his lap. And what, Jared suddenly wanted to know, was Deirdre doing in a tavern?

At the Derbys' he had been determined not to leap to her rescue. She wasn't a child, after all, and she had stubbornly refused to listen to anything he'd told her. She had to learn some lessons the hard way, just as he had. Jared's eyes narrowed as he remembered the hard lessons he'd been forced to learn. Lessons about how one's parents could so easily leave you penniless and burdened with estates and titles that only served to encumber you further. And about the price of making terrible choices out of desperation. Choices you naively believed could somehow be made good, despite the obvious wrongness of them.

He could spare Deirdre that. Why should she suffer it, when he knew the pitfalls and pain better than anyone? He couldn't imagine her without her spirit, that indomitable belief in life and herself that seemed ever present. Then a disturbing memory came to mind, and its impact was like a blow. It was the image the first time he'd seen her. She had seemed distant and unhappy that night as she'd entered the ballroom. The beautiful bird who, caged, could no longer find joy in life. That was how she would be—her spirit broken by the impossible situation her parents had left her in. She was too proud to sell him Ramshead. He suddenly understood that. Doing so would be an admission of failure on her part. For the sake of her pride, she would rather convince herself that she could make a marriage of convenience work than free herself financially by selling her home. It was a belief that Jared understood completely. Just as he now understood the fatal flaw of such thinking.

Pressing his stallion into a gallop, he headed for Charles's office. He would have the paperwork on his offer sent over to the Derbys', and then he would leave for Ramshead. He would go after her. For whatever good it would do him. He was likely to be the last person on earth she'd want to see. Except for Anson Reece, he thought, with more than a touch of pleasure. The warning bell in his brain told him that he was mixing business with something else, something deathly dangerous. But it wasn't really business anymore, Jared reasoned. He no longer wanted Ramshead for the sake of its excellent location or the fertile valley in which it lay. He wanted it as protection. Protection for Deirdre from the world that threatened to destroy her.

Eleven

It had dawned a beautiful day, and after a light breakfast for both Deirdre and Avis the little group was on its way again. This second half of the journey was more familiar to Deirdre. The countryside soon became the rolling hills of the midlands in which Ramshead was located, and Deirdre watched out the carriage window, her happiness unbounded. "Look, Avis," she said, pointing as they passed a pasture filled with grazing cattle. "Aren't the little calves adorable?" She counted more than thirty of the spindly-legged babies before the herd passed out of sight. "I can't wait to reach Ramshead. It's been so long."

"It has been a long while it seems," Avis agreed. "Doesn't feel nearly a year gone since I saw my family."

"Tonight you must go down to their cottage and surprise them! They'll be so happy to see you."

"Aye, my mum has been ill, and I've been worried I'd not see her again."

"Then you must go for certain. And you'll stay the night with them." Avis gave her a doubtful look. "Truly," Deirdre encouraged her. "There's still more than enough food for supper in that picnic basket, probably enough for two suppers."

"Well, we'll see how things are when we get to Ramshead."

Smiling, Deirdre nodded. "You won't have long to decide then, the gates are just over this next rise." It was true. The carriage topped the hill and suddenly the entrance to Ramshead was in full sight. Peters knocked on the carriage roof.

"My lady, the gates are padlocked. Is there another entrance?"

"Continue down and to the left," Deirdre instructed. "We can drive up through the tenant road. It's perhaps two miles farther."

"Very good," Peters responded. Deirdre stared at the thick chains that locked the gates. The entrance seemed so cold and foreboding—not at all like the Ramshead she knew. Never in her entire life had she seen the gates closed, much less locked to keep people out. A twinge of apprehension curled in her stomach. Would it be so different? Would it, as Jared had claimed, be abused and rotting? She couldn't believe those words. When she had left last year the house had seemed strange to her, devoid of the familiar objects she'd grown up around. It could not be very different now than it had been then. What could happen in a year? But the apprehension stayed with her, refusing to be dispersed.

The carriage turned up the road that led to the house by way of the tenant lands and the small village that offered limited services to Ramshead's residents and farmers. The village—not more than a handful of small thatched structures that contained the blacksmith and a tavern that was, in reality, only the front half of a cottage—was unchanged. The tenant lands, as well, were as she remembered them, neat squares of carefully planted fields segmented by thick hedgerows of holly, hawthorne, and dog roses with a small thatched roof house at the near corner. They soon passed Ramshead's three enormous barns. But they were unnaturally quiet, empty of the life that should have been there.

Deirdre's gaze stayed on the empty barns until the coach rounded a curve and started up the hill that would lead them to the house. Soon, she knew, they would come upon the wide swath of manicured lawns that surrounded the house for half a mile or more. Deirdre rapped at the carriage roof for Peters's attention.

"Could you please stop?" she called.

"My lady?"

"Could you please stop, Peters."

She felt the horses slow and the wheels of the carriage creak to a stop. Nils appeared at the door. "Why do you wish to stop, m'lady? We're nearly to the house."

"I know," Deirdre told him with a soft smile. "I'd like to walk from here."

Nils regarded her with disapproval. "Peters says 'tis nearly a mile!"

"That's all right. I want to walk." Looking to Avis for approval, Nils pulled down the steps and handed his mistress out of the carriage. "I'll watch for you to make sure ye don't run amok of trouble," he added, clearly thinking of the previous day's events.

"There won't be any trouble," Deirdre assured him. "I'm home now."

Waving them off, Deirdre watched the carriage kick up dust as it continued along the gravel road. Stepping into the hip-length grass, Deirdre let her fingers trail through the green seed heads and watched the grass sway slowly at her touch. The air smelled so sweet after the long months in London that Deirdre couldn't get enough of it. Taking deep, long draughts of it into her lungs, she felt the weight of the past year begin to lift from her. She tugged at the pins that held her hair in its elaborate coiffure and shook it loose. Then, feeling like a young filly suddenly giddy with freedom from saddle and bridle, she plopped herself in the grass and yanked off her slippers and stockings. She wiggled her toes along the roots of the grass, feeling the coolness of the soil against the soles of her feet. Then tucking one stocking into each slipper, she climbed to her feet and started again toward the house.

She enjoyed strolling through the long grass, noting each

familiar landmark as it came into view. But it occurred to
her as she went that she should have reached the scythed
lawn by now. She recognized trees and bushes that were
part of the formal lawns surrounding the house. Then it
struck her that there would be no scythed lawn. There was
no one to cut it. The tenants were here to work their plots,
but there was no reason, and no hired help, to cut the lawn.
It would be long right up to the cornerstones of the foun-
dation.

The thought saddened her. Ramshead was so beautiful—
or it had been. It was stately and graceful in an aged sort
of way. She didn't want to see it unkempt. Her concerns,
though, were confirmed as she came around the next bend.
There before her was the house. Twin wings of grey stone,
softened by age-old ivy that shook in the warm breeze, were
connected by the main entrance. Pink clouds of roses clung
to arched windows which were shaded by an open portico
supported by thick stone pillars in the Ionic style. Ramshead.

But two of the upper story windows were overrun by ivy,
and weeds had settled into the crevices of the walkways
that circled from the imposing front entrance to the walled
formal gardens on either end of the house. The closed
leaded-glass windows reflected a darker sunlight, as if in
acknowledgment that behind them lay only empty, lifeless
rooms.

It was her home, and it was not. It seemed older to her,
stooped, as though it had aged a decade in a single year.
Tattered and slightly shabby. The orphan left to its own
devices and found wanting. Not the breathtaking estate it
had always been before. She would have cried, had tears
been her way. Had she done this, she wondered. But she
knew the answer. All of Jared's words rushed back to her
again. How had he known? Had he come here? Seen it?
And why hadn't she understood how quickly a place as

wonderful as Ramshead could become only a sad shadow of itself?

Her gaze drifted from the house to the stunning view that stretched behind it. Located as it was on a long ridge, woods and fields and uncultivated pastures spread out below the house for as far as the eye could see both to the north and south. *This* was Ramshead, Deirdre thought as she slowly scanned the horizon. The land and the air, the pastureland and fields, the lakes and ponds. It wasn't merely a house or a lawn, but much more. So much more. Her resolve strengthened, her chin tilting stubbornly skyward. What had been lost could be found again. What now lay fallow could be planted. She would not let her home crumble like a faded flower that soon is nothing more than dust. She would find a way. She *would*.

"Lassie?" A tickle of joy raced up Deirdre's spine at the familiar voice. Turning, she found Bert standing in the drive behind her, dressed in brown knee breeches and the same well-worn boots that had long ago conformed to the bow of their owner's legs. "Lassie, what are ye doin' here, and why did ye not send word you were comin'?"

"Because it was a little last-minute. But Bert," she said, nearly jumping in her excitement, "I've come to stay."

"Stay? How would that be? Did that solicitor of your father's find a stash o' pounds sterling that your parents didn't know of?" At the crestfallen look on Deirdre's face, Bert pursed his lips. "I'm sorry, lassie, 'twasn't a worthy thing to say. Things 'ave just been a bit hard here the past year, what with the payments ye have required of the tenants."

"Payments?" Deirdre knit her brow, perplexed. "I don't know what you're talking about."

"The five guineas you've requested that each tenant make a payment of twice a year." Deirdre stared at Bert in disbelief.

"I haven't required any such payment, Bert! Why, it's bad

enough that I can't offer the tenants work at the manor house! I would never ask for a payment from them."

Bert's heavily seamed face settled into an angry scowl. "It's that damned solicitor, then. I told 'im I wouldn't believe you'd do such a thing to us. I knew ye wouldn't lass. But 'e insisted that you needed it to live on down there in London. Said ye were barely makin' ends meet. And so, the tenants and meself, we all made the payments. We didn't want to think of ye suffering any more than ye already have."

Deirdre thought of the armoire brimming with gowns and the beautiful bedroom she slept in at Selda and Felix's home. "Bert, how much did we make on the last oat and wheat crops last summer?"

Bert shrugged. "I don't have the exact figure in my head, but it was somewhere around £1,200."

Shaking with fury, Deirdre clenched her teeth to keep herself from using language Bert would have been disturbed to think she knew. "Our Mr. Benchley has been skimming the cream from the milk, so to speak, Bert. And I have been fool enough to think he was looking out for the best interests of myself and all of you." Deirdre recounted the clues she had seen at Mr. Benchley's office yesterday. The freshly painted office and the new pair of chairs at his desk. Even the town house's black trim had been newly repainted. Never, she reminded herself. She was never going to trust anyone ever again. "Never mind." Deirdre crossed the drive and, taking his hand, gave it a warm squeeze. "We'll talk about it later. For now, I'm just glad to be here."

"Aye," he agreed. "The house 'as been needin' a bit o' life in it."

"That it does."

Four hours later, Deirdre and Avis had succeeded in unsheeting what little furniture remained in the house and hauling the pile of dusty linens to the laundry house, where, Avis advised, they should deal with them later. As each room was dusted and swept, Deirdre threw open the windows, letting the hilltop breezes blow away the smell of stagnant air. She unpacked most of her belongings herself despite Avis's constant, distressed flitting.

"I have to learn, Avis!" Deirdre declared, impatiently waving her away. "You can't do everything for me. There are only the two of us here and a great deal of work to be done. It's high time I learned to manage for myself at any rate," she proclaimed. "I intend to learn to cook and wash and farm." Avis rolled her eyes in mock horror. "You may make jest if you like, but that is my intention. We'll start tomorrow with the marketing."

"No, we won't," Avis stated flatly. "The market is open but one day each week and that is not until two days hence."

"Oh. You see! I must learn, and that is what I will do." Having thus made her intentions clear, Deirdre pointed to the door of her bedroom. "Now, it will be dark soon, and you must organize the things you'll be taking down to your parents. You're staying there tonight, remember?"

"I don't think it's a good idea to leave you here alone. My parents can see me tomorrow," Avis protested.

But Deirdre would have none of it. Setting her hands on her hips, she gave Avis a stubborn stare. "You are going."

"Not until I've fed you."

"There is more than enough from the basket Maggie packed." Avis glared, but she was no match for Deirdre's determination. "Promise me you'll not leave the house."

"I promise."

"And you'll lock every latch. Close all the windows."

"Except for the ones in my bedroom."

Avis sighed in defeat. "All right, then. But I'll be back by dawn tomorrow."

"Wonderful. It's better if we get started early." Then, tilting her head, she added uncertainly, "Isn't it?"

Avis grinned and the two women chuckled in unison.

"Aye. 'Tis better to get the work done before the heat of the day."

As Avis turned to go, Deirdre added, "Say hello to your family for me."

The sun was just dropping behind the midland hills as Deirdre strolled down to the stables in search of Peters and Nils. Checking on them, she'd decided, did not qualify as "leaving the house," which she'd promised Avis she wouldn't do. "Have you eaten?" she asked the duo as she rounded a stall and found them tackling the unused bridles and harnesses with soap and oil.

"Yes, m'lady," Nils replied. "Bert's wife, Marta, brought a large basket of food up not an hour ago. We helped ourselves, if you don't mind, but there's plenty left of it."

Deirdre nodded absently and wandered down the row of empty stalls, her fingers tracing the names inscribed on brass plates nailed to each door. "It's so empty."

"Well, I believe your mare is pleased to be home again," Peters commented. "She had a fine roll in the pasture this afternoon, then went racin' and kickin' up her 'eels like a filly what's got 'er legs all crinked up from never bein' outside. And all that after she's come nigh to thirty leagues in the last two days!"

Deirdre laughed. "Then that makes two of us who are glad to be back."

"We'll be stayin' ye know, my lady," Peters added. "Until we see that yer settled and safe. Lord Derby gave us strict orders."

"I know," Deirdre responded, smiling softly. "And I'm grateful that you are. Right now it all seems a bit overwhelming. Well," she said, brightening, "I'm off to delve into Marta's basket!"

On the long chopping table set in the center of the kitchens, Deirdre found the promised basket, and it was, indeed, full of wonderful treats. Though not as elaborate as the contents of Maggie's basket, it held a wealth of freshly made bread, cheeses, and freshly picked strawberries that made Deirdre's mouth water just to look at them. She made herself a plate with a little of each and poured a cold glass of cider left over from the day before. Then, supper in hand, she headed for her father's study.

Lighting the oil lamps that sat on either corner of the desk top, she perused the scattered papers. She hadn't come back into this room since her first encounter with Mr. Benchley on the day she'd received the news of her parents' deaths. The untidy mass of correspondence was precisely as her father had left it when he'd last been there. Tearing off a piece of bread and placing a slice of cheese on top of it, Deirdre took a bite of her supper at the same time she lifted the topmost letter. Three hours later, she was still reading, each letter or memorandum going onto one of three neatly piled stacks, and any others finding a home in the trash receptacle by her feet. Bert's knock at the door made her jump, but as soon as she saw him, she relaxed.

"What are ye doin' in here, lassie? Marta seen the light burning and sent me up here to check on ye."

"I'm fine, Bert. I'm just going through Father's papers."

"Aye, so I can see. It looks a dauntin' task to me. And ye ought to be gettin' a nip o' sleep. Ye traveled far today and overdid yerself from what Avis tells."

"I'll go up in a few minutes. I've got just about half the desk sorted. I'll finish this half and then go straight to my room. I promise," she said with a solemn face.

Bert walked over to the chair on the opposite side of the desk and lowered himself slowly into it. "What's yer plan, lassie? Tell me 'ow it is yer thinkin' to stay."

"Do you remember teaching me my ciphers, Bert?"

"Aye, I do."

Deirdre leaned forward, her eyes lighting with excitement. "You taught me on the ledgers of Ramshead. You always made it profit. And I want to do that again. Start the estate up again, get it back to making money. Bring it back to life."

Bert sat back in his chair, one gnarled hand rubbing the bristles along his chin in thought. " 'Tis not so simple, lass. We've no stock left but a few old cows, and there's nary a lamb to be found 'cept the two old ones Seamus has on 'is plot. Still, it could be done. 'Ow much money have ye left after the sales and debts 'ad been paid off?"

Deirdre ducked her head and winced. "Only £730."

"Lord, lassie! What do ye think we can be doin' with that? We need coin to pay the plowboys and shepherds, and then there are the harvest laborers. We'll be needin' ta pay 'em all before we get a single quid for a crop!"

"Isn't there something we can do? There must be some way to get a crop to market and pay them after? If I signed them each a note of guarantee myself, would they trust me?"

Bert made a face which Deirdre knew indicated that he was deep in thought. "Well-l-l-l, I need ta sleep on it. But there might be a way." He gave her a reassuring smile. "Let's not be diggin' ourselves a grave just yet. Now! Get yerself to bed, lassie! 'Tis after midnight, and yer goin' a have a busy one tomorrow."

"I'll go in a minute." Rising, Bert pinned her with a reproachful look. "I will!" Deirdre promised.

"G'd night, then," Bert said with a nod. "And, you'll be 'appy to know there's not a man, woman, nor child what's not pleased as punch to see yer back."

Deirdre smiled at that. "Thank you, Bert. It's good to know."

The dream brought her wide-awake and sitting bolt upright in her father's chair. Bright sunlight streamed through the paned windows, printing a pattern of squares across the desk where moments ago her head had lain on a pillow of

letters. She'd been dreaming about Anson, a grotesque
dream in which he was surrounded by naked women feed-
ing him champagne which appeared to squirt from their
breasts.

Deirdre shivered and shook her head to clear it of the
hideous image. Her gaze came to rest on the pile of letters
she'd been reading when she finally fell asleep. They were
all from a Mr. Delwin Jones-Hale, solicitor. She had found
several unopened letters from Mr. Jones-Hale first, and
then, digging deeper into the disarray of papers, she'd discovered nearly a dozen letters covering the course of more
than two years. Realizing that this was the solicitor who'd
handled her father's finances prior to Mr. Benchley's being
retained, Deirdre had been certain she would find the culprit
responsible for the enormous financial debts her father had
incurred and which she had paid off last summer. Unfortunately, reality was not as Deirdre had hoped—or believed.

The earliest letters she found made reference to correspondence from her father authorizing Mr. Jones-Hale to
take whatever steps necessary to secure the funds required
to pay a variety of outstanding bills which were overdue.
They also referred to her parents' impending departure for
France and the fact that her father had indicated he would
need at least £6,000 for the extended trip. Mr. Jones-Hale
went to great lengths in those early letters to explain to her
father that the estate was doing quite well, but that the earl
and countess were overspending. Apparently, Deirdre's father thought this concept pure rubbish since the following
few letters confirmed that, as per the count's wishes, Mr.
Jones-Hale had obtained increasingly larger loans and had
used, as instructed, various valuables owned by the earl and
countess as collateral. In each letter, the solicitor warned
that the debts were growing and that regardless of the profit
made by Ramshead, the earl was overspending—a habit
which Mr. Jones-Hale strongly recommended he curb.

Apparently, her father disregarded his solicitor's advice,

Deirdre had realized, as there was an ever-growing sense of frustration and urgency communicated in the solicitor's letters. The last letter she had read, though, had been the hardest. It was clearly a response to a request made by her father. A request that Ramshead be mortgaged to provide the funds he and her mother needed. Mr. Jones-Hale was quite emphatic in his response. No, Ramshead could not be mortgaged. It was entailed by the deed signed by his father, which stated clearly that the estate was only Morgan Ramsey's for his use during his lifetime, after which it would pass to his heir. It was his to use, but not to sell, mortgage, or otherwise encumber.

Her father had been willing to lose Ramshead. The betrayal Deirdre felt was all-consuming. How could they have even *thought* to do such a thing? Ramshead had been in her family for a hundred years. But they hadn't cared. Not about Ramshead and not about her. What would they have done with her if Ramshead was sold or lost to debt? The answer was obvious and painful. She would have been deposited in a London town house with a handful of servants to look after her while her parents gallivanted through Europe. Deirdre stared stoically at the letters while her mind reeled. She had thought her parents were so wonderful. She had focused on their beauty and their charm. Paying attention to that had enabled her not to look at the other side of them. The parents who left her alone for months at a time. The parents who left her with nothing but their debts.

But she was not her parents, Deirdre told herself. She loved Ramshead. Her grandfather had loved it, she knew that. There were eleven books of her grandfather's in the library. Books filled with handwritten notes detailing every decision he had made here. Every lamb purchased, every crop sown and reaped, every construction undertaken. And he had put the entailment on the estate, making it impossible for his son to mortgage or sell the property. Deirdre chewed her lip thoughtfully. Had her grandfather suspected that his son did not have the same love for the estate that he had? Deirdre knew, from Mr. Benchley's detailed explanations, that there was no such entailment on her ownership of Ramshead. It was hers outright, to sell or not as she pleased. He had insisted on discussing that point at length after Jared's first offer was made on Ramshead last summer.

Funny, she thought. Her father would have mortgaged it or sold it, but he was prevented from doing so. She, on the other hand, had no such restriction, yet she knew she would never sell Ramshead. If she had been determined not to sell it before, her conviction was redoubled by what she had learned last night. By dint of will she would bring it back to life. Someday she would pass it on to her own child. That was a new thought for Deirdre. Her own child. She imagined a little boy—her little boy—running through the fields as she had, learning to add the long columns of numbers in the ledgers she would make.

Deirdre smiled. Ramshead would belong to her child one day. She would make sure of it. Then the smile vanished. There would be no child for her. No husband and no child. Her decision to come to Ramshead had been an acknowledgment of being alone for the rest of her life. She could not have all the things she dreamed of, but she could have some of them. She would have Ramshead.

The padlocked front gates posed no problem at all for Jared. In a single bound, his stallion was over the low stone wall that ran along the property line, and he was cantering casually up the drive. The road ran uphill, cutting through a dense woodland for almost a mile. Its similarity to the entrance to his estate, Jerseyhurst, was one of the things he found so likeable about Ramshead. The forest had been cut back fifty feet or so on either side of the road, but the grass that replaced it was up to his mount's hocks. The woods gave way, at last, to open land punctuated by hundred-year-old maples, lindens, and chestnut trees, whose graceful limbs spread heavy blankets of shade across the untrimmed lawn.

Jared slowed his horse to a walk as the house came into view. It was a bit old-fashioned in its style and more relaxed than most estate houses of the aristocracy. Jerseyhurst was considerably more imposing than Ramshead and at least thrice the size. But Jared liked the more casual look of this house. He could imagine Deirdre as a little girl serene and undisturbed by the formality most parents required of their children.

His gaze roving over the estate, he saw someone step through a gate at the far end of one wing of the house. A serving girl, or one of the tenant's daughters come to work at the house he thought, then he realized there wouldn't be any servants here. It was Deirdre he saw walking, twin wicker baskets looped over her arms. She wore a simple cotton gown devoid of the numerous underskirts normally worn beneath a woman's dress, and her hair hung loose to the middle of her back, held out of her eyes by a triangle of cloth tied at the base of her neck. She wore a pair of cotton gloves as well, protection for her hands.

Coming to the trailing roses that climbed the front pillars, she set down her baskets and proceeded to begin trimming flowers from the vine. Spent roses went into one of the baskets and a few choice blossoms were carefully set in the other. Jared rode toward her, watching as she stooped to reach the lower blossoms, then knelt. Producing a small hand rake from one of the baskets, Deirdre began to work the soil around the roots of the rosebush, diligently loosening it to give the plant more room for growth.

"These gloves do not work!" she declared in frustration to no one in particular as Jared pulled his stallion up twenty feet from where Deirdre knelt. Yanking one off, she inspected her thumb, stuck it in her mouth, sucked on it, then pulled it out again.

"Leather would serve better against thorns," Jared offered.

Snapping her head around, Deirdre's gaze settled on Jared, her expression one of intense displeasure. "If you have come to convince me that I should sell Ramshead to you, you have wasted much time and effort. It is not for sale. In fact, it is less for sale now than it was three days ago, or four, or five, or one year ago. And it was not for sale in the least even then. I suggest you turn your horse around immediately and head back for London." She adjusted the offending glove back over her hand and returned to her task.

"I haven't come to buy your home," Jared countered. "I've come to help."

Shoving the hand tool back into a basket, Deirdre rose. Jared watched with keen interest as she sauntered over to him, one hand on each hip in a gesture meant to be defiant, but with another effect all together. A very nice effect to Jared's way of thinking as he watched her hips sway provocatively from side to side. She was more slender than her ball gowns and city clothing had revealed, he thought, noting the fine bones that outlined her shoulders. Her cheeks bore a touch of color from a day spent in the sunshine, and one tendril of her thick mahogany hair trailed past the gathered neckline of her cotton dress, leading his eyes to feast on the rounded curves of her breasts.

"The kind of help we need is of the sort I'm certain you would not have the least interest in," she snapped, coming to a stop before him.

"And what kind of help is that?" he inquired, with a speculative quirk of one brow.

"Toil. Physical work. You would most likely perspire, my lord. Are you, perchance, familiar with sweat?"

It was all Jared could do to keep from laughing at her ire. "Sweat?" he repeated, knitting his brow thoughtfully. "Isn't that what common laborers do?"

"It most certainly is," Deirdre declared triumphantly. "And you can't work up a sweat writing out bank drafts at your desk, Lord Montgomery. So, I'm afraid you've come all this way for naught."

Jared calmly watched Deirdre turn on her heels and march back to her roses. Swinging off his mount, he followed her. "I thought you knew nothing about roses."

Deirdre halted mid-stride. "I don't recall saying that."

"Yes, you do. You told me so at the Cavendeshes' ball—when I suggested you might be able to offer some advice to my gardener."

"Oh." Deirdre looked over her shoulder at him. Her gaze began at his feet and slowly made its way to his face. When she finally looked him in the eye, she took a nervous nip at her lower lip. "I just don't know anything about *foreign* roses," she explained lamely.

"I see." Jared pinned her with an accusatory gaze. "Do you recall our discussion in the park?"

"Of course. I recall everything about our *encounter,*" she said, emphasizing the last word. "I remember you chasing me. I remember you scaring me half out of my wits, and I remember—"

"Do you remember saying that I was not a villain?" Jared interrupted.

Deirdre glared at him. "Yes."

"And do you recall that I asked you simply to watch me? To see what it is I do. I promised you that by doing so you could easily know who I am and whether or not I am deserving of your trust. Is that not correct?"

"It is," she replied, although she stuck her chin out at a mutinous angle, as if acknowledging that her admission went against her inclination.

"Then I expect you to do so," Jared finished firmly.

"I am not yours to command!" Deirdre sputtered in a rage.

"A disadvantage I admit."

"Oh-h-h-h! You are insufferable, sir."

"I don't think so, Deirdre. I am merely right. Have I yet done anything to warrant your distrust?"

She glared again. "No."

"Then do as you promised. Trust me." He saw the fear in her eyes then. Fear of him—not for who or what he was, but simply because he asked for her trust. Why was he even here? he berated himself as he watched her. Deirdre had given the best part of herself to a handful of people who had abused it, and now that she understood that, she was afraid. Afraid to be hurt more. This was the last thing he needed. To attach himself to a woman. Woman! Hell, she was barely more than a child, so innocent and protected was her outlook on the world. And one who was emotionally injured, who needed patience and nurturing before she would even begin to be ready to trust again. What on earth was he doing trying to convince this *innocent* to trust him? Jared Montgomery, who made a habit—no, a lifestyle—of only dealing with self-interested, experienced women.

Yet the answer was right in front of him. He could easily have killed those fools for what they'd done. For stealing the sparkle from her eyes and the carefree smile from her lips. He wanted to wrap her in his arms, barricading her from a world that was full of people like that. He wanted to heal her wounds, soothe her and pet her and promise her it would never, ever happen again. But he knew he couldn't. There were too many people who would hurt her and never give it a second thought. Only Deirdre could learn to recognize them and steer her course away from them.

What he could do, though, was to guard her from them until she learned for herself. If he didn't, she would become what he had become—hardened and cynical of everyone's motives. He had been that way when he'd first come to Ramshead, intent on buying the property for his own uses and utterly unconcerned about the desperate situation a young countess was in because her parents had abused their responsibilities. But he had changed. When? When he had seen her coming down the staircase at the Whitmores' ball? When he'd handed her his handkerchief after she'd gotten ill? When he'd seen her gaze in wonder at a rose mallow flower? In fact, he had changed each of those times, becoming more and more entranced by the rare combination of spirit and innocence that was Deirdre Ramsey.

He would protect her.

Even though he would likely have to shove his protection down her stubborn, hurt throat.

Twelve

"I'd like you to show me the estate."

Enraged that he was again *demanding* that she take him on a personal tour of her property, Deirdre glowered at him. Every vile, hateful invective she could think of raced through her mind, but judging by the impassive expression on his face it was clear that nothing she might say or do was going to budge him from this place. Her last hope was that if she placated him and gave him what he wanted, he would become bored or find it to his disliking—and leave. Pinning him with one final, fractious stare, Deirdre stomped into the house, sweeping up her baskets as she went. Twenty minutes later she stomped back onto the drive. Jared was sprawled casually on a stone bench on the walk, the reins of his stallion's bridle looped over the branch of a convenient mulberry tree.

"I'm ready," she snapped.

"Your horse?"

"Will be here any moment," she finished with a sullen look. As though he'd been waiting for her cue, Nils appeared with Iris in tow. "Here you go, m'lady." Handing the reins over to her, Nils bowed politely to Jared and left.

Without waiting for Jared, Deirdre mounted and turned her mare west, toward what had been the wheat and oat fields, and cantered off. Her ire didn't last long, however. The day was warm without being hot, and, as always, the beauty of Ramshead soon mellowed her mood. She had

heard Jared ride up behind her, and as they reached the
bottom of the valley she pulled Iris to a walk. Turning in
her saddle, Deirdre pointed to the fallow fields on their left.
"I'll put wheat, oats, and barley in these fields. Hay over
there," she added, indicating more fields to the right.

"Why have you chosen these fields for each crop?" Jared
asked.

"Because that was what was planted here before."

"Then you should plant the hay here and the oats, barley,
and wheat over there," he told her, indicating the exact opposite of what she'd just said.

Rather than let herself get irritated, Deirdre ventured a
question. "Why would you suggest so?"

"Every crop leaches different nutrients from the soil.
They also return different benefits to it. By rotating the
crops, you'll yield a better harvest."

"Truly?" she asked in surprise.

"Yes," Jared told her with a slow grin. "Truly."

"Then thank you for the advice."

"It's my pleasure."

He smiled broadly at her, and Deirdre's heart skipped a
beat. Why was he so handsome? He probably turned the
head of every female whose path he crossed. The contrast
between the pitch-black color of his hair and the lightness
of his grey eyes was disturbing, she decided. But not as
disturbing by half as his smile. When he smiled at her, as
he was now, she was nothing more than butter left in the
hot sun. She melted—from the inside out—and all she
could think of was the delicious taste of his mouth on hers.
Deirdre gave her brain a good shake. What was she thinking? She wanted to get rid of him! She wanted Jared
Montgomery to depart Ramshead as soon as possible and
leave her alone. "We'll ride to the pasturelands now," she
told him, a tinge of irritation creeping back into her voice.

With little more than a nod, Jared followed her. As they
cantered past three ponds, each one smaller than the pre-

vious and fed by a series of small waterfalls, Jared called to her, "Deirdre, when were these ponds created?"

Deirdre pointed to the rustic folly built of stone and tree branches. "The pavilion was built by my grandfather when I was very small. He said that he built it just for me. As a playhouse. He'd created the ponds years before as a gift for my grandmother. My father said the three ponds were meant to symbolize their family—my grandfather being the largest pond and my father being the smallest. The waterfalls were meant to show that they were all connected, a family." Deirdre fell silent as the smile faded from her lips.

The silence drew out for long minutes as they passed the folly and its ponds, until at last Jared spoke. "What are you thinking of?"

Deirdre looked away, wary of putting her thoughts to voice.

"Perhaps it will help to talk about it."

"Do you have any family?" she asked, her voice low and very quiet.

"No, I was the only child. My mother died giving birth to my younger brother. He only lived a week."

"And your father?" Deirdre asked gently, aware that they shared at least one similarity.

"My father died when I was twenty-four. Does that answer your question?"

Embarrassed at being so forward, Deirdre pursed her lips. "I didn't mean to pry. It was just that I was looking for a comparison." Haltingly, she continued, feeling her way as though through a dark room. "I have discovered some things about my family—my parents—that are not what I had expected. Not what I had believed. And it's made me wonder whether I ever really was part of a family."

Falling silent again, Deirdre considered her life. It seemed now, after all she had come to see, that she had not. Not in the sense of the ponds—an interconnected group of three. There had never been much interaction between her parents and herself. The water had flowed only between the two of them. None of it had come to her.

"Did you come here often?" Jared was asking.

Deirdre glanced at him and then averted her gaze. "Yes. I loved my folly. I'd play for hours and hours here."

"What did you play?"

She shrugged, the hurt rising fast into a knot at the back of her throat. "Sometimes I'd play with my dolls, but more often than not, I'd dance barefoot in the folly or hunt for polliwogs along the edges of the ponds." Taking a deep breath, she blurted out the deeper truth. "Mostly I played make-believe," she told him in a choked voice. "I would make-believe that I had friends to play with."

"So did I," Jared responded softly.

She looked at him in confusion. "What do you mean?"

"I was the only child and the heir. I was forbidden from playing with children below my station, and I was often lonely. Even as an adult, I have been lonely more often than not. Show me the pasturelands," he directed, changing the subject quickly as he set his heel to his stallion's flanks.

They cantered off again, but this time a strange sense of community settled over Deirdre. He was like her—a little. But hadn't she sensed that from the moment she'd set eyes on him? And had that been why she'd confided her fears in him just now?

Deirdre looked over at Jared as they rode side by side. Until now she'd never asked him anything about his family or what his life had been like growing up. The only thing she'd known was that he had been married to a beautiful woman whose death he still mourned. That must have been what he meant when he'd said he was lonely even as an adult. He must miss her terribly, she realized, noting that once again he was dressed in black, except for his white linen shirt. And she didn't even know what his wife's name had been.

Pursing her lips, Deirdre tried not to think about his wife.

If she were still alive, Jared wouldn't be here at Ramshead riding through the fields with her. For some ridiculous reason, Deirdre was suddenly very glad that he was here. There was so much she didn't understand about him. Why was he really here? If he truly was here to help, as he claimed, why was that? Surely, Jared Montgomery, marquess of Jersey, had other things to do than spend his day galloping across hill and dale with her. Maybe he was no different than Stewart Benchley, looking for someone to use. But then Jared certainly was not in need of making a little cash on the side. Deirdre immediately determined that this evening she would find the answers to her questions. She was learning quickly that the best way to learn anything about Jared was to ask him outright, and, she decided, that was precisely what she would do tonight.

Tonight. The word suddenly presented her with a new problem. What was she to do with Jared tonight? He certainly could not stay at Ramshead. Not with only herself and Avis in the house. That was unthinkable. Besides, she added to herself belatedly, she didn't want him there. They reached a hilltop from which Deirdre could point out several miles of pasturelands. Slowing to a walk, indicating the rolling hills that had served as Ramshead's grazing heaths, Deirdre asked, "Should I change these also?"

"Change them?" Jared asked as their horses walked side by side along the high ridge.

"You know, as you said with the crops. Would I do well to put crops here and the livestock where the fields are?"

"No," he responded, laughing. "It's too much work. You see, the fields have been tilled for years. The rocks and tree stumps are long ago taken out and the soil is easily turned because it has been each spring. The soil beneath your meadows is hard and full of stones. It would not be wise to switch them. Tell me what kind of sheep you'll raise, though. There are some new breeds which produce excellent wools."

"Bert has raised Shropshires, Hampshires, and South—South something," Deirdre recited, recalling the names from the ledgers.

"Southdowns." Jared quirked a black eyebrow. "I'm impressed that you would know the names of the breeds."

Pleased by his compliment, Deirdre brightened. "I admit to knowing nothing else about them except that their black faces are sweet. When I was six, Bert let me nurse two orphaned Shropshire lambs. Lord Mutton and Lady Sutton." She chuckled at the memory, a warm blush coming to her cheeks. "I adored them. I even smuggled them up into my room and let them sleep on my bed. The housekeeper nearly had apoplexy when she found them. She reamed Bert up and down for it, claiming it was his fault for giving them to me in the first place and then for forbidding me from sleeping with them in the barn. Can you imagine?" She beamed. "Oh, but I thought they were so-o-o-o soft, and they even smelled good to me—like warm milk mixed with honey. They were just like two little woolen muffs fitted with legs and a tail."

Jared chuckled along with her, his eyes never leaving her face. What a treasure she was. She sparkled with happiness, the memories of her lambs lighting her like nothing he'd seen before. She had meant it when she said she loved this place, and he now understood why in ways he hadn't before. She was meant for the countryside. Though she was stunningly beautiful in a ball gown, the image held no comparison to the one he feasted upon now. The late afternoon sunlight bathed her in a golden glow that gilded the soft waves in her hair, reminding him of autumn leaves stirred in the breeze. Her eyes sparkled like twin sapphires, and he would swear that the soft blush the summer sun had lent to her cheeks was the exact shade of peach he'd just imported roses from France to capture. Jared stared, transfixed by her spirit as much as by her beauty. Deirdre Ramsey was not created for the city. Its soot and confines only muted her incredible beauty. It was here that she belonged, out where the sun could shine on her and the hillshire breeze toss her hair.

Deirdre squinted at him, lifting one hand to shield her eyes from the sun's rays as she watched him. "Perhaps we should turn back. We've at least a thirty-minute ride to the stables, and the sun will soon begin to dip."

But Jared didn't want to go. He didn't want the moment to end. "Tell me about your other pets," he responded, holding his horse where he was.

"Well, if you count the innumerable polliwogs that turned into frogs, there were too many to recount in a mere day, my lord. Every kitten born to the barn cats or pup that would one day watch the sheep was mine for a while. I would play with them and coddle them from the time their eyes were still shut until they were a few months old and ready to be put to work or given to a tenant in need of a mouser or a dog."

"Did you never have a pet of your own?" Jared asked, thinking how very sad it must have been for her to always lose her pets before they were full-grown.

"No," Deirdre replied with a shake of her head. She was still smiling, but it was a bittersweet smile now. "But I was happy with what I had. How many other children of similar families had such experiences as I?"

"That's true," he replied. "You were very lucky to have all this."

They rode back at a leisurely walk, while Deirdre pointed out various landmarks on her property. When they arrived back at the stables, Nils was seated outside the stable door, apparently having a lazy afternoon repairing a carriage harness, but Deirdre was certain, the stableboy had been watching for them. "Nils, please rub down Lord Jersey's stallion and put him in Destrider's old stall—the biggest box at the end of the row. Lord Jersey will be staying in the gatekeeper's cottage. Perhaps Peters could see to taking Lord Jersey's luggage there as well."

Without looking at Jared, Deirdre turned and headed toward the house. The last thing she wanted just now was a confrontation—in front of Nils—over her decision that he should stay at the gatekeeper's house. But Jared made no comment about her arrangements at all. He simply instructed Nils that he could find his valise by the front door of the house.

She had started off a few paces ahead of him, but it took Jared no more than a handful of long, powerful strides to catch up with her. Placing his hand at her elbow, he leaned to her ear. "Am I also banished to the netherlands for supper?"

Deirdre gave him a sideways glance and found a lazy smile crooking one side of his mouth. "You are more than welcome to sup with us," she responded, placing an emphasis on the plurality of diners.

Jared regarded her for a moment. "Are you afraid of me, Deirdre?"

"Certainly not," she objected, her tone overly emphatic. "It is simply that Avis is here, and Peters and Nils as well. I have extended an invitation for them to sup with me each night since I cannot pay them and also 'tis more economical to serve one meal for many rather than the other way around."

Flustered by his closeness as much as by the fact that he was exactly right about his assessment of her state of mind, Deirdre reached down to hand him his valise. The leather satchel wouldn't budge. Abandoning that tactic, Deirdre turned in the entrance of the house as if to form a barrier blocking his entry. "Nils will show you to the gatekeeper's cottage. It is quite presentable for guests. I will have Avis come down to be sure you have everything you need. Now, I must change for supper. We dine at eight," she blurted. Even to her own ears she sounded hasty and defensive.

Jared gave her an easy smile. "I shall see you at supper then."

Deirdre watched him heft his valise and start down the gravel drive in the direction of the gatehouse. "I didn't mean that you should walk," she called out. "And Nils or Peters will fetch your bag."

Still striding down the drive, he looked back at her and grinned. "It's a fine evening for a walk, and the case is no trouble at all."

"But the gatekeeper's cottage may be locked," she said, cupping her hands around her mouth so he could hear her. Frustrated, she found herself stuck between beckoning him back and sending him on a useless journey of at least a quarter mile only to find his assigned quarters bolted shut.

Jared stopped, nodded in agreement, and casually turned in the direction of the stables. "Then I shall get Nils, or . . . Pender?" he asked trying to recall the other manservant's name.

"Peters," she corrected softly.

"You see, Deirdre. I'll be fine. I'm here to help you, not frighten you or cause havoc. Just watch me." He grinned at her, a smile so devastating in its effect that Deirdre felt her heart flutter like butterfly wings and her knees nearly buckle beneath her riding skirt. She watched him go, swinging the valise over one shoulder and sauntering off to the stables as though the bag which she had not been able to so much as shift weighed nothing at all. In his loose white shirt, black breeches, and boots, he looked unbelievably athletic and *nothing* like a male member of the *ton*. There was nothing about him that didn't emanate power. Not his personality, not his way of speaking, and certainly not his body or the way he used it. Swallowing, Deirdre turned away in search of Avis and instructions on how to gather water for her bath.

* * *

It wasn't that she was afraid of Jared, Deirdre told herself, an hour later as she stepped into a simple gown of lilac piqué trimmed with cream-colored lace at the neck and wrist. Critically evaluating herself in the tall mirrored glass in her room, Deirdre smoothed the bodice once and then went to her dressing table to put a pair of unadorned amethyst teardrops on her ears. She admitted that she had chosen this dress because Jared was here. Had it been only herself, Avis, and the others, she'd have settled for a simple cotton gown like the one she'd worn to do her gardening this morning. It was what she was feeling that scared her. He already could make her go completely senseless with nary more than a smile, and she was incessantly watching him, aware of his every action and the effect it had on her. Yes, she was afraid.

But her fear was more of herself and the pain she might have to go through because of him. The things she had felt toward Anson Reece were little more than a sense of friendship at first. And, she admitted, after the Cavendeshes' ball, a bit of wonder if something might possibly develop between them. Yet the pain of betrayal she had felt when she'd found Anson fondling that girl in the alley had been terrible! She had felt as though someone had ripped her heart out. The hurt—and the anger—had been ghastly, and her sense of betrayal overwhelming. Deirdre shuddered at the memory of those feelings. She knew now how betrayal felt. She knew how rejection and sadness felt. She didn't want to feel those things again. Not because of Anson Reece. Not because of her parents. And not because of Jared Montgomery.

And Jared Montgomery could hurt her. She knew it with a certainty that broached any logic or argument. From the moment she had first seen him and every time since, he had affected her. One minute she thought him wonderful, like today, as they had ridden across Ramshead. And the next she hated him. Deirdre's wry smile was soft as she thought of the innumerable times since they'd met that his demanding, plainspoken words had incensed her. Oh, how he could hurt her. And it was that of which she was so deeply fearful.

Jared knocked twice at the door before letting himself in, assuming that Deirdre was still refreshing herself. It was the first time he'd been inside this house, and, as with the exterior of the structure, he found the rooms very much to his liking. The decor was understated in its elegance. Mellowed with age but perfectly maintained. It made no difference to him at all that the rooms were devoid of furnishings and not a single painting hung on the walls. The house was exceptionally airy. The wide marble hallway gave way to an expansive drawing room that would be brilliantly lit each morning by sunlight streaming through the long line of arched French doors. At one end of the hall, he found the study, and at another end, the dining and morning rooms. But no matter how devoid of furniture, each room held at least one vase filled with freshly picked flowers. Jared recognized the roses he'd found Deirdre clipping in several arrangements, along with early summer irises, marguerite daisies, and sweet-smelling lavender. Beyond the morning room he discovered the kitchens, where he gave a start to the unsuspecting maid who'd recently provided him with fresh linens and water at the gatekeeper's house.

"Your lordship!" Avis gasped as she managed a quick curtsy. "I didn't hear you arrive."

"I knocked," Jared assured her. "But I thought it would be best to let myself in. Lady Ramsey gave me the distinct impression that this household is being run on a more casual basis. Given the circumstances, I hope you'll look upon my visit in the same manner."

"As you wish, my lord."

"Supper?" he asked, inhaling a delicious scent wafting from the pot over the fire.

"Aye, my mum sent up a mutton stew for us. Thank God for that, there's not a lick of food in this house."

"I hope it's not Lord Mutton or Lady Sutton we'll be dining on."

Avis's eyes nearly popped out of her head, then a quick smile spread across her face and her small brown eyes lit up with a laugh. "So she told you about those two, did she? My mum near to collapsed when she walked in with Deirdre's breakfast tray and found two lambs dancin' about the room." She eyed him with renewed interest. "I don't believe she's ever spoken about those lambs to anyone before." Jared made no response to that. Instead he asked if there was any brandy to be found in the house. "The earl's study is at the far end of the marble hall," Avis directed. "You'll find a decanter and glasses on the sideboard. I'd be happy to fetch it for you if you like, my lord."

"Thank you, but I can get it myself," Jared replied. He was the one who was surprised this time. Striding into the library, he found Deirdre perched on a small pair of steps by the bookshelves.

Looking up, she flashed him a brilliant smile. "I knew they must still be here!"

"Who is 'they'?" Jared asked, casually pouring himself a brandy.

"Not *who*," she explained. *"What.* My grandfather's journals," she indicated, excitedly waving one. "He was meticulous about recording everything that was done here."

Crossing to where she sat, Jared bent over her shoulder to see the yellowed pages of the leather-bound diary.

"You see," she said, quoting from an entry dated September 10, 1738. *"Purchased twenty-five new Milking Shorthorns. Plan to crossbreed with Hereford bull by spring.* Those are the cattle grandfather raised," she told Jared proudly. "I can learn so much from these journals. I'll know just what seed he purchased and which crops were the most successful. I can follow his breeding plans exactly." Her enthusiasm growing by the moment, Deirdre fingered through several more pages.

"The journals will be helpful, but don't count on them entirely," Jared cautioned.

"Why not? My grandfather is the man who made Ramshead so successful."

"But 1738 was nearly fifty years ago. Much has changed in animal breeding and agriculture since then. The sheep your grandfather raised here, for instance. They're all good breeds, but the finest wool now comes from merinos, a breed which didn't even exist in your grandfather's day."

Deirdre nodded, understanding the importance of what Jared had just told her. "Then I'll learn. But for now I just need to get one crop in and have enough money to pay the workers." She closed her eyes, as though offering up a silent prayer.

"Let me help." Jared's voice was low and husky. Looking at Deirdre's grandfather's journal afforded him an enticing view of the valley between her breasts. Her perfume filled his senses, a subtle blend of lilies that scented the simple upsweep of her dark hair. Jared took a long sip on his brandy in a futile attempt to cool the raging desires that had suddenly been fanned. It would do no good to kiss her now, he told himself, though he wanted to badly. He wanted to do much more than just kiss her. He wanted to feel her pressed against his entire length, feel the wild beating of her heart against his chest as he had in the conservatory and hear her moan softly beneath her breath just as she had in the park. But he had promised that she could trust him.

Damn him for making such a promise, he cursed. He had built his life on *never* promising anything to anyone. Promises were cheaply given and more cheaply taken back, and he had avoided them for that very reason. But he had promised Deirdre Ramsey that he was worthy of her trust. No one of importance in her entire life had proved to be so, and Jared was determined that he would not be another of the many who caused her disillusionment and pain. But when she was ready, he would be there. Until then, he would have to tamp down his desire for her, no matter how it raged.

"You have already helped me immeasurably," Deirdre said, turning to look at him. "You have offered advice which I will take, and you are here, offering . . ." Her words trailed off, leaving her staring down at her grandfather's journal in silence.

"What is it I'm offering?" Jared asked, softly repeating her words.

"Companionship." It was a whisper, choked with emotion.

Jared reached down, turning her face up to his. He stared into the crystalline blue of her eyes, eyes full of clashing emotions. In them he saw her want, her desire for him, and it caused his own desire to roar into an inferno so hot his hand nearly trembled. But he saw her fear as well. Fear of him. Fear that he might be like her parents. Or like that lying fool, Reece, who'd dared to whisper promises to her he never meant to keep.

His thumb caressed the line of her jaw. Her skin was satin beneath it. "Companionship," he promised. "And much more. When you're ready." Despite her fear, Jared knew he could not stop himself from kissing her now. It was an impossibility.

Bending to her, he slid his fingers along her jaw until they cupped her small chin. His gaze met hers, and he saw that she watched him. Her eyes searched his as their sapphire depths shone with the tears of a lifetime of hurt held captive by her will. He saw another emotion as well as he gazed down into her eyes. What he saw was hope. A bright, shining hope that still lived within her heart. A hope that existed despite the shambles which others had made of her life. A hope that made him want to enclose her in the circle of his arms where no harm and no hurt could ever reach her again. His gaze dropped to her lips, soft and warm. Lips that he could not resist. Sweet, generous lips.

Her heart beating like a mad drum in her ears, Deirdre watched, mesmerized, as Jared's mouth came ever closer, until it captured her own in a kiss that sent molten lava rushing through her veins. Like a river gone wild, the fevered warmth rushed over her as the kiss went on and on, growing in its demand. His lips parted, and she knew their intent—knew she desired it as well. The moment that her own parted under his demand, his tongue slipped between them, thoroughly exploring every rise and hollow therein. With a groan, Deirdre returned in full the passion of his kiss, which only resulted in Jared's increasing the pressure and insistence of his lips upon hers. Gently, he pulled her lower lip between his and suckled at it, sending a jolt of pleasure slamming through her body.

If his kisses before had seemed like explorations into heaven, this was a sensation which sent her far beyond. This was not the companionship he had spoken of, but that other. That "more." His kiss was both tender and unrelenting, giving her no quarter except to respond honestly with the full measure of her intoxication. And she did, joining her tongue with his and even delving into the recesses of his mouth, where she found new, wonderful sensations that made her head spin.

It was Jared who broke the kiss at last. Taking his lips just far enough from hers to prevent her from pursuing them, he drew a ragged breath. "When you are ready," he repeated in a husky voice, leaving his hand to linger on her shoulder as he straightened.

Deirdre ran her tongue over her lip in an unconscious savoring of his kiss that nearly sent Jared over the edge of caution. He wanted her—this independent, irrational, maddeningly naive woman—more than he had ever wanted anyone or anything in his life. But he wanted her only on terms which were unlike any other relationship she had known. He wanted her only when her trust could come as well. A trust that was given—not out of duty or because she thought she should—but because she knew it would be honored.

Thinking that somehow she had done something wrong, Deirdre averted her gaze and searched for something to break the silence. "Are you hungry?" she asked at last.

"Famished."

"I think the others may have already started." Climbing down from her perch and away from the warmth of his hand, Deirdre started for the door. Halfway there she stopped and turned self-consciously to Jared. "Will you come?"

Raking his fingers through his hair, he smiled. "You couldn't keep me away." Expecting a noisy kitchen filled with people talking and eating, Deirdre was surprised to find the room empty save for the pot of stew bubbling over the fire and a basket of bread, cheeses, and fruit on the chopping table.

"It seems we've missed them entirely," Jared pointed out.

"It appears so, doesn't it?" Deirdre agreed. "But that would make them rather quick eaters, don't you think? And the other night when we picnicked on our way here both Nils and Peters easily spent three-quarters of an hour eating." Tapping her finger against her lips, Deirdre considered their options. "It's quite warm in here for eating, perhaps they took their meals outside."

"That," Jared announced emphatically, "is an excellent idea."

"We could join them."

A slow smile spread across Jared's face. "I have a much better idea." Grabbing the basket of food with one hand, he nodded toward the stewpot. "Can you find two bowls and napkins?"

"I think so."

"Good. Then fill some bowls and follow me. There's a terrace beyond the drawing room, isn't there?"

"Yes," Deirdre responded, but Jared was already gone. Securing two bowls from the cupboard was quite easy, but locating a pair of napkins was a bit more difficult until Deirdre recalled the times she'd seen the housemaids put them away in the linen chest in the butler's pantry. Having found all the required materials, she filled the bowls with a large portion of steaming stew and then located a flat-bottomed basket for carrying them. Pleased with her success, she headed for the drawing room. But Jared was not there.

Spotting an open French door, she crossed the empty room and stepped outside. The scene she walked into stole her breath away. The basket of food Jared had snatched sat, untouched, on the uppermost of the wide, stone steps leading to the formal gardens. On either side, where the balustrade ended, he had set every candlestick in the house. The thirty or so flames of pale gold danced in the breeze like bright fairies come to life in the gathering dusk.

"Dinner *al fresco,*" he announced from behind her. Whirling, Deirdre found him standing in the doorway, two glasses in one hand and a bottle of wine—located, Lord only knew where—in the other.

"It's beautiful," she whispered, nodding toward the steps.

"It will look much more beautiful once you are a part of the scene."

Blushing, Deirdre carried the basket containing the stew to the steps and sat down. Jared joined her, the two baskets between them. He handed her a glass and poured them each some of the fine French wine he'd found, while she sliced cheese and bread for them.

Taking their first bites of their supper, they looked out toward the horizon. From where they sat there was a fine view of the lower formal gardens, yet even in the evening gloaming its ill-kept appearance was obvious to Deirdre's eye.

"I've only been back a day, and already it is beginning to seem overwhelming to me," she sighed. "There's so much to do." She stared out over the gardens, her supper forgotten in her lap. "I thought it would be a matter of two or three things. Sow a few fields with wheat and purchase a small herd of sheep. I thought that would get us through the hardest part. But I was wrong wasn't I?"

Turning to Jared, she waited for him to confirm her doubts. When he said nothing, she continued. "It's not just one crop I must plant, but barley and oats as well as wheat. Else I will not have fodder for the animals. And I must find the right sheep if my wool is to demand the greatest amount at market. Then there are the laborers and the household.

"Even this summer we must keep the orchards up or we will lose fruit trees and berry bushes that have taken years to yield a full harvest. And the gardens . . ." she paused, her voice saddened by what she saw before her. "They were always so beautiful. It brought such peace to my soul just to stroll through them. When will Bert or I have the time to care for these gardens? Look!" she said, stretching her arms to take in the endless hedgerows of bayberry and roses that created diamonds and curlicues. "I will need the dozens of servants my parents employed to maintain all of this, and it may be years before I can afford them. By that time, it will be too late." Looking over at him, she found Jared's shoulders shaking with ill-suppressed mirth. "What is funny in that?" she demanded.

"First you insist upon coming out here with the barest minimum of help, despite the advice of everyone around you. And now you have given up before you have even begun!"

"I have not given up!" she insisted. Then suddenly her wrath dissipated into the night air. "Although it must sound as though I have." She managed a self-effacing smile. "I must seem an utter nitwit to you."

"Not a nitwit, Deirdre. But a woman who feels deeply. I would never fault you for that trait, it is far too rare. Look," Jared pointed overhead.

"The stars are so bright here," Deirdre murmured, gazing at the black sky studded by diamondlike drops of light.

"There's Cygnus."

She looked at him, surprised. "You know the constellations?"

Jared grinned. "Better than you."

"I wager otherwise."

"Beware, lady, I never wager that I do not win."

Her eyes twinkling, Deirdre pointed to a cluster of stars just above the horizon. "Cassiopeia, and there," she announced her finger indicating another grouping, "is her daughter Andromeda."

"Pegasus, the winged horse," Jared countered, indicating the constellation. "Lepus, the hare, and Cetus, the sea monster."

Deirdre searched the sky. "Uhm-m-m-m. Oh! The bear. What's it called? Ursa!"

"That's too easy, my lady. Can you find Draco, Lyra, or Aquila? And what of Ursa's young brother?"

Deirdre threw up her hands in defeat. "Where did you learn so many constellations?"

"I was tutored by a long line of interminable men. All of whom I was certain had been hired specifically to bore me to tears. I learned about the stars despite their best efforts to keep my mind on more important tasks."

Deirdre looked over at Jared. In the fluttering candlelight, his face was a constantly changing silhouette of contrasts. Dark shadows interchanged with brightly lit surfaces that enhanced the strong lines of his handsome features. Dark and light. Black hair and light grey eyes. A body that exuded power and indomitable strength, yet a mouth that offered kisses so warm and gentle they turned her will to water. A man capable of hard, hurtful words and yet also capable of heartfelt praise. This was the Jared Montgomery she was coming to know.

She was glad that he had come. Despite her glowering upon his arrival, she admitted now that she had been irrationally pleased to find him here. If, she thought with a shudder, she should not prove able to keep Ramshead, she would rather that Jared Montgomery have it than anyone else. He had already shown her his knowledge and ability in matters of land management. And he had shown her more. He'd let her see his understanding of what she held dear here. The meadows and forests. The flowers and the endless views. And the stars.

Watching him as he scooped up the last of his stew with a chunk of bread, her eyes fell upon his mouth, and she felt the sudden rush of heat as she thought of his kisses. She wanted him to kiss her again. She willed it. *Kiss me.* The cooling night sent a chill up her spine, or was it her thoughts? *Kiss me. Wrap your arms around me and warm me.* What wanton notions! she chastised herself. How could she think such things? But she did.

As if reading her thoughts, Jared looked over at her. In the darkness, his eyes seemed like liquid silver. "You're cold."

"No," she countered with a small, self-conscious shake of her head, followed by a shiver.

"Yes, you are. I'll be of poor assistance here if you become ill because I kept you outside too late. Come, we'll go in. It's time I was banished to the gatekeeper's cottage at any rate," he told her. Standing, he took her hand, drawing her up beside him.

"Jared?"

"Yes?"

For a long moment the silence stretched between them. Deirdre did not know what she'd intended to say. It was only that she didn't want him to go. But she couldn't say such a thing, could she? He looked down at her, expectant. And yet, she wasn't sure of what. Did he want her to tell him she desired his kiss? He had never waited for her to ask before. In the past, he had always taken. Yet now, when she wanted him to pull her into his embrace and warm her mouth with his, he did not. Breaking their gaze, Deirdre picked at the lace on her sleeve. "Good night," she whispered, looking away as she spoke.

"Good night, Deirdre." While she had not known it, he had moved. And now, as he spoke, she could feel the warmth of his breath against her cheek. She looked up, and in that instant he brushed a wisp of hair from her forehead and kissed her. A chaste kiss upon her brow. "I pray your dreams are sweet tonight." Before she could speak, she heard the clip of his boots on the drawing room floor and then the solid sound of the front door closing behind him.

Thirteen

Deirdre arrived in the kitchen just after seven the next morning ready for her first journey to the market. Avis was already there, and her sister was with her. "Maris!" Deirdre exclaimed in delight. "I'm so glad to see you!" Giving the young woman a warm hug, Deirdre stood back and assessed the girl who was not more than two years older than herself. "You look wonderful. Life must be well for you."

"Marriage is well for her," Avis chimed in with a wink.

"You've married? Tell me who? Is it someone I know?"

"Aye," Maris told her, blushing with pride. "I married Bob Hardy. His father's a tenant, my lady, and my Bob is the blacksmith's assistant. He apprenticed with 'im for six years and he makes the finest things you've ever seen."

Deirdre smiled warmly. "That's wonderful, Maris. I am truly so very happy for you."

"Maris is come to help me here at the house," Avis announced. When Deirdre immediately began to protest, Avis wagged a finger at her. "Maris and me have discussed this and we're in complete agreement. Her Bob 'as a fine job, but Maris hasn't been able to find work this past year since you closed Ramshead. Now she's expectin' their first babe and she can't be trudging off to some other household, not with 'er being in a delicate way. So, she's goin' to help me here. At least it gives her somethin' to do, and she won't be forgettin' her skills either."

Deirdre contemplated this a moment, then nodded.

"You're right. Maris can't work anywhere else in her condition. So, I'll pay you each £1, 2 pence a month. I know that's a bit less than you were receiving before my parents' death, but if it will do . . ."

"There's no need to pay us so much, my lady," Avis interrupted. "It's enough that we're both here at Ramshead and near our family."

"Aye," Maris agreed.

"No—£1, 2 pence each," Deirdre proclaimed with finality. "Because there's so much to be done." The two sisters nodded, touched by their mistress's generosity. "Now," Deirdre asked, the matter of wages settled, "when do we leave for the market?"

"Peters will take us at eight. But you need breakfast before we leave." Avis set a plate of buttered toast and a bowl of strawberries sliced in fresh cream before Deirdre.

"I'm not terribly hungry," she countered. "Although strawberries are my weakness."

Maris and Avis chuckled in unison. "You need to eat, my lady," Maris told her. "If you don't, you'll end up purchasing three times what we need. The market is so full of smells and luscious things to eat that if you don't fortify yourself, you'll not be able to resist any of it."

Acquiescing to their experience, Deirdre dipped her spoon into the delectable strawberries. "Have either of you seen Lord Jersey this morning?" she ventured in as nonchalant a manner as she could muster.

"Aye," Avis nodded. "Mum saw 'im heading to Bert and Marta's cottage a'fore dawn this morning."

Deirdre regarded Avis in surprise. "Before dawn? To Bert's?" Avis nodded. "And he has not appeared for breakfast since then?"

"No. I've no idea where he's gone off to."

"Oh," was all Deirdre could think of to say. Despite her strong desire to see him this morning, she couldn't very well go traipsing off to Bert's looking for him. What would she say was her reason for seeking him out? No, there was no choice but to wait until he appeared. Resolute, Deirdre put Jared out of her mind—or tried to. Peters's knock at the kitchen door assisted her efforts somewhat.

"The carriage is ready, my lady."

"Are you ready, Avis?" Deirdre asked, excitement evident in her voice.

"That I am."

Deirdre ran to collect a shawl and wide-brimmed hat while Avis instructed Peters to put several baskets in the light, two-wheeled carriage. It was an hour's drive to the small village where the market convened once a week. Although she had lived at Ramshead virtually her entire life, Deirdre had never been to the market. Left with the responsibility of watching over the count and countess's only child, Bert had issued a strict edict disallowing Deirdre from any markets or fairs before she was even four years old. His reasoning had been quite simple. The hubbub of the market, let alone a fair, made it too easy for wily gypsies to whisk away a small child. Such things happened with startling regularity across the countryside, especially when the child was well dressed and clearly of the gentry. Bert had no desire to write his employer with the news that his child was being held for ransom or had simply disappeared while backs were turned.

This, then, was an event of huge proportion for Deirdre. For countless years she had listened with eager ears to young chambermaids relate with exuberance the thrills of the fairs and the excited bustle of the market. And at night she would lie in bed imagining what it would be like. For Deirdre, the market had always sounded much more exciting than a ball, and so, as the carriage came up over the hill and they could see down into the village, she was delighted to find it just as noisy and pandemonius as she had dreamed it would be.

As soon as the carriage was parked at the edge of the

market grounds, Deirdre and Avis dived into the bustle with enthusiasm. With Peters following behind them, they decided to explore the dairy stalls first. Butter, milk, cream, and cheese all had to be purchased, Avis explained, until Deirdre could acquire some cows of her own. Given the price of the goods all together, multiplied quickly in her head by fifty-two weeks' worth of visits to the market, Deirdre determined that she would do well to purchase a few milking cows as soon as possible.

Next they visited vendors hawking grains, flour, lard, and other comestibles for the table. Deirdre spied a fishmonger and they selected several fine brook trout as well as oysters and a pot full of clams. There followed stops for honey and sugar, a visit to the candle and soap makers' booths and more. Through it all, Deirdre found it nearly impossible to take in all the sights and sounds. Her head snapping from side to side, her eyes grew rounder with each passing hour, and her endless questions finally drove Avis to threaten her with leaving early if she didn't desist.

Although they did not stop at any of them today, there were entire stalls devoted to selling ribbons of every color and fabric imaginable and an entire lane set up by the spinners and weavers. Even the leather workers had their wares out, displayed to best advantage across long tables or hanging from poles. There was a flower stall filled to the brim with heavenly, fragrant blossoms from which Deirdre could barely tear herself away. And then there were the smells, as Avis and Maris had promised. Delicious scents from the pie maker's stall or where a wizen lady roasted chestnuts and spiced walnuts to be eaten warm. Along the rim of the marketplace were areas where farm implements and livestock were traded. Horses, cattle, sheep, and pigs were all for sale. Deirdre even found a small boy, who could not have been more than seven, seated in the dirt beside a wooden crate overflowing with squirming puppies.

"Could you use a good sheeper, m'lady?" the young boy

inquired with a shy smile. "These here pups are from a fine mum. Pure sheep dog she is, and a fine herder as well. Only a ha'pence for a pup."

"And do you know who the sire is?" Deirdre inquired, bending to tickle the soft belly of one.

"The dad, m'lady? Well, me own dad tol' me to say he was a sheeper, too. But," he told her in a conspiratorial tone, "it ain't true, and I wouldna want to be telling a fib to a nice lady such as you. We don't know who the dad is. But what I said about the mum is true as can be. She's the best sheeper in all the village."

"A halfpenny, did you say?"

"Aye, m'lady."

"Here it is, then. Take this brown-and-black one to the carriage at the end of the lane." A bright smile on his dirty face, the boy scooped up the pup and hightailed it for the carriage.

"What 'ave you gone and done now, my lady?" Avis admonished, as Deirdre returned to the stall where she had been haggling over the price of a barrel of salt. "You've no sheep for that pup!"

Deirdre smiled, a look of pure satisfaction lighting her face. "I know, Avis, but by the time he's old enough to herd, we will have some. And they'll be merinos."

It was late afternoon by the time the marketers returned. Exhausted, Deirdre lifted two baskets from the back of the carriage, one containing a very frisky and unruly pup, and carried them into the kitchen. "Has Lord Jersey returned from Bert's?" she asked the moment she saw Maris.

"No, m'lady. I've not seen a sign of 'im. But perhaps Nils would know where he was."

"Thank you, Maris." Depositing her hat and shawl in the butler's pantry, Deirdre picked up the pup and headed for the stables. There she discovered that both Bert and Jared had ridden out to look over the summer wheat fields. "How long ago was that?" Deirdre asked.

"They left no later than nine this mornin'," Nils assured her.

"They've been gone that long?" Deirdre couldn't imagine what would take Jared's attention for the entire day, and now she was determined to find out. Depositing the puppy on the floor of his new home, Deirdre went to get Iris from her stall.

"Would you like me to curry her for you, m'lady?"

"No thank you, Nils. You know I like to do it. But you could bring her tack for me. I think the market wore me out a bit." Happy to oblige her, Nils disappeared into the tack room.

It wasn't long before Iris was groomed and saddled. Deirdre knew that she should go back to the house and change into a riding habit. The dress she'd worn to the market was made of too light a fabric for riding. But she wasn't going far, she reasoned, and her curiosity demanded that she not waste the hour it would take her to change. As Nils helped her into her sidesaddle, her new pup came scampering after her, clearly determined to go wherever it was she was going.

"You'll have to put him in Iris's stall, I think," Deirdre directed Nils. "Otherwise. he's likely to get lost."

"Aye, m'lady. He's attached to you already!" With a chuckle, Nils collected the pup and took him inside.

A late afternoon breeze freshened, and a bank of clouds gathered along the horizon as Deirdre set off for the western fields. It felt good to canter slowly over the hillocks since she'd missed her normal morning ride today. Watching for any sign of Jared and Bert returning, Deirdre's eyes scanned the hills and valleys. But it wasn't until she was nearly upon the field that she saw Jared.

At the sight of him, her breath caught in her throat, and for a moment she didn't breathe at all. The reins gone slack in her mistress's hands, Iris came to a halt. Burying her nose in the tall grass, the mare yanked a mouthful of grass from its roots and began chomping happily.

Deirdre simply stared in admiration at what she saw. Jared, alongside twenty of Ramshead's tenant farmers, was helping to harrow the field into long straight furrows for planting. He was bared to the waist, his shirt discarded under the heat of the summer sun. Staring, she drank in the sight of his body. He was magnificent. Godlike in his build. Speechless, Deirdre watched him lift the pick over his shoulders and then slam it into the earth. Again and again, he hefted the tool; each time, the heavy muscles that ran between his shoulder blades and down his arms flexed and bunched, their contours glistening with sweat in the dying sunlight. His skin was the color of glistened bronze. His black hair was wind-tossed, wild tufts of it aiming in every direction while, around his face, damp strands clung to his skin. And the only thought in her mind was that he was so *beautiful*.

He looked up then, as though he had felt her watching him. A broad smile creased his face at the sight of her, and, handing the pick to one of the men working beside him, Jared started toward her. He stooped to collect his shirt from a dirt clump, hooking it carelessly over one broad, sun-browned shoulder with a finger.

"Hello," he said when he finally reached her. He placed one dirt-encrusted hand on Iris's neck. "Was your day at the market a success?"

A warm smile spread across Deirdre's face, and she felt her heart fill with a special peace. "Yes, it was a success and a trial and an event all wrapped into one."

"Good. I want to hear all about it. Just let me get my horse." A few minutes later they were headed back toward the house, the wind at their backs now, the dark clouds that threatened a thunderstorm behind them. "So, what did you buy?"

"I'm afraid *I* bought very little," Deirdre explained. "Avis was quite definitely the expert today. I merely tagged along."

"Why was Avis the expert?" Jared queried.

" 'Twas my first trip to market."

"Truly?" he asked in surprise. "I would have thought it a favorite pastime of yours."

"I wasn't allowed to go as a child. So, it was quite an experience. And I don't mind saying it exhausted me! I don't understand how Avis bargains. One vendor gives a ten percent discount and she is happy, but another one gives her twice that and she grumbles the whole way home. How does she know what is a fair price? And if everyone expects to bargain, then how does each marketer set his price? 'Tis a mystery to me!" she admitted with a shake of her head.

"It's called bartering, Deirdre. And it is an art, I'll grant you that. But it won't be long before you'll be right in there haggling over the difference of a farthing. And I'd wager as well that you'll become the bane of every vendor. For once you understand it, I've no doubt you'll get the best price of anyone for the goods you buy."

Deirdre felt a swell of pride at Jared's words. Did he truly think her so astute? Unexpectedly, she giggled, and at Jared's questioning glance, she burst forth with a full-fledged fit of laughter.

It was a magical laugh, Jared thought as he gave her a half smile and creased his brow, perplexed by her sudden outburst. Like the sound of a thousand tiny bells blown in the evening wind. Her eyes sparkled as her mirth redoubled and she tossed her head back, wrapping one arm about her waist as she shook helplessly. At last wiping tears from the corners of her eyes, Deirdre gasped for breath, her smile so wide and so happy it tugged at Jared's heart as nothing else could. *She should laugh so thoroughly all the time,* he thought.

"I'm sorry," she declared gaily. " 'Twas just that your remark was so kind, and so confident of my abilities," she stopped, trying valiantly to suppress another fit of laughter. "But then I thought of what I did select at the market."

"And?" Jared prodded, beginning to chuckle himself for

no reason other than the infectious nature of Deirdre's amusement.

"Well, I bought some fine brook trout for us to enjoy."

"Good. I love trout."

"But, my lord, I know not the first thing about how to prepare it!" The admission out at last, Deirdre burst into another series of uncontrollable giggles. "What are we to do?" she gasped. "Avis and Maris are already on their way down to their parents' for supper, and Peters and Nils are supping with Bert and Marta. I fear we'll starve, but not for lack of food. Only for my inability to cook it!"

"I'll cook it," Jared said, softly.

Deirdre sobered in surprise. "You know how to cook?"

"Don't misinterpret my abilities. I'm sure I'm not much better than you in this field. But I can cook a freshly hooked trout."

Deirdre's smile changed from one of enjoyment to one of warmth. "You would cook supper for me?" she asked, finding the thought so romantic her heart ached.

"I will cook the trout for *us*," he corrected. "You must prepare the other accoutrements of our supper."

"Oh." His statement took a bit of the romantic edge off of his offer although Deirdre still thought it something out of a fairy tale that he should be willing to do anything other than sip his brandy in the study while she slaved over their meal. However, the problem of the *accoutrements* loomed large in her mind for, just as with the trout, she hadn't the first idea of how she would successfully accomplish her portion of the duties. Concentrating all of her thoughts on this issue, Deirdre fell silent for the rest of the ride home.

Jared found it surprisingly pleasant to ride in this companionable silence with her. Too often women felt the need to talk constantly, as if silence was a thing to be avoided. They talked at breakfast and at supper, at balls and on carriage rides, at the opera—where they were *not* supposed to talk—and even in bed, which only prompted an early de-

parture on Jared's part. In the end, their constant need for
conversation only made him crave solitude, not them, which
was why his affairs had never continued for very long.
Women felt abused if they didn't hear from him for six
months and, inevitably, when he reappeared they either
wanted assurances he had no intention of giving or they
had moved on to accept the attentions of some other man
in Jared's absence. But Deirdre seemed not to mind the long
silence that existed between them. A fact Jared found wonderful.

He stretched in his saddle, weary from the long day of
manual labor. His muscles ached from use and his skin
tingled from hours under the sun. But it was a feeling he
enjoyed. Nothing made him feel more alive than to be bone
tired from physical labor at the end of a hot, summer day.

Nothing except lovemaking.

Jared's gaze settled on Deirdre, who rode just half an
arm's length in front of him. It had taken every ounce of
will to walk away from her last night. And he knew he
didn't want to do it again. The day of labor with pick and
hoe had been more than just lending another able body
where needed. It had been the only way he could make
himself sane again. Last night he'd lain awake in his bed
at the gatekeeper's cottage knowing that Deirdre slept in
hers a half mile away, but she was beside him in his mind.
The scent of her perfume lingered on his skin and his chest
seemed still warm where her breasts had pressed against it.
The calm night air was like her breath—the slightest movement of warmth against his cheek. Thus had he lain
throughout the night, hard with his need for her.

Having barely slept, he had risen before dawn once more
furious with himself for the stupid promise he had made to
her. A self-imposed promise to be worthy. And he had been
angry at her as well. Angry because she had chosen to trust
people who had not deserved her trust, people who were
not worthy at all. His ire at Deirdre had covered every year

she had spent believing in useless, selfish people no matter what they did to her. And now, because of those people, she was afraid to put her trust fully and without reserve in him. Digging the end of his pick into the unyielding soil, he had attacked all of the hurts she'd ever known, hurts that had left her needy of promises. But only needy of promises that were kept.

He had desired her from the moment he had set eyes upon her. Then, at the Whitmores' ball, his desire had only been for her beauty, but it was a deeper thing he craved when he looked at her now. Now he knew how indomitable a spirit she possessed. He had seen her tilt her chin in proud disdain of a society that thought nothing of ruining a young woman's future with a single word. He had experienced firsthand her willful determination and seen her childlike exuberance for nature and a simplicity of living that he well understood. And in yesterday's twilight he had seen the essence of her soul through her own eyes—the home that she loved so desperately. No, it was far more than her beauty he craved possession of now. It was her spirit and her will which he desired. And he desired them given willingly and in faith to him, and him alone.

Deirdre glanced at him from over her shoulder. "What precisely did you have in mind when you mentioned accoutrements?" she inquired. "Do you care for asparagus?" Jared made a face. "Roasted potatoes?" she tried. "And please," she declared in exasperation, "don't tell me you crave anything sauced or minced because I doubt greatly that I can manage it."

"I was hoping," Jared said, straight-faced, "to begin with a sherried turtle soup followed by a selection of sweetmeats to accompany the trout, truffles—since it is that time of year—cockscomb, a basket of fruits picked fresh from the orchard by your own hand, and then a tansy for dessert."

"Tansy and truffles and—!" Deirdre burst out in near hysteria until she saw the gentle rocking of Jared's broad shoulders. Shaking her head in reproach, Deirdre joined in his joke. " 'Tis a shame we've no game, sir. I could whip up a fine pie of minced partridge and create a splendid poach of pullet. They're quite tasty prepared according to my unique style—charred black!"

"Between us," Jared laughed, "I think we're safer with potatoes and trout and a large amount of wine to kill off any poisons we might accidentally produce from our cooking."

They stopped, having arrived at the stable yard. Jared swung one long leg over his saddle, dismounting fluidly, and then reached up to assist Deirdre. His palms closed around her waist, and he realized as he lifted her down, that his hands nearly encircled her waist. She was as light as a feather, and the thin muslin of her robin's egg blue gown left little to his imagination. Jared let her slide against his chest as he slowly lowered her to the ground, letting his hands slip from her waist up to the soft curve of her bosom.

Breathless, Deirdre stared up at him, her hands pressed against his shirt as her feet finally touched the ground. His eyes had turned the color of smoldering ash, intense and warm and beneath her fingers, she could feel the hard curve of his chest. Indomitable, just as he was. He smelled of sun and sweat and skin, mingled together in a scent that was intoxicatingly male. And she knew she was lost. She watched his mouth lower to hers, knowing what was to come, and found herself hungry for the taste of him. She lifted onto her toes, anxious to receive his kiss. When it came, it plundered her senses with its intensity.

Her lips parted, welcoming his tongue as it dived hot and hungry into her mouth, drawing a gasp from her as she leaned into him, molding her body to his, surrendering to the power of their kiss. She remembered how he had suckled at her lip last night, and, desirous of having him feel the same melting warmth trickling through him that he had brought to her, she captured the corner of his mouth between her teeth, gently nipping at it. With her tongue she traced the outline of his mouth, tasting the sharp tang of salt from his day's labor. Her efforts were rewarded, for Jared groaned, a rumbling from deep in the back of his throat. His arms slid around her, crushing her against him as he cupped her buttocks, one in each hand. "Deirdre," he whispered against her mouth. "My God, how I want you."

She was about to respond in kind when a sharp yap and the insistent tugging at the hem of her gown broke the spell of the moment.

"What," Jared growled with displeasure at having been interrupted, "is this?"

Stepping away from him, Deirdre stooped to gather her wayward puppy into her arms. "This is my dog," she explained as she received a thorough face-washing from the pup's perpetually moving pink tongue.

"A market purchase I take it?"

"Yes!" Deirdre declared as she tried unsuccessfully to contain the mongrel's enthusiasm. "His mother is a prize herder. He'll be perfect for my merinos."

"Your merinos?" Jared repeated.

"Yes. You said they provided the finest wool in all Europe, so I've decided that my herds will be only merinos." She chuckled softly to herself, and then, looking up at Jared, she beamed. "No one will be able to forget the name of the best wool in England, you know. Ramshead wool. It has a ring to it, doesn't it?"

Although his agitation at having their kiss brought to such an abrupt conclusion was great, Jared knew that he had been close to going beyond all reason and taking Deirdre's virginity hard and fast here in the stable yard. And he doubted that Deirdre would think anything of that except that she had been badly used by him. The last thing he wanted was to frighten her or hurt her. Her first time must be just the opposite. Raking his fingers through his dirt-flecked hair, Jared sighed as he watched Deirdre bring the pup into submission by scratching his round belly in long, calming strokes. "So you bought this pup for your nonexistent sheep?" he asked, pointedly.

"And because he'll be mine forever." When she looked at him then, he saw bright tears shining in her eyes and that willful determination of hers. No one, it said, was going to take *this* dog away from her.

"Then he was an excellent purchase," Jared told her gently.

Deirdre regarded him with a tender look of gratitude. "The only problem, apparently, is going to be keeping him in the stables where he belongs."

"Why is that?"

"Because Nils put him in Iris's stall to keep him from following me and, as you can see, he didn't stay there long."

Frowning, Jared led their horses into the stable while Deirdre followed close behind. It didn't take them long to discover the puppy's escape route. Claw marks and gashes from his milk teeth marked the small square opening through which the horses were given their oats each day. "Well, at least we know he's a smart little nip. He clawed his way into the hay trough and then made his way out of his prison through this opening."

Deirdre judged the distance from his escape route to the stable floor to be nearly three feet. "He could have broken his leg jumping down from there!" she declared. Then, wagging a finger at the pup's innocently happy face, she warned, "There will be no more of that!" At the woebegone look her scolding brought to his big brown eyes, Deirdre hugged the pup to her neck and planted a kiss on one slightly shaggy ear.

"Do you think the tack room might be a better home for him?" she asked Jared.

"No, he'll be lonely and probably howl until everyone on the estate goes mad. Leave him with your mare tonight. I think all he wants is company."

Together, they brushed down the horses and turned them into their stalls, where Nils had filled their bins with oats and hay for the night. Deirdre was surprised, again, that Jared, unlike the other aristocracy she'd met in London, didn't balk at doing the work of caring for his stallion. In fact, he seemed quite adept at it. Leaving the stables, the pair sauntered slowly toward the house. As they approached the split in the drive where one side led to the gatekeeper's cottage and the other to the main house, Jared stepped toward his quarters. "Has Avis already left for her family's home?"

Deirdre bit her lip uncertainly. "I believe so, but I'm not certain. I'll look for her in the house. If she is still there I'll ask her to fetch you some water for a bath."

"No," Jared countered. "If she is there, you will want her to see to your needs. I can avail myself of a fine bath on my own."

"Are you certain?" Deirdre asked, thinking that she couldn't imagine that he would want to lug buckets of water into the house for his bath after slaving all day in the field. But Jared just winked at her, a mischievous grin on his face.

"I'll see you at eight then. And don't worry, I won't smell anymore!"

Fourteen

Deirdre found both Avis and Maris still at the house awaiting their brother, who had promised to collect them on his way back from working in the fields. Dispatching Maris to the gatekeeper's cottage with instructions to fill a tub for Jared and take fresh linens down as well, Deirdre and Avis set about getting Deirdre ready for supper. "Will you be all right about supper without Maris and me here to help?" Avis asked, a doubtful expression on her face as she tested the bathwater.

"We were fine last night," Deirdre told her proudly, then added, "I want to put some of my lilac-scented oil in the water tonight."

Avis suppressed a knowing smile. "Well, you managed to eat, I saw that much. But I've got my doubts about the rest of it."

"What do you mean?" And then, "Do you think my spring green gown is too formal for here?"

"I mean, this mornin' I found nary a candle in the entire house. But all of them collected *outside* on the terrace. And, no, I don't think the green gown would be too fine for this evening."

Chagrined, Deirdre ducked her head as she climbed into the tub of scented water. "I'm sorry, Avis. I brought in the bowls and goblets, I must have forgotten about the candlesticks. . . . Perhaps I'd do better to wear the apricot gown with the tangerine trim."

"What are you plannin' on serving his lordship for supper, if I might ask?"

"He's cooking for me," Deirdre told her with a brilliant smile. "He said he knows how to prepare trout. I suppose he's fished for it often at his estate."

"Well, that at least makes a bit o' sense. What about the rest of the meal?" The face Deirdre made told Avis everything she needed to know. "So, you are to do those honors, are you?" She shook her head in dismay. "What was it you were thinkin' of fixing?"

"Potatoes?" Deirdre suggested.

Avis's mouth moved in a semi-approving motion. "And?"

"I haven't gotten any further. I saw some asparagus in the garden this morning, but he doesn't care for it."

"Are you plannin' to dine outside again this evening?" the spry maid inquired, giving Deirdre a sharp look.

"No," Deirdre told her just before she slid beneath the surface of the water to wet her hair. "We'll just eat in the kitchen."

"Humpf! The kitchen! Yer gonna put your hair up and wear a fine gown so that you and his lordship can have supper in the kitchen? Not while I'm workin' at this household!" Avis muttered to herself as she waited for Deirdre to resurface. Still mumbling about candles and kitchens, Avis soaped Deirdre's hair, mixing in a tiny amount of the patchouli oil and essence of spring honeysuckle to scent it as well as her skin.

Just as Deirdre climbed out of the tub, Maris knocked twice on the door of the suite and let herself in. "I saw to Lord Jersey's bath, my lady, and left fresh toweling for him. I waited quite a while so as his bathwater wouldn't get cool, but he never arrived."

"He wasn't there when you went down to the cottage?"

"Nay, he wasn't. As I said, I waited nearly three-quarters of an hour for 'im. I was afraid I'd miss Raymond and me Bob comin' to fetch us. I'm sorry, my lady. I filled the tub and left the linen and returned here." Maris twisted her fingers into a knot. "Did I do wrong, my lady?"

"No," Deirdre assured her. "You did the right thing. I just wonder where Jare—Lord Jersey went."

"No matter," Avis interceded brightly. "Come on now," she admonished as she hurried Deirdre to the dressing table. "We've got much to do and only a little time. Maris," she said, holding out one of Deirdre's hairbrushes, "you must do this while I attend to a few things downstairs. And don't fret about Raymond and your Bob. I'll give them each an ale to quench their thirsts, and they'll be happy to wait a bit for us." At the door, Avis turned back. "Wear the green gown," she instructed in a no-nonsense tone. "I'll bring up a branch of blossoms from the garden, and Maris can weave a few sprigs into your coiffure."

An hour later, Maris beamed as she watched Deirdre turn before her long mirror. "You look a vision, my lady. You should be goin' to a grand ball tonight, not spending your evenin' here in an empty house in the country."

Deirdre gave Maris a glowing smile. "I wouldn't trade the grandest of balls for an evening here."

"Ye look lovely, indeed," Avis agreed, coming into the room. Without ceremony, she grabbed her sister's hand and hurried her toward the door. "Well, you're on your own for the evenin'," she declared. "Raymond and Bob have been havin' a fine time of it restin' in the shade with their pints. But young Kyle has just arrived, sent up by our mum, so we're off."

Deirdre waved the two women good-bye. "Have a wonderful time and don't worry about me. I promise not to burn the house down tonight."

Maris laughed at the comment, but Avis just rolled her eyes and applied her knuckles to the heavy walnut door. "Aye, I hope not!"

* * *

From her bedroom window, Dierdre watched Avis and Maris along with their two brothers and Maris's handsome, young husband stroll in the near darkness down the path leading to the tenant road. How happy they all seemed. Comfortable with one another's companionship. Here at Ramshead their parents and grandparents had been born, lived, and, in some cases, died. It would be the same with them. Deirdre was certain that the coming child of Maris and Bob's would be but the first of many. One day their little cottage would be full of children.

Leaning against the window frame, she stared into the night. It would not be so with her. Remembering her daydreams of coming back to Ramshead, Deirdre's soft smile was suddenly touched by sadness. A spinster puttering in her gardens, that was what she would be. She would not go back to London; she knew that with a certainty even greater than what she had felt when she'd decided to come back here. She wouldn't leave Ramshead ever again. She belonged here.

But without London there would be no husband for her. Not that any eligible man would have her once it was known that she was running her own estate. Keeping books, bartering with common folk for food and services, raising sheep, growing crops, and marketing her wool in the city, no lord would be caught dead with a wife who doubled as a solicitor and bailiff rolled into one. Ramshead wool.

Closing her eyes, she leaned her head back and sighed, imagining Marvella Bowers's appalled reaction when she learned that Deirdre was engaging in free enterprise. Such things simply were not done by ladies of quality. Her previous suitors, Lord Hale and George Dimock, though long since disinterested in her, would be similarly shocked. And Anson Reece—Deirdre shuddered at the memory.

She didn't regret her choice. She knew she would make the same one again and again should time have turned back to a few days ago. But the finality of it weighed heavy on her just now. She would indeed be a spinster. Quite alone once Jared left.

Once Jared left.

Looking down at the soft folds of her gown, with its inches of fine, cream-colored lace spilling from the three-quarter-length sleeves, she admitted to herself just how much she had enjoyed his company the past two days. He was as warm as he was hard. As open as he was impenetrable. He was as handsome as gossip had made him out to be, but far more interesting and far more compelling. Deirdre didn't dare allow herself to believe that he would stay. He had only come to help, as he'd made very clear. He had his own home—an estate probably twice the size of Ramshead if Felix's comments were anywhere close to accurate. He had his friends, his businesses.

And the memory of his wife.

Her thoughts turned to his kisses and to the passion she saw in his eyes when they darkened like rain-heavy clouds. Why was it that at times she found him so difficult, so unyielding, so completely devoid of understanding and yet an hour or a day later he would be warm and gentle and more filled with comprehension for her feelings and her needs than any person she'd ever known? How was it that one moment she wanted him as far from her as the world was wide and the next moment she desired nothing so much as for him to pull her close and smother her with his very soul?

Turning away from the night that lay beyond her window, Deirdre drew a heavy sigh. She did not know what to make of him, nor of her feelings for him. But tonight she would do everything in her power to make the evening memorable. She would at least have this when she grew old, and hers were the only footsteps which echoed through the halls of Ramshead. She would have a few days of memories.

* * *

Taking each step on the staircase slowly, Deirdre stooped to peer through the banister in hopes that Jared had not yet arrived for supper. She wanted at least thirty minutes to evaluate the possibilities in the kitchen before he appeared. Relieved to find that he had not yet arrived at the house, she headed for the kitchen. It was already fully dark outside, and the storm that had hung in the distance earlier that afternoon now blotted out any light from either star or moon. Avis and Maris had lit several branches of candles before they left, providing illumination in the marble hallway. As she passed the dining room, Deirdre noticed a light emanating through the double French doors that led to the empty room. Pushing the doors open, Deirdre stepped inside. There at the far end of the long chamber was a perfectly arranged table for two.

A vase filled with lilacs, iris, and roses sat in the center of the small table, which she recognized as the cherry tiptop that usually held her father's brandy decanter. Her mother's crystal stemware reflected the soft light of twin candelabra perched upon the mantelpiece, and a low-built fire added to the light and intimacy of the setting.

"It's lovely."

The sound of Jared's deep, resonant voice sent a shiver of pleasure up her spine.

"Avis did this," she said softly as she turned to greet him.

Standing with her back to the fire, Deirdre was a vision more beautiful than anything Jared had ever seen. Her dark hair was swept into a simple knot into which tiny white blossoms had been woven. Light stars in a mass of dark curls. The firelight outlined the height of her cheekbones and the slender curve of her neck for him, and his eyes followed the soft crescent shape of her cheek as though it was his hand that caressed her rather than the light. His eyes dropped from her face and he noted the dark shadow that marked the place where her breasts dipped beneath the fine silk of her gown, then, going even lower, his eyes narrowed at the golden outline of her narrow waist and softly curved hips. Desire raged through him, and had he not spent the last hour in the icy cold of her grandfather's pools, he'd have swept the fine china from the dinner table and taken her here. But reminding himself of his promise, Jared drew a hard breath instead.

"It's lovely," he repeated. "But not nearly so lovely as you."

Impulsively, Deirdre plucked a pure white rosebud from the vase and walked to him. "You are lovely," she whispered, sliding a hairpin from her coiffure and using it to secure the rose to his lapel.

"Men are not lovely, Deirdre."

"Aren't they?" She blushed. "I fear you are, my lord. Yet you are more a man than anyone I've ever known." She gazed up at him, her hand resting against his chest just below the rosebud she'd attached there. Silence, potent as a drug, stretched between them. Neither spoke, unwilling to let the moment pass. At last, Deirdre let her hand drop. "We still have supper to prepare."

"You must be a more tidy cook than I," Jared ventured. "Otherwise, you would not have put the future of such a stunning gown in jeopardy."

Deirdre laughed. "From what I saw of Avis's confidence in my abilities, I wager we'll find a pair of aprons awaiting us in the kitchen." Her intuition was straight to the mark, for lying across the chopping block were two aprons. Along with the aprons, however, were the half dozen shucked oysters they had purchased at the market, carefully set upon a bed of shaved ice. There were still-warm buns as well, a delicious-smelling roulade of roasted potatoes with sprigs of rosemary, a bowl of wilted lettuce topped with bits of pan-fried meat, and a large helping of trifle.

Viewing the array of goods set out for them, Jared pursed his lips and eyed Deirdre speculatively. "Are you certain you didn't profess your dilemma to Avis and beg her to provide a respite for you?"

Deirdre, who was as much surprised by the bounty as he, shook her head in disbelief. "I can only tell you that she was unimpressed by my plans for our meal."

Jared could not help laughing at that. "Either that or she is set on making a match for us," he told her, indicating the two bottles of French champagne that sat cooling in a pail of water by the window.

Deirdre blushed profusely at the suggestion. The intimate candlelit table for two in the dining room as well as the preparations before them here did indeed sniff of matchmaking, but Deirdre could not imagine that Avis would do such a thing. "I think she is just being motherly," she told him lamely.

"Next time, I must tell her that I do not appreciate having all your work done for you while she has left the fish untouched."

Deirdre's eyes lit with humor. "I told her you were adept at food preparation. She must have thought you would be sorely irritated should she touch your fish."

Jared, who was busy releasing the cork from the first bottle of champagne, shot her a look full of ire. "Then I will be sure to correct her misassumption. To killing any poisons I may inadvertently create," he announced, handing her a glass.

"This is the first champagne I've tasted since the night I became ill," she told him.

"It will taste much better."

"Why do you say that?"

"Because that night you drank too much in an effort to be merry when you were not. It is a ploy that never works." Deirdre's gaze met his over the top of her glass. "Tonight you are relaxed. It's an entirely different thing."

Deirdre sipped her wine and discovered that he was right. It no longer turned her stomach, nor reminded her of the sickening feeling of emptying her stomach over the Whitmores' balustrade. Jared drew a three-legged stool over to the chopping block and helped her onto it so that Deirdre could watch as he prepared the trout. He worked with the skill of a surgeon, never hesitating in his motions, and Deirdre realized that he must have done this innumerable times before. Adding salt and pepper, a bit of butter and a touch of minced onion to the fillets, he deftly sautéed them over the kitchen fire. It seemed only a few minutes before they were seated at the intimate table in the dining room with their meal before them.

Raising his glass in a toast just as the first bolt of lightning split the blackness of the night, Jared looked deep into Deirdre's eyes. For an instant she felt naked before him, as though the lightning had stripped her bare and he saw everything that she was, and knew her more intimately than anyone had ever known her before. Then, just as suddenly as the darkness returned, the impression was gone. "To our first supper together."

Deirdre smiled. "To our second."

"You're right. To our second."

The meal was delicious. The trout melted in her mouth as did everything Avis had left for them and they were well into the trifle by the time the streaks of lightning that regularly rent the blackness became a full-fledged storm. The rain beat steadily against the full-length windows that lined the far wall as Deirdre created swirls and peaks in her trifle. *This is what it feels like to be completely satiated,* she thought. She was pleasantly filled with a delicious dinner made by the hands of what she had just decided quite emphatically was the most handsome man on earth. The fire warmed her to the perfect degree, she was safely ensconced in her own home where no one could malign her or comment on her or disabuse her. She was seated across the table from a man she judged to be not only handsome beyond compare, but wise, kind, and hardworking. And she was feeling delightfully carefree—a result, she suspected, of the three glasses of champagne she'd imbibed during the course of their meal. But unlike the Whitmores' ball, when too much champagne had done little more than make her ill, tonight she felt quite well. Exceedingly well, in fact.

"Do you think I can do it?" she asked, languidly putting her index finger in her mouth and then running it slowly around the rim of her champagne flute to elicit a tone.

Jared's eyes followed her finger from the glass back to her lips, where she wet it with her tongue and back again to the crystal. Didn't she have any idea what effect her actions had on him? Did she expect him to sit watching her when his fingers already itched to touch her? He watched in fascinated torture as the warm, moist tongue that had sent shivers up his spine last night moistened her finger yet again.

Shifting in his chair, the toe of Jared's boot crushed something beneath it and he realized that Deirdre had once again shed her slippers. He considered searching about for her foot, but rejected the idea, knowing that should he discover that she wore no stockings, he would be lost.

"Yes, I think you can do it. You are bright, Deirdre. And you are already very knowledgeable about the estate. The only thing you need is some capital to see you through the first year, and if you will allow me, I'd like to help with that." He saw the light immediately dim in her eyes and a dark defensiveness dropped over her face. "Deirdre," Jared ordered, reaching across the small table to take her hand in his. "Look at me."

It was a command again. And although she wanted to hate him for it, she did as he wished.

"I did not say 'I want to buy Ramshead' did I?" Deirdre shook her head, but the near grimace on her face did not change. "I want to help you. I don't want to buy Ramshead. It's yours. Even if I had been able to purchase it from you, I realize now that it would never have been mine. It belongs to you. It is your heart and your soul, I have seen that these past few days. You were right in that, and I was wrong."

Deirdre looked into the silvery depths of his eyes, surprised by his words. She had never thought to hear him admit wrongdoing. And his acknowledgment made him a greater man in her eyes. Others, no matter how evident their error, would not have relented for fear of making themselves seem inept. Jared had no such fears. "If you lent me money," she responded, emphasizing *lent,* "what would your terms be?"

Jared considered for a moment. "I would require some say in the spending of the loan. The funds could not be used to hire household servants or furnishings. They would be earmarked for sheep and cattle. Also for seed and field laborers."

Deirdre nodded. His terms were more than fair. He was only ensuring that he would see his monies returned, knowing that he would receive no recompense from the purchase of gowns, or, she thought with a smile, dining room tables. "Then you would want to see the ledgers at the end of every season."

"No. I would want to see the ledger every fortnight. If I waited a season, the damage would be done by the time I knew of it." He still held her hand in his and he squeezed it now, his gaze becoming intense as he leaned toward her. "I promise you, Deirdre. I do not wish to take your home from you. I only wish to help you accomplish your goal. Believe me, you cannot succeed with £730. But you can succeed with your wit, Bert, and the monies I will lend you. I have no doubt I will receive my investment back."

The nearness of him as he gazed at her so intently was making Deirdre's face go hot and her breathing come in quick gasps. His effect on her was more powerful by far than a physician's powder. She felt drugged by the very essence of him. He was power and knowledge and intensity combined. It emanated from him like heat from a flame.

Intelligence, solidity, and *warmth*. That as well. How could he be gentle and strong at once? She didn't know. But she felt it. Felt it, and her attraction to it, like a magical spell put upon her. One which she could not resist, and which she wasn't certain she wanted to.

"I'm afraid the day of marketing has had an effect on me," she explained, pulling her hand from the grasp of his fingers. "I'm very tired." Not wishing to look at him for fear he would see her lame excuse for what it was, she collected her napkin and made much of setting it beside her plate.

Jared rose as she did. He didn't speak, but looked at her with those penetrating eyes, as though waiting for something. A flash of white-hot lightning streaked across the sky, illuminating the empty room in a sheet of pale light. A crash of thunder followed close upon it. Deirdre jumped. Her eyes locked with his. Breathless. "Good night," she said, and turned, knowing she must flee or else throw herself in his arms. It had to be one or the other.

Her bare feet moved quickly, out of the room, up the stair, down the hall. Safely in her suite, Deirdre leaned against the door as it shut. She threw her head back, her breathing coming in great gulps that made her sides ache and her hands quiver. What had she run from? What was she so afraid of? She had promised to make this night a memory. But it was not a complete memory, and she knew it. It was her deepest recesses that quivered for him now. A need ancient in its origin and nearly undeniable in its strength. Only being separated from him by thick walls and dark hallways kept her from begging him to fulfill her need.

She crossed to the window and threw it open, heedless of the rain as she drew its cooling effect into her lungs. The sky was lit by another bolt of lightning, another crash of thunder.

"Deirdre."

Standing in the doorway of her room, one hand braced

against the wall, Jared stared at her. Never in his life had he wanted anything with the passion he possessed for this woman. Not money or success or lover. She was fire and ice. Spirit and innocence. He craved her. Craved to possess her. "If you want me to go, you must say so. I cannot make myself leave."

"Stay. Please."

He did not wait for her to reconfirm her words. In an instant, he was across the room, tearing her hands from the window latch, pulling her into his arms, crushing her against him as the storm within him, like the one outside, raged. His mouth swooped to seize hers with tender fervor. "Deirdre," he murmured against her lips. "I want you. My God, how I want you, Deirdre." Her name was like a balm, soothing the beast's soul that roared within him. His hands shifted over her body, discovering the feel of her, committing to memory every inch of her perfect form. Sliding his hand down her side he cupped one buttock, disbelieving of how perfectly it was shaped to his palm, while with his other hand he loosened the pins in her hair until it came tumbling down, a cascade of dark silk that fell to her waist.

Deepening his kiss, Jared plunged his tongue into her mouth, demanding that her own meet his—that tongue he had watched all through supper. And when it did, he closed his mouth around it, sucking hard and fast. The skies above them rumbled and flashed and he heard her moan at the same moment her body melted against his. The sensation of her hips against him caused him to rise harder and hotter than he had thought possible, taking him to the very edge of the breaking point. To a place beyond reason. He swept her into his arms and, without looking, found the bed. He laid her there, lowering himself onto his elbow beside her. It was only then that he pulled his mouth from hers and stared deeply into her eyes.

She saw his question, bold and yet, unbelievably, somehow tortured. The same question his gaze had spoken to her at supper and last night and, she realized with a jolt, every time he'd bent to kiss her. But this time she understood its meaning. He would not force himself on her, no matter how he wanted to. And she knew in an instant what her answer was. She did not speak it. She wanted no words at this moment. Nothing said that would ring false with the dawn. Instead she answered his gaze with her own. And he read it. Knew it.

It was as though the dammed river had suddenly broken its bounds. An explosion of need, as sharp and jagged as the lightning bolts outside the window, assaulted her mouth as he brought his down on it, raw with hunger. His fingers dug into her hair, grabbing a great handful of it and then opening to press her closer to him, her mouth harder against his. His kisses were nearly violent in their demand, suckling at the corner of her lips, plunging his tongue deep and hard into her mouth, then racing it along the edges of her teeth. His hand glided along her thigh, upward, always upward, caressing everything he touched until it reached her breast. He cupped the fullness of it and Deirdre felt the rush of sensation to the tip of her nipple as it hardened in response. His mouth tore away from hers, trailing across her cheek, to her temple, then finding the lobe of her ear. He ran his tongue up along the sensitive outer rim and plunged it into the crevice there, sending a shiver of pure, exotic sensation racing through her.

Deirdre began to move beneath his ministrations, unable to hold herself still. She wrapped one leg around his thigh, dragging the skirt of her gown over him. Her arms reached around him, wanting to enclose him. Wanting to hold him as he held her. Completely. Yet his back was too broad and so, instead, she spread her fingers across his shoulders, pressing him down on top of her. Urging him closer.

Jared leaned back on his elbow, slowing his kisses, banking the fires that threatened to spark out of control. His head still bent over hers, he kissed her neck and down across her shoulder. Slowly, his fingers dipped beneath the cream lace at her neckline, tantalizing her with the touch of his fingertips against her bare breast. When she drew a sharply ragged breath, Jared stopped his kisses long enough to gaze at her, an essence of regret on his lips. "I'm sorry, my love." And then in a single swift motion he curled his fingers over the lace edging and tore the moss silk to her waist.

Deirdre jumped for a moment and then, letting out a tiny laugh, she murmured, " 'Twas too fancy for the country at any rate."

His eyes were the color of smoke now, and his gaze intense despite the shadow of a smile that lingered there. "You are beautiful, Deirdre. So beautiful." His gaze swept slowly down the length of her revealed by the torn gown. Then he spread the fabric and reached for her breast, cupping it now, skin against skin. Rubbing his thumb across the spiked nub, he smiled when it peaked further in response. "Take it off," he murmured softly. "I want to see all of you."

Deirdre's gaze roved over his, searching for reassurance there. Seeing her sudden fear, Jared sat up, giving her time. Casually, as though giving no thought to her presence, he pulled off first one boot and then the other. Then he rose from the bed, taking her hand as he did to help her rise with him.

Standing face-to-face, mere inches separating them, Deirdre felt the coolness of the storm's breeze on the bare, exposed skin of her breasts, and she wondered how she dared do this. But Jared was reaching for her, hooking his fingers around the shoulders of her gown and drawing it slowly, seductively down her arms until it dropped into a lake of pale green around her ankles. She would not hide what he desired to see, she told herself. And so she stood proudly, letting his gaze burn a hot path over every inch of her skin, praying that he found no flaw in her that would turn him away.

Instead of turning from her, he took her hand, curling

her fingers around the fabric of his shirt. "You must do the same," he urged.

Her fingers shook. She knew she did not have the strength to tear his shirt from him. But she could undress him, and that, she realized suddenly, was what he desired. She stepped closer to better deal with the row of linen-covered buttons. At first her fingers were clumsy, then, as his arms came around her and he returned to caressing her and warming her she became more adept. His touch sent sensations such as she'd never dreamed of flashing through her, and she had to force herself to concentrate on her task rather than letting his caresses sweep her into mindlessness. In a moment the shirt was free of its buttons and she laced both hands under its fine weave, caressing his chest and then his shoulders as she freed him of it.

As he had done, she found she could not take her eyes from him, nor stop her hands from exploring the curve of his muscled shoulders and the soft, dark fur that matted his chest.

"Are you pleased?" he asked, his voice softly curious.

She only looked at him in response, her eyes luminous with arousal. "You are the beautiful one," she murmured. "I thought it today when I saw you in the field. That I have never seen a man of such beauty before."

Although he had heard her say similar words earlier, they still shocked him. Women called him "hard" and "cold." Dangerous. They admired his strength for the pleasures he gave them, for the thrill of riding a man so powerful. None had ever termed him *beautiful*. Jared reached for the laces of his breeches and slowly loosened them. His eyes never leaving hers, he removed the pants, tossing them carelessly on the floor. Deirdre stared at him, at the enormity of him. The corded muscles in his thighs were thick and heavy, and in the single step he took toward her, she saw the power of them. And between them, his rigid erection. Stilling the cry of fear that rose in her throat, Deirdre turned her gaze to his face. Locking on that. Recalling the image of herself as a spinster. Alone.

He did not wait for fear of him to overwhelm her, but came to her immediately, wrapping his strong arms around her until she was enveloped once more in his embrace. Crushed against him, she could hear the pounding of his heart against her cheek and the deep rumble of his voice as he spoke to her. "You must trust me, Deirdre." She looked up at him, so tall that, even when she stood on tiptoe, the top of her head barely skimmed his chin, and she nodded. Then his mouth dipped to hers once more and her fears fled at the onslaught of his passion. Once more he gathered her close against him and carried her to her bed, but this time there was no hesitation in his actions. He lay against her, trapping one leg beneath him, his knee between hers. His hands caressed her buttocks, and drew her hips against him until she could feel the insistent press of his erection hard against her thigh. Jared dipped his mouth to her breast, drawing a gasp from her as he circled first one nipple and then the other with his moist tongue. His mouth closed over her breast, drawing hard as he suckled. Deirdre moaned and laced her fingers through his hair, pulling his mouth tighter against her as she arched into him, wanting more as wave upon wave of pleasure washed over her.

Her reaction nearly drove Jared to insanity. She writhed beneath him, wanting things she did not know of yet. Slowly, he glided his hand along the soft, milky whiteness of her waist, eliciting a moan from her as he trailed his fingers across her flat belly and down to her thigh. When he touched the soft curls between her legs, Deirdre stiffened. But releasing her breast from his ministrations, Jared moved his mouth to cover hers, murmuring against it that she needn't fear his touch.

Indeed, as if by magic, his words and his touch combined to send a raging fire surging through her veins. Wrapping her arms tightly around his neck, Deirdre closed her eyes and clung to him as his touch incited a hunger deep in the very wellspring of her being. With a sob of pleasure, Deirdre arched against the need that grew within her until she feared she would shatter from the bliss of it.

Knowing she was ready, Jared moved, settling himself over her, his knees coming between hers, his erection poised just at the apex of her thighs. His movement drew Deirdre's eyes open, and she saw him above her, his grey eyes smoldering, his mouth a hard slant across his face. His gaze went deep into her, touching hidden places and feelings, reaching to an intimacy that was at once both irresistible and terrifying. And Deirdre gave back, staring deeply into him, seeing who he truly was, reaching for the part of him no one touched as he cupped his hands beneath her hips and drove his throbbing shaft hard into her, breaching her maidenhead.

He heard her gasp of pain and felt her freeze beneath him as the pain of his entry coursed through her. Pulling her close, Jared tried to press every inch of his flesh against hers and enclose her in the safety of his embrace, offering what comfort and warmth he could against her pain. As the pain passed and she became once more pliant against him, he began to move inside of her. Slowly at first, sliding against the walls of her warmth in a torture so sweet it was excruciating. The feel of her around him was like the heat of the sun deep within him. With each stroke he drove deeper. With each rhythmic thrust, he tortured himself further. He withdrew until just the tip of him remained inside her, then slid, hard and fast into her. Deirdre's hands slipped over his buttocks clasping him to her as he drove into her, sheathing him in her softness. As he withdrew, she arched upward, her hips moving in unison with his, creating a dance of intimacy that was intoxicating and hypnotic. It was a miracle, this rhythm of theirs. And unlike anything he had ever experienced before. In her totally unselfish innocence she was creating an arousal in him that threatened to erupt in a fiercely violent torture of utter, unbelievable pleasure.

Deirdre felt her legs shaking under the onslaught of the passions he had aroused in her. Higher and hotter, the swirling pleasure swept through her as she moved with him seeking a need she did not understand, only knowing it was near and that she could not be at peace again until she found it. Jared's movements quickened, turning insistent and driving. And she knew he, too, sought that thing. Urgently, she moved to the pulsing beat that vibrated deep within her, matching its tempo to his. Seeking together.

Faster, deeper, harder they drove. More. And more. And more still until suddenly the building heat within her exploded, shooting hot, sensuous liquid warmth snaking wildly through her in a flood of unbelievable pleasure. It racked her body with wave upon wave of incredible sensation that robbed her of her breath and stole away her reason. She clung to Jared, unwittingly sheathing him deeply in the throbbing, pulsating spasms of her pleasure.

Near mad with passion and need, Jared drove into her, unable to control his thrusts any longer as he felt her reach her fulfillment. He drove deep, pulled back, drove again, as the tight feel of her around him sent bolts of hot pleasure slicing through him. He felt himself rise to the peak of pleasure, hovering for one flash of a moment at the precipice of arousal, and then he slammed over the edge. Hot, jagged stabs of pleasure racked through him and his body jerked spasmodically as, at last, he allowed himself the piercing satisfaction of release. Explosion upon explosion tore through him and he pulled her fiercely against him, burying his face in her hair, breathing her in, driven by a possessiveness and a need he had never known before as he poured himself into her.

Fifteen

The storm had abated. As Deirdre stood at the tall window in her room all that remained of the tempest were distant flashes of blue light that outlined heavy thunderclouds now miles away. Her arms hugging the lawn wrapper she'd donned, she gazed at the dark outline of Jared's slumbering form in her bed and felt a stab of need so poignant, so unutterably sharp, that it ached unbearably. *What had she done?*

She turned away from him, finding greater comfort in gazing out at the receding storm. Deirdre had thought she knew what would come of this night. She'd believed she was in control. She'd believed that if she had no expectations beyond this night, that if she was not misled by promises, she could not be hurt. But she'd been very wrong. She hadn't known she would feel like this. Like a rosebud unfurled to the sunlight. She had wanted to know the touch of his hand, his body upon hers. A touch that she could carry with her forever. But she had not known that his possession of her would reach to her soul.

Deirdre closed her eyes, inhaling the dampness of the night, lingering in the time that was a new day yet unborn. She had thought this a safe thing because she had not entered into this union with any false illusions of a future. He had not plied her with silly lies, falsehoods that were meant only to lead her on as Anson had. In those moments when passion had risen like a rush of need between them, he had told her that she was beautiful. He had caressed her as though she was a treasure of immense value. Even when he'd hurt her, he had held her, gathering her pain against himself to soften it. His essence was like an elixir to her. Filling her with want for more. More than just one night. More than only a few days of intimate dinners and long, peaceful rides across the countryside. And this need that flamed within her was the very thing she feared.

She had made a terrible error tonight. Not because she was now a "ruined" woman, no longer eligible for a husband. She was ruined the moment she decided to come home to Ramshead and run it as a man would. But because she had thought she could armor herself against any hurt she might suffer from Jared. She had believed that if she expected nothing more of him than this night, she would be safe from pain. But she wasn't. She did not want him to leave. She thirsted for this feeling, this fulfillment she felt when she was near him, and tonight had only made her need for him total.

She had not spared herself at all.

What was worse, he had asked that she trust him. Demanded the thing she had vowed never to give again. As he'd risen above her, his eyes and words had demanded it. Staring deep into their silvery depths, she had known that he would accept nothing less from her. If she could not trust him, they could not come together as one. In return he had offered himself, his eyes an open doorway that let her seek what she needed. There had been no words of love. No promises made. They would only have deterred her. She had needed his honesty, and he had given it.

Likewise, she had given him her trust. Given it with the same willingness by which she gave her body to him. Unafraid. Now, though, in the aftermath of their lovemaking, she found herself scared again. Scared by the need in her. Scared of the hurt that it could inflict.

"What are you thinking about?" Jared's arms closed

around her, cradling her in their warmth. Deirdre turned her head, resting her cheek on the broad plane of his chest and closed her eyes, reveling in the feel of him.

"Hurts," she replied honestly.

"I'm sorry that it hurt, Deirdre. But only the first time hurts. It will be better next time."

A sound, almost like a whimper, escaped her lips. She didn't want any apology for the pain of his entry. She couldn't imagine anything more wonderful than the sensations he had roused in her. "It's not that pain I was thinking of. The true hurt is yet to come, I think."

Jared tightened his arms protectively around her, an ache growing in his chest, while he silently cursed the events that had caused her such pain. Despite her willingness to trust him, to give herself so utterly and passionately to him, she was still afraid. Afraid of what that trust might do to her. How it might hurt her. Bending to kiss the rim of her ear, Jared whispered huskily. "I won't hurt you like that, Deirdre. I prom—"

"Don't!" Then more softly as she turned in his arms and pressed her fingers against his mouth. "Don't. I don't want that. I just want you to hold me. Please." Rising onto her toes, she slipped her arms around his neck, her face upturned. Expectant. Hopeful.

With a groan, Jared captured her mouth with his. His hands slid to cup her breast as Deirdre twined her fingers through his hair, drawing him down to her like a whirlpool drew the helpless victim. No longer was she the frightened virgin, unsure of what was to come. Now he found a woman in his arms, a woman who knew and wanted. Her tongue darted into his mouth, inviting, teasing, sliding along the sensitive inner wall of his lips, imitating the ways in which he had kindled her passions. His arousal was immediate and intense. She rained kisses on him. Kissing his cheek, his neck, pulling his head down so she could dip her warm tongue into his ear until he felt gooseflesh cover his arms.

She nibbled at the lobe of his ear, always drawing him closer, always awakening a greater need in him. Her breasts pressed against his chest, titillating in their softness. Her hands ranged over him, sliding across his neck, caressing his shoulders, tracing the pattern of his muscled ribs, kindling a raging fire in him. A fierce, aching hunger. He was throbbing, nearly senseless with arousal, as she intentionally worked to please and excite him. Her hands ranged lower, exploring, seeking, learning, until her fingers touched his arousal. For an instant, she faltered, then her hand closed around him and Jared lost all control.

Bending her back in his arms, he pulled her wrapper open, revealing the glory of her body. Jared drew the length of her nakedness hard against him. He drove his tongue deep into her mouth, then pulled it back and drove again. Harder. With fierce demand he emulated the act they would soon share. And Deirdre returned his passion with her own, wild need. Groaning, he dug his fingers into the thick mass of curls and buried his face in her neck, kissing and nipping. He bent lower, devouring her breasts, running his teeth over their peaked nubs as his hand kneaded them. And then he lifted her. Not to the bed they had shared, but to him.

Instinctively, Deirdre wrapped her legs around his hips as he lowered her, sliding her hips against his, cupping her buttocks, drawing her apart so that he could slip inside her. As she felt his erection touch her, she tensed reflexively. But then he was easing into her, slowly so as not to hurt her, and it was a sensation of slow, seductive heat that only made her crave him more. Fully within her now, with his mouth hot upon her breast, Deirdre felt Jared begin to move rhythmically as he held her aloft. She clung to him, her arms wrapped around his shoulders and her legs locked around his hips as they moved together. Deirdre arched against his deepening thrusts, his movements sending streaks of hot pleasure rushing through her until suddenly the universe exploded and a pleasure, heady and intoxicating, took possession of her as Jared buried himself deep within her and, with convulsion upon convulsion, poured his lifeseed into her.

They clung together. Upright. Connected. Breathless. Jared was overwhelmed by the passion her attentions had brought him to. He pressed a kiss against her neck and then another one to her mouth. At last he let her slide to the ground. The minute her feet touched the ground, he led her silently to the bed, where he pulled her down on top of him. Jerking the coverlet over them, he tucked her head beneath his chin and enclosed her in the safety of his arms. Gently stroking her hair, he kissed the crown of her head. "Go to sleep, Deirdre," he told her softly. "No one is going to hurt you."

Deirdre awoke tangled in her sheets, one leg and one arm exposed, her fingers curled over the pillow where Jared had slept last night. His clothes, along with any other sign of the intimacies they had shared, were gone. Pulling the pillow closer, she wrapped her arms around it and buried her face deep in its folds. He *had* been here. She could smell him, the wonderful maleness of him on the pillowcasing, and she inhaled it, letting the scent of him bring a rush of sensations back to her. A knock on the door brought Deirdre upright as she yanked her sheets to her chin. In the few seconds afforded her by Maris's struggles with her breakfast tray, Deirdre pulled the heavy goose-down coverlet up as well.

"Good mornin'," Maris sang out brightly, as she backed into the room. Turning, she took in the disheveled bed and the twin pink stains on Deirdre's cheeks. Blinking once, she hastily turned her head. "I'll just set this here on the table, my lady. You can help yourself in a bit. I think I'll fetch your bathwater." Without looking back, Maris scurried from the room.

Dropping her face into her hands, Deirdre moaned. She

hadn't thought about Avis and Maris. What would they think? Would they even stay on at Ramshead to help her? With a sinking feeling, Deirdre looked around her room. Jared must have picked her torn gown up off the floor. But the fact that it was tossed over her reading chair in a mass of wrinkles wasn't much of an improvement. The bed, which normally was barely mussed, looked a disaster. The coverlet was askew and two pillows had been cast unwanted, onto the floor. Suddenly miserable, Deirdre cast her legs over the edge of the bed and attempted to run her fingers through her tangled hair. It was a useless effort. Rising she retrieved her wrapper, which Jared had also thrown over the armchair, and sat down to brush her hair.

She had only gotten a small section brushed out when Maris returned with water. Keeping her eyes averted, she busied herself with preparing the bath. "Would you like help bathing, my lady?" Maris inquired when the water was ready.

Deirdre shook her head. "I can manage, thank you, Maris."

At the door, the housemaid hesitated. "Would you be wantin' to learn how to bake bread today?"

"Oh, yes! I'd love to learn. Everyone has been wonderful to bring bread and meals up to the house, but I've got to start learning to do for myself. If you don't mind teaching me, Maris."

"Nay, I don't mind at all. But, I'm planning to start a few loaves soon. It promises to be a wickedly hot day today and the bread will do better if it's finished before the worst of the day's heat is upon us."

"Then I'll be quick with my bath," Deirdre promised.

Thirty minutes later Deirdre was in the kitchen. She'd taken a brief bath, whisked her hair into a queue, and donned another of her cotton gowns as well as a pair of leather slippers. Maris was just introducing Deirdre to the benefits of leavening when Avis burst into the kitchen in her normal fit of energy. "His lordship has been meeting with Bert all morning, and by the looks of it, I'd say he will be there until midday at least," she announced specifically to Deirdre.

Deirdre blanched at Avis's assumption that she was interested in the marquess's whereabouts and tried to change the subject. "What have you been doing, Avis? Is it something I should be learning?"

"No," Avis replied nonchalantly. "I was just finishing up the washing."

"The washing?" Deirdre repeated, her face warming at the thought of Avis cleaning her bed linens.

"It's all done. And 'tis better that you learn to bake." Grabbing up a broom, Avis attacked the kitchen floor with a vengeance. "I take it your supper was a success."

Deirdre beat the dough Maris handed her as though her life depended on it. "Yes. Thank you for everything. The food was delicious."

"Our mum whipped it up. Cooking keeps her mind off her illness." A long silence stretched out in the big kitchen, each of the three women throwing themselves into their work as though the devil himself was watching. Finally, Avis stopped her frantic sweeping. The broom handle grasped in one hand like a staff, Avis cleared her throat and she squared her shoulders, waiting until she had complete attention.

"I've watched you come home from those fancy balls in London this past year. It was clear to me from the start that you weren't gonna find yourself a husband there. I know that's what all the other young ladies do, but you were never like those others. You'd come home from those balls and whatnots all glassy-eyed. Why, they bored you stiff, those gentlemen. And I just want to say that sometimes when the right thing happens, it just does." Her statement made, Avis set the broom back in its corner and dusted off her hands.

"Well, I think I'll fetch some beets and apples out of the root cellar."

She disappeared, leaving Deirdre scarlet-cheeked for the third time in less than an hour. It was just past noon when Deirdre and Maris put the last of the plump round loaves to cool on the open window ledge. "I think I'll take this basket of hard sausage and bread down to the stables for Peters and Nils," Maris said. "Perhaps you should take one of the same to . . ." Letting her sentence trail off, she curtsied as Jared entered the kitchen.

"A plowman's lunch sounds perfect," Jared responded to Maris's unfinished suggestion though his eyes remained riveted on Deirdre. Deirdre stared self-consciously at her hands, aware that her face was once again hot with embarrassment. When Maris had grabbed the basket of food and departed, Jared moved to her side. "How are you today?" he murmured, pressing a kiss to her temple.

"I'm fine."

"You sound upset."

"They all *know*," she said miserably.

Jared's brows came up. "Why don't we take our lunch outside? There's a huge chestnut tree I passed on my way from the gatehouse, and a bit of a breeze. It will be ten times cooler beneath its limbs than in here." Collecting a basket, bread, and several slices of meat, Deirdre let Jared lead her outside. "I missed you this morning," he murmured as he nuzzled a tender spot on her neck.

"I missed you."

"I'm sorry I wasn't there when you woke, but I thought it best if I left before Avis or Maris arrived."

"I don't think it matters much; as I said, they all know."

"Is that very bad?"

"Yes!" Deirdre shot him an incredulous look. "How could it not be so? I know I made my choice. And I promise you, I will never say otherwise! I willingly gave what you took from me." She knit her fingers together, her shoulders drooping in frustration and misery. "But I didn't think of them," she admitted in a near whisper. "I was thinking only of me. Of how *I* felt. But now they will all know me for a . . . a . . ." She couldn't make the name come out of her mouth and she sighed, dropping her chin to her chest. "Avis even tried to tell me she wasn't going to judge me the worse for it."

"Whatever they think, they won't think it for long." Jared had risen before dawn, well aware that he could not be found in her bed when the two serving maids arrived from their parents' cottage. The first streaks of light were just touching the sky when he had collected the torn gown and the wrapper that had slid from her shoulders when her kisses had turned him into a madman and laid them both across the small fabric-covered chair. Then standing at the foot of her bed, he'd watched Deirdre sleeping, her dark lashes lying like thick fringe against the warm peach of her skin. She was completely unlike the jaded women he'd bedded before. Never before had any woman freely given herself to him. Everyone before Deirdre had come with a price—some more dear than others. But Deirdre had not asked for anything, either before or after. He'd enjoyed the most passionate night of his life, and he had been surprised to discover that it hadn't a thing to do with sexual prowess. But with something much more deeply mined. He'd told her she could trust him. And she had. He had watched as she searched deep within him and found something there that she could believe in. That alone was a gift worth keeping through a lifetime.

He would not take only.

"Why won't they say it for long? I don't care what London may say," she admitted. "But I do care what Bert and Avis and Maris and all the others say. They have been my family since long before my parents' death, and I didn't think about how my choice would affect them."

"They won't say anything for long, if they do at all, because soon you will be my wife," he told her. "And then there will be nothing to say."

She stared at him, not believing what her ears had heard. Not daring to believe. "You want to marry me?" she asked, incredulous.

"Deirdre, you are beautiful, intelligent, energetic, and determined. Look at what you are undertaking here!" he said, his arm encompassing everything they could see. "Marrying you will hardly be a burden."

Deirdre's smile was touched with melancholy. Foolishly, she had hoped for a declaration of love. An admission that he could not go on without her at his side. Realistically, what he told her was more appropriate. Jared had offered her a business partnership last night at supper, and she had accepted. This was the same. A business dealing. He would marry her, she would have Ramshead, and she could be with him forever. "When will the wedding be?" she asked in a subdued voice.

Jared laughed and planted a kiss on her temple. "Would you prefer a London wedding or something less ostentatious?"

"No London wedding, please. I would have no one to invite save Selda and Felix. Although if you would prefer it . . ."

"No," he told her, taking her chin between his fingers and tilting her face until she was forced to look at him. "I would much prefer that we marry quietly."

"Here?" she ventured, thinking how nice it would be to stand with him in the formal gardens.

"If you like, yes. I think that would be a good choice."

"And may I invite Selda and Felix?"

"Of course." His eyes going stormy and dark, Jared dipped his mouth toward hers. Deirdre let her eyes flutter closed, waiting for the warmth of his mouth on hers. It came, and when it did it was exactly as she knew it would be. A kiss that caused her to melt.

"I'll take care of making the arrangements. I'm sure Avis and Maris will help. Would Thursday be too soon?"

Thursday? The word sent waves of shock rolling over her. That was only three days away! Two days to prepare for her wedding! Then she calmed. What was there really to be done? Select a dress from those she already owned, send a message to the local minister, arrange a small supper for the tenants and whomever Jared might invite. "Thursday will be fine," she told him. "Will you be inviting anyone?"

Jared chuckled. "No, I haven't any family, and my friends don't need to be here. It will be our wedding, Deirdre. It need not be elaborate."

The three days until the wedding flew by. Avis and Maris threw themselves into a flurry of activity, making up beds, cooking, and assigning an unimaginable number of chores to Peters, Nils, Bob, Raymond, and even young Kyle. The news of a wedding gave their mother something to look forward to as well. She came to the house each day to help in whatever way she could. Gifts of food and other simple, but welcome, offerings flowed in from the tenant families. For Deirdre's part, she tried not to think about her impending marriage, concentrating instead on the management of Ramshead.

It was Selda and Felix's arrival that jarred Dierdre back into thinking about the wedding. "My dear!" Selda cried, throwing her arms about Deirdre in a warm embrace. "I am *so* happy for you. I know you couldn't have had time to have a dress made, so I took it upon myself. Madame Solie is a treasure! She actually put aside her other work to create a miracle from one of your gowns. Look!" Opening the trunk she'd brought, Selda lifted one of Deirdre's gowns from the top of the pile of clothes.

It was the biscuit-colored silk Deirdre had worn the first night she'd ever seen Jared. The talented dressmaker had embellished the sleek gown with a moiré train trimmed with silk cream-colored rosebuds and a profusion of seed pearls. "It's beautiful," Deirdre murmured.

"I always thought you looked ravishing in it." The corners of her aunt's smile drooped with emotion, and she sighed. "You will be the most gorgeous bride." Embracing her again, she whispered, "I am truly so, so happy for you. The marquess is a good man, although for the longest time I had thought him too bereaved to marry again." She shrugged. "Ah well! That only shows how wrong a person can be." Stepping back to hold her at arm's length, Selda tilted her head. "You don't look like a woman who is about to become the bride of London's most handsome and sought-after gentleman."

"I'm very happy to be marrying the marquess." Spending the rest of her life with Jared was a dream come true, she thought ruefully. It was just that she was miserable with fear that her marriage would only lead her to more pain. Although she was certain Jared held an abiding affection for her, she suspected that he had proposed because he had lain with her—not because he loved her. The night they had made love, she had not wanted any words of love because she would not have believed them. But marriage was somehow different. She imagined it as two people who loved each other. But Jared's proposal had not included a declaration of love. Worse, he had as much as stated he considered her a suitable wife because she would manage Ramshead. Deirdre wanted to know that he needed her with the fierceness of her need for him. But everywhere she looked was proof that just the opposite was true.

The specter of Daphne rose before Deirdre, elusive and frightening. How could she ever hope to replace a love that lasted through three years of mourning? A love that he wouldn't allow to die? "Do you know what his first wedding day was like?" she asked Selda quietly.

Giving her an understanding smile, Selda took Deirdre's

hand and led her to the bed, patting a place next to her as she sat down. "I wasn't there, mind you. But I heard . . . and read all about it."

"Please tell me," Deirdre requested, the pit of her stomach lurching miserably at what she suspected she was about to hear.

"Well, it was the talk of London—all of England really—for weeks before and after. Nearly a thousand guests were in attendance at the ceremony and afterward! There was a reception at the marquess's home in London, and then a week long celebration at his estate. Nearly three hundred of his closest friends and relations were there! They say the champagne and feasting never stopped. It was lavish, my dear. Absolutely lavish."

"And his wife?" she asked, already feeling ill at her aunt's description of the event.

"Lady Daphne Blandford. Daughter of Baronet Richard Blandford. She was, um, well . . ."

"Very, very beautiful," Deirdre finished for Selda.

"Yes. And enormously wealthy. A woman of extraordinary power among the *ton*. Even though she was young," Selda continued, with an amazed shake of her head. "She had such control. The parties didn't start until she arrived, and they were over the moment she left. Of course, from the first everyone assumed they would marry."

"Why?"

Selda shrugged. "He was devastatingly handsome and she was breathtakingly beautiful with white-blond hair and emerald green eyes. Besides, apparently he was quite taken with her. And she made it known that she wanted him. Daphne Blandford always got what she wanted."

"I see," was all Deirdre could manage to say.

"My dear," Selda proclaimed, patting her hand, "this is totally different. You simply cannot make comparisons."

"It is, isn't it? Different, I mean. Totally different." A pasty smile plastered to her face, Deirdre helped Selda hang her wedding dress in the armoire and discussed what flowers she would carry. At last Selda suggested that a rest prior to supper would be refreshing after her long trip. Deirdre, however, was anything but tired. As her aunt headed for her rooms, Deirdre's only thought was to escape the house. In a matter of minutes, she was down the stairs and out the drawing room doors.

The fresh air felt wonderful, but it did nothing to calm the sickening fear that continued to grip her. The moment she was down the stone steps on which she and Jared had shared their candlelit supper of stew and bread, she burst into a run. Holding her skirts high, she ran until she came to a wide expanse of grass bordered by tall cypress trees. At the far end of the lawn a fountain tinkled, and beside it was a stone bench. Deirdre threw herself onto the bench, wrapping her slender fingers around the edge as she rocked. Back and forth, back and forth she rocked, searching desperately for a way to stop the wild hysteria inside her.

She was frightened. It was a horrible, terrible fear that was eating away at her. A fear that, rather than lessening, had only grown more monstrous with each passing day because the awful truth was that she was terrified of marrying Jared Montgomery.

Deirdre inhaled deeply, ordering herself to be calm. Hysterics would do her no good at all, she berated. She must try to be rational. Rational and calm and reasonable. Feeling the angst that had gripped her subside somewhat, Deirdre drew another calming breath. She listened to the splash of water against stone and stared at the fountain which Bert and Nils had just cleaned. She had come here often as a child, assigning names to each of the fat goldfish that used to inhabit the small pond at its foot and spending hours trying to catch one to pet.

A high-pitched yap at her feet drew her attention, and, with a shake of her head, she scooped up her puppy, whom she had recently christened as Tyler. "How did you find me again?" she asked. Bringing him to eye level, Deirdre looped her thumbs under his front legs and held him so that the rest of his body hung just above her lap. Peering eye to eye at him, she pinned him with a chagrined look. "Nils is doing a poor job of making a stable dog of you. Every day you escape and end up at the house. I tell you," she warned, "Avis is nearly at her wits end with you."

The puppy yapped again and began to pedal his hind legs in a frantic attempt to give her face a washing. "No," she reprimanded gently. "You must learn your manners, sir. No more face-licking. But if you will be still, you may lie in my lap and have your ears scratched." Placing him on the folds of her dress, Deirdre began to administer long, slow strokes to the back of his head.

"I'm getting married tomorrow," she murmured to the little dog although he had dropped into a sound sleep. "Just as every young woman dreams. Why, then, am I so afraid?" But in her heart Deirdre knew the answer. How well did she really know Jared? As well as she'd known her parents? She'd thought she knew them better than anyone, but she had selectively chosen to know the things she wanted to know about them, ignoring the parts that would hurt her. The same had been true of Anson. Now, looking back, she could recount numerous signs that warned of the type of man he was. The way he drank at the balls. His penchant for charming all the women around him. She thought of the young women they'd passed in his carriage, wondering now what his relationship with them had been. But she had overlooked those things, choosing to see only that he was a familiar face.

She didn't want to make those same mistakes again. They only resulted in terrible hurt. Part of her wanted desperately to believe Jared when he said he'd never do anything to hurt her. Hadn't he proved his trustworthiness in innumerable ways since they had met? Hard though the things he said to her sometimes were, she had learned that they were the truth. About her parents. About Anson Reece. About Ramshead. She hadn't wanted to hear any of it. She had slapped his words away because they made her a person used, a person unloved and uncherished, a person with dreams that could never be made real. She had hated him for his honesty. Yet that was all it had been. Honesty. He had given her the truth in each of those instances, not candied words that were false.

But would she live to regret trusting him, Deirdre wondered. Was he really different from the others she had trusted and been hurt by? She had survived those disappointments, bitter as they were, but each had taken a piece of her. Now she was not certain she could bear the hurt if Jared deceived her or in any way proved unworthy of the trust he had demanded from her. That was her fear. The horrible, gripping terror that would not let go of her. Now that she had trusted again, given her faith into Jared's hands, she stood once more in the open field where she could be struck down by so many painful things. A dread lived deep inside her, curled like a frightened child in her heart. Because deep in her soul she was absolutely certain that one day he, too, would hurt her.

The past three days she had hoped for some indication that he loved her. His proposal had been so nonchalant. So businesslike. Since then, he'd stayed away from her. There had been no more nights of lovemaking, no kisses stolen when they were alone. Not even a shared meal. Jared was gone before dawn, either out in the fields or locked with Bert in the study. He worked until long after dark and then went straight to the gatekeeper's cottage. The only time they had spent together was when he wanted to go over some aspect of the estate with her. Though Deirdre paid diligent attention and asked pointed, well-considered questions, Jared treated her much as she would have expected him to treat another man, but not the woman he was about to marry.

And then there was Daphne. Selda had been right when

she'd said there was nothing similar between this marriage and Jared's marriage to Daphne. Clearly he had adored Daphne. He had reveled in showing her off to the world, taking her to balls, hosting a lavish wedding that London was still talking about years later. There was to be no such wedding for her. He hadn't invited even one of his friends. Deirdre ran her index finger along the puppy's spine all the way to the tip of his black-and-brown tail. Why was she suddenly yearning for a spectacle when she knew she would hate such a wedding? *You are being petulant and childish, Deirdre!* she chided. *You want proof that he loves you. But you should be happy with the fact that he wants to marry you.*

Deirdre chewed on her lower lip unconvinced by her own chastisement. She and Daphne didn't even look alike. Daphne had been tall and fair with jewellike eyes, while Deirdre was petite and dark-haired. And Daphne had been effortlessly comfortable in the one place Deirdre was not—society. Why then would Jared want to marry her? Deirdre could account for only one reason. It could only be because she was so unlike Daphne. Because she was so different, she would never remind Jared of the woman he had loved so much that he still wore only black.

What was she to do? she wondered brokenly. She could not bear to think of her life without him. Yet neither could she endure a life *with* him, knowing that he did not love her and that he pined for a woman who was gone to him forever. *But he had promised that she could trust him.* Promised he wouldn't hurt her. And it was up to her either to believe him or not. If she did not, then she would be a fool to marry him, for she would only be giving him permission to hurt her. Just as she had allowed her parents and Anson to do.

But if she did believe him, if she truly trusted him, then she must do so completely. She must believe that he would never hurt her. And that he would be worthy of her trust.

If she were to trust him, it must be a total trust. She could not shelter a part of herself from him. She could not give him only so much and keep the rest tucked away in case he proved otherwise. She could not do that to herself, nor would she do it to him. He had asked her to trust him and by sharing a bed with him and accepting his offer of marriage she was as much as saying that she did. Cradling the sleeping pup in her arms, Deirdre began to walk slowly in the direction of the stables.

She would trust Jared. She would trust him because he had asked her to do so. If she wasn't prepared to give him that trust, she should have refused it long before this.

And also, she admitted, because she was very much afraid that she was falling in love with him.

Sixteen

Jared scanned the newly cropped lawn looking for his wife. The grassy expanse was filled by Ramshead tenants and the handful of other guests that had been invited to the wedding. He found Deirdre standing with several of the tenants' wives, her perpetually active pup tucked under one arm while she balanced a glass of champagne in the opposite hand.

Watching her chat congenially with the other women, a possessiveness he had never experienced before rose inside him. Deirdre was not only beautiful, she was respected and loved by the people who lived and worked on her property. Standing in her wedding gown, her thick, dark hair piled high on her head and encircled by a wreath of ivy and pale ivory roses, she could easily have passed for a queen. Yet her graciousness with those of lower station than herself was genuine. As he watched, Deirdre tossed back her head laughing at a quip made by one of the women. She was so different now from the withdrawn young lady he'd first seen in London. Her cheeks blushed peach in the afternoon sun, and there was a sparkle to her personality that had been dampened and nearly extinguished in London.

Staying away from her for three days had nearly driven him mad. Only the depth of her concerns that these people would think badly of her had kept him away. The feel of her pliant, warm body sculpted against his was the first thought he'd had every morning when he woke and the last image in his head at night. It had taken long hours of manual labor combined with nightly plunges into the icy waters of the three ponds to control his hunger for her. Yet despite his efforts to stay as far away from her as possible, Deirdre had seemed to have other plans. Breakfast, lunch, and dinner she had appeared either with a tray or basket of food and a cold jug of cider or ale. Neither his growled claims that he was too busy nor his refusals to eat with her deterred her in the least; for at the next meal she would be there again, smiling and delightful in every sense of the word.

Avoiding her had not been his only problem. Even when he managed long hours without running across her physically, he was regularly subjected to overhearing parts of conversations about her—Nils and Peters discussing her excellent abilities on a horse; Bert relating story upon story of Deirdre as a young, headstrong beauty running wild in the forests and glades of Ramshead; even the tenants commenting proudly on their mistress's fair nature and pragmatic attitudes. He was somewhat suspicious that at least a portion of these exchanges were executed specifically for his benefit, a sort of affirmation by the residents of Ramshead that he had chosen wisely. Regardless of their intent, the constant reminders of Deirdre had only served to make it nearly impossible for Jared to have a moment of peace from his desires.

Glancing at the cloudless sky, he thought of the hours still remaining before he would be able to take her to bed. Too many. But seeing how thoroughly she was enjoying her wedding day, he was determined not to cut the celebration short. She'd had too few happy days in the past year; he could wait until darkness fell.

Bert came up beside him, looking uncomfortable in his coat, breeches, and stockings. He gazed across the lawn with Jared. "Betty, the cook ye had come from your estate, said to let ye know that the supper will be served in thirty minutes. She's wantin' to feed all these folks afore dusk so as they'll be able to start the dancin'.'"

Jared nodded. "Is my wife's surprise ready?"

"Aye, that it is. In fact, I'd think you'd be wantin' to give 'er the gift now, as it's gettin' to be a mite messy out front."

Jared chuckled softly. "In that case, I'll give it to her immediately. Once it has been presented to her, the mess will be her problem!" Sauntering across the grass, he made his way toward Deirdre. The gentle music of her laughter soothed something deep in his soul as he stepped behind her and wrapped one arm around her waist. "Ladies," he said, with a nod of his head. Each of the women dropped a curtsy and, eyes averted, murmured their congratulations. Jared thanked them and then turned to Deirdre. "You haven't asked about your wedding gift yet."

"Wedding gift?" Deirdre looked up at him in unabashed surprise. She turned to look across the lawn now set with long trestle tables and benches and then back at Jared, a light of deep gratitude and affection in her eyes. "I thought *this* was my wedding gift. Believe me, my lord, it is more than I ever dreamed of."

"This is simply our wedding feast. I have a gift for you as well, but you must come with me to see it." Taking her by the elbow, Jared excused them from the women and led her through the drawing room doors. "Now you must close your eyes."

"Close my eyes!" Deirdre laughed. "Why I'll trip and fall and then you'll have to explain to all your friends why you married a woman with a crooked nose."

"You won't fall. I have told you before, you must trust me."

For a moment, Deirdre's heart caught in her throat. He was so handsome, so wonderful in more ways than she could recount. And she wanted desperately to trust him. She *did* trust him. It was just that lingering fear which made his words feel like pinpricks against her stomach.

Pushing her fears away, Deirdre gave her new husband a bright smile. "If you insist, my lord." Snapping her eyes shut, she held out her hand. "Lead on!"

Jared led her through the house, winding through a few unnecessary rooms in order to confuse her before he stopped at the front door. "You must understand," he cautioned, "that this is not a typical wedding gift. But then, there is nothing typical about you, my dear."

"You must give me a clue," Deirdre insisted as she stood beside him, her eyes demurely closed.

"It's something you told me you wanted."

Making a face, Deirdre tried to guess what his gift might be. "A cook!" she declared gleefully. "Oh, I know! A pistol for the defense of my person against unsavory characters who might attempt to ride me down in a park!"

"No," Jared responded chuckling. "Although I don't doubt you are in need of both items."

"Then I am at a loss, my lord. You must show me."

Opening the door, Jared led Deirdre down the front steps and onto the crushed stone drive. The instant she heard the high-pitched bleating of a lamb, her eyes flew open. "Merinos!" she cried in delight. There were not just three or four of the famed sheep milling about, but more than two hundred spread over the drive and across the front lawn all the way to the edge of the woods—each wearing a bright blue bow tied about its neck. Deirdre threw her arms around Jared's neck and kissed him again and again. "Thank you! Thank you so much. A bride couldn't have a finer gift on her wedding day."

"Ramshead Wool," Jared murmured against her mouth.

"Yes," she agreed smiling from ear to ear, her arms still twined around Jared's neck. "The very first of Ramshead Wool. Someday it will be considered the finest wool in the world."

If he heard her claim, Jared didn't acknowledge it. Deirdre looked up to find that her husband's eyes had turned smoky and her heart leaped with joy to see the desire she had feared gone forever burning in their depths. She didn't have to reach for his kiss. It descended upon her with fierce intensity, sweeping her into the sweet oblivion.

"My lord?" Bert cleared his throat and made much of shuffling his boots in the gravel. None too pleased at the interruption, Jared released his wife and gave the bailiff an unappreciative look. "I'm sorry to be interruptin' you, this being your weddin' day and all. But that Betty, she's gonna be fit to be tied if she can't start handin' out the meals, and she won't begin until the two of ye have been seated and said a few words."

"We're coming," Deirdre responded. "We'll only be a moment. And Bert," she added as he turned back toward the house, "can we get my sheep into the pasture?"

Bert nodded his head. "I'll see to it, don't you worry, lassie. But I'm not worried about the sheep just now. It's Betty what's got me shakin' in my boots. I'll wrestle any ten rams over gettin another one o' those glowering looks from 'er!"

"Then here we come." She laughed.

But Jared didn't move as Bert disappeared into the house. "No cook of mine is going to keep me from kissing my wife," he declared, pulling her into his arms once more. "Now, where were we?"

"I believe you were kissing me, my lord."

"Ah, yes. I think you're right." And he proceeded to kiss her until her knees went weak and her head was spinning. "Now," he said, releasing her at last, "we can go to supper."

The assembled guests, numbering close to one hundred, were all seated as Deirdre and Jared took their places at the head table set upon a dais close to the house. Jared remained standing and raised his glass to the gathering. "To Lady Deirdre Montgomery, marchioness of Jersey, countess of Ramsey, and my wife. And to all of you, who have helped make Ramshead great and will help it become great once again!" His toast met with a roar of approval. Glasses were raised, and the celebrating began again as servants, newly imported from Jerseyhurst, scurried to bring forth the enormous amounts of food Jared's cooks had spent the day preparing.

As Jared accepted the congratulations of several men, Deirdre looked down at the simple gold band encircling the fourth finger of her left hand. Until he had said it, she had forgotten that she was now Deirdre Montgomery and a marchioness in addition to being a countess. She looked out over the lawn filled with the people she had known her entire life. The only sign of aristocracy here today beside themselves were Selda and Felix. The rest of the guests were the local tenants and villagers, invited to celebrate her wedding day and this new beginning for Ramshead. Her heart bursting with pride, Dierdre scanned the gay faces of her guests. Jared could have done far less and they would have been ecstatic over being asked to join the celebration, but he had insisted that they be treated to the finest meal available. Deirdre had no doubt that they had never before, nor would ever again, enjoy a feast such as they would eat tonight.

Servers bore enormous trays of roasts of goose served with a stuffing of bread and cherries and whole venison shanks with roasted potatoes and root vegetables seasoned with sage and hyssop. There would be turkey, lark, partridge, pheasant, a full roast of beef, and salmon, turbot, trout, and stewed carp as well, along with cheeses and bread. The meal would finish with an enormous spiced wedding cake and fresh berries from the gardens. Ale, wine, beer, and hard cider ran plentifully, and Jared had arranged for the tables to be cleared away after the meal so their guests could dance long into the warm summer night. She would not trade her wedding or these guests for a London spectacle, even if the king were to come.

Hours later, as Deirdre chatted comfortably with Selda,

Jared placed his hand over hers and leaned over to whisper close to her ear. "I hope you have enjoyed yourself today."

"Oh, yes," she responded, her eyes shining with gratitude and happiness. "It has been the most wonderful day of my life."

"Will you always think so?"

Deirdre's smile softened. "Nothing will ever change my feelings about today."

"Perhaps you would like to freshen yourself a bit?" he suggested.

Deirdre had already seen the smoldering darkness she had come to understand was desire burning deep in his heart. "I think I'll retire for the evening." She smiled. "Give me thirty minutes."

Jared quirked a brow. "I hope I can wait that long."

Sitting before her mirror, Deirdre let Avis remove the rosebuds and ivy twined through her hair and then gently begin to brush it out. Nothing *could* ever change the way she felt about today. No matter what tomorrow brought, her wedding would forever remain a treasured moment. Everything she loved most was there. Her home, the people who lived here and toiled for its success, and Jared. She could not wait for him to come to her. For three days she had thirsted for his touch and fretted madly over her fear that he no longer desired her. Now that she knew what it was to feel his hands on her, to sleep with his arms wrapped around her, she could think of nothing else.

Finishing with her hair, Avis laid out the incredibly delicate nightgown Selda had brought as a wedding gift, while Deirdre used a cloth dipped in cool lilac water to refresh herself. A knock on the door brought Deirdre's heart into her throat, but it was only a kitchen girl bearing a platter of cold meats, wine, and cheese from the onerous Betty. " 'Tis for a midnight respite should you and his lordship be wishing it, my lady," the young girl explained. Deirdre instructed her to set it on a small table by the windows, thinking it would stay coolest there.

"You look more lovely than anything I've ever seen," Avis declared, folding her hands in front of her and taking a long look at her mistress. Deirdre blushed. "Yer in love with 'im, aren't ye?"

"In love with him?" Deirdre didn't know how to answer that statement. She knew she was at least a little bit in love with him. But there was that part of her that didn't want to feel too deeply for Jared. Didn't want to need him too much.

"Aye," Avis said with a sturdy nod. "Yer in love with 'im in a mighty way, and if yer not admittin' it to yerself, then yer a foolish thing. I saw 'ow he made you go all warm in the face the first day he came to the Derbys'. There you were, tryin' to hide your bare feet behind the pianoforte and then callin' him every name you could think of! I never saw you so angry at anyone in all my days. 'Twas then I knew for sure."

"Because he angered me?" Deirdre asked incredulously.

"Aye! And remember that night you came home from that ball sayin' how you met a man who was different from anyone ye ever knew before. That was 'is lordship, wasn't it?"

"I had forgotten about that."

"Well, you can't be forgettin'. You've got a long road ahead now. Knowin' you the way I do and seein' what I have of him, it won't always be an easy one. You've got to know what it is you've got in here." She pointed to the valley between her breasts. Leaving Deirdre with that thought, Avis took her leave, closing the door softly behind her.

Deirdre looked at the bed, carefully turned down now, and her heart began to hammer. Would it be the same? Would they come together as well as they had, or had their one night together been a moment that would never repeat itself? Would it be different now that they were man and wife? And how would tonight compare with Jared and Daphne's wedding night? Daphne had been the toast of London, a renowned beauty. Deirdre lifted a thick strand of her own hair and inspected its dark highlights. She was pretty; she knew that to be true. But she was petite while Daphne had been tall and willowy. She was dark-haired and too much sun turned her skin golden while Daphne had been as fair as the petals of a moonflower. She could never compare with Daphne's elegant beauty.

The click of the door latch made Deirdre jump, and she bit her lip as Jared walked in and closed the door behind him. He was bare-chested, having taken a minute to refresh himself in one of the other bedrooms, and Deirdre's eyes widened as she drank in the sight of his broad chest and the dark mass of hairs that covered his flat stomach and led her eye to the waistband of his breeches. Swallowing hard, Deirdre snapped her gaze back to his face and found him watching her intently. The slightest hint of a smile touched one corner of his mouth.

Crossing to her, he slid his arms around her waist and pulled her against him, dipping his mouth to capture hers in a succulent kiss that went instantly from tender to treacherous. Taking his lips from hers, Jared looked down at her. "Was your wedding day to your liking?"

"Everything I wished for and more," she murmured, gazing at him from beneath long, dark lashes. Deirdre began to ask him if their wedding had pleased him as well, but logic stopped her. She knew that this small party of one hundred villagers could never compare with an enormous wedding at Westminster Abbey attended by the country's most illustrious aristocrats. Only she would find their wedding in the formal gardens and the following casual celebration preferable.

"And your gift? You don't mind that it was sheep and not diamonds you received?"

Deirdre laughed at that. "What use would diamonds be to me?" Glancing over either shoulder, she raised one eyebrow. "I do not see anyone whom I could impress with them here. I'm far happier with my herd of merinos. After all, it is a wedding gift which will continue to grow with each passing year. Each spring there will be new lambs, and every summer fresh wool for the market!" The corners of her husband's eyes crinkled as he smiled broadly, but Deirdre's mouth tipped into a frown of concern. "But I did not buy a gift for you."

"I have my gift," he confided.

"That's true," Deirdre responded, nodding thoughtfully at this statement. "You have Ramshead since, as my husband, all that I own is yours. So it isn't as though I have not presented you with a wedding gift and dowry of sorts." She smiled, pleased that she was not coming to him empty-handed.

Jared shook his head. "Ramshead is yours, Deirdre. I told you that I realized the first day I was here that I could never take it away from you. It shall remain in your name only. You still have to make it profitable again. I expect you not to abandon your quest."

"Nor will I!" she declared adamantly. But before she could enumerate exactly how she would live up to his expectations of her, Jared kissed her again. This time, longer, and with an intensity that let Deirdre know with no uncertainty that their conversation was ended, displaced by more urgent desires of her husband's.

"Will you make me tear your clothes tonight?" he whispered, his voice husky as he caressed the rim of her ear with his tongue and cupped her breast through the sheer batiste. With a shake of her shoulders, the loosely constructed chemise slid to the floor, leaving her naked in his arms. It took Jared no time at all to peel off his breeches, leaving them on the floor beside Deirdre's chemise. Naked, he scooped her into his arms and carried her to the bed.

The feel of his skin against hers was more tantalizing than ever, and Deirdre let her fingers trail up and down his back, memorizing the location of each muscled rib, the shape of his narrow hips. Jared, too, explored. But he used his tongue for his journey. Starting at her ear, he burned a path along her neck down to her breast, where he stopped to apply both tongue and teeth to the rosy nub of her nipple, making it rise hard with desire. Then, slowly, leisurely, he continued on, trailing lower along the flat plane of her stomach and across her hips to the vortex of her thighs. Gently spreading her legs with his hands, he first used his fingers to bring sweet, hot need boiling to the surface. Then he dipped his tongue there, using it to awaken new sensations within her. Feelings so heady that Deirdre feared she would cry out in ecstasy spun through her.

He brought her to peak after peak of pleasure. Jolting waves of piercing heat swept over her, uncontrollable, intoxicating sensations, until her need of him was so great she couldn't bear not to feel him take her. Frantically, her fingers searched, raking over his ribs, racing across his stomach, until she found his manhood, hard and enormous with his want.

Jared's sharp intake of breath as her fingers closed around him told her how great his need was. He did not need to be guided to her, but shifted between her legs eagerly. Neither of them waited, for they were both beyond reason in their need of each other. Jared slid inside her, gasping as she sheathed him fully. Then they began to move to the rhythm that pulsed through them. The music of their desire for one another. Together they moved—arching, sliding, driving, seeking—until they peaked together. Jared drove hard into her as Deirdre arched, accepting the warm stream of life that flowed from him and releasing, at the same time, her need. Hot, piercing pleasure drove through them both, uniting them, creating a fierce bond of need that neither, at that moment, fully understood.

* * *

Deirdre awoke to a brilliant, cloudless morning and her husband's leg pinning her beneath him. For several minutes she contemplated this dilemma. There was a great deal to do today; besides, judging by the slant of the sun's rays through the window, it was well past the time that Avis or Maris usually appeared with a breakfast tray, and she did not want them walking in to find Jared sprawled naked on top of the sheets. Shifting slightly, she looked at Jared's slumbering face. But there was no sign that he was close to waking. She squirmed again, but this time the results were very definitely the opposite of what she had intended. Instead of freeing her, his arm came around her waist and his hand found her breast, catching her nipple between his thumb and forefinger as he cupped it. Sighing, she waited several minutes more before attempting to extricate herself from their bed.

"Where do you think you're going?"

Deirdre glanced up to find Jared looking down at her with one eye open and a look of extreme displeasure on his face. "It's very late and there is so much to be done. The tables in the yard must be taken away and I must look in on my sheep and—"

"It can wait."

Deirdre gave him a dubious look. "It can?"

"Yes. There are more important things to be seen to this morning."

"Such as?"

"Such as your husband," he explained with a half grin. Taking her hand, he guided it to his engorged manhood.

Deirdre's eyes widened in shock. "Avis or Maris is bound to appear at any minute with our breakfast!" she declared adamantly.

"If they are foolish enough to bother with breakfast or to come in here without knocking first, I guarantee they

won't do it again. And I seriously doubt that either Avis or
Maris is so dawdle-brained that they would come anywhere
near our rooms the day after our wedding."

"But—but it's broad daylight!"

"You don't think the only time I want to make love to
you is under the cover of darkness?" Jared asked, turning
her so that her breasts were pressed against the matted fur
of his chest. "I can't think of a time of day or night that I
won't be desirous of you, my dear. And as I said, other
things can wait."

As his tongue dipped to taste her mouth, Deirdre realized
the truth of what he said. The cold supper Betty had sent
up had gone untouched last night, Jared's hunger being ori-
ented toward a taste for her instead. Groaning, she gave in
to him as his ministrations inflamed her own desires.

Two hours later, Deirdre finally appeared in the kitchen,
famished. "Is there anything to eat?" she asked, unable to
stop the blush that crept up her face.

"Aye," Maris replied. "I'll fix you toast and chocolate if
you like."

Glancing about the kitchen to assess what was available,
Deirdre ducked her head and casually asked, "Would there
be any muffins or biscuits?"

Maris began to grin. "Aye, Betty made a batch last night
that are still good. Would you like anything else?" she asked
innocently.

"Well, if there are any cold meats . . ." Deirdre suggested.

The other woman began to chuckle heartily now. "Oh,
aye! Go and have a seat in the morning room, my lady. I
think I'm understanding what you'd like for breakfast now."
Still chuckling, Maris shooed Deirdre out of the kitchen
and a few minutes later appeared in the morning room with
a large silver tray. It was laden with cold ham and pheasant,
three muffins, two slices of toast, a bowl of ripe berries

with cream, and an extra large pot of chocolate. Deirdre
ate it all save for the third muffin and one slice of ham.

Her ravenous hunger sated, Deirdre set about recording
the acquisition of her herd of sheep in the estate ledger,
along with the names of the new laborers Jared had signed
on this week. She worked quickly and efficiently in her
father's study, making certain that she cross-referenced
every entry against the loan Jared had made to the estate.
But when she was finished Deirdre remained at the big,
mahogany desk, her face grave.

She could not banish thoughts of Daphne from her mind.
Deirdre knew she could never be what Daphne was to Jared,
and it hurt. What had Daphne done to make Jared love her
so completely? she wondered. Despondent, Deirdre realized
that no matter what she did, she could never be Daphne. It
was an impossible task and she would only assure herself
of defeat if she tried to emulate Jared's first wife. All she
could do, she decided at last, was to make her husband
proud of her. The fact that she would forever have to step
in the footprints of another love and another wife was her
problem alone. And one that had never been denied by anyone. After all, she chided herself, she had known from the
first night she'd met him that he'd had another wife and
loved her deeply.

She couldn't tell Jared about her dilemma, she thought
glumly. He wouldn't understand what she was faced with.
He was her only husband. No one had ever been to her
what he was, nor would they be. But she would live in the
shadow of Daphne her entire life. And, Deirdre admitted
heavy-hearted, it would always be Daphne first in Jared's
heart. Dispirited, she paged listlessly through the ledger,
finally closing it and staring silently at the wood-paneled
wall opposite her.

If only Daphne had never existed. If only she could have
Jared completely and totally as her own. Deirdre couldn't
imagine anything as blissful as that. She pictured the two

of them working side by side to make Ramshead better than it had ever been, raising children—and spending long, passionate nights wrapped in each other's embrace. She sighed, how wonderful that would be.

How wonderful to be able to tell Jared that Avis had been right, that she *was* in love with him. Deeply in love with the man she was married to. And, Deirdre admitted silently, she would do anything in the world to make sure he never regretted marrying her. Even walk in Daphne's shadow forever.

Seventeen

Jared and Bert sat astride their horses at the corner of the last field they needed to inspect. The better part of the day had been spent riding the length and width of Ramshead in order to assess the progress being made in readying the fields for sowing winter wheat next month. "This one still needs a bit o' work," Bert noted, pointing out a large section that had not been tilled yet.

"Overall, I'm pleased with the work that's been done," Jared complimented the bailiff. Then he added, "Do you think you have everything you need to get the estate back to full production?"

"Aye, except for a nice herd of cattle."

"I'll take care of that as soon as I've discussed it with Deirdre. She has to make the final decision on the breed she wants to raise here."

Bert nodded. "The oxen and draft horses you purchased are fine animals. I couldn't ask for better."

Jared swung his horse around and started back toward the house. He was well pleased with Bert's efficiency and the willingness of the tenants to work hard for Ramshead's betterment. If things continued to progress in this manner, Ramshead would be profitable by next September, sooner if the merinos wintered well. Jared turned to Bert, assessing him one last time before he continued. He felt comfortable with the bailiff, but his next question would reveal whether Jared's appraisal was correct. "Will you be able to handle the estate on your own after we've left?" he asked, watching the bailiff's reaction carefully.

Bert raised his eyebrows and drew his mouth down. "Aye," he replied after a thoughtful pause. "I'm good for a few more years, I think. But ye'll be needin' to consider my replacement soon. I'd like the chance to train 'oever yer select, and I been thinkin' that two years is what I'll be needin' to do it right."

It was the answer Jared had expected. It would have been a bad sign if Bert had implied that he could continue as bailiff indefinitely. He was only a handful of years from fifty, and Jared couldn't afford to have Bert take all his knowledge of Ramshead with him to the grave. "Is there someone you'd recommend as an assistant?"

At mention of an assistant, Bert's eyes lit up, and he rubbed one soil-blackened hand across his jaw thoughtfully. "Well, now, I admit to bein' partial, so ye must take that into consideration, but my oldest son, Martin, is workin' as bailiff at the estate of Baron Davies. He's a smart young man and I think he'd not be a disappointment to you, your lordship."

"Then hire him on as your second-in-command," Jared told him.

"Ah, your lordship," Bert declared with a broad grin. " 'Is mum will be pleased as puddin' to hear he's come back to Ramshead. Got a wee one on the way, he does!"

Jared smiled, continuing toward home in silence. The stables were nearly in sight when Bert cleared his throat meaningfully. Jared seemed not to notice, so the bailiff coughed loudly and cleared it again. Jared glanced at him, his brow raised. "Beggin' your pardon, your lordship, but I was wonderin' if you've decided when you're leaving Ramshead?"

"By the end of the week, I hope."

"And 'ave you told the lassie? I mean, her ladyship the marchioness."

Jared chuckled at the endearment Bert used for his wife,

but his laugh died on his lips as he realized that he had completely forgotten to tell Deirdre about his plans to move them to Jerseyhurst. "No, I haven't told her yet."

"I know it's none of my affair and all, but it's my own opinion that yer ought to be breakin' the news to her as soon as ever you can. I don't think it's occurred to her that she might be living elsewhere, my lord, and she's a bit on the headstrong side."

Jared laughed at the bailiff's understatement. "That I do know, Bert. But I admit I overlooked speaking to Deirdre about leaving Ramshead. There have been other things on my mind this past week."

"And don't I know it!" Bert agreed with a sharp nod. "What with yer weddin' and gettin' Ramshead back to a state of activity. It's like I said, I don't mean to be stickin' my nose where it oughtn't be, but I know 'er well, and I've been thinkin' you need to break it to her in a gentle way. If ye do that, she'll be more likely to understand it's not about takin' her 'ome away, but about a woman's duties as a wife." His spate of advice given, Bert awaited some sort of response from the marquess, whom he had already judged to be a reasonable and intelligent gentleman.

"Thank you for your insights, Bert. You can rest assured I'll put them to good use."

"Good!" Bert declared, with a satisfied nod of his head. " 'Twill make it a might calmer around the place for all o' us."

Jared suppressed an urge to chuckle at the older man's blatant honesty. But he was right about the need to speak to Deirdre as soon as possible. Jared didn't want her to think he had intentionally misled her. It was the last thing he wanted.

Deirdre could not shake the despondent mood that had hung over her all day. As she dressed for dinner, she found herself nearly in tears because she could not find the citrine earrings she had thought to wear this evening. She had dressed carefully, choosing a jonquil-and-white-striped gown and weaving butter-colored blossoms into her hair. But looking in the mirror, the only thing she saw was a dour face and a pair of lifeless blue eyes. "How will he bear being married to you if you are constantly sullen and dejected?" she asked, staring at the image in the mirror. Grabbing a gold pair instead, she angrily put them in her ears and glared at the mirror. "I must stop this!" she declared with determination. "If I cannot change what is, and I can't, then I must find another way to deal with it. I must come to terms with Daphne; otherwise, I will drive myself and Jared to insanity!"

Her mind made up that she would not mope a minute longer, Deirdre squared her shoulders and set her chin at a determined angle. Just then, Jared came through the door. He wore a loose, white linen shirt that was open halfway down his chest, and his hair was windblown from riding. Deirdre jumped up from the dressing table bench and started to run to him, but halfway there she stopped herself. She couldn't behave like a besotted girl! Daphne sounded as though she had been the epitome of sophistication, and Deirdre was determined to be as close to her in her actions as possible. Therefore she greeted him with a warm, but not overly anxious, kiss. "Did you have a good day, my lord?" she asked politely.

Jared frowned as he watched Deirdre's sudden change in her reaction to his return. "I much prefer that you throw yourself at me when I come home," he teased. "Although you may have to put up with a soiled gown or two in that case."

"If you would rather that I greet you with greater enthusiasm, then that is what I shall do. I confess to having a great deal to understand about your preferences. But I will

do my best to learn them," Deirdre told him, smoothing
away an imaginary wrinkle in her gown.

"The only thing you need to learn, Deirdre, is that I want
all of your attention when we are together," he told her,
sweeping her into his arms. "If you are able to do that, you
will have seen to all my preferences and all my needs." He
kissed her warmly, but just when she thought that he would
take her to bed again, he released her. Giving her a chagrined look, he stepped back and crossed the room. "You'd
better wait for me downstairs before I ruin your gown and
everything underneath it," he warned.

Thinking of the cost of gowns and her meager resources,
Deirdre began to exit the room although had he made love
to her, she would have felt more assured of his affection
for her. "I will wait for you on the terrace."

Jared watched her go, a vision in her simply cut gown.
He would have to see to it that he had a dressmaker create
several new outfits for her once they were settled at Jerseyhurst. Now that she was his wife and not a demure debu-
tante, he would like to see her in gowns that were a bit
more sophisticated. Something cut a bit lower in the bodice
and created to exhibit her stunning figure to better advantage. Even if it was just the two of them at dinner, he looked
forward to feasting his eyes on her every evening and making love to her every night.

Stripping off his shirt, he winced at the thought of telling
Deirdre that they would not be living at Ramshead perma-
nently. Until Bert had mentioned it, it hadn't occurred to
him that she would assume they'd live here rather than at
Jerseyhurst, but this morning Bert had been right when he'd
implied that Deirdre might consider it a betrayal of sorts.
Ramshead was where she lived. It was her home, and it
was unlikely that she'd made the connection yet between
marrying him and living at *his* ancestral home. He knew
he would have to explain it to her as soon as possible.

Taking a quick bath and changing into a fresh shirt and

breeches, Jared met Deirdre on the terrace less than an hour later. She handed him a glass of brandy and turned to gaze out over the gardens. "It's a gorgeous night, isn't it?"

"Yes," he responded. "Beautiful. Deirdre, there are so many beautiful parts of England," he began, thinking to tell her about Jerseyhurst immediately. "I think you will enjoy seeing them."

But Deirdre hadn't heard him. Her mind was back on Daphne. Waiting for Jared, she had decided that she could only free herself from her fears of Daphne by getting Jared to talk about his first wife. Although Selda and Felix had revealed a great deal about Daphne, Jared had never uttered a single word about her. And trying to be sensitive to his feelings, Deirdre had been wary of bringing the subject up for fear it would either depress or enrage him. But she could not cope with her fears if she didn't hear from his own mouth about Daphne. She knew that she chanced having him tell her outright that he loved Daphne more than he could ever love anyone. But, Deirdre reminded herself, Jared had never told her that he loved *her*. She would be no worse off than she was now if he told her the truth. The only thing that would change was that now she still harbored the prayer that he would utter those words to her someday. If he told her that he still loved Daphne, she would not have even that meager hope to cling to.

She turned to him, her first question ready, but her mouth suddenly went dry and her tongue became leaden. She couldn't ask it. Not now. The evening was too beautiful. The mood too intimate. She had seen the small table for two set in the dining room, a bouquet of flowers freshly picked just for them, and a bottle of fine wine to share. She didn't want that taken from her. Not just yet.

Smiling, she looped her arm through his. "Supper is waiting for us," she said.

For a minute, Jared considered delaying their meal so he could explain to her about their future living arrangements, but he was famished, and they had the entire evening for talking about Jerseyhurst and Ramshead. "Good, I was not looking forward to cooking tonight. I'm hungry enough that I'd be forced to eat the meat raw."

"You needn't worry; Betty has made a feast for us."

They dined by candlelight, although it was somewhat different from their first dinner. The liveried butler Jared had sent for served and removed the various courses, while seeing to it that their glasses were never empty.

Afterward, when Jared had finally banished the servants, he took Deirdre by the hand and led her to their room. He made love to her, and, once again, it was magical. Hearts beating together, bodies moving in unison, creating a bond that was rare and precious. But no matter what Deirdre did, nor how much she enjoyed their shared passion, she could not banish Daphne from their room. In every sound Deirdre made, every response Jared evoked in her, Deirdre found Daphne.

Had she responded in a more artful way to Jared's lovemaking? Had she known of ways to please him which Deirdre had no idea of? And worst of all, as he attained his release and poured himself into her, Deirdre had not been able to stop herself from thinking that Jared had done this with Daphne—shared this sacred bond, given to her what he gave to Deirdre. Afterward, Jared wrapped his arms possessively around her and fell asleep, but Deirdre lay awake in his embrace for a long time before she drifted into a fitful sleep, where she dreamed of beautiful white doves that winged their way toward the sun while she stood earthbound below them.

Lying in the darkness with Deirdre snuggled close against his side, Jared tucked one hand behind his head and stared at the ceiling as he recalled the ardor with which Deirdre had responded to his lovemaking. Each time they made love he was surprised by her responsiveness, and her unrestrained desire to please him. His lovers had always been

experienced sexual partners, women who knew every trick
to bring a man to the pinnacle of passion. Even Daphne,
who he had foolishly believed had only been with him when
they were wed, came an experienced lover to their marriage
bed. The women he slept with knew how to moan and thrash
about until he was sometimes tempted to look out the window in case the world was coming to an end. But Deirdre
was completely different. Hers was a quiet, nontheatrical
passion, yet it moved him as nothing ever had before. Never
before had a woman looked deep into his eyes at her moment of greatest pleasure the way Deirdre did, as though
she offered him her ecstasy to be shared together.

But tonight, despite their shared climax and the intensity
of their lovemaking, he knew that something had disturbed
her. Even now, she was not sleeping soundly. As though
sensing his thoughts, he felt her lift her head and look at
him.

"Are you awake?" she asked softly.

"I think you were having a nightmare," he told her. "You
cried out a while ago, and the sound woke me. Are you all
right?"

Deirdre would not meet his gaze. "I'm fine."

"No, you aren't. Tell me what is bothering you."

Hesitating, Deirdre snuggled deeper into his arms and
Jared closed them tightly around her in response. After a
long silence, he heard her draw a deep breath. "You'll think
me silly," she began. "I will sound petty and foolish if I
tell you."

"No," he told her, gently stroking her hair. "I promise
you I won't think you foolish." He was certain now that
she had heard somewhere that they would be moving to
Jerseyhurst as soon as Jared was assured that Ramshead
was adequately staffed and funded for Bert to manage, and
he braced himself for what he thought would be her angry
response to this news. Therefore, his shock at the words

she whispered against his chest was so complete that for several moments he didn't even respond.

"Tell me about Daphne," she said so quietly he wasn't even sure he'd heard correctly.

"Daphne?" he managed at last, his voice hoarse with surprise.

Deirdre propped herself up on one elbow and looked at Jared, assessing the degree of his anger with her. His first wife's name had come out like a growl torn from deep within him, and Deirdre was certain that she had drastically overstepped her bounds. "I'm sorry, Jared. I should not have brought her up. I know how you mourn her death, how difficult the years have been since she died. I know that her death hurt you so much that you never even speak her name. I'm sorry," she adjured miserably. "It's just that I can't get her out of my mind."

Staring at her, Jared pushed himself up in the bed until he was seated and leaning against the ornately carved headboard. "What?"

"I'm sorry," Deirdre repeated sitting up also. "I should never have brought up her name. I swear to you, Jared, I'll never do so again." Terrified now that she had breached a chasm which would afford her no return to the companionship and passion she'd shared with her husband, Deirdre jumped off their bed, wrapping her arms protectively around herself, and began to pace the room.

"Deirdre!"

At the sound of Jared barking out her name, she jumped and spun around, staring at him wide-eyed with fright.

"Come here," he commanded more gently. Frantic, Deirdre shook her head in refusal. "Come here," he repeated. Slowly, Deirdre stepped toward him. Reaching out, he closed his hand around her wrist and pulled her down on the bed. "Look at me, Deirdre. Do you think I'm angry at you because you spoke Daphne's name?" Deirdre nodded slowly, her eyes never leaving Jared's face for an instant.

He let out a snort, which made her jump again, and then slowly shook his head. "I'm not angry with you. It's those gossiping fools in London I'd like to draw and quarter. Now, tell me what you've heard about Daphne."

Deirdre swallowed hard as she perused his face, trying desperately to read his thoughts. She was terrified of what he would say, yet she was more frightened of not knowing. She had wanted to hear it from him, she chided herself, and now she was about to. There was no turning back. She would either have to live with her fear or live with the truth, and after all that she had learned this past year about hiding from truths, she knew that she would be better off with the truth no matter how difficult it might be to bear. "I know that you were married to her and that three years ago she died in a tragic accident."

Jared raised one brow. "Is that all?"

Miserable, Deirdre shook her head. "I know that she was beautiful. The most beautiful woman in all of England and Europe combined."

Jared barked out a laugh. "She would have loved to hear you say so," he declared, with a sardonic twist of his mouth. "Go on."

"And you loved her deeply. So deeply that you have never recovered from your loss."

"Is that what they say?"

"You lavished gifts on her and took her out every night. You were wed before a thousand people and you celebrated for a week afterward. The two of you were never seen apart—you were inseparable." Finished, she dropped her chin to her chest and let her shoulders droop unhappily. She could feel Jared's gaze on her, and she was certain he was assessing how best to confirm that he did, indeed, love Daphne beyond all reason. She knew that her worst fears were about to be confirmed.

At last he pulled her into his lap and tucked her head

beneath his chin. "Deirdre," he started softly, "I have done you a grave injustice."

Pulling away, Deirdre forced herself to meet his gaze. "I know," she cried. "I know you love her still and that you can never love me the way you do her. But, I swear, Jared, you have done me no injustice. I knew long before you asked me to marry you that I would never be first in your heart and I—"

"Stop," Jared commanded, his voice stern but quiet. Pressing his finger against her mouth to silence her, he shook his head. Then his finger slid from her lips to her chin and he applied pressure there until she was forced to meet his gaze. He looked deep into her eyes and, as he had so many times before, she felt that he saw through the doorway of her soul. He drew a long breath before he spoke, his gaze holding hers. "I have done you a disservice, Deirdre, by not telling you about my marriage to Daphne. Foolishly, I thought that you either hadn't heard of it, or that you would not care. I rarely speak of Daphne to anyone, that much is true. But it is not out of a broken heart that I remain silent. It is because I have always considered it no one's business. But you are my wife now, and, of course, you must understand the truth."

"No," Deirdre declared brokenly. "It is not my business unless you make it so. Your feelings for Daphne are yours and yours alone. I have no right to intrude upon them."

"But I would like to tell you what those feelings are, if you will allow me."

Deirdre looked at him, a look filled with such forlorn despair it nearly broke Jared's heart to see. Finally, she nodded. "All right," she whispered. "Because I need for you to tell me."

Jared waited a moment, watching for her full attention, waiting until he was certain that she could not mistake what he was about to say. "I hated Daphne."

Deirdre's entire body jerked, and her mouth dropped open.

"But I didn't hate her as much as she hated me."

Deirdre could not believe her ears. "You *couldn't* have hated her!" Her entire body was shaking with emotion.

"Why not?"

"Because," she stammered. "Because everyone *saw* you. They saw the two of you together, they went to your wedding, they . . . they . . ." She let her sentence trail off into confused silence.

"What they saw," Jared stated bluntly, "was a perfectly orchestrated deception." Deirdre stared at him in disbelief. What he was telling her was too far from everything she'd believed and heard for her to grasp at that moment.

"Unfortunately, it's true," Jared told her. He slipped her hand into his and squeezed it. "I'm not proud of my marriage to Daphne. She made a fool of me, and there was nothing I could do to stop her that wouldn't have made me even more of a fool."

"I don't understand," Deirdre told him as she searched his face.

Jared sighed and raked his fingers through his hair. "Do you remember me telling you that my father died when I was twenty-four?" Deirdre nodded. "Well, like you, I was left with a title and an estate that required thousands of pounds each year to run. Jerseyhurst, however, never made money like Ramshead did. All through my father's life and his father's before him and back through the last hundred years at least, Jerseyhurst devoured cash. It was inefficiently run by bailiffs who often took much of the crops and dues for themselves since my forefathers never seemed to notice. Somehow they managed to muddle through, though. They accumulated debts and repaid most of them—or at least enough to keep their creditors at bay. From what I can tell," he said with a caustic laugh, "I come from a long line of men who are particularly adept at cards and marrying young women with large dowries and a taste for titles.

"I intended to be different. I was fascinated by agriculture and the intricacies of breeding to produce a better animal. I wanted to make Jerseyhurst more than just a place for hosting lavish weekend hunting parties. But there was no money, and my father had stretched the patience of the moneylenders once too often. The rate of interest they wanted for loans to me was ridiculously high. Somehow Daphne found out that I was looking for money."

"She was wealthy wasn't she?" Deirdre said, recalling something Selda had mentioned about her father.

"Yes. And she was beautiful, although hers was a kind of beauty that held little appeal for me. Even when I first met her, she seemed brittle and hard." He paused for a moment, and Deirdre knew he was imagining the way she had looked.

"She appeared one evening at Jerseyhurst. It's quite a trip from London," he explained. "Even farther than coming to Ramshead. I was there alone, working on some plans to add to the number of acres we were planting, and she just appeared. She stayed the night and the next day told me that nothing would make her as happy as becoming the marchioness of Jersey." His mouth hardened as he remembered it, and his eyes turned leaden. "I thought I would be getting the best of everything. Her dowry would pay off all the debts already accumulated and provide the wherewithal to turn Jerseyhurst into my dream.

"It wouldn't have been so bad, if I had kept the whole thing a business transaction. But I didn't. I confused Daphne's desire to be a marchioness with her having some feeling of affection for me, or even just behaving respectably. But she never had any intention of doing either thing, and she made sure that I understood exactly how she intended our marriage to be."

Deirdre watched Jared's face carefully. She had never

seen a look of such unholy anger before. His eyes were like shards of ice, and his demeanor was as cold and hardened as iron. "How did she do that?" she asked gravely.

"I learned on our wedding night that I wasn't the only man she'd slept with. In fact, she laughed when I suggested that she would be monogamous. We had an arrangement, she explained, that was all. She had needed a title, and I had needed money. I got my money, thus she had lived up to her end of the bargain. In order for me to live up to mine, I could never divorce her. If I did, she would stop at nothing to publicly disgrace me."

"And did she?"

"In every way except publicly. She was so certain she had the upper hand the night of our wedding that she bragged to me about her lovers. There were three that she was currently sleeping with, she announced. One man, she declared, was not enough for her. She didn't understand me very well, however," he said, his mouth a hard line across his face. "And she forgot the one thing I did have control over—her body."

Deirdre pursed her lips as Jared spoke. She could well imagine his fury at being so deceived. He had married Daphne in good faith, meaning to be a good husband, and she had humiliated him. Ridiculed him. Laughed in his face when he'd said they would have a real marriage. Deirdre trembled just thinking of how angry he must have been. Daphne had broken his trust. Hadn't she understood the kind of man Jared was? Hadn't she realized that he would *never* allow her to live as she intended and publicly, or privately, take lovers? Jared was proud and deeply possessive. Any woman who could not see that clearly in her own husband must either have been a simpleton or simply did not care. Deirdre doubted that Daphne was the former, and the thought of the latter so incensed her that Deirdre would have throttled the woman herself had she been standing with them just then.

"I would not be cuckolded," Jared told her, biting out the words with controlled fury. "And there was only one way for me to be certain that she did not sleep with other men. The couple that the *ton* saw were blissfully happy. Much as I preferred staying home, it would have raised eyebrows if we disappeared from the social scene, and I wanted no questions asked. So she never went out without me. During the day, she was confined to her rooms unless I was available to accompany her when she shopped or took care of other errands. And, at night, I was ever the devoted husband, constantly at her side. I saw to it that we attended every function of the Season. That is the sham your friends saw and believed. But behind the doors of our home, it was very different."

"Then she was faithful to you."

"Oh, yes. She was faithful to me, though not by her own will. I never touched Daphne again after our wedding night. Just looking at her repulsed me. I was determined that she would never know the feel of a man's hand on her again. I honestly wanted her to boil in her own flesh. She could go insane from want for all I cared. After a few months, she began to warm to me. I think that once she realized I meant for her to be celibate, she became desperate. But nothing could have made me sleep with her again."

"Were you faithful to her all that time?" Deirdre asked, although she was already certain of the answer. Jared was too virile a man to be sexually abstinent, and he was not punishing himself. It was Daphne who had struck the first blow.

"No," Jared replied quietly. He stared into the darkened room. "I took discreet lovers. To my knowledge, there was never a rumor of my infidelity while Daphne was alive. I doubt that even Daphne could have sworn I was not as celibate as she."

"But if you were always together, where was she going the night she died?"

Jared cocked his brow and let out a derisive snort. "That's a good question. I still don't know what she was doing on the road to Brighton. I thought she was in her room."

"You didn't know she'd left?" Deirdre stared at him incredulous.

A harsh, short laugh escaped from Jared. "For six years I watched her like a hawk. Six years! And in those six years I learned that she was completely without scruples. She would do anything to thwart me. I became as much a prisoner as she. I couldn't leave her alone either in London or Jerseyhurst, and, as a result, I was in London more than I cared to be because my associates had to come to me. When I did go out, I confined my business and personal pursuits to no more than three hours, never letting her know when I might leave so she could not plan an escape." He shook his head, remembering. "It was insanity.

"The night she died, we were in London at home. Charles Ellis was coming over to discuss some legal issues with me and Daphne complained of a headache." Jared's fingers closed into a fist and Deirdre watched the vein in his temple tighten until the blood pulsed through it like an angry, throbbing river. "I should have known better than to believe her that night. She was never ill. Her hatred of me kept her at a vibrant hum. But I was preoccupied. Preoccupied and sick to death of watching her every move.

"She either paid my coachman an outrageous amount of money to help her escape or she took him to bed as payment. I had recently hired him, so he had no allegiance to me, and Daphne had yet to loosen her acid tongue on him. I don't know when they left or where they were headed. The authorities arrived at the house about four in the morning with the news that my carriage had been found tipped over in a ditch and burned. One door was only partially destroyed, and that was where they found my coat of arms."

"Then the coachman died as well?"

"I rode directly out to the accident. It was a deserted

stretch of road, deeply rutted and slick with mud from the recent rain. Everything was destroyed. Even the horses hadn't escaped. The fire roasted them in their harnesses. Mick must have been knocked out when the carriage overturned. There was nothing but ash and a few charred pieces of wood." Jared's gaze met hers for the first time since he'd begun talking about Daphne's death. "Daphne and I shared no affection for each other, but I wouldn't wish that death on anyone."

"I know." Deirdre reached up to smooth the deep lines from his brow. "I'm sorry that you had such an unhappy marriage. And I'm sorry that she died so horribly."

As she ran the palm of her hand down the side of his cheek in a caress, Jared turned his head and kissed it. "I'm sorry I never told you," he murmured, bringing her wrist to his lips. "I'm sorry you suffered even one minute of anguish over Daphne."

"And *I'm* sorry I didn't ask you sooner. I made her into a goddess whom I could never equal."

Jared scoffed and pulled her into his arms his hand settling gently at her breast. With a sharp intake of breath, Deirdre felt her breast swell to fill it. "You are the one who cannot be equaled," he murmured as he pressed languid kisses along her jaw. "Don't ever worry about Daphne or any other woman again. I've given you my word that I will not hurt you. You can trust me, Deirdre."

Deirdre turned her mouth to meet his and gloried in the feel of his lips upon hers. Once her confused disbelief that Jared had *hated*—not loved—Daphne had subsided, wave upon wave of relief had washed over her, followed closely by a delirious joy. *She did not need to be second in his life and his heart!* The door was thrown wide for them because his affections were not preordained to another woman. His story of Daphne's treachery had broken the barriers that Deirdre had so painstakingly constructed to diminish her feelings for Jared. And now as she twined her fingers around his neck and pressed herself against him, she knew that until tonight, until she could truly believe that he would not hurt her, she had not let herself admit the intensity of what she felt for this man. And what she felt was a love that was fierce and enduring.

Daphne's ghost was gone and, with it, Deirdre's fears and restraint. Pulling back, she looked deep into Jared's eyes and felt her heart fill to bursting with her love. He was proud and demanding and, yes, brutally honest, but she no longer wished to change the least thing about him. His pride allowed him to understand her own pride, and if he was demanding of her, it was no less than what he expected of himself.

Taking his face between her hands, she sprinkled kisses everywhere. She rained kisses on his cheeks and his nose, his eyelids and the lobe of his ear, then she trailed her tongue along the curves and valleys there until Jared groaned with pleasure. Straddling him, she set about caressing his shoulders with her tongue, eliciting shivers of pleasure that sent gooseflesh rippling over his muscles.

"Deirdre," he moaned hoarsely as she caused his desire to flare wildly. "My God, you are so wonderful." His fingers closed around a fistful of her thick, mahogany hair as her tongue flicked across his nipple. But when her mouth closed around it and she nipped its peak, he went crazy. Dragging her mouth to his, he plunged his tongue hungrily into her mouth. He rolled her onto her back and pulled her hips hard against his. She was everything he'd ever dreamed of—innocence and fire, pride and humility, fierce passion and gentle warmth—all gathered into one immensely pleasurable package that seemed to fit him as though she had been created exclusively for him.

Covering her body with his, he succumbed willingly to the pulse of the passion they created. He felt Deirdre tighten around him. Her nails raked his back as her legs wrapped around his waist, clinging to him as he drove into her and brought her to her climax. Then, just as her pleasure burst through her, she pulled her mouth from his and stared into his eyes, letting him see the resplendent ecstasy he gave her. Straining for control, Jared watched until the clear blue of her gaze told him she was satiated, and then he drove into her, spilling himself deep within her as he experienced a throbbing pleasure that went far beyond what he could have ever described in words.

When they finally slept, it was the deep sleep of utter contentment; their arms and legs twined together, head tucked under chin. All the ghosts that had haunted them were at last banished, all fears scattered to the nether ends of the earth so that all which remained between them was their need and the first blossoming of a true faith in one another.

Eighteen

Deirdre picked the last strawberry of the summer and dropped it in the basket by her side. Humming, she stood and made her way to the rhubarb. Cutting three of the ruby pink stems, she decided that she would try her hand at pie making today. A rhubarb pie with a few strawberries added in for sweetness would make the perfect dessert for the picnic lunch she was planning.

Jared had woken her with a kiss this morning. A kiss that led to lovemaking. With the first rays of sunlight slipping through the window, he had taken his time, letting both of them enjoy a long, lingering passion that even now made her heart leap. Kissing her lightly, he had stroked her, his fingers running up and down each of her limbs until she could not bear it any longer. Then, when she reversed their roles, he had lain perfectly still, allowing Deirdre to explore his body from head to foot. It was only when she focused her attentions on his engorged shaft that he had at last groaned and lifted her by the hips until she straddled him, his swollen manhood within her.

With her newfound freedom from Daphne's ghost, Deirdre's feelings for Jared were a thousand times stronger than they had ever been. She no longer needed to protect herself from the fear that he would hurt her, or that Daphne would stand between them forever. Those fears were banished—all of them. Their absence left Deirdre feeling as light and carefree as a butterfly. And deeply, deeply in love. It was as though a door had been opened to a future that could be all things wonderful. Yesterday she would never have believed she could be so blissfully happy. But a tremendous burden had been miraculously lifted from her, and all that Deirdre could think of now was how splendid a future lay before her. She was so caught up in her thoughts, that she didn't even notice when Avis slipped through the garden gate to snip a few lettuce leaves.

"So I was right then, was I?" Avis pinned Deirdre with a knowing look.

"Right?" Deirdre asked innocently, as her cheeks warmed under Avis's perusal. "About what?"

"About you bein' in love with the marquess," she declared.

Deirdre made much of collecting her basket before finally turning to Avis, a timid smile on her face. "You were right, Avis. I am *so* in love with him. More in love than I ever imagined possible."

"In a mighty way."

With a sheepish grin, Deirdre recalled Avis's words from her wedding night. "Yes, in a mighty way."

"That's good," the tiny maid declared stoutly. "And do you recall what else I told you that night?"

Deirdre knit her brow before giving her head a rueful shake. "I'm sorry, Avis. I don't remember."

Rolling her eyes in exasperation, Avis sighed. "I said you'll be needin' to remember how much you love 'im when things are difficult for you."

"And I will," Deirdre assured her. "I could never forget how much I love him. I love him too much."

"And do you think he loves you?"

Deirdre blushed again. "Yes," she replied softly, thinking of the way Jared looked at her with such desire, and of all the things he had done to help her with Ramshead. She had never said it before. And until he had told her the truth about Daphne yesterday, she hadn't even dared to dream it. "Yes, I think he loves me."

"Well, he does. Just in case you're havin' any doubts."

"Avis!"

"Everyone can see it plain as can be! He's fairly mad with love for you. And I don't just mean that *other*," she pronounced, making a face that was meant to convey exactly what that "other" was. "He loves you for what you are."

"I'm glad you think so," Deirdre managed, at a loss for anything better to say.

Waving her hand in dismay, Avis heaved an agitated sigh. "It's not *me* who needs to think so. 'Tis you." Reaching out, Avis took Deirdre's hand, her stern face softening as she looked at her young, willful mistress. "Have you thought about what it means to be his wife?" she asked gently. "It's more than just lovin' him. You're a marchioness now and you have at least three homes."

Deirdre's head snapped up, bewilderment in her eyes. "Three homes? What are you talking about, Avis?"

"I'm saying you've got Ramshead *and* his house in London *and* his family's estate. The place *he* grew up at and loves. What will you do when he wants you to live there with him?"

Deirdre rubbed the toe of her slipper into the dirt path they stood on. She hadn't thought of that. She hadn't thought about anything at all except how wonderful it was to be with Jared and to be his wife. But now she suddenly realized the import of what Avis was saying. She was Jared's wife, and they would naturally live at his estate. Yes, Jared loved Ramshead, but he had wanted to buy it as an addition to his other estates. He had never wanted it as a home for himself. He had a home. And that was where they would live.

"He hasn't mentioned anything to me about leaving Ramshead," she said. But the excuse sounded lame even to her ears. Whatever the reasons that he had not brought up eventually living at Jerseyhurst, it still stood to reason that they *would* live there.

"Aye, he's not mentioned it yet. What do you think he suspects your reaction will be? He knows you'll like as not go into a raging froth at the idea of leavin' your precious Ramshead!"

Deirdre blanched at Avis's harsh words, a rash denial on her lips. But her disavowal stuck in her throat as she caught sight of the maid's solemn countenance. Avis was right. If Jared had come to her an hour ago and told her they would be leaving Ramshead, she would have been hurt and furious. "I've been very selfish, haven't I?" It was a statement of self-reproach.

"No one's sayin' you haven't had your reasons. And good ones, at that. But now you've got yourself a fine man for a husband, and you need to be thinkin' of pleasin' him."

Deirdre nodded. Yesterday she had been determined to please Jared by being as much like Daphne as she could possibly manage. But it wasn't Daphne she needed to emulate. It was Jared. Hadn't he proved over and over again that he cared about her by giving her what she needed? He had given her the ability to bring Ramshead to life again, and he had openly told her about the ugliness of his marriage to Daphne—a thing many men would have hidden. But she had needed to know, and he had understood her need.

Now it was her turn to prove that she could give. Any man would expect his wife to take her place by his side. And for Jared that place was at Jerseyhurst and his town house in London. He had promised her that she would always have Ramshead. But she would be living at Jerseyhurst.

"So," Avis asked, seeing that her meaning had finally gotten through to Deirdre, "what will you be doin' about it?"

Deirdre raised her chin. "I suppose I must choose between my husband and my estate."

Avis nodded, keenly aware that Deirdre's willful nature could wreak havoc on the happiness that she had so recently found.

"It's no choice at all, then," she said, with a trembling smile. "I will stand by my husband's side, wherever that is."

Releasing the breath she hadn't even realized she was holding, Avis wrapped Deirdre in an embrace and planted a kiss on her cheek.

"Will you come with me?" Deirdre asked, her face forlorn.

"Aye," Avis laughed. "I've been taggin' along with you since you were a babe. Do you think I'd abandon you now? I've seen enough of you sad and alone. I want to be there to see you happy and watch you raise a family!" Deirdre gave her a tremulous smile, her eyes shining with love for the tiny woman who had always been with her. "Thank you for reminding me that my place is with my husband."

Avis cheerfully waved Deirdre's thanks away. "What are your plans for that rhubarb?"

Deirdre glanced down at the forgotten basket in her hand. "Pie," she pronounced.

Avis made a considering face. "I think you can manage a pie."

Three hours later, Nils dropped Deirdre at the top of a hillock overlooking the meadow where her sheep grazed peacefully. The ancient oak that topped the rise provided shade, and a refreshing breeze stirred here, making it a perfect location for a picnic. Handing her down, Nils retrieved the heavily loaded basket and a cotton spread from the light trap. "Can I help ye with anythin' further, milady?"

"Would you mind helping me spread this blanket?"

" 'Twould be my pleasure," he replied, grabbing up two corners of the spread and shaking it until it float down over the short-cropped grass. He anchored one corner with the picnic basket and then bowed shortly to his mistress. "What time shall I return for ye?"

Deirdre looked out over the hazy meadow. She did not want to hurry this afternoon. She planned to tell Jared that she would happily go to Jerseyhurst with him, and then she hoped they could spend a lazy afternoon enjoying each other's company. "Don't come until six, Nils. Even if his lordship has some more work to attend to, I won't mind waiting. It's such a beautiful view from here."

"As you wish, milady."

Dierdre watched as Nils turned the trap and headed back toward the house. Looking east, she could see it from where she stood. Its grey stone walls were imposing even from this distance. Ramshead. She would miss it. There was no use denying what was the truth. But her place *was* with Jared, and since she had come to that understanding this morning, her sadness over leaving her home had diminished. It wasn't like the last time she had left. Then she hadn't known either her fate or her home's. But now she knew that Ramshead was safe and would always be there. For her children. The thought sent a warm tingle through her. She and Jared would keep Ramshead, make it work, and someday give it to one of their children. Laying a hand over her flat belly, Deirdre wondered if even now a child might not be growing inside her. A glow settled deep inside of her that would not leave.

Turning away from the view of the house, she scanned the horizon for Jared. She spotted him riding through the herd of merinos, his white shirt and black breeches making him easy to see. He had given her so much already. The loan for Ramshead, her sheep, the hours of labor he'd put into the estate just in the last week. It was definitely time for her to give something to him.

Jared swung from his saddle and a moment later Deirdre was in his arms. Between the enthusiastic kisses she pressed on him, he chuckled warmly. "You may greet me in this manner anytime you wish, my dear, but beware that the hunger your affections awaken might not be slaked by what you've brought in the basket." Her arms wrapped around his neck, Deirdre raised her gaze to his, her face glowing with a look of such tenderness that Jared's heart leaped into his throat. "You have made me very happy," he murmured huskily.

Deirdre kissed him again, this time slipping her tongue into his mouth, an action that brought Jared's arms around her in a crushing embrace. "You are playing with fire, little one."

"So long as it's a fire of your making, I know it will not burn me."

"So, then, you think it safe to persist?" Quirking one brow, he shot her a wicked grin. "I'm glad to hear that you won't mind having your gown torn from you and making love under the midday sun."

Jared burst into a deep laugh as Deirdre's eyes grew round with shock. "It would still be a fire of my making," he teased. His wife danced away from him, luring his thoughts from lovemaking with a chilled bottle of wine.

"Do you have much time to spare today?" she asked him shyly.

Jared drew his brows together, wondering at this meek demeanor she had suddenly acquired. "I have nothing pressing."

"Good. I was hoping we could enjoy a leisurely lunch. Betty has packed a wonderful meal for us and," she announced, her chest puffing with pride, "we have pie for dessert!"

"Pie?" Jared asked, peering at the blackened, circular disk in Deirdre's outstretched hands. "That looks more like something an errant cow left behind."

"Something a cow left behind!" Deirdre croaked in dismay. "It is only a *little* burned around the edges! Not at all bad for a first try!"

"You made this?"

"I was a bit remiss in watching the time," Deirdre admitted, an abashed flush rising to her cheeks.

Jared chuckled and pulled her into his arms once more. "Then it will be delicious." He kissed her thoroughly, and then dipped his head to her neck. "Do you think," he murmured in a guttural voice, "that we should have our wine?"

"It will probably make the pie taste better," she suggested, with a demure smile.

Jared laughed and kissed her on the nose before releasing her. As he uncorked the wine, he watched Deirdre kneel beside the picnic basket pulling plate upon plate of food from it. Her hair was loose today, the way he liked it. And she was dressed in another of the simple cotton dresses that clung to the delicious curves of her breasts and hips. Chuckling to himself he noted that her slippers lay abandoned at the foot of the oak while ten perfectly formed toes peeked from beneath the hem of her gown. "I fear you'll always be a bit of a wood nymph," he told her as he handed her a glass of wine.

"Of course!" she agreed, setting out a cold, sliced loin of veal. "But I assure you I will keep my shoes on at any of the social functions we attend."

The mention of social functions reminded Jared of the unpleasant job that lay ahead of him. He had yet to tell Deirdre about his plans to move to Jerseyhurst. Stepping around the picnic blanket, he sat down beside her and leaned back onto one elbow, stretching the kinks out of his long legs. He reached for a strand of her hair, curling it around his finger as he enjoyed the satiny feel of it. This newfound affection between them was almost hypnotic in its effect. So much so, that Jared was wont to destroy it. But he'd be damned if he was about to let his wife throw a fit over something as normal as being expected to live at *his* home. "Deirdre," he started, immediately realizing that his voice had already turned harsh.

She turned to look at him, her face gone pale. "What is it?" she cried. "Is something wrong?"

"No," he responded, deliberately softening his tone. "There are some things we need to talk about." The last of the lunch retrieved from the wicker basket, Deirdre settled comfortably next to him and sipped her wine as she waited for him to continue. Jared eyed her suspiciously. He had expected her to turn obdurate the moment he raised the issue of a discussion. "Have you considered the fact that because we are now married certain adjustments must be made?"

"Yes, I have. It would be unnatural if nothing changed except for the fact that I now wear a wedding band on my finger."

Growing increasingly wary of this unexpected complacency, Jared continued. "I've told you that Ramshead will remain yours." Deirdre nodded. "But you will be coming to live with me at Jerseyhurst. I know that is probably not what you have been thinking would happen, but it would be ridiculous for us to reside here when my family's seat is Jerseyhurst."

"I agree completely." Jared's astonishment at Deirdre's strange amicability left him momentarily speechless. "I know that we can't live at Ramshead," she continued in the face of Jared's silence. "Jerseyhurst is your home, just as Ramshead has been mine. But my place is beside you, and that means that Jerseyhurst will become my home." Laughing at the look of shock on his face, Deirdre leaned over to kiss him. "I know I'll miss Ramshead. But at least I know it's here, and perhaps, if you feel it's all right, I can come for a visit."

The smile that spread across Jared's face reached all the way to his eyes, lighting their smoky depths with a silvery twinkle. "You'll *have* to come back, Deirdre. Ramshead is still yours to operate, and you've a sizable loan to repay to an extremely unyielding lender," he said, reminding her that he still expected full repayment on his investment.

Deirdre jumped up in excitement. "You mean that I'll be coming regularly?" she cried in delight.

"We'll be coming regularly. I think a two-week stay every two or three months would be about right."

"Oh, thank you!" Deirdre threw herself into her husband's lap and wrapped her arms around his neck. She could hardly believe his generosity and thoughtfulness. All told, they would spend nearly three months out of the year at Ramshead, which, she reasoned as she scattered wild kisses all over his face, was nearly like living here. "When will we leave for Jerseyhurst?" she asked, still kissing him.

"I thought we'd leave on Sunday if you can be ready by then."

"Sunday?" she repeated, presenting him with the warmest smile he'd ever seen. "Sunday will be fine."

"Good," Jared said, rolling his wife onto her back as he gave in to the urgent need her kisses had incited within his loins. "Let's hope we're back from this picnic by then."

Nineteen

"Jerseyhurst is located in the Vale of Jersey," Jared explained as their carriage, bearing the Jersey coat of arms, rolled through the verdant countryside.

Deirdre, who had only seen the countryside surrounding Ramshead and, on the road back and forth to London, could barely keep from poking her head out the window as she craned her neck to see everything. They had spent most of yesterday circumventing London to their north, and this morning had crossed a high ridge of hills that brought them to the entrance of the endless valley Jared called the Vale of Jersey. A wide ribbon of blue curved in a graceful serpentine down its center for as far as she could see. "It's so beautiful," she murmured. "What is the name of that river?"

"The River Byrne."

"Does it lead to the sea?"

"All rivers lead to the sea, Deirdre," he explained gently.

Embarrassed, Deirdre buried her nose in Tyler's furry neck, and the puppy let out a delighted yap. "I know they all end at the sea somewhere," she explained. "It's just that I've never seen a river that actually looked like I might be able to *see* where it went to the sea."

Jared chuckled and ran a finger along the curve of her jaw. "Well, you can't quite see where the Byrne meets the North Sea from here, but we can visit the shore later this summer if you like. I'll take you to the mouth of the river so you can see the two waters mingle before your very eyes."

"Could we?" Deirdre asked in delight. "I would absolutely love to go. I've never been to the shore." Her enthusiasm for everything she saw was like a tonic to Jared's soul, and he relaxed back into the squabs of the carriage, thoroughly enjoying the delight she exhibited over every newly discovered detail of the landscape. He loved this country as much as Deirdre loved the rolling hills that surrounded Ramshead, and it had been years since he'd had the opportunity to share it with anyone, much less a person who appreciated its beauty as much as he did.

"What is that?" Deirdre asked, pointing out a collection of buildings midway down the valley. "You didn't tell me there was a village so close to Jerseyhurst."

"There is, but it's farther down the valley and much smaller than what you see," Jared told her, and then, at her look of bewilderment, he added, "that is Jerseyhurst."

Her mouth dropping open, Deirdre turned to stare out the window again. "That—that village. That *town*," she sputtered, "is your home?"

"There was a great deal of accumulated wealth at one time."

"Ramshead is well over a hundred years old and it looks nothing like that. *That*," she declared, "is a palace."

"The main house was begun eighty years ago and construction wasn't complete until nearly twelve years later. It's quite new by some standards."

"Your family has only owned Jerseyhurst for eighty years?"

"No," Jared explained casually, "the holding is ancient. The original castle is standing. You can see it on the southernmost edge of the compound."

"I do see it!" Deirdre exclaimed.

"My forbearer was a knight of William the Conqueror. He was instrumental in William's defeat of Harold II at

Hastings. As a reward, William granted him title to whatever property he cared to claim on English soil. According to legend, the grant was to be a piece of land the size of which was determined by how far my ancestor could see." Deirdre blinked in disbelief at the enormity of the gift the Norman king had granted to Jared's relative. "When the king asked him why he selected this location, the knight informed the king that he had ridden over every mile of England and from the ridge we just passed he could see more land than from any other site in the country."

Deirdre jerked her head around and ran her gaze over the broad valley spread below them for as far as she could see. "Are you saying that *all* of this is yours?" Jared nodded. "What was this relative's name?"

"Norris Montaigne." Deirdre knit her brow, perplexed. "The name was anglicized sometime between 1066 and now."

"He must have been quite a man. I can see how the two of you are related," she quipped as she returned to staring out the carriage window at the enormity of the estate Jared owned and of which she was now marchioness. It was nearly an hour before the four perfectly matched horses clattered over the wide, stonework bridge that crossed the Byrne and marked the official entrance to Jerseyhurst.

More awestruck by the moment, Deirdre swallowed back the lump of growing intimidation as they approached the building where she would live. She could not think of it as a manor or even a hall. In her eyes, it was nothing short of a palace. Why there were easily a hundred windows on the front of it alone! "I fear you've made a dire mistake, my lord," Deirdre whispered dazedly. "I can't possibly be the mistress of all this. I haven't the . . . the training, or the background. And I haven't the least notion of how to even begin to manage the staff required for a home like this."

Jared placed his hand over hers in a gesture of reassurance. "You will do a wonderful job," he told her. The staff was assembled in a half circle at the front of the house when they rolled up the drive. "Hello, Winston." Jared nodded to the steward as he handed Deirdre out of the carriage.

"Welcome home, my lord."

"Deirdre," he said, as soon as she had both feet on the ground, "this is your steward, Winston. He will see to it that each member of the staff is personally presented to you for approval, and he will answer any questions you may have about how Jerseyhurst runs. Any changes you care to make, you need only convey to Winston."

"Winston," he said, turning to the steward who had managed Jerseyhurst for the last three years, "this is your new mistress and marchioness, Lady Deirdre Montgomery. And this," he announced plopping her squirming pup into the steward's unsuspecting arms, "is her dog."

Having been informed several days ago of the marquess's impending arrival with his new wife, Winston presented Deirdre with a dignified bow while he struggled to subdue the disgruntled Tyler. "If I may speak for your entire staff, we are delighted to welcome you to your home."

Deirdre's relief at not being rebuffed by a glowering, malevolent staff was enormous, and she took an immediate liking to the steward. Tucking her hand into his elbow, Jared led her around to the front of the carriage, where he made a general introduction to the staff. Deirdre was welcomed with a warm round of applause. That task completed, he escorted her up the front steps and into a great hall, resplendent with marble statuary and thirty-foot fluted columns. Winking, he bent to whisper in her ear. "I think you have the staff in the palm of your hand already."

"That is impossible," Deirdre responded flatly. "All I did was stand there and smile. I haven't said a single word."

"I believe the smile is what did it. Now, would you like to see your bedroom?"

"Most certainly, sir." The curving staircase was wide

enough for two full-grown men to lie head to foot across each step, and exquisite tapestries of famous battles hung from the walls all along the stairs and the upper hall. "Ancestors?" she queried, nodding toward a life-size painting of a man and woman with three children at their knees.

"My great-grandparents," Jared affirmed. "And their family." He stopped at a pair of heavy mahogany doors. "Our room."

Deirdre stepped inside, her eyes darting from wall to ceiling and corner to corner. It was an enormous room that very definitely belonged to Jared. At the center of it was a huge four-poster bed draped with a cobalt brocaded spread that matched the long, silk drapes held back by gold roping at the windows. From where she stood, Deirdre was afforded a view of a smaller room, which she assumed Jared used as a study judging by the ornately carved desk at its center. Every piece of furniture in it was masculine. Even the black marble mantelpiece spoke of his tastes. At the sound of the door closing behind her, Deirdre turned to Jared. "This is lovely," she said. "Are my rooms adjacent?"

"There are rooms for your use through those doors," Jared told her, nodding. "But you will sleep in here with me."

A seductive smile touched her lips. "I was hoping you would say so."

Two days of travel had not afforded Jared nearly enough hours of holding his wife, and the invitation in her eyes was all he needed to sweep her off her feet and carry her to their bed. Lifting one dark brow and giving the bodice of her traveling suit a contemplative look was all that was required to send Deirdre scurrying to remove her clothes. "Are you developing an ability to read minds?" he teased, loosening his ascot.

"Only yours, my lord," came his wife's saucy reply. "Only yours."

* * *

In the two weeks that followed, Deirdre found a happiness so profound that sometimes she caught herself doing nothing but savoring the intensity of it. She wanted to catch it somehow and put it in a place of safekeeping, where nothing could ever destroy it or rob her of it. But her blissfulness was like sunlight, something that could not be held. It streamed over her and through her, but she could not put it away to be taken out as needed.

With so much to see and learn, her days had been very full. Jared was busy as well, but neither of them was so busy that there was not a great deal of time dedicated to long, luxurious hours in bed. Deirdre had concentrated on learning everything she could about Jerseyhurst and Jared's family history. She wandered from room to room looking for family likenesses in the tapestries and studying the oil portraits and statuary that decorated every room. Just yesterday she had gotten quite lost wandering about in the west wing. Fortunately, Winston had anticipated just such an occurrence and Deirdre only suffered thirty minutes of acute anxiety over how exactly she would find her way back to the main hall before a servant, having been dispatched to locate her, happened along.

She was convinced that Jerseyhurst was one of the most exquisite estates in all of England, and she was growing accustomed to the formality of life here. But today, as Deirdre made her way to the Green Salon for her daily meeting with Winston, she had specific plans in mind. With a house staff of thirty-five it was difficult to feel that she was ever truly alone with her husband unless they were in bed, and today she was determined to remedy that situation. "Good morning, Winston," she greeted the steward.

"Good morning, my lady," he replied, bowing as she took a seat behind the delicate French desk Jared had purchased last week expressly for her use. "There are several items for us to review today. Perhaps you would like to begin with the menus for the week?"

"That would be fine," Deirdre nodded. "In fact, I was hoping to enlist your assistance in the matter of supper this evening."

"Whatever you wish," he told her with an agreeable smile.

"I would like to surprise my husband with a . . . private supper tonight. Nothing elaborate. In fact, the simpler it is, the better. I was thinking of eating on the balcony outside of our rooms." Winston raised his eyebrows, and Deirdre bit her lip nervously. "Do you think that can be arranged? I mean, if it wouldn't be too much trouble."

"Of course it can be arranged, my lady."

Having met with success so far in her plans, Deirdre plunged onward. "And do you think we might have something *simple* for our meal. Something," she suggested, "that we could eat without three or four footmen in attendance."

A light of understanding coming to his face, Winston suppressed a smile and nodded. "I believe I understand exactly what your needs are, madame. A private meal outside. Simple, yet elegant. Perhaps a bottle of champagne or an especially fine French wine would be appropriate."

Deirdre gave the steward a glowing look of gratitude. "Exactly!"

"Consider it done. Now, as for the rest of the week's menus, here are Betty's suggestions." He handed her a sheet that detailed a daunting array of foods covering every breakfast, supper, and late-night snack for the next seven days.

"Oh, dear," Deirdre groaned, perusing the list. "I forgot to tell you that his lordship has arranged for a few of his friends to come for the weekend. They will be arriving Friday in the afternoon, I believe, and departing Sunday—also in the afternoon."

Unflustered, Winston noted the change in plans in his household journal. "Do you know who the guests will be?"

Deirdre thought for a moment, wanting to get everyone's names right. "Lord Harelton?" she suggested, looking to

Winston, who nodded. "And Viscount Marlot. Also the Earl and Lady Cavendesh, the younger earl."

"Lord Andrew and Lady Elizabeth," the steward offered helpfully.

"Thank you," Deirdre said with a wry smile. "There is still so much to learn."

"If I may say so, you are doing an admirable job, my lady. But since there will be entertaining this weekend, I won't bother you with approving this list. I will confer with the kitchen staff and present a revised plan in the morning."

Relieved to have that chore delayed for a day, Deirdre happily plunged into the other issues Winston wanted to discuss, and by the time they were finished, it was nearly noon. Just as Deirdre was getting up from her desk, a chambermaid appeared to announce that the seamstress had arrived. A light repast was served while she went over the seamstress's sketches, and by the time she had finished selecting fabric for a dozen new gowns, four riding habits, two capes, and several jackets and breeches for Jared, it was nearly six in the evening.

Rushing to her room, Deirdre found that Avis had begun to fill the brass tub with warm water from the plumbing works Jared had just recently installed throughout the house. She chose a salmon silk gown with matching slippers, and, because of the warmth of the day, Avis pinned her hair into a loose coil on the crown of her head. For earrings, she made do with a pair of gold teardrops that had once belonged to her mother. Hearing Jared arrive in his rooms, Deirdre grabbed Avis's hand. "Winston was supposed to have a table set for Jared and me on his balcony, but I'm not sure if he had time to do so."

"Everythin' is arranged," Avis told her authoritatively. "He said to tell you 'Just open the balcony doors' and ring when you wish to be served."

Her heart fluttering madly, Deirdre checked her reflection once in the mirror, and then walked to the door that connected her room to her husband's. She felt as though she was back at Ramshead on the night Jared cooked trout for them. Her stomach quivered with the anticipation of surprising her husband and enjoying a leisurely evening alone together. She knocked once before letting herself in.

Jared walked naked, and dripping wet, from his own bathing room and grinned broadly at the sight of his wife. "Did the seamstress come today?" he asked as he planted a wet kiss on her lips.

"Yes. You were far too generous in what you instructed her to make for me. What will I do with a dozen new gowns?"

"Entice me to tear them off of you, I hope," he teased as he dried himself and stepped into a pair of breeches.

"At what it will cost you for these gowns, I don't think you'll wish even to wrinkle them!"

"I will consider it a personal challenge, then, to severely crease every one of them. Then, if they don't come off quickly, I shall hold you responsible, my dear." The glint of humor in his eyes turned to smoldering ash as he pulled her into his arms. "Are you pleased with the things you selected?" Jared murmured, enraptured by the blueness of her eyes and the starkly contrasted black of her long lashes.

"How could I not be?" she said softly.

"There is something else you will need to go with your new gowns." In response to her furrowed brow, Jared held out a plain, velvet-covered box. "I didn't really think that sheep were an appropriate wedding gift. They aren't very wearable."

Slowly, Deirdre opened the box revealing a suite of necklace, earrings, bracelet, and tiara, all created from the most stunning array of sapphires and diamonds she had ever seen. She gasped, unable to believe that Jared would be so extravagant. "They're so beautiful. But—"

"Those are for whatever occasion you choose, my dear." His voice was like the deep pool of a spring stream. "But this is for always." Taking her hand, he slid an enormous square sapphire flanked by diamonds onto her fourth finger. It fit perfectly against the plain gold band he had given her at their ceremony.

"Jared, I—"

Her husband looked deep into her eyes and shook his head. "Just say thank you."

"Thank you," she whispered. Then, smiling softly, she added, "I have a gift of sorts for you as well." Delighted by the look of surprise on his face, Deirdre crossed to the doors leading to the balcony and swung them open, praying all the while that Winston had understood what it was she wanted. He had.

An Aubusson rug had been placed in the center of the tiled balcony floor and, atop it, a small table. The gold brocade tablecloth and the matching china service would have suited a king. At each end of the balcony stood enormous vases filled with the flowers Deirdre had picked that morning, and silver candelabra, as tall as a man, had been posted at each corner.

A lump of emotion constricted Jared's throat as he looked out on the magical scene Deirdre had created. His wife was forever astounding him. When she was not determinedly conquering the nuances of managing a house the size of Jerseyhurst, she was inquiring after the health of the servants' families. At every opportunity she begged for stories of his ancestors, echoing names and dates in an effort to memorize his family tree. And according to the seamstress's estimated bill, which Winston had presented to him less than an hour ago, Deirdre had ordered not only clothing for herself, but several pieces for him as well. In fact the most costly item was not a gown for herself, but a greatcoat lined with the fur of wolverine that was to be his Christmas gift.

More amazing than all those things combined, however, was the abandon with which she gave herself to their lovemaking. She was becoming skilled at knowing when he desired her and at pleasing him in every way. And if he was not mistaken, the dinner she had arranged tonight would be a prelude to another night of unequaled loving.

Hours later, as Deirdre lay sleeping in his arms, her leg thrown over his and her fingers curled in the matted hair on his chest, Jared thought he had never known such a sense of peace as he felt with her. He could easily lie here, just like this, for hours or even days. The sound of her gentle breathing was a balm that soothed the restless beast that for years had driven him. For the first time in his life, he no longer felt compelled to journey across sea and continent in search of something he had never been able to define, but which he knew intrinsically he could not rest until he found. That he had found it in the embrace of a saucy, headstrong woman with eyes like sapphires and lips that inflamed his soul, was unfathomable. Unfathomable and godsent. "I love you, Deirdre," he whispered, bending to kiss the crown of her head. "I will never hurt you. Never. On that you have my most solemn vow."

They had just finished breakfasting in bed when Winston knocked on the door of Jared's suite. "Your pardon, my lord," he said through the door in a low voice. "But if I might see you."

Knowing that his steward would only intrude on his mornings in a dire emergency, Jared quickly pulled on last night's breeches and shirt. "I'll be back soon," he told Deirdre as he stepped into the hall.

"A messenger has arrived from London. He is in the first state room. It seems quite urgent," Winston explained, wasting no time on formalities.

Jared took the stairs two at a time and snatched the missive out of the messenger's hand. The man looked as though he had been chased by the devil. Breaking Robert Harelton's seal, Jared turned the parchment over and read. *Come to London immed. Meet us at White's. RH.* "Us," Jared knew, meant Robert and Will. Other than that, there was no clue as to the reason why he was urgently needed in the city. It occurred to Jared that this might be some sort of prank on the part of his friends. A form of postnuptial ribbing, but it was an elaborate length to go to for a joke. "What time did you leave London?" he asked the courier.

"Three in the morning, sir."

"You are under the service of the Viscount Marlot, aren't you?"

"I am, sir. The viscount bade me ride with all urgency and convey to you that you must come immediately."

"Do you know what this is all about?"

"No, my lord. I'm sorry that I can give you no further information."

"All right," Jared said, running his fingers through his still-uncombed hair. Walking to the door, he summoned a butler. "Take this man to the kitchen. See that he is well fed and given a place to rest should he care to sleep for a bit."

"Thank you, sir," the messenger said, following after Jared's butler.

"Winston," Jared barked. "Have my horse saddled and ready to leave within the half hour." When he strode into his room a few minutes later, it was empty. He found Deirdre in her room, just buttoning the cropped jacket of her riding habit.

She smiled brilliantly at him, the blush of their morning lovemaking still in her cheeks. "I thought I'd go for a ride this morning. It seems that you'll be quite busy."

"I have to go to London." At her look of surprise, he tried to downplay any problem. "It's just a business matter that I forgot about. It shouldn't take more than a day. I'll be back tomorrow. I promise." He bent to plant a quick kiss on her mouth. "I'll just change into fresh clothes, and then I'm on my way."

Jumping up, Deirdre followed him into his rooms. "Jared?" She said his name so softly that he immediately stopped and turned around. She came up to him, sliding her arms around his neck as she rose on tiptoe to kiss him. "Last night I dreamed that you told me you loved me," she said shyly. "I know it was only a dream, but I had to tell you that I *do* love *you.*" The corners of her mouth trembled ever so slightly as Jared stared down at her. "I love you very, very much."

"That's good, my dear," he murmured, tucking a strand of her hair behind her ear and then running the back of his hand down her satin cheek. "Because you weren't dreaming." Dipping his lips to hers, he kissed her. A long, lingering kiss full of promise. "I'll be back tomorrow."

Jared covered the distance from Jerseyhurst to London in five hours. Swinging down from his saddle, he turned the stallion over to the waiting stableboy and strode into White's. At this hour of the day, most of White's regular customers were just thinking about rousing themselves from their library chairs, so the establishment was nearly empty. William and Robert had spotted him the moment he was in the door and were already on their way to greet him.

"Thank God you received our message," Robert said, shaking his hand.

"Jersey," came Will's clipped greeting. "Let's go into one of the back rooms. Even these few people are too many."

His brow furrowed, Jared followed the other men into one of the rooms White's provided for private meetings. The minute they were in the room and the door was closed, Jared swung around like a caged animal. "What is this all about?" he demanded.

"Sit down," Robert suggested.

"I don't want to sit down, damn it. I want to know why the pair of you are acting like the king has just died, and there's no heir. And I swear, if this is some sort of prank, I'll kill you both. One at a time and very, very painfully."

"There's no prank, Jersey. But it is the worst sort of trouble."

"Just what you'd expect from her," Will bit out.

"Just what I'd expect from *whom?*" Jared repeated with emphasis.

"Your wife."

Jared blinked once at Robert Harelton and then started to advance on him. "I told you what I'd do if this was a joke."

"It's no joke," Robert declared, backing up as he spoke.

"My wife is five hours away, probably lost in some wing of her home."

"Not *that* wife," Will interjected. "Your other wife, the darling Daphne."

Twenty

Jared stopped cold in his tracks. When he finally spoke, it was in a voice that dripped ice. "Daphne? Daphne died in an accident three years ago."

"She's not dead, Jared. I don't know where she's been or why she came back, but she's here," Will told him.

"Where *exactly* is 'here'?"

"At your house on the Pall Mall. She said she'd be waiting for you there."

"She came to my town house last night just as I was leaving for the theater," Robert explained, as Jared prowled across the room and back again, his anger leashed so tightly that Robert could see a muscle in his cheek jump. "She acted as though it was the most natural thing in the world for her to pop up. Then she wanted to know where you were."

"You didn't tell her about Deirdre, did you?"

"God no!" Robert raked his fingers through his hair.

Jared took in his friend's appearance. There was a day's growth of beard on his chin, and he was still in yesterday's clothes. Will didn't look any better. Turning, he crossed the room in two long strides and slammed a fist against the mantelpiece. "If she's not dead, where the *hell* has she been for three years!?"

"Good question," Will noted dryly.

Lancing his friend with an unappreciative look, Jared headed for the door. "I'll be back."

* * *

Daphne lounged in the oversize leather chair that flanked the fireplace in her husband's bedroom, a bottle of his best French champagne iced in a bucket beside her. He was always so *male,* she thought, running a finger along the brass tacks that decorated the arms. She could hardly wait to see the expression on Jared's face when he walked in. She smirked, remembering that face. God, but he was handsome. If the rumors she'd heard in Austria were right—and she paid well to see that they were—he had only grown more handsome over the past three years. More handsome and wealthier. Much, much wealthier.

He should have arrived by now, she thought, unless Robert Harelton had somehow misconveyed her message to Jared. Irritated, she flicked a piece of lint from the bodice of her shimmering aquamarine gown. The gown was too formal for early afternoon, but it showed her cleavage to excellent advantage and she wanted Jared to see everything he'd denied himself during their mockery of a marriage.

Jared slammed the front door to his house so hard the building shook. In response, the butler came running down the hallway from the kitchen. "My lord. I'm so glad you're here. The marchioness, ahem, I mean the former marchioness—"

Jared didn't wait for the confounded servant to finish his sentence. "Where is she?" he demanded.

"In the master bedroom, my lord." His eyes narrowed dangerously, Jared stared up the staircase with such a look of loathing that the butler muttered a quick prayer.

"I want every person out of this house *now,*" Jared growled. "Did you hear me? *Every person.*" The butler fled, and Jared started up the staircase.

"Why hello, darling," Daphne purred, as Jared came into the room. Jared gave her an impassive stare, his face utterly devoid of reaction as he closed the door behind him.

"Aren't you even going to say hello?" she taunted. "Ah, you're still angry that I managed to slip away from you. Sorry." Daphne rose and poured herself another glass of his champagne. "But I'd had just about enough of your childish games." Crossing the room, Daphne leaned against him, the inside of her thigh against his. With one finger she drew a line down his chest. "They were right, you know; you are more handsome than ever. And hardened. I wonder if I did that? I imagine I did." Smiling at the thought, she tossed back her head and caught his gaze with hers. "You were much warmer when we first met. And so full of dreams! Too bad your dreams were so lofty, Jared. Had they been a bit more hedonistic, I think our arrangement would have worked beautifully. You were a wonderful lover."

Jared wrapped her arm in a vise grip and blatantly forced her to step back. "Don't bother with your seduction tactics, Daphne," he mocked through clenched teeth. "You hold about as much appeal for me as a viper."

Daphne formed a pout that was so flagrantly false, Jared was tempted to take her by the neck and squeeze the life out of her once and for all right there. "Don't tell me your little virgin has you so enamored you've actually given up your other lovers?" Jared's eyes narrowed dangerously. "Surprised again, my darling? Oh, I know all about your new wife." Her laugh was obscene. "Why do you think I came back from the dead?"

"Falsifying a death is a criminal offense, Daphne. Or didn't you think about that? You would have been better off remaining where ever you were."

"And you aren't the least bit curious where that was?"

"No," he stated flatly.

He hadn't moved an inch, Daphne chafed. He hadn't changed the bland, bored expression on that handsome face of his a whit. He should be sweating by now. He should be at her feet!

"My only concern is getting rid of you, Daphne."

"Getting rid of me? Jared," she said feigning a demure look, "don't let the constables hear you say that. They might think you were the one who plotted to exterminate me three years ago! After all, you had what you wanted from me. Why not pass me off for dead and then drag me off to some deserted castle to rot?"

Her patience with Jared was running thin. He always thought he had the upper hand. Always thought she couldn't affect him. She hated him. So cold. So aloof. So *superior.* Suddenly she wanted to scratch his eyes out. She wanted to scream and throw things, make him pay for treating her like a common slut he was too good to touch. Anything to force him to react. Daphne closed her eyes and drew a deep breath. *She* had the upper hand now. She had to remember that. Soon enough Jared would be begging for mercy.

"What is it you want?" Jared asked, implacably, as he watched Daphne through narrowed eyes. She'd never had an ounce of self-control. If she didn't get what she wanted immediately, she became a caustic-tongued bitch. It was only a matter of time.

Daphne drained the champagne glass and set it on the table. "You know, my darling *husband,* when we married you were in dire need of money. You had your precious home and your plebeian ideas about farming, your only problem was that you were a little short on resources. *I* gave you the money to make all your dreams come true." Jared's only response was to lift one black eyebrow.

"It's *true!*" she screamed, all her control vanishing. "Without me you'd be nothing! And you wanted me to rot in that mausoleum you call a home! You locked me up like a mouse in a cage!" she ranted.

"Like the vermin that you are," Jared responded dryly.

"You think you hold all the cards, don't you Jared? You always have! You with that damned face of yours. Never showing *any* emotion! You thought you were going to keep me like that forever. But you didn't, did you?" She tossed her head, a look of rabid hatred mixed with triumph in her eyes. "I won. I bided my time, and just slipped away. God, it was so *easy!* And what will everyone think when they discover that the great marquess of Jersey was duped by his wife?" When Jared made no reply, Daphne let out a deep, throaty laugh of triumph. "Nothing to say, my dear?"

"All your dowry money was returned—in full—after your death, just as you and your father had requested before we married. It seems to me, Daphne, that you never really intended to stay married to me. But I really don't care one way or another. Now, get out of my sight."

Unperturbed by Jared's demand, Daphne walked to the window and held one perfectly manicured hand up to the afternoon light, admiringly. "Not quite yet, Jared." Turning, she gave him a calculated smile. "I'm sure you want a divorce. After all, you can't go around a bigamist, and it's obvious you hold some unfathomable affection for the little strumpet you just married. I'll gladly oblige you, save you all that *nasty* scandal. All you have to do is pay me £200,000. Then I'll slip up to Scotland, obtain a nice, quiet divorce, and you'll never see me again."

"Blackmail, Daphne? Why is it I'm not surprised?"

"Don't attempt to intimidate me by looking down that superior nose of yours," she retorted. "You have until Friday, Jared. If I don't hear from you by then, I'll be making an appearance at the duke and duchess of Marlborough's ball Friday night. As you know, the duchess is an old acquaintance of mine. Why I've even heard the king will be there." Daphne raised one perfectly etched brow. "Do you have any questions?

"No, I thought not. I'll be staying here until then," she continued. "Your willing captive until you can get me my money. I'm sure two days is more than enough time."

Jared eyed her coldly. "Go stay with one of your friends. If you have any."

"And leak the news early that I've returned from the dead? No, I don't think so. Besides, this is still *legally* my home."

Jared's brows came together in an angry slash over his eyes, his face frigid with control. "You should have stayed dead."

Charles Ellis tapped the nib of his quill against the inkpot as the marquess finished explaining his predicament and silently thanked God he wasn't part of the aristocracy. Theirs was a world of never-ending backstabbing and intrigues that, frankly, made chills run up his spine. It had been bad enough when the unheard of occurred and the marquess appeared at his offices an hour ago instead of sending a short note that Charles's services were required. But the scenario he had just recounted was so bizarre that Charles was finding it difficult even to comprehend it, much less come up with a solution.

"I want to file for divorce, Charles. Immediately. And I'd like you to handle it."

"I assure you it will be handled with the utmost discretion. But it's impossible to obtain a divorce by Friday."

Jared let out a derisive laugh. "Daphne will discover that she doesn't hold the trump card she thinks she does. I don't give a damn what anyone thinks of me! She can parade herself all over London for all I care. My only concern is getting her out of my life once and for all. And she's deluding herself if she thinks I'll succumb to blackmail." Jared shook his head in disbelief. "She must be desperate to have come up with that."

"What about Lady Deirdre?" Charles ventured, aware that he was bringing up a delicate subject.

Jared shot him an angry look. "What about her?"

"What will she do when you tell her about this?"

"I hope not to tell her until it's over and done with. That's why I want this divorce handled quickly. Once it's official, she won't need to feel threatened."

"There is one problem I foresee," Charles said, considering Jared's words. "You mentioned that Lady Daphne said something about making it appear that you had orchestrated her disappearance."

Jared leaned forward, his elbows on his knees, and for a moment rested his forehead in his hands. "She said people might think I arranged for her disappearance so that I wouldn't have to put up with her anymore."

"Do you think that's possible?"

"That the magistrate would think *I* faked her death?" Jared snorted in disgust. "Daphne can talk an unsuspecting man into anything."

Charles scratched a short note on the paper that sat on his desk. "In order to procure a divorce, all you need is proof that she has in some way broken her marriage vows. But currently we don't have that proof. We also have no proof that she planned her escape and falsified her death.

"In addition," he continued, "if Lady Daphne were to claim that *you* were responsible for her disappearance and that for three years she's been imprisoned somewhere . . . We might have a problem." Jared's jaw tightened in mute fury. "It might appear that you *were* trying to be rid of her. It would make your recent marriage and your bigamy, look very—um, intentional." At the deadly look in his employer's icy eyes, Charles added. "It is my job to present you with all the possibilities, my lord, however unsavory."

"Then we prove that she planned her demise so that she could escape our marriage. Isn't her desertion of that marriage grounds enough for divorce?"

"Certainly. There's not a magistrate in the land who wouldn't grant a divorce to a man whose wife had run off intentionally."

Jared gave Charles a thin smile. "Then we have to prove it." A long silence filled the room as the two men searched for a solution to the problem before them. At last, Jared stood and crossed to the brandy decanter that stood on a sideboard in Charles's office. "May I?"

"Of course, my lord. I apologize for not offering before."

Pouring the amber liquid into a glass, Jared drew his brows together in thought. "The night of the accident," he said in a measured tone, "Daphne took one of my carriages and my coachman. I thought Mick was dead, along with Daphne. The carriage was so badly burned that it was obvious nothing remained of either of them. But if the fire was a ruse—"

"The coachman is still alive," Charles finished for him. Coming out of his chair, Charles joined Jared at the sideboard. "What was his name?"

"Mick—Michael Browley. He'd be about twenty-eight now. Medium height. Fair hair."

"Scars? Missing teeth?"

Jared lampooned his solicitor with a deprecating look. "I hope I have the brains not to hire coachmen who look like footpads," he told him dryly.

"My apologies, my lord," Charles said, turning a deep shade of red. "It's just that my brother dabbles a bit in this sort of thing and sometimes, I get a bit carried away with the descriptions of the characters he runs across."

"You brother is a footpad?"

"No, no, sir! He sometimes, *finds* people, so to speak. Or things. He's something of the black sheep in my family. A good soul, I assure you, my lord. Just someone who doesn't deal well with rules and schedules and that sort of thing. I daresay he has some fascinating tales about things he's witnessed, or been involved in," he amended, "along the waterfront." Charles swallowed an embarrassed lump in his throat at Jared's blank stare. "I'm carrying on again. I'm afraid it's becoming a habit."

"Could your brother find Mick Browley?"

"We haven't much to go on."

"Finding Daphne's accomplice is key. See if your brother will do it. I'll pay him well for his services." Tossing back the last of the brandy, Jared gave Charles a sharp nod. "I'm taking a room at White's. If you need me for anything. You can find me there."

"I will go to my brother's house immediately."

An hour later, having ordered a bath and a brandy, Jared walked into the room he had rented at White's and stretched out on the comfortable bed. Despite his long ride and the handful of infuriating meetings he had held today—including the one just now with a very tired Robert and Will—he crackled with an energy born of pure fury. He didn't doubt for a moment that, somehow, he would find Mick Browley. And when he did, Daphne was going to regret ever crossing him. Until then, he needed to put every resource and every bit of energy he had into finding his former coachman. Tonight he would eat a quick supper and then go to the waterfront himself. But before he did, he needed to send a courier with a message for Deirdre.

Just the thought of her name brought a vision of her to him. She was so warm, so loving, and so very beautiful. Not the cold beauty that had already begun to fade in Daphne, but a warm, fiery beauty that reflected the spirit that burned so strong within her. Her eyes shimmered with the color of the ocean five days out to sea. And her lips begged to be kissed no matter how many times he had already kissed them. She was as free of spirit as a wood nymph and as stubborn as an old crone all twined together in the form of a woman who was constantly stealing his breath and leaving him to marvel at her uniqueness. The last thing he wanted was for Deirdre to hear rumors that Daphne had returned from the dead.

One of White's butlers arrived with Jared's bath and his brandy, both of which felt extremely good tonight. Grabbing a quick supper in his room, Jared dressed, intent on combing the docks along the Thames for any news of Mick

Browley. He was just shrugging into his jacket when someone knocked on his door.

Jerking it open, he found Charles standing on the other side. Slightly behind him stood a man whose only resemblance to the solicitor was his extreme gauntness. He was shorter, with sharp dark eyes that took in the room and Jared in a single glance. The man Jared assumed to be Charles's brother was devoid of Charles's carrot-colored hair, and he was rougher. He wore a threadbare jacket with dark breeches, and his shirt sported a workman's collar.

"My lord, I'm sorry to disturb you," Charles explained. "But we thought it best to come directly to your room, that way we might talk in private." Jared stood aside, indicating that the two men should enter. "This is my brother, Edmund. Edmund, the marquess of Jersey."

"Sir." Edmund met Jared's gaze evenly. A man from the middle classes who chose to live on the seamier side of life.

"Have you discovered anything?" Jared asked, indicating that the two men make themselves comfortable.

"No," Edmund told him frankly. "I intend to start nosing around as soon as we're finished here. But before I began, I wanted to meet you. It's a policy of mine," he explained. "I've been hired on false pretenses more than once, and I find that people who aren't really after what they say they are, are easy to spot in person."

"And do I pass your test?" Jared asked coolly.

Edmund smiled. "You do. Now, is there anything that's come to mind since you spoke with my brother?"

Jared shook his head. "Believe me, I've racked my brain for some other distinguishing marks, but Mick Browley was only in my employ for a few weeks."

"What about other things. Things that might help us find his trail. For instance, how do you think your wife convinced the coachman to help her escape?"

"She either paid him handsomely or slept with him."

"And how would she have paid him?"

A light sparked in Jared's lead grey eyes. "She would have had to use her jewelry. And," he continued as the pieces of her deception fell into place, "I noticed when I saw her today that she wasn't wearing the diamond I gave her as a wedding gift." Jared's mind flashed back to Daphne standing before the window as she admired her nails. Her left fourth finger had been unadorned.

"Is it possible that she would not wear the ring because she considered herself no longer married?"

Jared's derisive bark spoke volumes. "Not Daphne. That diamond was her most prized possession. It was worth a fortune."

"Then she probably wouldn't have used it to pay off a servant."

"True. But her emerald necklace and earrings were missing from the safe after the accident. If she was desperate enough, she may have parted with those. Although"—Jared shook his head—"I just don't believe she'd give up her jewels."

"Well, I'll see what I can find." Rising, Edmund walked to the door, then turned. "I imagine you were thinking of going to look for Browley yourself. Don't. You'll stand out too much down by the river. And if word gets out that a member of the peerage is looking for Browley, we may never find him."

"A very astute observation," Jared complimented Edmund. "I'll remain here, then."

"He's quite bright, despite how he looks," Charles told Jared in a low voice as he followed after his brother. "I'll be in touch as soon as we have something."

Restless, and feeling ineffectual with nothing to do, Jared decided to go down to the public rooms. A brandy and a card game might help his agitated state. He wasn't surprised to find Will and Robert there.

"Any news?" Robert asked.

"No," Jared responded, giving him a complete perusal. "But you look considerably more fit for company."

"A bath and fresh clothes, to say nothing of a few hours' sleep, does wonders."

"Well?" Will asked, impatient as always. "Have you heard anything?"

Jared shook his head. "Not yet. But I will. You are both still planning to come to Jerseyhurst for the weekend, aren't you?"

"With all this going on?" Robert looked at Jared in surprise. "I thought you'd cancel."

"The last thing I want is for Deirdre to think anything is wrong. Besides, she has been looking forward to meeting both of you again, in more casual surroundings," Jared emphasized.

"Well," William declared, running a finger along the edge of his ascot, "I don't know about the two of you, but since there is nothing we can do but wait, a few rounds of cards sounds like an excellent diversion."

"There's a fast game of loo going on in the back," Sheldon Austin, viscount of Marley told them as he passed. "I've just left."

"You?" Robert said in surprise. "You usually win."

"Usually, but not tonight. At least I'm not being raked as badly as Reece. I'm afraid he'll be bagged for good after Sexton finishes with him."

"Anson Reece is playing?" Jared's eyes narrowed dangerously as the name rolled off his tongue.

"Being fleeced would be a more accurate term."

"I can't believe he's got anything to play with. I played him a month ago and he didn't have a shilling. Had to put up his carriage and pair up just to stay in the game, and he lost that before the night was out."

Austin shrugged. "Sexton lent him £3,000. Although Sexton is beating him so badly I'm sure he'll have his money back with interest before dawn."

"What's the collateral?" Will asked, amazed.

"The same collateral he's been using at every tailor and gaming establishment in town. His fiancée's estate."

The implacable mask of disinterest on Jared's face dissolved, replaced by utter and vehement fury. His eyes turned to black coals and his mouth slanted in a slash of unleashed rage as he headed for the room where Anson Reece had just signed away his wife's estate. Jared had Reece by the lapels before he even knew what was happening.

"Jersey!—"

"Shut up!" Jared spit out the words like ale gone rancid as he jerked him out of his chair. "Sexton," he commanded, not even looking at the man, "give me the note this *ass* signed." The document was obligingly placed in Jared's outstretched hand. Crumpling it like the useless bit of trash it was, he jerked it to within an inch of Reece's face, his balled fist between the paper and Anson's nose. *"Fools* like you shouldn't be allowed to live. You are nothing but an affliction, a disease. This loan you have made is not backed by anything. Nothing. You have no fiancée!" Anson choked and sputtered, his face growing redder by the moment.

Jared tightened his grip on the fabric of Reece's shirt, twisting it. "Tell him! Tell Lord Sexton that you've been lying to him and everyone else in town." Reece gagged and began to claw at his throat. Jared flung him into his chair in disgust. He turned to Sexton and dropped the note on the gaming table in front of him. "Unfortunately for you, this is a useless debt. Reece has no more right to the estate he signed as collateral than he does to Buckingham Palace."

"Are you sure, Jersey?" Chad Sexton demanded.

"Quite. Ramshead is owned by my *wife."* Turning on his heels, Jared departed the room, slamming the door as he went.

"So much for cards," Will muttered, as Jared returned to his drink and tossed down the brandy in a single swallow.

"I'm sure there's some ball the two of you can find tonight," Jared declared, his voice still frosted with icy anger. "I think I'll wait for news from Charles's brother." Taking the decanter from the table between them, Jared strode off, leaving his friends to their own devices, plans to wash all memories of this hellish day from existence foremost in his thoughts.

It was late the next afternoon before Edmund Ellis knocked on Jared's door. He took one look at Jared as he opened the door and drew his own, painfully accurate, conclusions. "I'd say you flushed more than three-quarters of a brandy bottle through yourself last night."

"What have you found out?" Jared asked, pinning him with an unappreciative look.

"Some."

"Where's Charles?"

"Preliminary meeting with the magistrate in your behalf."

Jared grunted his approval and sank into a chair. "Sit down, Edmund. You're right, I had a lovely evening with a decanter of brandy as my guest. Now, what have you learned?"

"Well, Browley's description didn't get me far until about two hours ago when I mentioned to a 'gentleman' I know that your coachman may have come across some jewelry he'd want to sell. That brought to mind an incident he encountered just about three years ago.

"As it turns out," Edmund explained, leaning forward in his chair as his voice filled with excitement, "there was a fellow who somewhat matched Browley's description trying to sell some jewels. Emerald and a very large diamond. Problem was, the stuff he had wasn't real. It was paste. He wouldn't believe it at first. Kept saying he'd gone right to the source for them. But after three different jewelers told him the same thing, the fellow was more than a little angry."

Sitting back in his chair, he waited for the marquess's re-action. It wasn't long in coming.

A slow, cold smile spread across Jared's face. "How exactly like Daphne. She even duped the man who helped her. But we still don't have Browley."

"No, but now we know that your man isn't beholden to the marchioness anymore. If he had gotten what he wanted out of the bargain, it would be much harder to find him. He might even have left the country. But, he ended up with nothing. No job. No name. And no jewels. If I were this coachman, I'd be looking for just one thing."

"Revenge," Jared finished for him.

"Precisely. I believe I can find him in the next two to three days."

"Good. I'm leaving for Jerseyhurst in the morning. Charles knows how to reach me. In the meanwhile, I'll see that you receive a partial payment for your work, as well as a stipend to cover your expenses."

Twenty-one

Deirdre sat at her desk in the Green Salon poring over the packet which had just arrived from Bert. She had decided to run duplicate books on Ramshead in order to stay abreast of the estate's progress between visits. The agreed-upon procedure was that every fortnight Bert would send a packet containing a complete description of the work accomplished over the past two weeks, and a copy of all entries made to his ledgers. Deirdre would then copy them into her set of ledgers at Jerseyhurst.

Painstakingly she copied the list of supplies Bert had entered on July 5. An improved seed type for the winter wheat which Jared had recommended, three scythes, twenty new head of cattle, and a harness for one of the plows. The tip of her tongue clenched between her teeth as she concentrated on accurately transcribing the numbers into her set of ledgers, Deirdre didn't look up when she heard the door open.

"Just put the lemonade on the small table with the statue of the third marquess, please, Della," she requested as she copied another entry. "I can pour myself a glass in a bit."

"Is that any way to greet your husband when he's been gone a day longer than expected?" At the sound of Jared's voice, Deirdre jumped up from her chair and flew into his arms.

"I've missed you so much!" she cried, drawing his head down so she could reach his mouth with her kisses.

"Not nearly so much as I've missed you."

"Really?" she asked, her eyes sparkling with delight. "You know I've worn myself thin trying to carry this enormous stone around on my hand all day," she teased, waving her sapphire ring at him.

"It's better than trying to wear one of your sheep!" Jared reminded her. Deirdre laughed happily. It was such a wonderful sound, Jared thought. So utterly different from the caustic noises Daphne made. The difference between an angel and a demon. One was all light and joy, the other nothing but bitterness. One was born of a heart pure and unsullied by greed or envy, the other knew nothing but. "I think we should retire to our bedroom," Jared whispered close against her temple as he nuzzled in search of the rim of her ear.

"But we have guests arriving at any time!"

"All the more reason we should confine our lovemaking to the privacy of our room. They might find it disconcerting to walk in and find their hosts stretched lengthwise across the desk." He ran the tip of his tongue along her ear, and Deirdre melted against him with a moan of delight. Scooping her into his arms, Jared took the stairs two at a time, only setting her down when they reached his room. It took Deirdre less than five minutes to divest herself of her gown and several underskirts. The moment she was naked she went to their bed, proud of the love they shared. Proud of the pleasure she gave her husband.

Lying down beside him, she splayed one hand across his chest. It was like polished granite beneath her fingers, and his face darkened with desire at her touch. Jared drew her hard against him, cupping her buttocks so that his manhood pressed insistently against her hip. Deirdre leaned against him, letting her warm, pliant body mold to the hard contours of his own, reveling in the heat they created together. Slowly, Jared used his tongue to trace the curve of her neck, bending until he brushed it against the tip of her nipple, while his fingers gently caressed the soft folds of her womanhood.

Deirdre gasped at the heady rush of sensation that he created within her and a thick haze of desire descended upon her like a mist upon the moors. He turned to the other breast, bestowing equal attention upon the deep rose of its peak, his fingers becoming more insistent as they delved deep within her. Rivulets as warm as butter left in the summer sun coursed through Deirdre, taking her to the place only he could take her, lifting her closer and closer to the sun until gasping and breathless she shattered into a million newborn stars.

Now, urgent with need, Deirdre's hands ranged wildly over her husband's perfectly formed body. She trailed her fingers down his back, tracing across a rib to find the flat, hard valley of his stomach. Then, boldly, she roamed lower, until her fingers lightly caressed his engorged shaft, signaling her need. Arousal crashed through Jared like a bolt of lightning to his soul, freeing the desperate need he'd felt all day. Never in his life had he been so driven. Driven by a madness that could find peace only in this unique union. Only with her in his arms. Only when he knew that she was completely and totally his.

A man possessed, he covered her mouth with his, his tongue delving deep into the recesses of her warm, wet mouth, twining his tongue with hers in a dance of passionate intimacy. He felt her arms slip around his neck as her fingers found the nape and caressed him in a way that sent desire snaking through him. Rolling her onto her back, he spread her legs and drove into her, knowing she was well ready for him. Jared buried himself deep inside her as he fought to control his need.

But today there was no such thing as control. A force beyond his understanding had possession of him now. He could not get enough of her. Could not stop his urgent need to fill her with his seed—his life-giving completion. Jared drove into her. Each time reaching deeper, filling her more completely. Deirdre clung to him, her legs wrapped around him, arching each time he withdrew, tightening each time he drove into her. Jared dragged his mouth from hers and stared into her eyes. He was aware only of her now, her and the rhythm of their union, which moved to the beat of his heart, his need, and his craving. Her name on his lips, he cried out, shuddering as he drove deep within her one last time and freed himself. Still joined to her, Jared buried his face deep in the dark, fragrant mass of her hair. "I love you, Deirdre. My God, I love you so."

Jared slept for nearly an hour. The stress of the past two days had left their mark on him, and his mind and body needed replenishment. When he opened his eyes again, Deirdre was seated on the edge of the bed, a vision in one of the new gowns he had purchased.

"You were sleeping so soundly, I didn't want to disturb you," Deirdre told him softly. "Avis tells me our guests have all arrived. Refreshments are being served to the gentlemen in the west study. I thought perhaps I would join them as soon as Lord and Lady Cavendesh came down."

"Let's go down together." Jared stretched, rising onto an elbow. "I don't want you to have to make introductions alone. I won't be long."

"I've met Lord Harelton and the viscount before," Deirdre reminded him. Then with a self-effacing smile, she added, "And I think I've grown more socially adept since I married. I think it's because I no longer need to worry that looking at a man sideways will lead to hours of boring discourse on his favorite hunting dog or the merits of whist over ecarte."

"Robert may still bore you with those topics."

Deirdre gave a blithe shrug of her shoulders. "But I can spend my time looking at you while he rattles on."

Jared burst out laughing. "They will adore you."

"I hope so. I want them to. After all, they're your best friends."

"Deirdre?" Jared's voice lowered to a strange, new tone; one which Deirdre could not recall ever having heard before. It was a tone that contained an unfamiliar urgency. The same urgency that had flavored their lovemaking earlier.

"Yes, my love?"

"Do you remember the day in Kensington Gardens?" Making a face of sham vexation, Deirdre nodded. "Do you remember when I told you a time might come one day when you might have reason to think me a villain?"

Deirdre knit her brow. "I do, but Jared, if I did not think you a villain then, how could I ever think you one now?"

"Sometimes things are not always as they seem."

With a somber nod, she agreed. "That is one thing you have taught me quite well. You needn't fear I'll give sway to those who aren't deserving ever again. Besides," she added, leaning to kiss him gently, "I have you to watch over me." Rising, Deirdre crossed to her dressing room, a warm contentedness glowing deep within her. "I thought to wear the sapphire necklace and earrings you gave me. Would that meet with your approval?"

Jared nodded. "Not only with my approval, but with my wholehearted endorsement."

"Good. Now, you promised to hurry. Winston told me you are meticulous about being on time, and I don't want your friends thinking that I am the cause of your tardiness." With a quick wink, Deirdre disappeared into her room.

As promised, Jared bathed and dressed quickly, donning a handsomely cut evening coat, breeches, and tall, polished black Hessians. The wide ruffle at the cuffs and neck of his white linen shirt only emphasized his masculinity. "How handsome you are, my love," Deirdre said, joining him so that they might descend to greet their guests.

"I must look equal to the job of acting as your escort," Jared responded.

Her eyes lighting with mirth, Deirdre slipped her hand into the crook of his elbow. "My lord, there has never been any doubt that you are more than equal to that task!"

Arm in arm, and with eyes only for each other, Jared and Deirdre greeted their guests. Robert Harelton and William Marlot were extremely cordial, though Deirdre felt that both men seemed somewhat distracted this evening. Andrew and Elizabeth Cavendesh had just returned from a six-month voyage to the Mediterranean, and Deirdre was immediately taken with Elizabeth, who had studied the antiquities in depth and was fluent in both Greek and Latin. Similar in age and stature to Deirdre, Elizabeth's auburn hair and deep brown eyes were warm and friendly, and she immediately put the entire group at ease by telling an outrageous story about one of Andrew and Jared's more audacious exploits while at Oxford.

Deirdre held her sides and rocked with laughter as Elizabeth concluded her tale. "I don't believe it!" she cried, wiping tears from her eyes. "You should both have been sent down!"

Jared grinned wickedly at his wife. "I imagine we should have, but the wife of the schoolmaster was rather taken with Andrew. She interceded on our behalf."

Andrew Cavendesh turned a brilliant shade of red. "I'll thank you not to remind me of that, Jersey!"

Seeing the butler signal that supper was ready, Deirdre gave Viscount Marlot a melting smile and asked if he would do her the honor of escorting her into supper. Utterly charmed by this never-before-seen side of Deirdre, Will presented his elbow and, with a smug look, preceded the rest of the party into the second state room.

Deirdre had chosen the room for their meal because it was much more intimate than the formal dining salon—a room which easily seated twenty for supper and was extremely imposing, with its marble and gilt walls. The room she had selected, while still quite grand, was warmer, and had six large windows that looked over the south reflecting pool. The table was set with Sèvres china and sterling utensils on a heavily brocaded cloth shot with silver threads. Four footmen stood at attention, one at each corner, ready to see to their every need.

As the others followed Deirdre and Will in to supper, Robert leaned over to Jared. "Just think, at this very moment your reputation is being slaughtered by our beloved Daphne. What do you think the king will say when she claims you to be a bigamist?"

"I don't give a damn what he says," Jared stated emphatically. "And I don't give a damn what kind of fool Daphne makes herself into tonight."

Robert put an arm around his shoulders. "If I were in your shoes, I honestly don't think I'd give a damn either. She's a delight, Jersey," he said, nodding toward the door that Deirdre and Will had already disappeared through. "I can barely even believe she's the same woman who used to stare glassy-eyed at the walls of every ballroom in London last season."

"She says that she was forced to act that way because you all bored her to tears."

"Did she?"

"A bit less bluntly, but yes," Jared said with a satisfied grin.

Robert chuckled good-naturedly. "Well, considering what you've told us about her preference for the country, I suppose I can believe that we did. I take it we won't be seeing much of you in town in the future."

"Not in town, but you know you're always welcome here or at Ramshead."

Robert smiled. "I'll be sure to take you up on it, Jersey. You know, marriage is agreeing with you so much that I

must ask your wife if she has a friend for me, someone
with a similar demeanor."

Jared chuckled as he stepped into the state room. "What?
You think you'd be interested in someone who's as cold as
a witch's tit?"

Robert blanched at the friendly jab. "Sorry, about that,
old fellow," he said recalling the remark he'd once made
about Deirdre. "I could hardly have known. . . . You have
an irritatingly good memory, Jersey."

Jared burst out laughing at the discomfited expression on
his friend's face and headed for his seat at the head of the
table.

As soon as they were seated, the first course, a delicate
creamed soup, was served, followed by a poached turbot
with lobster sauce. The meal proceeded accordingly, each
course served with a fresh bottle of either red or white wine
as the menu dictated. They were just starting in on the duck-
ling when there was a huge crash and the sound of glass
splintering in the hall. Everyone at the table went perfectly
still. A second crash echoed through the room, followed by
angry voices. Jared was halfway out of his chair when the
door burst open. He froze where he was, his face nearly
black with fury.

Deirdre's stare went from her husband's face to the two
people standing in the open doorway. One was a very disheveled and angry Winston. The other was the most per-
fect-looking woman she had ever seen. At Deirdre's elbow,
William groaned and put his head in his hand, while Robert
Harelton went absolutely pale. Elizabeth looked to Deirdre
with as much confusion as Deirdre felt, but it was Elizabeth's
husband who spoke first, enlightening the two women.

"My God! Daphne!"

Deirdre's head jerked around to stare at the woman standing so regally at the entrance to the room, and she knew,
as surely as she knew that winter followed the autumn, that
she was looking at Jared's first wife.

A very much alive first wife.

"Get out of my house!" Jared ground out the words slowly, so that each syllable carried the full weight of his fury.

Daphne raised one curved eyebrow and rolled her eyes in a display of utter tedium, then she turned to Deirdre. A slow, predatory smile touched her features. "You must be Jared's new little wife. Too bad," she added with a pout, "that he neglected to tell you about me."

Deirdre gripped the arms of her chair until her fingers began to go numb and for a moment her mind went totally blank. "He . . . he did tell me about you."

"Did he? And did he tell you I was alive and well in my little hideaway? My, my how very sweet of you not to mind sharing him."

Very slowly Deirdre shook her head, her brow knit in a deep knot of confusion so complete that she couldn't find her voice.

"I mean, darling," Daphne continued, "it *is* going to present a few, shall we say, uncomfortable moments now that I'm out of hiding. But, if you don't mind sharing your husband, I'm certainly game. Actually," she declared, putting the tip of her finger to her cheek and running her tongue across her lips, "a trio sounds deliciously naughty!"

Shock and disbelief brought Deirdre to her feet as Daphne's words jarred her from the fog that had frozen her brain. Her entire body shaking, Deirdre turned her gaze to the other end of the table. Jared stood there, shoulders squared, refusing to look at her. His face was a mask, utterly unreadable and completely devoid of remorse. And it was that cold, closed expression on his face that told her that he had known Daphne was not dead. An expression that tore straight to her heart.

He had lied to her. Lie upon lie upon lie.

The room suddenly tilted wildly and a buzzing filled her head as though a thousand bees were inside it. For an instant, she couldn't see anyone, and black blotches filled the place where Jared's unyielding visage had just been.

Do not faint! she commanded herself. She had never fainted in her entire life, and she would not do it now. She would not give them the pleasure of seeing her crumple under the onslaught of her husband's horrible betrayal. By the strength of her will alone, Deirdre dragged a long, balancing breath into her lungs. She forced the insistent buzzing from her head and brought Jared's face back into focus.

"My dear, you look positively *pale!*"

It was Daphne's voice. Silky and mocking and utterly sure of herself. She continued her one-sided dialogue, but Deirdre no longer heard the words. Instead, she concentrated every ounce of her being on removing herself from this room. She had to get away from the droning of that slippery-smooth voice, from the iron-cold ice of Jared's eyes, from the censure of his friends.

Slowly, as though moving in a dream, she stepped away from the table and moved toward Daphne. She did not look at her, did not acknowledge the presence of Jared's *true* wife. Her chin held at a regal tilt so as not to let them see the tears that burned in her eyes and tore at her throat like the ruthless claws of a beast, Deirdre walked through the doorway. She didn't notice that Daphne stepped aside, a bewildered look akin to fear in her face. Nor did she see Winston bow to her in a statement of utmost respect and admiration.

She just walked away.

Walked away from a hurt too deep and too heart-wrenching to acknowledge.

She wasn't sure how she got to her bedroom. She had no memory of passing from room to room, nor of climbing the wide stairs. Standing perfectly still, she allowed Avis to take off her gown and drop a soft, lawn chemise over her head, and for once Avis had nothing to say. No advice to offer. Slowly, as though in a trance, Deirdre walked into

Jared's room and a pain so acute that it robbed her of her breath stabbed her heart.

I should want to put him as far from me as I can, she thought. *I should hate him and rail against him. Steel myself from all the hurt.* All the terrible, horrible hurt.

But she couldn't.

In Jared she had found something so fine that she could not build a wall within her. She could not hate him. She had believed completely in him. Had given totally to him, and she could not tear away what had become a part of her soul.

She wanted only to be where he had last been, remember everything that they had shared in the magical time when there had been no Daphne and no deceptions. The time when there had been only them, together. Her eyes settled on his bed. In the entire time she'd been at Jerseyhurst, she'd never slept anywhere but here. With him. Even when he'd gone to London, she had slept in his bed, finding security in the knowledge that his belongings surrounded her. The shirt he'd worn today lay across the foot of the bed, and she picked it up, closing her eyes as she pressed the fine linen to her face. It smelled of Jared, that unique blend of scents that was his. A sob tore from her breast, and then, with shaking fingers laid against her lips, she forced herself to be silent.

How she ached for him even now. How strong and mystical was this love that would not let go of her. His shirt still clutched in her hand, Deirdre moved through the room. Her fingers trailed over his dresser, caressing the cuff links that lay in an open box and the small gold stickpin he sometimes wore in his jacket. Her gaze went to the balcony doors, and she crossed to them, determined to recall every wonderful moment they had shared.

To make herself insane with the thought of him.

She needed him with such an all-consuming need. Loved

him with such an earth-shattering love, that not even this, this inconceivable deception, could diminish what she felt.

At the balcony doors, she drew a breath and then pulled them wide. For an instant she thought she saw into the past. Thought she saw the two of them as they had been the night before he left. She saw the way the candle flames had danced as the night's breeze carried the scent of the flowers to them. They had spent the long, unhurried night with nothing to do but touch and talk of tomorrow, and all the tomorrows to come.

But the vision passed. There was nothing but blackness on the balcony now. A void where they had once been and now would never be again.

Deirdre heard the door open and shut. She felt Jared come to stand behind her. She basked in the warmth of his body as he encased her in his embrace.

"Deirdre," he whispered.

She swayed against him, letting his strength support her. She concentrated on memorizing the feel of his chest against her back, the caress of his fingers along her jaw. Closing her eyes, she inhaled, committing to memory a million things which she would need later. Things of him. The color of his eyes, the texture of his hair. The effortlessness of his smile. Just for this moment, she wanted to pretend that Daphne had never been. That no deception lay between them. Just for this moment she wanted to put them back in time. Back in the place that was theirs alone, and where nothing could harm their love.

"You must listen to me," Jared murmured, but Deirdre turned in his arms and pressed her fingers to his mouth.

No more words, she thought through the numbing haze that had settled in her brain. Never again words. Never again promises.

Drinking in the feeling of him close to her, she closed her eyes and laid her cheek against his chest, letting the heavy, constant drumming of his heart blot out all reality, all future, so that she could exist only in this moment.

This last moment of oneness with him.

Jared held her there on the balcony, never speaking, until Deirdre's soft measured breathing told him she had fallen asleep against him. As her knees gave way beneath her, he scooped her into his arms and carried her to his bed. Lying down beside her, he gathered her into his arms and held her. Refusing to let her go. Knowing that she slept a mercifully dreamless sleep where demons dared not go.

But Jared was granted no such respite. Instead, he lay awake all night, hounded by the wrongs he had committed. How many times had he asked for her trust? How many times had he sworn he would not hurt her? It didn't matter that he had thought Daphne dead or that he had not intended to inflict the wound that bled within her. It was there, and he had held the knife just as much as Daphne. It mattered very little that he had not wielded it with the lust or intent that Daphne had. It was his crime as well.

Deirdre's expression had spoken all that her voice did not when she had looked from him to Daphne and back again. And he hadn't been able to look at her for fear of what he would read in her eyes. But even as he turned away, he had felt the moment when Deirdre believed he had betrayed her.

He'd realized the moment Deirdre was gone that nothing he could do to Daphne would ever be fitting retribution. There had followed a long silence as Jared counted out the seconds it would take Deirdre to get to the far end of the house. Then he had unleashed every ounce of the formidable fury he'd held in such tight control in the presence of his dark-haired wife. Without a limit, or judgment that would be suitable punishment for the heinous injury Daphne had inflicted upon Deirdre, Jared didn't even try to control his wrath. But the fury that came out was not what any of the people in the room had expected.

In a barely audible tone, Jared told Daphne that she would

never get a farthing of his money, nor would she bear his
name for one day longer than was required. She could say
or do whatever she wanted, but in the end he would see to
it that she was nameless and without a shilling that had
come from him. And then he had told her to get out of his
house and off of his property.

He didn't know where Daphne was now, nor did he care.
He had practically chased her to her carriage and then had
posted riders to see to it that she departed his property. He
dispatched guards to every road, ordering them to check
every rider and every carriage that attempted to cross his
land. If they were to find Daphne in any carriage, they were
to take her directly to the local constable, where she could
rot in prison for all he cared.

But it was all of little use.

The damage had been done, just as Daphne had intended.

Sometime in her plotting and planning, she had suddenly
realized that he didn't care if she maligned him before the
king. And then she had figured out exactly where his weakness was.

Only by destroying Deirdre could she destroy him. And
that was exactly what she had done. Staring up at the grey
light of dawn that bathed the bedroom ceiling in the color
of rain, Jared waited for Deirdre to wake. Waited to face
the look of betrayal in her eyes and to beg for forgiveness.
Yet it was the only thing on earth that could have taken
him from her side that did. Winston rapped twice on the
door and then announced in a whisper that Edmund Ellis
had arrived.

Jared walked into the red writing room, and for a moment
thought he was alone. Then the slightest movement in the
far corner caught his attention. Edmund Ellis moved out of
the shadows.

"I've found our man."

Jared raked his fingers through his hair in relief. "Is he
here?"

"No, you have to come back to London with me. He wouldn't come here. He's scared to death you'll kill him on sight for deceiving you. But I've explained to him that your wife has returned and that she's claiming you planned the accident and her disappearance. He was quite indignant at that. And Lady Daphne has been very busy. The rumors are already spreading. If you don't get Browley to the magistrate and soon, you'll be fighting public opinion as well as that of your peers. It will be ugly, I guarantee it."

"When is the latest we can leave?" Jared asked, already knowing the answer.

"Now."

Jared wasted no time—he wanted Daphne legally disjoined from him, and now was not too soon. He also wanted Deirdre to see that he had not intended to be married to two women at once. Striding down the upper hall, Jared headed for his bedroom, but he suddenly found himself toe-to-toe with Avis. The tiny self-appointed guardian had positioned herself in front of the door, her arms crossed one over the other in an attitude that reeked defiance.

"She's sleepin', your lordship. Sound as a babe. And I'll not have anyone wakin' her."

"I have to leave, Avis. And I need to talk to her before I go."

"I'll tell her whatever it is she needs to know from you."

For a minute, Jared thought about picking Avis up and moving her out of his way, but there was more to what she said than her words implied. She was protecting Deirdre from things she could not bear right now. Deirdre had been like a wraith last night, holding her emotions bottled deep inside her. She had not cried or screamed. She hadn't even mentioned Daphne's name. Any other news about Daphne might very well push her over the edge of sanity. "All right, Avis, tell her I'll be back tomorrow. If this wasn't urgent, I'd never leave her."

"Aye, and it was urgent business that took you to London three days ago."

Jared looked away, his eyes narrowed. "I love her, Avis. You helped me woo and win her, you must have believed that I loved her or you never would have done that." The maid's stony face softened ever so slightly. "Please stay with her and try to help her. I love her. I swear it."

Despite her momentary sympathy, Avis continued to glare at him, refusing to budge. But as he turned to leave he was certain that he heard her mutter under her breath, "I'll try."

Twenty-two

The instant she woke, Deirdre knew something was wrong, but it was minutes before her mind allowed her to recall the horror of the night before. As it came flooding back to her, her heart clutched and her stomach heaved with such force that it was all she could do to push herself upright in bed, gasping for air. The last thing she remembered was Jared holding her on the balcony. The memory brought another unbidden sob to her lips, a sound so retched that Avis came running from the other room, her hand at her throat in fear.

"Are you all right?" she demanded, sitting down on the heavy coverlet of Jared's bed. Looking at Deirdre's dry eyes and stony countenance, she gently brushed a strand of hair from Deirdre's brow. "Aye, I can see that you're just as you were."

"Where is he?" she whispered.

"He said to tell you that he's gone to London on urgent business."

Avis's words were like an arrow shot straight to Deirdre's heart. "Daphne." She choked on the name, unable to believe, even after all that had happened, that Jared would be so cruel. That he would leave their bed to go to Daphne.

"Nay, my lady. Don't think that," Avis intoned as she read her mistress's thoughts. "It's something to do with her, but not that. It's you he loves. Not her."

Deirdre tried not to think of the look on Jared's face when

she'd turned there for reassurance last night—for any sign at all that this was as much a surprise to him as it was to her. But he hadn't even been able to meet her gaze, and that had told her all she needed to know. "When will he be back?"

"Tomorrow."

"Then we have plenty of time to pack."

"And where are we goin'?"

"To France."

Nothing Avis could say against her plans had the least effect on Deirdre. Not her railing that Jared loved her. Not her heated insistence that he at least deserved a chance to tell his side of the story. "Why do you believe that heartless woman over your own husband?" she demanded. "Why won't you listen to him! You don't know where he's gone! Maybe he's gone to shoot the bloodless witch!"

"He knew she wasn't dead, Avis. He knew."

"So you're not goin' to trust him. Not even for a day." Avis let out a growl of frustration. "Deirdre, I'll go with you to France or wherever it is you wish, but just wait for his lordship to come back. I don't want to see you throwin' your life away over that heartless woman."

Deirdre made no reply. Emotionless and detached, she moved around the room, methodically selecting gowns and slippers for her new life. For one logical reason or another, she painstakingly discarded each of the new outfits Jared had purchased for her, until two trunks were filled with items that would never remind her of the man she loved so desperately. And who had betrayed her so completely.

Winston protested Deirdre's plans loudly, but to no avail. In the end he managed to delay her departure for two hours, and then reasoned that with evening so close, it was too late for a safe departure. But his mistress only stood stonily at the door and repeated her determination to leave until he feared he would cry himself.

At last, the carriage was brought around front and a small meal packed inside.

It was almost, Deirdre thought hysterically, as though she was departing for a holiday at the shore. The thought brought memories rushing back—of the river's end Jared had promised to show her one day. Deirdre's hands began to shake uncontrollably as she climbed into the carriage. She chose the seat inside that looked forward, not back, and so she didn't have to see the stricken faces of the assembled staff as she left. Even Tyler was subdued, lying quietly in her lap.

"I beg you to reconsider, my lady," Winston said as he stood with the carriage door handle held in his gloved hand.

Deirdre gave him a wan smile and gave a nearly imperceptible shake of her downcast head. "Thank you for everything, Winston. You made it very easy for me here. Thank the rest of the staff for me also. I shall miss them."

"And, his lordship?" he asked boldly. "Is there a message I shall give to him?"

"No." Deirdre looked away until she heard the door click quietly shut. The driver overhead called to the team of horses, and the carriage rumbled down the drive as Deirdre stared in silent anguish at her slippered feet.

"You cannot be forever runnin' away," Avis finally said as they crossed the River Byrne, and then turned onto the unpaved road leading south. "Do you think he wants that shrew when he's got you who's so like him and so happy to be here?"

"Please don't, Avis."

"Then tell me, if you've got to get away from her, why it is we're goin' to France and not back to Ramshead?"

Deirdre stared out the window, the despair in her heart beyond her ability to express. "All I would do at Ramshead is think of him. He would be everywhere. The sheep, the garden, the fields, the dining room . . ." Her words trailed off as the images they evoked pierced her soul.

"So we're goin' somewhere where you'll not be around anything of him, is that it?" Deirdre nodded miserably. "And doin' that is goin' to keep you from ever thinkin' of him again?

"Oh, aye!" Avis continued. "You're never goin' to think of the love you had with him? Never goin' to remember how he made you laugh or helped you with Ramshead? Just like that, eh? That simple. Just run away and he'll be gone from your heart forever! You're never goin' to wonder whether it was him that tricked you or that Daphne who used you to get what she wanted from him."

"I love him too much, Avis. I can't bear the pain of knowing that he betrayed me."

Avis shook her head in bitter disbelief. "You're the one who's lying now, Deirdre. One big, fat whopper of a lie. And you're tellin' it to yourself. No matter where you go, he'll never be out o' your heart. And if you look deep within, you'll know that he'd never do such a thing. *I* know his lordship wouldn't hurt you in such a way. But you're tellin' yourself that you do not. All because them others hurt you so!

" 'Twas your parents who never cared a whit for you. And 'twas that Master Reece, what with his airs o' bein' so refined when all the while he was lyin' to ye and usin' you. *They* were the people who hurt you, and because o' them, you're unwillin' to trust the one ye should.

"You tell me that you love his lordship, but if you did, you'd listen to him. You'd trust him. O' course, perhaps you never were truly in love with his lordship after all, just like that Daphne . . ."

"That's not true!" Deirdre nearly shouted her denial. "I love Jared. I love him so . . ."

Her disavowal came to an abrupt end as she saw the blinding truth of Avis's words. Then her entire body began to shake, and no matter how intently she concentrated on stopping her hands and legs from quivering, she couldn't.

She *hadn't* given Jared a chance. Instead she had believed Daphne, a woman she didn't even know, and one who her husband had told her was not to be trusted. A woman who had deceived Jared in their marriage and even before that.

Why wouldn't she do it again?

Gasping for breath that was blocked by the enormous knot in her throat, Deirdre faced the truth of what she was doing. She was running away without even knowing what the truth was. Deirdre squeezed her eyes tightly closed. Jared deserved better than that. Trepidation filling her heart, Deirdre forced herself to look deep within her heart—searching for the truth. She would not let the pain of the past discolor her thoughts. It was time for the past to be left behind, and those who hurt her with it. She focused on Jared and on everything she knew to be true about him.

Would Jared really do such a thing? Had all the words he'd said to her, all the things he'd done, led her to believe that he would betray her at the first opportunity? Had his actions proved that he would tell a lie of such enormous proportion?

Then her heart answered her, and she knew that he would not.

It was Jared who had always been there for her. Jared who had never lied to her no matter how harsh his truths. Jared who had cared about her, confided in her, provided for her. It was Jared who had never, ever let her down. Who had always held tightly to her hand and seen her through the darkness and into the light.

The realization of what she had done fell like a crushing boulder on her heart. Suddenly she felt tears rising, hot and piercing, behind her eyes. Tears, not for what Jared had done to her, but for the terrible wrong she had done to him. And unlike the lifetime of tears that others caused, but which Deirdre had never allowed to fall, she couldn't stop these tears of her own making.

"Avis," she sobbed, her face pale, "I've done a terrible thing. We have to turn back."

That was all the little maid needed to hear. Frantically, Avis beat on the carriage roof. "Go back! Her ladyship says turn back!"

Bill, the coachman, opened the small trapdoor in the top of the carriage. "What did ye say?"

"I said turn back!" Avis declared in exasperation.

Like every other servant in the marquess's household, Bill had not approved of his mistress's sudden departure, although not a soul was unsympathetic to the poor marchioness's feelings. That witch what was once, unfortunately, the marchioness, had caused the whole problem. And, in Bill's opinion, it was *her* what needed to be put on the first coach to Dover and sent across the channel. And he would have been happy to be the one to do it, too. But he wasn't at all happy about taking a fine lady like the current marchioness anywhere but home.

Those thoughts foremost in his mind, the coachman wasted not a moment. If they were quick about it, they could be back at Jerseyhurst before his lordship returned, and the marquess need never even know that his wife had thought to flee. Though they were moving at a steady canter, Bill pulled hard on the harness reins of the four-in-hand team. The road was wide here and smooth. The land on either side was flat, and the regular traffic that passed along the road on the way to and from London had kept the grass low. The carriage began to turn in a wide arc that took them onto the grassy flatlands, then suddenly one horse stepped into a hole.

White-eyed with fear, the animal's foreleg buckled and it lunged to the right, dragging the other horses with it. Bill whistled and called out as he attempted to calm the team, but the injured gelding lurched again, and the other three horses were pulled out of their rhythm. The leader crashed into the shoulder of the injured horse and the other pair, feeling the extra weight no longer being borne by the others, began to rear. The carriage careened wildly off the road. Fighting frantically to keep the carriage from rolling onto its side, Bill hauled at the reins and shouted again and again to his team, trying to steady them. But the horses were thrashing in different directions as they tried to get their legs beneath them.

Inside the carriage, Deirdre and Avis were thrown against opposite walls. Avis screamed and Tyler yelped as he was pinned between Deirdre and the heavy door. The basket of food upended itself, spilling buns and crockery everywhere. Deirdre threw her arms over her head, trying to protect herself, as she was thrown from one side of the carriage to the other. She heard a horse bellow in fear and the crack of a wheel as it buckled under the weight of the carriage. She was thrown again, and the hard edge of the far seat slammed into her ribs.

We're going to die, she thought.

And then, with a crystal clarity she suddenly knew that Avis had been right. No matter where she went or what she did, Jared would never be anywhere but nestled deep in her heart. Even in death he would be with her. They were bound by a love greater than any earthly thing could destroy.

"Jared!" she screamed, and the carriage rolled onto its side.

Twenty-three

Jared rode like a man possessed. Leaning over his stallion's withers, he pressed his heels hard into the horse's ribs. The guards he had posted to keep Daphne at bay had told him that they'd seen his carriage leave Jerseyhurst and head south along the road to Dover. Jared had known immediately that it could only be Deirdre inside and had ridden after her.

He would not lose her now, he vowed. Not when their future was so close at hand. Not when he had the signed divorce papers in the pouch tied to his saddle.

Thank God he had headed straight for Jerseyhurst after leaving the magistrate's offices. He had come back to tell Deirdre everything. He knew he had to explain what he had been afraid to tell her before—that Daphne had tricked him. He should have done it the moment he'd discovered Daphne was alive, instead of trying to protect Deirdre. Though it would have hurt her, the pain would have been far less than what she suffered last night.

When he had left Jerseyhurst this morning, he and Edmund had ridden hard for London. First they had gone straight to Mick Browley, who was anxious to have his own revenge on Daphne for leaving him empty-handed and a fugitive as well. He had readily agreed to speak with the authorities, who had promised that he would be held harmless in the affair.

The magistrate had listened intently to Charles's expla-

nation of the events of three years ago and to Daphne's
sudden reappearance last week. Then he had listened to
Mick Browley. When Browley had finished with his tale,
not only had the magistrate declared in favor of Jared's pe-
tition for divorce, but he had charged Daphne with willfully
misleading the law and theft of the jewels that he deemed
to be Jared's property as well.

Out of deference to her station, it was decided that
Daphne was to be held at a friend's house until sentencing.
She would be ordered to return Jared's jewels or repay him
for them if she no longer owned them. Jared wanted nothing
to do with the jewels, and had already instructed Charles
to sell them and donate the proceeds to the foundling hos-
pital. There was a chance that Daphne would spend several
months in the women's prison as well. Or, if the magistrate
saw fit to be merciful, Daphne might merely end up banished from England forever. Either way, Daphne could no
longer interfere with Jared's life, and she could never hurt
the woman he loved again.

But it would all be for naught if Jared didn't have Deirdre.

Coming over a rise he saw the carriage. Pressing his
thighs harder against his stallion's ribs, Jared urged him to
an even greater speed. As he rode after it, the carriage
slowed and began to turn.

Jared pulled his horse up. *She's coming back! Deirdre
wasn't going to leave him. She was turning around.*

Then, before his very eyes, he saw the carriage careen
suddenly off the road. His heart thundered in disbelief as
it teetered on only two of its wheels and the horses flailed
as the weight of the carriage dragged them down.

A sickening sense of the unreal spread through Jared as
he watched an accident occur. An accident that was supposed to have happened three years before, but never did.

Dear God, his mind cried out. *Don't let this happen now.
Don't let what was false before be real now.* As false as his

marriage to Daphne had been before, that was how real and vital his marriage to Deirdre was now. And he would not lose her. He would not let fate take her from him.

Spurring the stallion back into a gallop, he raced for the carriage, watching in disbelief as it tipped over and crashed onto its side. For long sickening seconds, as he closed the distance between himself and the overturned coach, he watched for signs of movement. Then he saw his driver crawl from the ditch into which he'd been thrown. He looked up and, seeing Jared bearing down on him, began to wave frantically. The instant Jared was upon the carriage he flew from his saddle, already on the ground before his horse had even come to a stop.

"My lord!" Bill cried. "The marchioness is inside with her maid!"

Jared climbed on top of the carriage's side and yanked the door open with a strength born of the terrifying fear that gripped him. "Deirdre!" he cried.

"Here, your lordship!" It was Avis who responded, not his wife. "She's here, but she's badly hurt. Her head is bleedin', and she won't come 'round."

"Let me go down, milord," Bill offered. "I'm smaller and I can hand her up to you."

Jared nodded and lowered the man into the broken carriage. He heard Deirdre moan as they shifted her weight. "Take care with her!" he warned. "She could have broken bones as well."

Slowly, the coachman lifted her so that Jared could reach through the door. He gathered her in his outstretched arms and carefully drew her out of the carriage and into the fading light.

"You go on and get her down, my lord," Avis commanded from below. "I'm fine but for a few cuts and scrapes. I can get out with just a little help from Bill here."

Jared didn't argue. Carrying the most precious burden of his life, he slid down to the ground. Deirdre moaned in his arms, her hand going to her head. "Don't touch, my darling. It will only hurt more."

"Jared?"

"I'm right here."

Deirdre's eyes fluttered open and for a moment she thought that she was in heaven, for her husband was right there beside her, his arms cradling her with such tenderness that she thought she could not bear it.

Slowly, she lifted shaking fingers to his lips, disbelieving when she touched flesh and not spirit. "Are you really here?" He nodded, unable to speak for the tears that choked him. "I love you, Jared. And I shouldn't have tried to run away from you."

"Hush, now," he whispered in an emotion-choked voice. "We can talk later."

"No." She tried to shake her head, but the movement sent a crashing pain tearing through her skull. Wetting her lips in determination, she drew his head down until her lips brushed ever so lightly against his ear. "You asked me to trust you. Do you remember?" Jared nodded, and he turned his lips to her forehead, pressing the gentlest of kisses there.

"And you did."

"Nay, I did not. I was leaving. I believed that you had lied to me, and I didn't want to feel the hurt. It was too great."

"You weren't leaving me," Jared intoned gently. "You were turning around."

Deirdre managed to bring the touch of a smile to her mouth. "I'm sorry, Jared. I'm so sorry that I doubted you. Whatever happened with Daphne, I believe that you did not intend for it to hurt me. I don't think that you would want two wives." Deirdre tried to smile again. "I don't even have any money."

"Deirdre, don't," Jared urged. "There will be so much time later. I need to get you home and fetch a doctor for you. I swear I won't lose you now, Deirdre. I love you," he vowed as a tear slid down his wind-roughened cheek. "I will love you until I die and far beyond then. I will love you when our children's children are grown and the world is a far different place than this. It will not matter what may happen."

Deirdre looked up into her husband's face and there, deep in his silver eyes, she saw the truth of his words. She saw the boundless love he had for her. A love that the past could not destroy any more than the future could—whatever it might bring. And at last she knew that here, within him, was a promise that would never be broken.

"How is my patient feeling today?" Jared asked as he pressed a kiss to his wife's mouth and sat down on the bed beside her.

Deirdre sat up and touched the bandage that slanted across her hairline. "I feel much better."

"Do you?"

She gave Jared a brilliant smile. "I do indeed."

"If you are trying to convince me to let you get out of bed," Jared warned with a knowing look, "it is not going to work, my little schemer. The doctor gave instructions for you to rest for another three days at least."

"But it is *such* a beautiful day outside! I could sit in the garden this afternoon and rest there." At the word "outside" Tyler lifted his head, his tail thumping against the rug at the foot of their bed.

Jared looked down at the fast-growing pup. "I don't know how you think he's going to become a sheeper if he's constantly with you."

"I've been thinking that perhaps his sons will have to do the sheeping. Tyler needs to stay with me."

"And I need *you* to stay with me."

Deirdre looked deeply into the charcoal eyes of the man

she loved so completely. "I will always be with you, Jared. Always."

"Then stay in bed like a good girl and get the rest you need," Jared commanded as he began to stand.

Deirdre pulled hard on his arm, bringing him back to the bed. "If you won't let me get out of bed, then perhaps you should stay here with me." She pinned her husband with a wicked look and ran her tongue across the edge of her lower lip. "Because I *am* feeling *much* better."

"I'll hold you for a while."

"I don't want you to hold me."

"Deirdre," Jared warned, "the doctor says—"

"The doctor," she interrupted as she began to press kisses against his shirt, "isn't inside my body and he doesn't know how much I miss having you close to me. Very, very close to me."

Jared hardened immediately. For a week his concern for Deirdre's health had kept him away from her, but her warm kisses and the pressure of her thigh pressed against his was nearly too much for him. "You're playing with fire, Deirdre," he groaned, as his fingers dug into the thick tresses of her hair.

"My love, I am alive with a fire that burns for you."

With a moan of surrender, Jared pulled her into his arms. "Do you promise?"

Deirdre dipped her tongue into his mouth, and then looked into his eyes. "I promise, my love. I promise."

About the Author

Elaine Kane lives with her family in Englewood, Colorado. She loves hearing from her readers, and you may write to her c/o Zebra Books. Please include a self-addressed stamped envelope if you wish a response.

JANE KIDDER'S EXCITING
WELLESLEY BROTHERS SERIES

MAIL ORDER TEMPTRESS   (3863, $4.25)

Kirsten Lundgren traveled all the way to Minnesota to be a mail order bride, but when Eric Wellesley wrapped her in his virile embrace, her hopes for security soon turned to dreams of passion!

PASSION'S SONG   (4174, $4.25)

When beautiful opera singer Elizabeth Ashford agreed to care for widower Adam Wellesley's four children, she never dreamed she'd fall in love with the little devils—and with their handsome father as well!

PASSION'S CAPTIVE   (4341, $4.50)

To prevent her from hanging, Union captain Stuart Wellesley offered to marry feisty Confederate spy Claire Boudreau. Little did he realize he was in for a different kind of war after the wedding!

PASSION'S BARGAIN   (4539, $4.50)

When she was sold into an unwanted marriage by her father, Megan Taylor took matters into her own hands and black-mailed Geoffrey Wellesley into becoming her husband instead. But Meg soon found that marriage to the handsome, wealthy timber baron was far more than she had bargained for!

Taylor-made Romance from Zebra Books

WHISPERED KISSES   (0-8217-5454-8, $5.99/$6.99)
Beautiful Texas heiress Laura Leigh Webster never imagined that her biggest worry on her African safari would be the handsome Jace Elliot, her tour guide. Laura's guardian, Lord Chadwick Hamilton, warns her of Jace's dangerous past; she simply cannot resist the lure of his strong arms and the passion of his *Whispered Kisses*.

KISS OF THE NIGHT WIND   (0-8217-5279-0, $5.99/$6.99)
Carrie Sue Strover thought she was leaving trouble behind her when she deserted her brother's outlaw gang to live her life as schoolmarm Carolyn Starns. On her journey, her stagecoach was attacked and she was rescued by handsome T.J. Rogue. T.J. plots to have Carrie lead him to her brother's cohorts who murdered his family. T.J., however, soon succumbs to the beautiful runaway's charms and loving caresses.

FORTUNE'S FLAMES   (0-8217-5450-5, $5.99/$6.99)
Impatient to begin her journey back home to New Orleans, beautiful Maren James was furious when Captain Hawk delayed the voyage by searching for stowaways. Impatience gave way to uncontrollable desire once the handsome captain searched *her* cabin. He was looking for illegal passengers; what he found was wild passion with a woman he knew was unlike all those he had known before!

PASSIONS WILD AND FREE (0-8217-5275-8, $5.99/$6.99)
After seeing her family and home destroyed by the cruel and hateful Epson gang, Randee Hollis swore revenge. She knew she found the perfect man to help her—gunslinger Marsh Logan. Not only strong and brave, Marsh had the ebony hair and light blue eyes to make Randee forget her hate and seek the love and passion that only he could give her.